FISHING *for* SOMETHING

FISHING
for
SOMETHING

ANDREW SCOTT BASSETT

LUMINARE PRESS
WWW.LUMINAREPRESS.COM

Luminare Press
442 Charnelton St.
Eugene, OR 97401
www.luminarepress.com

LCCN: 2020912160
ISBN: 978-1-64388-459-2

For my father,
his love for fishing and the outdoors and his life inspired
this story for the better and for the worse.

For my older brother,
more a father figure than my real father would ever be.
He's been there in the good, the bad, and the ugly times,
and lived to share and bear it.

For my wife and children,
their love and loyalty made this book a reality.
They've stayed with me through all the ups and downs,
inside outs and ridiculous revisions that a writer goes
through to get it right.

CHAPTER 1

J ohn Barrett stumbles through the last hour of his shift at the Sierra Northwest Paper Mill. He was up late the night before putting on cabinet doors at a client's home for his struggling handyman business; before starting to work bright and early with the planer saw at the mill.

Right now John is as sleepy as the town he lives and works in, Grants Pass. Although it's early June and summer is calling, the canopy of trees and hills that surround the little town in southern Oregon keep the temperature at a manageable eighty-something. Manageable is the key word since this is where John toils for decent pay each day, and the building he works in at the paper mill has no air conditioning to speak of. The muggy weather wraps around a person like a towel taken out of a dryer that is still-damp, but hot at the same time. John in his zombiefied state loses all track of time. It takes two taps on his shoulder to get his attention. John's shift manager, Del, is the one doing the tapping. He reminds John that it is quittin' time, time to go home. Del, who's worked with John at the mill since they were both snot-nosed kids, can tell that John is burning both ends of something; he's just not sure what.

John tries in vain to rub the exhaustion of life out of his eyes as he acknowledges Del's command.

John clocks out for the day, and although it's early morning when most people are getting up and readying themselves for the day, he's already anticipating with great relief in his head, making acquaintance with the soft pillow back at his apartment that will allow him to pass out and sleep the rest of the day away. Sleep is one thing that doesn't come easy these days for John as he deals with so many conflicting thoughts and frustrating ideas.

As John walks to his truck in the company's parking lot, he crosses paths with the paper mill owner's son, Darrell Sammons. Sammons' father, Fred, founded the mill some thirty years ago. Because of his advanced age, Fred lets Darrell run the daily operations of the business, which Darrell has for some time now.

"John, you just getting off?" Mr. Sammons shouts in John's direction.

John waves a hand up in the air, and in his tired stupor grunts some acknowledgement of his boss's words while continuing his slow but steady dragging of his rear end to his vehicle. But it's no use. Sammons is making a beeline to John. The boss man cuts off John's path to his truck. Darrell's in the mood for chit-chat, small talk, and bullshit, whatever. John isn't, but what choice does he have? It's his boss. Stopped dead in his tracks, he's so close to his truck door now that he can almost smell the stench from his dirty undershirt lying on the passenger seat of his F-150 for the last three days. If the boss wants to waste his time there isn't much he can do, at least not until his handyman gig is fulltime, if that ever happens at all. Right now it's a hit or miss side business, more tease than anything else. John is struggling to figure out if all the hours away from his family and the extra money it takes to run it make any sense at all.

His wife, Darlene, has separated from him and asked him to move out. Her constant attacks on him have as their main target; John's handyman business. Her final ultimatum before she nicely told him to leave was a choice, his obsessive work schedule; or her and the kids. When John refused to make such a choice, and said it was totally unreasonable for him to have to, Darlene made the choice for him. Hence his destination right now, if he can ever get away from Darrell, is a cheap, small studio apartment in downtown Grants Pass. It has wonderful views of traffic and flamboyant backpacked transients holding impassioned conversations with themselves at all hours of the day.

Darrell is invading John's personal space as he is often prone to do. He drones on and on about something related to working at the mill while John does his best to pretend to be listening. John nods, uh-huhs, and ok's while wearing a big butt-kissing smile on his face so Darrell won't notice John looking straight through him and at his chariot of sleep that awaits just a few feet away.

But then out of nowhere, like a flash of light in a dark sky, Darrell gets John's attention when he invokes Darlene's name into his little diatribe. Darrell tells John he just saw Darlene working at the Caveman Café. It's a tiny little diner on the outskirts of town near the freeway that's been serving up three meals a day for as long as anyone can remember. And unfortunately for John, in a smaller community like Grants Pass, Oregon, people often know too much about other folks' business. Darrell sharing that he saw John's wife working at the café is one of those times. John, his brain turned to mush from lack of sleep, tries to wrap his grey matter around the fact that his boss knows more about Darlene's comings and goings than he does. If this is true, it's news to John who doesn't know anything about his estranged wife taking a job at the diner.

Darrell continues, "John, don't take this the wrong way or anything, but I was just kind of wondering how you and Darlene were doing?"

Wondering how we are doing? Why are you wondering anything about me and my wife? John is thinking as Darrell's mouth keeps moving.

That is the first question that gets John's attention but not the last. Wait for it now, wait for it.

"I know you guys have been split up for a little while now, so I was wondering if me being you're boss and all, if it would bother you at all, if I asked her out? What do you say, partner?"

And now we have a new low. Not John's wife asking him to move out of their home they've shared for the last five years where they were raising their three kids together. Not working seventy hours a week chasing a dream that is probably driving him to an early cardiac episode or worse, whatever worse is. Not even finding out from your space-invading big-mouthed boss that your wife, and she is still your wife, has a new job that she didn't tell you about. No the low of all lows to date has to be this one, when your boss is asking you if he can ask your wife out. Yep, it doesn't get much lower.

At this moment John is fighting back the very real urge to see how far his fist can penetrate his boss's head. But of course John takes the high road, the road that keeps his steady paychecks coming, and respectfully tells his boss that he and Darlene are still working on things, which is true to a point. The point being Darlene is still leaving the door open, even if it is just barely cracked open a bit, for the two of them to work on their marriage. Their children deserve as much, she keeps reminding John.

"I didn't know you guys were still working on things, sorry, John, I didn't mean to…"

"It's fine," John tells Darrell as he sees his boss's embarrassment for asking in the first place.

Darrell nods, pats John on the shoulder, and slinks away. He leaves John alone so he can finally get to his truck. John is punched in the face by the mixed fragrances of male single life, which is stinky clothes and stale left over food. John opens his truck door and slides behind the wheel. He searches in vain for his American flag air freshener tree, vanilla scent, but it's to no avail. "I'll clean the truck out later," he vows to himself as he roars out of the parking lot and down the road.

His bed awaits him, and since he hasn't gotten to spend time with it very much lately, he is really looking forward to the reunion. John only hopes his exhaustion will overcome his thoughts. How his wife could start a new job and not even tell him about it. Why would she do that? What else is she not telling him about? He ponders these questions and many more as he makes it home and into bed, where he slowly slips away into the sweet peace of sleep.

———

"Bam-bam-bam-bam." And then again. "Bam-Bam-Bam." Followed by the relaxing sounds of a jackhammer; then the lovely beeping of construction trucks going backwards and the shouting of city workers suddenly conspire to separate John from his slumber.

His normally relatively quiet apartment in downtown Grants Pass has suddenly become a playground for loud sounds to enjoy. John tries all the common prescription cures for such a problem—pillow over the head, cotton balls stuffed into ears, and then two pillows over the head. That's all John has to work with, and he still can hear everything going on around him. Frustrated as hell, he flips over onto his back and yells out like a wounded Sasquatch in the woods. Wiping the good thirty minutes of sleep from his eyes, John considers his best options.

John's a man of truly few close friends, for reasons too numerous to go into right now. At this short notice there's only one realistic option for his plight. "Darlene," he mutters to himself.

"It's my home, too," he argues to himself as if building his case up before he faces his wife who will render the final verdict. "My name is still on the mortgage, and I pay most of the bills. She has to do me the favor and let me put down several hours of z's."

Good talk, John assures himself. He throws on some clean clothes since he collapsed into bed still wearing his dirty work clothes from the sawmill. He considers a shower but decides against it. A shower might wake him up a little too much and make it difficult to get back to sleep. And sleep is the whole point of his stepping out into the deep end of the pool and asking Darlene if he can crash at her place, their place, whatever.

No, just clean clothes and hair combed will have to do, maybe some mouthwash in case Darlene's in a forgiving mood, fat chance probably at this point.

Back to his chariot of sleep for another trip across town to the house he used to call home.

⌒⦵⦵⌒

Darlene rips the brush through her hair a few more times and double checks her face in the mirror making sure everything is where it should be. A profanity slips out of her mouth when she accidentally knocks over a can of hairspray sitting on her bathroom vanity. Her three children, just a week into summer vacation, are still asleep in their beds enjoying their morning freedom from school.

"Hurry up, Rose," she whispers to herself wondering why her mother-in-law hasn't arrived yet to watch the kids so Darlene can head to her new job at the Caveman Café. She's a waitress at the café. Darlene has experience since she waitressed in her college days up in Eugene while attending the U of O.

A knock at the door grabs her attention. "Finally, Rose," Darlene says out loud as she tiptoes across the squeaking old wood floors in the house trying her best not to wake the kids. But to her surprise, it's not Rose on the other side of the door, but Rose's first-born son John, or as Darlene calls him "my idiot husband who can't figure out what's most important in life."

Darlene is surprised John is over so early in the morning and without warning. "John? What are you doing here?"

John explains his noise pollution problem at his apartment and asks if he can get some sleep here, in the home where his name is still on the mortgage. Darlene grudgingly says okay, feeling sorry for his predicament, but warns him that the kids are asleep and could wake up at any minute and wake him. "You know how excited they are to see you, every time you manage to pull yourself from work long enough to come by."

John staring at her Caveman Café Uniform wants to get on the offensive and grill her about her new job. But

Darlene's the one playing offense right now, as is usually the case, and its John on defense trying to block the incoming shots she's firing at him. Too tired to fight with her and not wanting to screw up his chance to rest his weary head in what used to be their bedroom, John says nothing in his defense.

"Your mom is going to be here any second. I'll ask her to do her best to keep them from going into the bedroom and waking you up. I'll see if she can get them to keep the noise down."

John says, "Thanks," before escaping to the master bedroom, leaving Darlene still waiting for his mother to arrive.

Darlene sits down on her lazy boy and waits. She wonders why John said nothing about her uniform. Did he even notice the uniform? Not taking interest in anything but his things, started many fights between the two of them over the years. But John had to have noticed her uniform, even he isn't that blind Darlene tells herself.

Darlene has been waiting for the right time to tell John about the new job and all the things that went into her decision to start working again. She knows full well that John doesn't want her working, but with them separated and things between them not getting any better, she did what she had to. Part of her would like to barge into the bedroom now and make John see her uniform and come to grips with her independence from him, but the other part of Darlene, the more rational, reasonable part, knows that now is not the right time. She has to go to her new job in a few minutes and John is wiped out from work. No, now is not the right time.

Darlene hears Rose's car pull up and stands up and waits by the door. When Rose walks through the front door,

Darlene tells her about John being in the bedroom and trying to keep things quiet for him. Rose is thrilled that her son is home, and a little twinkle makes an appearance in her eyes. Darlene can see it; and quickly tries to make sure that Rose understands that she is just helping John out of a pickle. That she is just letting him get some sleep that he desperately needs.

Rose listens and acts like she comprehends, but Darlene can tell that Rose is hoping that she is making up a story and that John really spent the night there, last night. Rose thinks that for some strange reason Darlene wouldn't want to tell her the truth. Why Rose would think she would keep such news from her, Darlene has no idea.

Darlene picks her car keys out of her purse and thanks Rose again for agreeing to watch the kids on the days she works. "I'll see you when I get home," she says as she heads out the door to work, leaving Rose to babysit her four children, the three little ones and the one big kid now sleeping in her bed.

⁂

"TABLE SIX'S ORDERS READY, DARLENE," BILL, THE OWNER and manager of the Caveman Cafe shouts to his newest waitress. She scrambles to get back and grab the plates of breakfast delights and get them to their intended destination. Darlene can feel beads of sweat suddenly, slowly dripping down her neck, as she rushes from table to table. It's been a lot of years since she's worked in a restaurant or worked anywhere for that matter, and she certainly can feel that fact in her legs and knees. The Caveman Cafe has been a madhouse all morning, and she has barely been able to keep up with her tables. After nearly three hours of customers filling up the joint, it finally slows a bit between the breakfast rush and the lunch craziness to come. Bill allows Darlene to take a much needed short break. She slumps into a bar chair in the tiny employees room in the back and sips some black coffee. Lorinda, another waitress at the café a decade of years or so Darlene's elder, has kind of taken Darlene under her wing and is helping her get back into the working woman swing of things. Lorinda is one of those people who doesn't care what comes out of her mouth, and just about everybody in Grants Pass knows it. Lorinda will be sweet and sensitive to one of the regular lonely, elderly customers who make their way into the café one minute, listening to their problems making them feel important, even offering to pray for them. Then the next thing you know, she's swearing like a sailor on leave and trading dirty jokes with truckers who can't wait to drop-in and see her every time they stop in town off of the I-5 Freeway.

This particular morning, a trucker by the name of Mike Stillman comes strutting into the café. Strutting is the perfect word because Mike, who is without question easy on the eyes and a charmer, loves himself even more than many ladies in town do, which is saying something. Mike drives his big rig north into Canada and then all the way down to the Mexican border, but Grants Pass is where he lives and where he grew up.

Darlene and John went to school with him from junior high through high school, and Darlene has always known that Mike has had a thing for her.

Lorinda quickly leads Mike to his favorite place in the café, at the bar where he can flirt with the waitresses and complain to Bill about his food. Bill yells right back, telling Mike if he doesn't like the food or irritates the waitresses to much he can get the hell out. The banter back and forth is in good fun, mostly.

Mike was in, two days ago, when Lorinda introduced him to the new waitress. Mike of course, already knows Darlene but hasn't seen her in many years. Lorinda is already teasing Darlene that Mike has his eyes on her. Lorinda sees a look in Mike's eyes she says she has seen before when he sees a woman he wants. Darlene just laughs it off and tells Lorinda to take a shot at him if she thinks he's so hot. "I'm too old. Mike likes them younger or no older than he is at least. You're about the same age, you're perfect," Lorinda reveals to Darlene.

"I'm also married," Darlene reminds Lorinda.

"You're separated honey, and from what you have told me, it doesn't look good for a reconciliation."

Darlene doesn't appreciate her co-worker's interest in her personal life and says as much.

"All I'm saying, is you deserve to have a life, too. You have been eating the same thing on the menu for a long time; maybe it's time to try something different."

"And you think a guy like Mike Stillman is the right guy for me?" Darlene responds with a snicker.

"I'm not telling you to marry him. But it's okay to have a little fun once in a while. How do you know John hasn't since you kicked him out?"

"Because I know John," Darlene protests. "Not to mention he's too busy working; to see his kids, much less be fooling around. And I didn't kick him out, we mutually agreed."

Lorinda utters that you never know as Bill pokes his head into the room to announce to the ladies that they're getting busy again, and break time is over.

"Coffee, strong and black as always, Mike?" Lorinda asks with a smirk on her face as she walks by his seat at the bar.

"It's as terrible as always," Mike offers back.

Lorinda pushes the other waitress to the side out of earshot of anyone, especially Bill the owner, and with a wink asks her to make up an excuse so that Darlene has to wait on Mike. The other waitress understands and winks back. She tells Bill she needs to use the bathroom real bad, a female emergency she tells him. Bill like any man, will never argue with any woman dealing with the mysteries of being a woman, so he lets her run to the bathroom. Bill asks Lorinda to take care of Mike's order. Lorinda yells that she can't, that she's too busy with her own customers. She tells him to have Darlene do it. The master plan now is in full action mode with Bill having no clue.

Darlene does as she's ordered and walks over and hands Mike his menu.

"Hey, Darlene, this must be my lucky day," Mike says flashing his baby blues.

Darlene smiles but offers no response. She knows that it is no coincidence that she is all of a sudden waiting on Mike. She knows Lorinda made this happen on purpose. "What can I get you today?"

"You're probably speaking of food, huh?" he says with a laugh. "Seriously, it's great to see you again. How's the new job working out for you?"

Darlene responds with the standard fine for an answer. Then goes back to pressing him for what he wants to order.

Mike ends her suspense. "Your attention, silly," he says with a devilish smile.

Darlene isn't buying what he's selling, but isn't about to offend one of Bill's best and most regular customers; on this, her second week of work. "You have it fully," she whispers back.

"But if you could try real hard and order something off

the menu, it would really make me happy."

Mike flashes the pearly whites again at Darlene's request, and he finally tells her what he wants to eat.

Lorinda who couldn't help but hear the whole conversation between Mike and Darlene puts her two cents in. "Wow, honey, you're made out of ice; I haven't seen too many ladies freeze out old Mike like that before."

"He's cute, but even more conceited," Darlene shares. "And I'm still married."

"Again, honey, you're separated, as in no longer together," Lorinda enunciates.

"We're separated, but we're still married," Darlene fires back as she heads to take another diner's order.

"Variety is the spice of life they say," Lorinda calls out with a tee-hee.

Darlene isn't too happy with Lorinda's meddling but considers whether she could be right about John. Is it possible that he could be seeing someone else, already? No, she tells herself. He's always working and always exhausted from working, so no, right?

Lorinda can see Darlene is getting a little upset and drops the topic for now. Lorinda walks over to Darlene and squeezes her arm in the way people do when they are comforting each other.

For the next hour, Mike Stillman does everything in his power to be sweet and charming to Darlene who waits on him. No off-color jokes, no sexist statements, no boorish comments come flooding out of his mouth as his reputation says they might. No, Mike is a perfect gentleman as he enjoys his huge plate of eggs and hash browns as he and Darlene reminiscence about growing up in a little town. He reminds Darlene of stories and episodes that happened to them when they were back in school, causing her to giggle. She can't help herself. Then one of them would ask the other if they've seen or heard from so and so, who used to be friends with them back in the day. The answer is almost always no. When people make it out of Grants Pass, they usually don't come back.

When he's finished with his meal, Mike drops a twenty on the counter, and then wishes her a good day. Mike makes sure to tell Bill and anyone else who's listening how great a job Darlene is already doing working at the café. Bill grunts his agreement, and waves to Mike as he's leaving. Lorinda, passing by Darlene as they are waiting on tables, elbows her gently, "It seems like you two got along."

Darlene stops long enough to look pleased and say, "Yeah, I was surprised," before getting back to her customers waiting anxiously for her presence at their tables.

"Let's remember to clean up everything real good before the lunch rush starts," Bill hollers from the kitchen.

The rest of the day Lorinda can't help herself. She just has to keep bringing up how good-looking and what a doll Mike Stillman is to Darlene. By the end of their shift, Darlene is telling her, "Enough already," and imploring her to drop the subject. But of course she never really does.

CHAPTER 2

John is in the thick of a dream. This is not just any run-of-the-mill dream either; this dream has the sizzle and spitting of bacon frying up in mouth-watering deliciousness. He is with Darlene and the kids at their favorite breakfast place. No, it's not the Caveman Café. No, this is a place down in Medford that specializes in every kind of pancake you can imagine. As great as the food is, the smells emitting from other tables and the kitchen are even better. The whole family is laughing and happy, the way it should be. Darlene is looking good in a tight skirt with a pretty flowered blouse that matches perfectly. John feels the soft touch of her skin as he cops a feel of her thigh from under their table, without the kids even knowing. The smell of bacon fills the air. Is there a better morning fragrance in the world to a man than bacon? He declares to Darlene in the dream.

"Dad, Dad, what are you doing here?!" "Dad, hey wake up!"

John opens his eyes just enough to see his youngest son, Kyle, sitting on the side of the bed. The smell he was dreaming about is still hanging in the air like mist in a rainforest.

"Nanna's making breakfast for lunch. Do you want some, Daddy? Nanna said you can keep sleeping if you want."

John struggles to his feet and struggles even more to get on his Wranglers. They fall to the floor more than once, as he battles to get the second leg in.

John hunts for his watch on the bedside table to check the time. He feels like he just got to sleep when Kyle woke him. His son hands him his cell phone. "The time is on this, Daddy."

John, non-techie as they come, reluctantly takes the phone from his son and checks the time. "Why is Nanna making you breakfast at four-thirty in the afternoon?" he asks his little boy. Kyle explains that Nanna feeds them when they are hungry and always asks them what they would like her to make. "Today, me, Cody and Courtney all wanted breakfast stuff."

John just looks amused at his son's explanation. After a pit stop in the bathroom, John follows his son out to the kitchen following the wonderful scent to its place of origin. John's walking slow, still shedding the last remnants of his slumber when he walks in on his mother in full cooking mode.

John's mom, born and bred in Britain, England to be precise, greets him as she often does with a, "Hello, ducky."

His other two kids, Cody, the oldest child at eleven years young, and Courtney, the youngest at six, are already sitting like soldiers at attention at the kitchen table, waiting for Nanna's grill to start serving happiness. Kyle joins in and plants his bottom between his brother and sister.

"Hi, Mom," John says as he takes one of the remaining chairs left.

"Hungry, dear?" she asks him.

"I could eat a little," John responds making his mother very happy. Like many women from European descent, Rose lives to cook and serve her family.

"How did you sleep? Was it quiet enough for you?"

"Good, Mom, it was fine."

Rose piles the food onto the kid's plates and then John's. John snickers at how, as usual, his mother's portions are so ridiculously huge. "The kids can't eat this much. I'm not sure I can."

Rose just sneers at her son's assertion and tells John the kids are growing all the time and need lots of food to keep up with their spurts. The kids dig in. The two little ones hum loudly as they eat as fast as they can, acting as if someone's going take their plate away from them in a second. John warns them to slow down and try taking a breath between bites. Rose happily scolds John and tells him to just let them be.

Rose is thrilled to see John at the house, sitting at the table with his children. It's been months since she's seen this sight. "It's wonderful to see you home, Johnny, like this," she tells him.

John is happy too but knows that nothing has changed yet between Darlene and him and doesn't want his mother to get her hopes up, at least not yet. He tries in vain to get this point across to Rose, but she isn't convinced and says as much.

"I'm telling you, Mom, I want to come back home just as much as you want me to, but Darlene and I have to work through some things first."

Rose is tired of hearing about all the work they have to do and reminds John for the umpteenth time how hard all this is on their three children, as if John isn't already aware of it. Then as is often her tack, Rose begins to push the blame onto Darlene for the whole situation. "I can't understand for the life of me why you and Darlene can't 'work on things' while living in the same home. You know, ducky, that I love Darlene very much, but she can be so stubborn sometimes."

John doesn't want to dispute that point with his mother, especially since he essentially agrees with his mother about his wife's stubbornness. But something inside him tells him he better stand up for Darlene or it may come back and bite him in the ass. "It's both of us, Mom. We just need to work things out before we're back together, that's all."

Rose sighs and shakes her head, clearly not happy with John's words. "I just hope your children can wait."

The kids are still pigging out at the table, so John wanting to talk to his mom without them listening, asks her to follow him into the den. After refilling the kid's glasses with more orange juice, she does.

Once in the den, John has to plead with his mom to stop cleaning up and checking out the messiness of the home long enough to listen to him. John wants to pump Rose for information about Darlene's new job but can't do that if he can't get her attention.

"So why didn't you tell me about Darlene?" John asks her.

Rose pretends to have no idea want John is talking about as she gives him a look like she's coming out of a fogbank or something and trying to get her eyes right. John isn't falling for her act, so he asks again. When she still acts like she doesn't have a clue, John gets straight to the point, no more messing around. "Why didn't you tell me Darlene got a job at the café?"

Rose starts to get busy again, a good way to avoid discussing things she doesn't really want to talk about. She picks up a dust rag and complains about all the dust, here and everywhere in the home. John presses her some more and finally gets his mom to come clean.

"Darlene made me promise not to tell you," Rose says.

Why, John contemplates, would she do that. What is his wife trying to hide?

"So I did as she said, Johnny. I guess, duck, that she wanted to be the one to tell you."

John considers if there is anything else that Darlene hasn't bothered to tell him about, like a boyfriend for instance. He shudders at the thought.

He knows his mom has been watching the kids since Darlene started work again, and now he wants to know if there are any other secrets his mom isn't sharing with him. But before he can put her on the spot, Rose's cell phone rings and she happily picks it up and turns her back to him. John can hear from the other side of the room his mom's enthusiasm for the call. He knows it's someone on the other side of the line that she is thrilled to hear from. Rose says something about seeing the person tomorrow before ending the call. She rushes back to John almost bouncing through the living room with glee. She can't wait to serve up the "'good news'" to him. "Your brother is coming here tomorrow!"

John is surprised by the news for a second and not really sure how to take it. He and his little brother haven't really spoken in over two years after a falling out about trying to locate their dad. Their father, Raymond Barrett, abandoned the family more than fifteen years ago when John and Audie were still just teenagers. As the oldest, John took on the biggest burden to help his mom and help provide for the family. John's brother, Audie, was too young to work and didn't face the same pressures that were forced upon John. As the years went by, Audie discussed connecting with their father many times, but never has. John is still angry at his father, and has refused to meet with him. John often held his mother in his arms when she was so depressed she could hardly get out of bed in the mornings. He cooked, he cleaned, he took care of his little brother, and he gave his mom every dime he made from his numerous part-time jobs after school, to help make ends meet. John isn't sure if it is fair to be upset with Audie for wanting to get in touch with their dad, but he can't help feel the way he does. And now Audie is coming here for the first time in three years to visit. Rose, well aware of her son's' bickering, warns John in advance to be kind to his brother. John doesn't address her concern and just asks when Audie will be arriving in Grants Pass. Rose answers that it will be tomorrow evening, between six and eight. She warns John a second time to be on his best behavior toward Audie.

"Okay, Mom, I'll try."

Rose wants more than "I'll try," coming from his lips. She wants a promise that he will talk to Audie and be nice to him. "You two haven't spoken in donkey years, and that's got to end tomorrow, Johnny. You're brothers, the only brothers that each of you has, and you both need to bloody well act like it!"

John dares not say anything back to his mom. He just offers his agreement as Rose storms back to the kitchen to start cleaning up from the meals. John considers his wonderful life right now. He's working himself to death for a wife who doesn't want him around and is living a secret life. He sees his kids only a few times a week, which eats him up inside, and now his pain-in-the-ass little brother is coming to visit with all this going on. It can't get any better than this, he thinks to himself. "I only hope Audie has a job now and isn't still gambling all his money away!"

"You be nice!" Rose yells from the kitchen.

"You do have plenty of alcohol in your house, Mom, right?!" John yells back.

Rose tells him again to be nice and leave things alone. "Go play with your kids. God knows they don't see you enough."

John can tell she's getting pissed and so he drops the subject and listens to his mother's words and heads back to the bedrooms to spend some time with his children. The kids are thrilled to see Dad sit down next to them. "We're having a 'Star Wars' binge party, Daddy," little Courtney announces to him.

John grabs her and places her on his lap. Then he sits back with his other two boys on both sides of him and joins in on watching a movie about a galaxy far, far, away. John wishes he could go to that galaxy, right now.

JOHN'S CELL DOESN'T BLOW UP ON HIM AT ALL WHILE he's at his old house. So without any side jobs to worry about, he sends his mother home for the evening and stays to watch the kids until Darlene gets home. Rose is more than happy to leave the children with their father as she hopes that seeing John watching the kids at the home might be something that impresses Darlene.

A couple hours go by and then Darlene pulls into the driveway. She is surprised to see John is still at the house. The kids are wrestling and laughing with their dad on the living room floor. She can't help but be pleased at the sight. But when John sees her he pulls away from the kids and puts the spotlight of attention on her. Darlene tells him, "as you were," not for a second wanting to take his attention from the kids and all the fun they are having.

"How was work?" John asks with two children wrapped around his neck and the other one sitting on his chest.

"Okay, but I'm tired, John, and I don't want to discuss my new job and why I took it, and all that stuff, alright?"

John hears her words, but like a rat nibbling around the cheese in the trap he just can't help himself. He pushes the kids off of him and tells them to go their bedrooms for a bit while he and Mommy talk. "I thought I was making enough money for both of us, and I don't see why our kids need to be babysat while you're off working some job."

Darlene is already getting irritated just by the tone of John's voice, much less his accusing her of not doing what's best for their children. She reminds him quickly that it is his own mother who is watching the kids while she works.

"You're making enough money for both of us. Listen to yourself. We're not even together right now, John! We're separated, and I don't know if we'll ever be together again. And the way you have no time for anyone in your life because of your work, I don't see us together, John I have to start planning my life without you. That doesn't mean we can't work things out, but I have to do things, like making my own way in life, as if we can't work it out."

John's blood begins to boil. He's afraid to show it to Darlene though, since that would just make things worse. How can she even consider that they won't get back together? How can she care so little for him and for what's best for the kids? Somehow he controls his temper and challenges not one point of Darlene's. "What do you want from me, Darlene? I'm working my ass off for you and the kids. I want us all to have a better life."

Darlene just shakes her head at his proclamation. She can't help herself. She's been listening to John say this kinda'-

of crap for several years now. "How about a better life now by just being in our lives? We can all have a better life right this minute if you could just see it."

John isn't sure what she wants him to see and tells her so.

Darlene considers why she keeps bashing her head into the wall over this same argument, again and again. "You're a workaholic, John, and you don't even know it."

John as he always does, defends his long hours and late nights. It's to make enough for Darlene and the children to live better than they do now, but Darlene isn't buying it. She never does.

"I don't care about that. I know the kids don't care about that, John. They just want to see their dad."

John always hates when Darlene uses the kids against him. Unfair fighting he assumes, since she knows how much the kids mean to him. "Everything I do, I do it for you and our kids!" he says in frustration.

Darlene, sick and tired of hearing that as his default comeback, yells at him. "You don't do it for me and the kids! We don't want you to work so hard, and we've never, ever, asked you to work so much! John, you do it for you and this ridiculous thing with your father!"

"My father? Why are you bringing him into this? He's been out of my life before we even met!"

Darlene has kept these thoughts to herself for a long time, but now in this moment with their marriage dangling by a thread, and in the heat of this very hot moment, she decides to not keep them bottled up anymore. "Because, John, your father is always with you and has been ever since we first met!"

John demands to know what in the world Darlene is talking about because he honestly has no clue at this point.

Darlene can read this on his face. Her voice lowers, and her anger starts to subside. It's replaced with sadness, sadness that the man she loves and has since she first laid eyes on him in high school English, can be so out of touch with his own feelings and motives. John is staring at her waiting for an explanation. He's not saying a word, only waiting. Darlene speaks softly now, "You've been trying to prove to yourself, as long as I've known you, that you're a better man than he was."

John keeps listening no emotion is on his face. Darlene can't tell if he's digesting what she's telling him or just getting really pissed. Whatever it is, she keeps on pushing forward, determined to find out. "John, you are a better man than your father. All the money in the world, all the things you can buy me and the kids isn't going to change that fact. Your father abandoned you, your brother, and Rose. I know you would never abandon your family. Don't you think I know that?"

John doesn't respond at all for nearly a minute. He still shows nothing on his face. Finally without saying a word he stands up and heads back to the kid's' bedrooms and says his goodbyes. Darlene can hear the kids begging him to stay, but John makes up some excuse that he has to go, work is calling or something like that.

John whispers to Darlene goodbye, still not giving a response to what she just charged him with in regards to his father. On the way out, Darlene lets him know that there oldest, Cody, has a baseball game at the park in only one hour. "If you're not busy working, I know it would mean a lot to Cody to see you out there."

John stops in his tracks at the front door and considers the request for a nano second. "I'll see you at the game."

24   *Andrew Scott Bassett*

Darlene suggests that he should just hang out with them at the house and then they could all go to the game together. John knows the right thing to say is "sure, why not," but he's still stinging from his argument with Darlene and for some reason, he's not even sure why, he says no. "No, I'll just meet you guys at the game."

Darlene shrugs but tells him that's fine. She's done fighting for the night. As John leaves, she wonders if bringing his issues with his father into the light of day for the first time was the right thing to do, or not.

CHAPTER 3

D arlene scans the ballpark looking for John. He's late as usual, but she tries not to show how upset it makes her feel to Kyle and Courtney who are sitting next to her in the stands. She's holding a seat for him but is about ready to let anyone sit there. If he comes much later, it will probably not be a good idea for John to be sitting next to her at all. Darlene's heart aches when she sees their son Cody look up into the stands for his dad. His mind should be on the game, not on whether his dad is going to be watching him or not. Darlene knows that Cody lives for his dad's approval, and this puts one more brick in the wall of separation between her and John, every time he lets his son down. "Where is he?" she whispers under her breath, hoping the kids can't hear.

JOHN WAKES UP IN A SUDDEN BURST OF ACTIVITY AS IF someone put the paddles on him and electrified his heart pump. He leaps out of his recliner, which he somehow dozed off in when he stopped for just a second to catch SportsCenter on TV. He moans and groans as he furiously looks for his car keys and wallet. John can't believe he fell asleep and is now late for Cody's game. He curses up a storm until he finds his keys and then sprints out the door knowing full well that Darlene is going to be waiting for him at the ballpark like the Indians were waiting for General Custer at Little Big Horn.

⎯⎯⎯⎯⎯

DARLENE IS INTENTLY WATCHING AS CODY CATCHES A pop-up near second base. Someone sneaks up from seemingly nowhere and asks if the seat next to her is taken. She looks up from her sitting position to see Mike Stillman standing over her with a delighted look on his face. Mike gestures to the chair next to her, again asking about its availability. At first instinct, Darlene is going to tell him that she's holding it for John, but then as upset with John as she is, she doesn't. Mike happily positions himself next to her. He asks her which one of the players is her son and Darlene proudly points to the boy on the end of the bench. Kyle and Courtney both in unison give their mom a look that asks who is this guy sitting in Dad's seat, but Darlene ignores them.

Mike comments on how proud she must be to see her son out there playing, and playing so well. He then makes a few quips about some of the other kids on the opposing team that makes Darlene chuckle, although she feels guilty for doing so. Darlene is surprised again by Mike. After all she's heard about him, certainly not always flattering, she's surprised at how decent he seems to be. She looks around again to see if there is any sighting of John. There isn't. Darlene knows if John does somehow make it to the game before it's over, he will not be pleased to see another man sitting and conversing next to her. She realizes that it isn't fair to put Mike in such an awkward position. "Mike," she says, ready to tell him about John possibly showing up and being jealous and angry.

John can't believe how many people on a hot summer night are here to watch a Little League game. John walks from one side of the stands to the other searching for his family. He yells out to Cody who's sitting in the dug-out. Cody smiles from ear to ear, happy that his dad is at the game, no matter how late he is. Finally John spots Darlene and the kids and begins to navigate through the stands toward them. He excuses and apologizes his way through the crowd as he climbs up the bleachers. Then he notices something else. A guy sitting next to Darlene stands up, gives her a smile and a laugh, and then looks for another seat. More noticeably, Darlene beams and grins back as she wishes him a goodnight. By the time John reaches Darlene, he remembers the face of the guy whose company she seems to be enjoying. Mike Stillman finds another seat above them at the top of the bleachers. John can hardly help but notice how different the look he gets when Darlene greets him from the look Mike got when he said his goodbyes.

"Oh, you decided to make it."

John's face has frostbite from the greeting Darlene gives him. He tries to apologize for his tardiness, but she won't give him the satisfaction of even listening. He sits down and although they are just a few inches apart in proximity, they could be a thousand miles apart in reality. Any volley of conversation John attempts is immediately batted down by her. When he attempts to change the subject and talk about his brother arriving tomorrow from Arizona, Darlene gruffly tells him she already heard the news from Rose. John wants to ask her about Stillman and the meaning of it, but he thinks better of it. After screwing up and being late, John knows any perceived criticism he might fire Darlene's way will end up being a bomb that comes back and explodes in his face. He lets her enjoyable conversation with Mike go. The next forty five minutes are painful. Darlene says nothing to him, and John is afraid to say anything more to her that might get the fireworks started. Their two kids sitting next to them watch the whole thing play out. It's not the first time.

After the game is over, John walks Darlene and the kids to their car. Cody is thrilled to have Dad there and is bubbling over with joy. John hugs him and tells him how great he looked playing tonight. He hugs Kyle and Courtney as well, but when he tries to open the door for Darlene, he's quietly rebuffed. She pushes him aside and tells the kids to get in the car. John leans through her driver side window after she lowers it for him. He attempts to apologize again for being late to the game. Darlene for the first time all night smiles at John, but then she says, "It's your world, John. You're the center of the universe, and we're just small little planets orbiting around you."

She rolls the window back up and starts the engine. Nothing more to be said, nothing more John can do. If life is like a baseball game then Darlene just pitched a shut-out on John. And John knows only too well that is exactly the case tonight. But tomorrow is another day and maybe his pitcher will have better stuff for the next game, he amuses himself with, as he waves as Darlene and the kids drive away.

THE NEXT DAY AFTER WORK JOHN HEADS TO HIS MOM'S house to see his brother, Audie. It's been quite a while since they've talked to each other and even longer since they last saw one another.

Audie leaps off of his mom's sofa to greet his brother when John walks into the house.

"Johnny! How the heck are ya?"

For an awkward moment, the brothers play a game of chicken with their respective greeting styles. Each brother ponders to himself if he should hug, fist pump, pat on the shoulder, or just shake hands the old fashion way. Audie, the more gregarious of the two, leans in but can sense the rebuff in John's body language and stops himself. He then realizes a quick handshake is the best he's going to get from his older brother.

Rose directs her boys to sit down as she makes them both a cup of her legendary famous hot tea. The two boys contend that it is too hot outside in the summer to drink hot tea, but Rose will not hear of it and moves to the kitchen to get the kettle going.

The two men measure each other for a second, like gunfighters preparing to draw.

"Johnny, I am surprised. You look great!"

John isn't sure if that's a compliment or an insult masquerading as one. "Thanks, I guess," John responds, stone-faced.

Audie tries to elaborate. "I mean, bro, mom's been telling me how hard you've been working and all. And you know with you and Darlene and everything, you just look good, man, that's all."

John thanks him for that, the best that he can.

"So how have you been?" John begins with.

Audie flashes his big toothy smile, the one he's had since he was a kid. He chortles hard at the question as if buying time while trying to come up with a clever answer. "Same old, same old, man."

John acts as if he understands, but as usual he has no idea what his kid brother is referring to, with same old.

"You still selling cars in Phoenix?"

Audie's teeth reappear again. "No, I quit a few months ago. I was sick of the grind, you know?"

"So what are you doing now?"

Audie suddenly jabs and jukes to a more philosophical and serious tone. "Taking a pause from the rat race man, and just watching the wheels as John Lennon once said."

"Is that code for you lost your job and can't find another one?" John asks him, his words dripping with sarcasm.

Rose hollers from the kitchen for John to be nice to his brother, but Audie just laughs off John's little jab.

"I didn't come all this way, Johnny, just to listen to your put downs, like always."

That leads then to the more important question John renders, why did Audie come to visit in the first place. John knows it's not because he misses his family.

"So, why?"

"Can't a guy want to see his family? I mean, it's been like a couple of year's dude," Audie confesses.

John has always been able to see through his brother's BS before, and he believes now is no different. He challenges Audie on the notion that he is just here in Grants Pass for a social call.

John point blank asks him what he wants, which bring more consternation from their mother, still in the kitchen preparing the tea.

"I know you, Audie. You want something. Do you need money? Is that it?"

Audie chuckles at the statement from John. "Not if you help me, big bro."

Now we're getting somewhere, John thinks to himself. Now we can get to the real reason for the visit and quit screwing around. John waits to hear more.

Audie swallows hard at being put on the spot by John. John's eyes are piercing through him right now as he struggles to find the right words to start his explanation with. Audie hem's and haw's before finding his foothold. He reaches for a large backpack sitting at his feet that John didn't notice until this moment. Audie pulls out a large manila envelope and unfastens it enough to reach inside and take some papers out. "Do you know what I have here man?"

Of course John has no idea. How could he?

Audie continues, "I'm the bearer of bad news, I'm afraid."

A big pause comes next as John waits for Audie to shed more light. Audie always one to love the spotlight, seems to be especially enjoying the attention he's getting from John as he slowly unwinds the threads of mystery. Audie yells to Rose to come in and hear this as well. He didn't really need to because she was already on her way back into the living room with the tea.

"What is it, dear? she asks as she places the tea and sugar cookies on a platter down in front of her two sons.

Audie asks his mother to brace herself at what he has to tell her. Rose gets fearful at what Audie is about to say, as John starts to get angry at his brother's stringing things out and upsetting their mom. He demands Audie just spill it; let them know what the hell he is talking about.

Audie without saying a word hands the papers from the envelope to his brother. "What's this?" John says as he takes them.

"I got it in the mail a few days ago," Audie replies.

John looks at the first page. The top of the page gets his attention right away. He can see it's from a law firm from Glens Falls, New York. John has heard through the family grapevine that their father lives near Glens Falls, so John instantly assumes it's from their father. Under further investigation John can see that it is a will. "Their father's will?"

Audie nods. The serious look on his face tells John that his assumption is right. Rose isn't following along with the conversation well enough to understand what Audie is holding in his hands. John then reaches for her hand and gently squeezes it.

"What? What is it, dear?" she asks John.

John looks at his poor mom, looking for the right words to tell her that the only man she ever truly loved is dead. "Dad has died. That is what Audie's here to tell us, Mom."

Rose shows no emotion at John's words. Her sons look at each other wondering what she's feeling and then look back to her to study her reaction some more.

"When?" she asks Audie.

"About a week ago," Audie answers.

"How did he die?" Rose questions.

Audie isn't really sure and lets them know that.

John, who knows his brother considered trying to get in touch with their father over the years, pushes to know any details that Audie might have. But Audie has no more to offer, at least not about the how's, or where's, or why's.

"Are you okay?" John turns and asks his mother.

Rose puts up a stiff upper lip and quietly says she is and then excuses herself and walks to her bathroom to be alone with her thoughts.

John thinks he should be sad, knows he should be, but just can't quite get there, not seeing his father in more than fifteen years has hardened him to anything involving dear old Dad, even his death it seems.

"Well, thanks for coming all this way to tell us, Audie," John tells his brother sincerely.

Audie responds that it was no problem, the right thing to do. And then shares with John his reason for traveling here is more than just breaking the sad news about Dad.

Watch out, John thinks to himself. Here comes the sales pitch. Even with the news of the death of their father still hovering in the air, Audie's about to ask for money. John contemplates if his brother has any shame in his short little body at all.

"You see bro, there's a letter that comes from Dad, well from Dad's attorney who was in charge of his estate and his will."

"How much?" John wants to know. "How much money do you need this time?"

Audie shakes his head at the accusation. "I don't need money, Johnny. It's about how much money you and I can make following dad's orders."

"What orders?" John wants to know.

"These orders, dude," Audie answers as he hands more paperwork to his brother.

This time it is a set of instructions and directions in the form of a letter that details people and places.

"What does this mean?" John asks him.

Audie begins to translate more clearly. "Dad has a list of people across the country that he wants the two of us to go see."

John asks why.

"He wanted us to break the news to them about his death. He also has a gift for each of them, for us to give to them."

John is so lost at why their father would make such a request and even more baffled at why he would think after abandoning the family more than fifteen years ago, that his two sons would go along with it.

Audie then clarifies. "We do this and we end up in Glens Falls in New York and get a check from Dad's attorney for fifty thousand each."

John slumps back in his chair. All this time when he thought about how his father might be doing these last fifteen years he never once considered the idea that his father might be a wealthy man. John could certainly use the money. Fifty thousand dollars could jump start his side business into a full-time gig, but it would mean being a hypocrite to his feelings. When Raymond Barrett left the family behind and high-tailed it away, John swore to himself and anyone who would listen, that he would never forgive his dad for what he did. At this moment John is remembering how much pain their mom went through when their father left. At just seventeen years old John became a breadwinner in the family and a therapist for his distraught mother. He's hated his father all these years for what he did, and now he wants him to be his errand boy and run across the country for him. Fifty thousand dollars is a lot of money, John realizes, but not nearly enough to pay for all the damage done. He leans forward and looks his brother straight in the eyes. "Not interested," he says.

Audie is dumbfounded at John's decision. How could anyone turn down fifty thousand dollars? Audie asks John to explain himself.

John says it again, and this time with a caveat. "You should be happy. That's one hundred thousand dollars for you."

But Audie's not happy. "It doesn't work that way, man."
John doesn't understand.

"It's both of us or nothing."

"What do you mean?" John replies.

"Dad wanted both of us to take this trip together. If I go alone, there's no money at the end," Audie discloses.

Why would their father do that, John contemplates. He asks Audie the same thing. Audie can only guess their father's reasons. "Maybe he wanted us to spend time together or something. I don't know, man. I just can't get my inheritance without your help."

This is crazy, John thinks. Audie sits quietly hoping for John to rethink his decision.

Rose, who's been listening to the whole conversation from another room in the house, wanders back in. She takes no time at all to put her two cents in. "John, you need to do this for your brother."

John now has two people pressuring him, and is surprised his mother would want him to do anything requested by dear old Dad. "I don't know, Mom…"

Rose cuts him off and again calls for his going with his brother. "Your father, God knows, owes you this much. Johnny, regardless how much bitterness you bloody well have against him, and you know, ducky, I have my share, following his wishes after he has died is the proper thing to do. You are a bigger man than he was."

Rose tears up as she says the words. John can see she is still coming to grips with her ex-husband having passed. Audie is still waiting for John's answer, hoping for a change of heart.

Audie's desire for his father's money carries little weight with John, but seeing that it is important to their mother means much more.

Rose, wiping away more tears, presses John further. "Audie needs the money, dear and so do you. Your father wanted you to do this, Johnny, and he wanted you to have this money."

Mom always lowers her voice when she is trying to make an important point, and she does the same thing here to get John's full attention.

"You're always telling me, dear, that you have a month of paid vacation coming from the mill."

She's right about that, but John had hoped to spend his vacation time if he ever could take time off from his side business, to have fun with his kids and reconnect with Darlene. "I'm going to have to talk to Darlene about this, you know."

Audie says he understands, confident that Darlene will see the need for fifty thousand more dollars in the family till. Rose chimes in that of course John has to talk it over with Darlene, but that Darlene and the kids could use that money as well.

"How long will it take?" John queries Audie.

Audie fights back exuberance, not wanting to tip his hand to much. He can see just by his brother's question that John's having a change of heart. "Probably a couple of weeks, I'd guess, man. There's one other thing we have to do with each person on pop's list."

John shrugs; he wants to know what it is.

"We have to go fishing with them."

"Why?" John asks. "Why would Dad want us to go fishing with people we don't even know?"

Audie has no idea why but that is part of the deal he tells his brother. Rose asks to see the list of names and does recognize some of them. "The ones I know were friends of your father from long ago."

"Fishing, that's a strange request," John states to his mom and brother.

Audie reminds John how much their father, like John, loved the outdoors and especially fishing. "You're just like him in that respect, bro. You and Pop would both rather fish than anything else."

John has no comment to that. He never likes to think that he and his father were ever similar in anything, but he knows Audie is right about fishing.

"So we're good, Johnny? I'd like to get going in the next couple of days, man," Audie adds.

John again tells him that it is up to what Darlene thinks. John, like Audie, could use the money, but he's not thrilled about being away from home for any amount of time, not with him and Darlene trying to "'figure things out.'"

Rose then tells John to go over to the house and speak with Darlene right now. "She's home, dear, and there's no time like the present."

Audie agrees with his mom.

"Alright," John says, "I'll go talk to her and see what she thinks."

"Good, tell her it's to help Audie," Rose responds, pushing her oldest to leave.

"So then we'll talk soon, bro," Audie promises as John starts for the front door.

John signals yes as he pulls out his car keys and takes off.

TWO MORNINGS LATER, JOHN AND AUDIE ARE PACKING up John's truck. They throw their luggage and fishing gear under the camper shell. Audie clutches close to him his large backpack with his dad's will and the letter with the names and directions on it that guide their trip. Audie also has some special items that their father requested they leave with each person they visit.

Darlene switched shifts at the café so she could be at Rose's home to see them off. She knows it's important for their children to say goodbye to their dad when he's going to be gone for weeks.

John can't help but notice how new all of Audie's fishing gear looks and comments on it to his brother.

"I'm not like you Johnny. I don't live in the outdoors all the time," Audie responds in defense of his going out and buying all new fish and tackle gear for the trip.

John shakes his head and sneers at his kid brother's defensiveness. Then after locking up the camper shell, John informs Audie that it's time to get going. Audie gives his mom a hug, which for some reason brings tears to her eyes. She pleads to him to drive careful and be safe. Audie just snickers. He reminds his mom that John would never in a million years let him drive his truck, so it's John she needs to remind to drive careful.

John overhearing the conversation agrees wholeheartedly with Audie about driving his truck. "Not in a million years," John says to his brother.

Audie pats John's kids on the head one by one and gladly receives a hug from Darlene. She whispers in his ear to take good care of John while there gone. "You got it," he whispers back.

John then says his goodbyes. First he squeezes the stuffing out of his daughter Courtney while simultaneously lifting her up into the air and twirling her around. Next he squats down and gives his younger boy, Kyle, a tight hug that gets Kyle's rain factory working from his eyes. Finally he pats his oldest, Cody, on the shoulder and tells him he's in charge of everything while he's gone. John shakes Cody's hand firmly, a real man's handshake he tells him before letting go.

Audie and his mother look at each other as if to say "gimmie a break." They then watch with fascination to see how John and Darlene's sendoff goes.

It's an awkward moment for both, especially with the audience of the kids, and Audie and Rose all there.

At first they appear to Audie and Rose to not be able to make physical contact of any kind, or at least not sure how to. John puts out his hand like it's a business meeting and they're trying to consummate a deal, but Darlene will have none of that. She moves in close and gives him a kiss on the cheek. "Take care of yourself, John, and take care of Audie."

John nods and promises her he will. He also promises to keep them all up to date on the trip by phone. Then a blubbering Rose, overcome suddenly by emotion, jumps into his arms. She begs him again to be safe and careful while crossing the country. She demands that he take care of his little brother, which John again promises he will. After fighting his way out of his mother's embrace, he and Audie say one last goodbye and then get into the truck and drive away. Through his side mirrors, John can see Darlene, the kids, and a still-crying Rose waving to them as they drive down the road.

Andrew Scott Bassett

CHAPTER 4

The rainclouds that keep Oregon nice and green follow the brothers out onto the interstate. The silence inside the truck is deafening, so Audie attempts to plug his cell phone into the truck's stereo. John, however, stops him in his tracks. "What kind of music are you putting on?"

Audie sighs. Here we go, he thinks to himself. We have barely got out of Grants Pass and already John is starting with his redneck crap. "Just some songs I like, man."

"You mean your hip-hop and rap crap," John comes back with sarcastically.

Audie has been down this road many times before with John and he already knows that he and John have very different tastes in just about everything. Still Audie's in no mood to get the trip off on the wrong note by fighting with his brother over choices in music. "I'm eclectic. I listen to pop, hip-hop, some rap, a little of everything man, except your hillbilly music," Audie answers.

John sighs at the very thought of that so-called music coming out of his speaker and tells Audie to keep it to himself. He orders his brother to listen through his earbuds and make sure that he can't hear it while he is driving.

Audie chuckles as he tells his brother he was going to listen to it that way, anyways.

"Well, alright then," John bellows as if he proved his point.

"Man, how can a brother of mine be so redneck about everything?" Audie mocks.

"Oh, don't start with that shit again," John tells him, not wanting to hear it. "Just because I know what good music really sounds like."

Audie laughs some more. "And what, brother, makes you the so-called expert on what makes good music?"

John is happy to make his argument and does. It's the same thing he's told Audie for years. Nothing new, Audie thinks to himself. Rap and hip-hop artists aren't musicians because they don't play guitars and the artists of today can't play anything or even sing without the aid of computers. Blah, blah, blah, Audie thinks as John goes through his usual list of rants.

"And country hick music and old time rock and roll is the real music, right?" Audie counters with his own sarcastic tone.

"Exactly," John replies. "Country music is about stories and real people."

Audie by this point is ready to let the discussion over music die its natural death. They've been arguing things like this forever, and nothing ever changes, so why bother. Audie changes the subject. "Darlene and the kiddie's look well."

"Yep," John replies, going along with the change.

"And I think I even detected some fireworks still there between you and Darlene when you we're saying goodbye."

John looks at his brother like he has no idea what he is talking about. So Audie keeps up with the positives about John and Darlene patching things up until John finally opens up. "I don't know where we're at right now."

"Well, you're working on things dude, and that's an okay place to be," Audie tells him trying to spin things into a good light.

"I hope so, but I don't know, I just don't know," John confesses to his brother.

Audie then assures John, to make him feel better about things with Darlene that he could definitely see some electricity coming from the two of them. John looks pleased. He knows what Audie is trying to do and appreciates it. "Thanks," he tells his brother.

Audie returns the look and tells him you're welcome, and then places his earbuds on and closes his eyes for a little r and r.

The first stop on their journey will take them to Northern California where they once lived as small children.

John looks up to the sky through his car window. The rainclouds are getting bigger and more ominous by the second. "Summer in Oregon," he says with laugh.

───⬡───

DARLENE IS WATCHING TELEVISION WITH HER THREE kids as Rose prepares lunch for them. Rose offered after John and Audie left, to feed Darlene and the kids, and Darlene took her up on it. She hops up from the couch leaving the children behind to see if there is anything she can do to help Rose. Rose being Rose, of course never needs any help from anyone in the kitchen. Still, Darlene asks before she takes a seat at the kitchen table after Rose tells her she's got it all under control.

Rose can tell something is bothering Darlene by the way she's acting and begins to hint around with her, trying to decipher what it is. At first Darlene says nothing, just the normal "I'm fine" that people always say. But Rose keeps poking and prodding her for more information, determined to get at the reasons for her unhappiness. "You can't be missing Johnny already, ducky?"

Darlene looks up from the table at the question and just tosses a grin in Rose's direction.

"Is that it really?" Rose wonders.

Darlene shakes her head. "No, not that, I'm not sure what it is. I guess I'm just worried that John's being gone for a little while will be too easy to deal with."

Rose is confused since it was Darlene who insisted that John move out a couple of months ago. "I thought you wanted time apart, to work on things, dear?"

Darlene agrees that she did, or does, but it's the fact of not having John around at all, that bothers her. But what if it stops bothering her, is her real fear.

Rose gives her a comforting squeeze on the top of her shoulder. She wishes she could come up with some powerful and poetic words for Darlene at this moment, but they're nowhere to be found. So Rose does the best she can with what she has. "You love Johnny. Being apart for even a short time will show you that."

Darlene isn't so sure but softly agrees with Rose. She knows it's what Rose wants to hear. Rose loves her and loves her son more than anything. She certainly wants everything to work out and for them to get back together and live happily ever after.

"Did you ever come to a point where you were happier when Ray wasn't around than when he was?"

Rose stops her sandwich making long enough to really consider Darlene's question.

"No," she says. "Ray was a bloody pain in the ass as husbands go. Think yourself lucky you have John, but I always loved him and I guess I still do in my own way."

"So you never thought about being apart from him, living your own life?" Darlene follows up with.

Rose chuckles as she considers the thought. "Every wife thinks about that, dear, but I never wanted that even after Ray left and I had no choice in the matter."

Darlene sees she's touched a raw spot in Rose and lets the subject go. "I guess I'm just being like every other woman who's separated from her husband?"

"Exactly, dear," Rose agrees as she places the tray of sandwiches on the kitchen table and calls the children to join them.

Like a herd of buffaloes, the kids come stampeding in. They know that no one makes better lunches than their nanna.

Darlene thanks Rose for listening to her. Rose just smiles and tells her it's going to work out all for the best. Darlene only wishes she was as positive about that as Rose seems to be.

⌘

THE SIGN WELCOMING THEM TO CALIFORNIA PASSES LIKE a blur. Soon they will be stopping and admitting that they have no fruit or anything else to declare. Audie thanks John again for coming on the trip with him.

"Mom asked me to do it," John answers curtly.

Audie still is thankful regardless of the reason. "This is going to be great, me and you out on the open road, criss-crossing the country."

"Our father just died, Audie, regardless of how we felt about him," John reminds him, curious why his brother is so happy.

Audie knows but is still excited at the thought of them embarking on this adventure, together. "We are like Bonnie and Clyde or something," he tells John.

John just shakes his head, not understanding the metaphor or the enthusiasm of his brother.

"How longs it been since you and I have done anything together?" Audie asks.

John forces out an, "I don't know," as he keeps his eyes straight ahead and his hands tight on the wheel.

"A long time, a long time," Audie responds, answering his own question.

John then pulls over to go through the state checkpoint. A few minutes later, after getting back on the road, Audie continues to ramble on and on, putting John in an even worse mood.

"It's cool that the mill let you have your vacation time on such short notice."

John nods.

"I wonder why Dad wanted us to do all this, anyhow," Audie contemplates, changing the subject matter hoping to find a topic that his brother will show interest in.

It's a one-sided conversation as John keeps quiet, just focusing on the road ahead.

Audie asks the same question again, but this time directly to John. John just mumbles he doesn't know and leaves it at that.

"Well, I'm still happy that we're doing this together, bro. The Barrett brothers are on the road, man!"

John shows no reaction. So far he's not enjoying himself, just as he thought.

THIRTY MINUTES LATER AND WITH THE CALIFORNIA

Andrew Scott Bassett

heat engulfing them, Audie declares, "God, it's a freakin' oven down here! It's just like Phoenix, man!"

The cooler climate of Oregon is behind then now as they pull off the road and into a truck stop in what seems like the middle of nowhere, surrounded by picturesque mountains all around.

"Happening place you picked to stop," Audie says sarcastically.

John responds by barking at him that they need gas. John tells Audie that they might as well get something to eat while they're here.

Audie could go for something, too, and follows John into the truck stop after his brother is done filling his truck's gas tank.

Once inside and after ordering from the lunch menu, John and Audie do everything in their power to not make eye contact with each other. John especially pretends to be distracted by looking at anything and everything on the walls of the restaurant. Audie begins to realize how stupid they are both acting and tries to start up small talk with his brother. He starts with the easy stuff, the non-controversial items to put up for discussion. "So, where exactly are we?"

John actually looks Audie's way and spouts, "Yreka."

"Not a lot here, I got to say?"

"Yeah," John grouses, starting to recall why he and Audie have talked so little in the last five years.

"How far to our first stop on the dead-dad tour, it's in Yuba City?" Audie says, unsuccessfully trying to inject some humor into the conversation.

"About two and half hours or so," John replies, still making more eye contact with the table they're sitting at than with his brother.

Audie remembers a bit about the family living in Yuba City when he was a small child.

Their father was stationed at Beale Air Force Base at the time. Audie asks John about how much he remembers from the time, but John gives him hardly any feedback. "What about the guy we're meeting there, Will Aldrich. Does he ring any bells?"

"Yeah, I remember him. He was a good friend of Dad's," John surprisingly answers.

Audie attempts a few more conversation talking points like John's work, his side-business, even John's kids, but gets almost no effort in return from John. John just sits there across from him acting like the kid in school who got in trouble and is waiting for the principal to call him into the office. After a few more minutes of stimulating discussion Audie's had enough and lets his brother know. "God, now I see it."

The fact that John has no idea what Audie is talking about gets his attention. John looks at his brother waiting for him to continue, to see what he's talking about.

"No, I get it. I really get what your biggest problem is," Audie surmises.

John asks him what he is talking about as their food arrives at the table.

"Johnny, look at you. You are so pent up inside. You can't even communicate like a normal person."

John isn't impressed with his brother's instant psycho analysis. "This is going to be a long trip, so why don't you just keep your liberal, hippie, let's-hold-hands-and-chant-together psyche-talk, to yourself!"

But Audie doesn't and proceeds forward, disregarding the caution signs ahead. "You are all uptight inside man,

Johnny. That's probably why you and Darlene are having so many problems."

Before Audie can utter another word, John slams down the bottle of ketchup sitting on the table. Other diner's in the restaurant turn their heads to see what the commotion is all about. John then forbids Audie to talk any more. Audie tries to apologize to his brother, but John won't listen to him anymore. He motions with his hand for Audie to not to say anything else. Audie seeing John's getting upset, obliges him. John then gets up from the table and announces he will be waiting for Audie in the truck. As he's walking out, John stops and turns around and marches back to the table. "You know what? I haven't even seen you in a couple of years or whatever and you have the balls to tell me about what my problem is and discuss my marriage with me!"

Audie tries to get John to calm down, but it isn't working.

"You keep your nose out of my business and my life, you got it?" John says with the voice of an iron fist.

Audie tells him sure, trying to defuse his anger.

John storms out, and as he said he would, waits for Audie outside in his truck.

Audie pays for his meal and then starts to leave. He passes a small gift shop and mini-market inside the truck stop; it is on his way to the parking lot where John is waiting for him. He pauses for a second and considers his options before heading back into the market area. He slowly walks over to the area in the back where different alcoholic spirits are kept. Audie checks out the selections for a second, debating his own thoughts. After glancing around in all directions and making sure John hasn't walked back into the truck stop, he makes his move. He grabs a bottle of "'Jack'" and goes up to the counter and pays for it. On his way out to the parking lot where his brother is waiting for him he hides the smaller bottle in the waistband of his shorts and under his loose-fitting tee.

John says nothing as Audie climbs into the truck and doesn't notice the hidden bottle he's sneaking in with him.

The next thing you know they're back out on the open road and heading south. The first stop on their father's list of friends to share the bad news with is two hours away. With each mile, the more south they go, the temperature outside seems to go a little more north. They can only pray that John's truck's air conditioning doesn't stop working.

It's quiet in the car with John not talking and with Audie lying low and just plugging into his iPhone, kicking back and relaxing to his tunes. It stays that way for the next two hours, all the way to Yuba City. The lack of conversation lifts John's spirit a bit and his mood gets better. The Barrett brother's do share one trait; they are both stubborn.

They make one more stop on the way to their destination. Audie makes John stop for a coffee in Gridley, north of Marysville. When he gets his coffee without John knowing, he slips some of the contents from the bottle still hiding in his shorts into his drink. "Ahh…that's what the doctor ordered," he tells himself as he strolls back to John and the truck. Audie feels better instantly. He's feels more ready to put up with his brother's attitude, thanks to his friend "'Jack.'"

———⊗⊗⊗———

BEFORE THEY KNOW IT THE BOYS ARE JUST OUTSIDE OF Beale Air Force Base's entrance. Audie has already finished his 'special-flavored' coffee.

John questions him about how he could drink something so hot on a summer day like this. If only you knew, if only you knew, Audie thinks to himself.

"So how do we get into the base? Do we call Mr. Aldrich or what," John asks Audie who has all the instructions from their father's will on his lap.

Audie studies the will's notes for a second before answering his older brother,

"We don't. He's retired," Audie responds with tone and words measured for correct enunciation and least amount of stammer, as to not tip off his brother about his ebbing soberness.

"He lives in an apartment complex down the road from Beale."

"GPS it," John commands.

Audie does and in a couple of minutes they are at the apartment complex looking for unit twenty-two, the home of one Will Aldrich. After John parks, he and Audie walk around searching for the right apartment. Audie spots it in the corner of the downstairs wing. He signals his brother over as he stumbles some walking toward the door. Audie deftly blames his jig on the 'damn weeds' growing from the sidewalk not an increased blood alcohol level from his 'spiced-up' coffee.

"Who's doing the talking?" John asks as he meets up with Audie on the doorstep of unit twenty-two. "This is big news. Who's better at breaking pretty terrible news to a complete stranger, well almost a complete stranger since we haven't seen him since we were kids."

Audie thrusts his thumb into his chest to show his vote in such a contest.

John gets his first whiff of Audie's breath and puts two and two together. "You put something in your coffee other than creamer, didn't you?"

Audie plays dumb and acts like he has no idea what John is talking about.

"It's probably better that I do the talking," John indicates as he knocks on the front door.

Audie chuckles at his brother's attitude of moral superiority. "Oh man, just untwist your panties, brother. I just had a little pick-me-up in my coffee. It's no big deal," Audie shoots back.

John looks him straight in the eyes and tells him that now is not the time to discuss this.

No one is answering the door so John knocks again. An older man with fishing gear in hand is passing by the boys, walking on the sidewalk in the front. The man spots them and yells out toward the brothers, "What the hell are you boys selling?"

John quickly turns to the man. "We are trying to locate the person who lives in this apartment. Any chance you know him?"

"Maybe, but why should I tell you boys where he is?" the man responds.

John bluntly asks him if he knows who lives here or not.

Audie sensing some tension between his brother and the older gentleman turns on some charm and takes a softer approach. "Look, sir, we're not here to cause Mr. Aldrich any trouble. We're not bill collectors or someone trying to leave him with a summons to appear. My brother and I are sons of one his oldest friends."

"Who is this old friend of his?" the man asks Audie.

John already has lost his patience with the cat-and-mouse conversation with the man and challenges what business it is of his to ask him and Audie so many questions.

But again Audie attempts to smooth things over and simply tells the man who they are. "The friend of Mr. Aldrich is Raymond Barrett. I'm Audie Barrett and this is my brother Johnny."

A big smile takes over the man's face. "Well, you boys are all grown up."

At that moment both John and Audie realize who they are talking to and why they were being peppered with so many questions.

John puts out his hand in front of him to shake Mr. Aldrich's. The man responds in kind and shakes John's. "Nice to meet you, sir."

"Call me Will, son. The last time I saw you two you were so little your mother was still wiping your butts."

John and Audie laugh at Will's recollection, but John assures him they were older than that.

"Well, whatever, it's been a hell of a long time."

John and Audie both agree it has been a very long time.

"So what brings you to my doorstep, and where the hell is your old man?"

Audie is happy to let John do all the talking right now. Will's smile starts to fade as he sees John struggle to respond to his question. He can tell that John has news for him that he probably doesn't want to hear. "Spit it out, son," he tells John.

John does his best to oblige. "There's no easy way to say this, but our father passed away, a few weeks ago."

Will is stunned by the news; he shakes in shock. "Son-of-a-bitch!"

He asks John how he died but John isn't even sure the cause.

Will wonders why after all these years, the boys are

standing on his front door step. "It's nice of you and your brother to come here in person and tell me this, and I am real sorry about Ray, but why?"

"But why are we here?" John replies back.

"Yes. I mean you boys could have just called me up and told me about Ray. Why did you come all this way in person?"

Audie decides to jump into the conversation. "Because our dad wanted us to come see you."

Will asks why. Audie tries to explain it. "It's in his will for me and Johnny to go across the country and visit some of Dad's old friends and let them know about his passing."

"Your old man wanted you to go across the country and break the news to his old friends, about his passing?" Will repeats.

Audie affirms he did.

Will tries to understand why Ray would give his son's such a task. John and Audie can't help him with the answer to that because they're wondering the same thing.

John tells him there's more. At that point, with his fishing gear still in hand, Will invites the boys into his apartment.

"Were you about to go fishing?" Audie asks.

"What do you think?" Will says with a laugh.

John then butts his way back into the discussion. "Funny enough, but our being here has something to do with fishing."

"How's that, son?" Will wants to know.

Will again invites them into his apartment. He offers them both something to drink. "Something cold or hot?" he asks them. John quickly tells Will that water is fine for both of them. John passes a dirty look in Audie's direction.

John doesn't want his brother to have any more alcohol.

John is for sure going to try to make it difficult for his little brother to have any more booze today if he has any say in it, and he's determined to.

"John Wayne and Audie Murphy, now I remember," Will recalls. "Your old man loved his western's, didn't he?"

With the boys named after two actors who were famous for being on-screen cowboys, John and Audie certainly couldn't quibble with Will about Dad's preference in films.

The boy's lay out everything they know about their father's will, and his instructions for this trip to meet Mr. Aldrich. None of them can understand the reasons for all of this. All the three of them can do at this point is conjecture why Raymond Barrett wanted all this to take place after his death.

"Well, boys, I guess the important thing here is to do as your dad wanted, and by gosh you are doing just that." Will says, proud of the boys for keeping his friend's wish. "Having to go fishing with everyone on the list is a funny thing, though."

John agrees with Will's thought and asks him why he thinks that would have been so important to their father.

"Ray did love to go fishing. It's the only time I saw him slow down for anything. A lot of my memories with him are the good times we had fishing out on the Feather River on our days off.

Fishing, drinking, chasing women, playing cards, and more fishing, and of those four endeavors boys, I think fishing was his favorite, slightly over the women."

John and Audie share a laugh at Will's account of good times with their father.

"Hell, if your dad wanted me to take you out and drown some worms in the water, then that's exactly what we are going to do." Will declares as he stands up from the table.

He asks the guys if they came prepared with their own poles and tackle. John assures him they are ready to go with all their gear in the back of his truck.

Then Audie remembers the special gift that their father wanted each person on the list to receive. John had already forgotten about it. Audie reaches into his backpack where he has all the items mentioned in the will. He finds the one marked with Mr. Aldrich's name on it and hands it to him. It's something small wrapped in thick white paper and taped like an old grandma would for a Christmas gift. Will tears it apart to reveal what's inside. "Oh my," he says with a chuckle. "I haven't seen this in years."

John and Audie take a look and see what appears to be a black race car toy. They can tell the item has significance to Will by the way he is ogling it from every direction as he hoists it up in the air with both his hands. The boys wait for Will to tell them what the gift means. After a few more minutes of studying it, Will can see that Ray's sons are waiting for an explanation. "I can see you're wondering. Come follow me into one of the bedrooms."

He leads them into the back bedroom in his apartment. "Take a look," he instructs the boys.

John and Audie glance in and see a huge slot car race track inside that has been fastened to a piece of plywood and has been painted to look like the city of San Francisco, Golden Gate Bridge and all. The track takes up most of the bedroom area, leaving just a little space for the racers to stand to the side of it. It sits up about waist high on large tables.

"Wow! This is really cool, Will," Audie can't help but say.

John with less exuberance still has to agree with his brother.

"And guess who helped me put this all together back in the early eighties?" Will queries, hinting they should be able to come up with the answer.

John and Audie glance at each other for a second before figuring it has to be their dad. Will is happy to tell them they are right.

"Your old man and I had so much fun over the years racing these cars. Hell half the guys on base over at Beale would be over here on a Saturday night wanting to get into the action."

"I guess that was before video games were popular, am I right?" Audie interjects.

"Video games…" Will says with disgust. "Ray and I made a lot of money hustling other servicemen out of their pay on this very track."

"Where did you fit everyone?" John asks.

Will reveals it wasn't in this apartment where they use to race. "I had a big house I rented back then. We had a huge game room that this baby stayed in. I was married back then, but after that divorce and a few more, this apartment is about all I can afford."

Audie tells him he's sorry to hear that, but Will wants no sympathy. "I did it to myself, so that's the way it goes. Like your old man, I always had to chase after the next pretty set of a legs that came along."

"Is that so?" John replies having had their mother confess to him many years back about their father's philandering ways with other women when they were married.

Audie recognizes that glint in his brother's eyes that says, he's about to guess pissed off. Just the idea of their dad cheating on their mom boils John's blood. Audie tries to push the conversation back to the track and the car their father wanted Will to have. "So what's so important about this car?"

Will puts the black race car onto the track and gives it a run around the huge raceway as the boys watch. "We had names for all the cars. This one we called the 'shadow,'" he explains to Audie. "We had a race car just like this one you just gave me from your dad. This car is exactly like the 'shadow' we raced back in the day."

"I take it this was your favorite slot car back then?" John assumes.

Will grins and says, "No, this was your old man's favorite. He never lost a race with this car. This black baby made us more money than anything else back in the day."

"I don't see the original 'shadow' here," Audie remarks as he scans the old slot car collection sitting on shelves in the room.

"No, one night an angry Marine who happened to be at Beale for something, came over to one of our parties. He got drunk and pissed off at losing all his money so he grabbed the original 'shadow' and smashed it into pieces. Your dad loved that car so much that he gathered the pieces up and buried them in my backyard."

The boys don't know what to say about that. It's a story about loyalty and love for something that they rarely remember seeing from their dad when growing up. After a moment of dumbfounded silence on the subject, Will breaks the ice and tells them to get their "crap" together for the fishing trip.

Twenty minutes later, John and Audie follow Will out from the apartment complex to waters unknown. Will is hauling his small fishing boat behind his old pick-up as the boys stay on his tail, fulfilling their father's wishes.

"Man, we haven't fished together in years, bro," Audie exclaims as he looks at his brother sitting across from him in the driver's seat.

John nods, saying nothing else.

"How long do you think?"

John isn't sure, but he knows it been a long time. "Probably about ten years ago, I think. You never were one much for fishing, Audie."

Audie can't argue that. It was always John who took after their father in the rugged male category of things. "Well, I guess we will make up for all the trips we didn't do on this trip, right, dude?"

John finally looks amused at his kid brother's expense. "Yeah, I guess so."

CHAPTER 5

The Feather River is calm with only a slight breeze moving over it. The breeze is certainly not enough to compensate for the triple digit weather. Audie tells Will that the heat reminds him of his home in Arizona. "It's a dry heat, just like in Phoenix."

John chimes in that it certainly isn't anything like Oregon where he lives. Will agrees with that and recalls the last time he was up in the Oregon neck of the woods. He tosses a few cold beers from an ice chest in the boat to John and Audie. John gives Audie a stern look that tells him he shouldn't drink anymore today, but Audie defies him and takes his first sip.

"Yeah your old man and I would come out here every chance we got when we were both stationed at Beale," Will tells the boys.

"Our dad loved to fish. That's something he and Johnny here had in common," Audie tells Will.

"You a big fisherman son?" Will asks John.

John admits that he is.

"I bet Ray took you out on the water a lot when you were youngsters?"

John shrugs, before confessing their dad did with him, but Audie was still pretty young.

"Old Ray was a hell of a fisherman, as good as I ever fished with," Will declares as he prepares his favorite lure to go and chase the striped bass that inhabit the river this time of year.

"You know your pop had an amazing fishing story that involved this river."

Audie and John are both curious what it is, so Audie asks Will to tell it to them.

Will is happy to do so and starts to tell them after finishing off his first can of Coors. He asks the boys if they knew their grandfather at all.

John says to Will that he barely remembers meeting him when he was a little kid on a trip back East with his mom and dad.

"Well, your grandfather was in the Air Force like your father," Will says as he starts to share the story about their father with them.

Neither John nor Audie had known that. They actually know very little about their father's dad. Their dad rarely talked about him.

Will continues with his yarn. "And your grandfather, believe it or not, was at one time stationed right here at Beale, just like your dad."

The boys are listening more intently now.

"Anyhoo, your granddad liked to fish as well. So one day he took your father fishing with him right here on the Feather River. Now your dad was just a kid at the time but old enough to be at his father's beck and call whenever they went fishing. Your grandfather would have little Ray get a beer when he wanted one, steer the boat when he closed his eyes for a few seconds, and jump into the water when your grandfather's line got snagged on anything. It's that last thing that makes this story so interesting."

Will can see by the expressions on the boys' faces that to use a pun appropriate to the situation, he's got them hooked on listening to the rest of the story.

So he goes on. "It was a strange day, weather wise, foggy and damp out with poor visibility for anyone who dared to go out that day. Your dad and grandfather had been out fishing for about an hour when your granddad slowly pulled the boat into a small cove at the side of the river. The water was still pretty deep even though they were close to the shore. It also was very muddy ground on the shore and the land near the shore. Your grandfather cast out first, but his line cast closer to the shore than he liked, so he began to reel it back in. Unfortunately for him, his line got snagged on something. Now between the foggy conditions and the muddy water near the shore, neither your pop nor your granddad could see what the line was caught up on. Of course after a few failed jerks of the line did nothing to free your grandfather's line, he ordered your dad, little Ray, into the water to unhook his line."

"I got a bad feeling about this," Audie moans interrupting Will's train of thought for a second.

Will remembers where he left off and starts again. "Right, so your pop isn't real keen on jumping into the muddy water and he told me years later that the fog sort of just floated over the top of the surface of the water, making for a real spooky effect."

"But I'm guessing he did, anyways?" John reckons.

"What else could he do? Your grandfather was old-school military. He would have taken a strap to your pop, so Ray does as he's ordered and jumps into the mucky water and swims like a frog toward the shore."

"Why like a frog?" Audie inquires.

Will thinks for a moment to what Ray told him years ago about the reason for the frog reference. "Oh, I remember now, the water being so muddy seemed dirty to your dad so he didn't want his head getting wet. So back to the story, your dad gets to the shore and finds the fishing line that your grandad cast and is snagged, and Ray begins to follow the line down."

"Why didn't they just break the line?" Audie asks.

"Your granddad was a frugal man from what Ray told me and never liked to waste anything that he thought he could reuse. So Ray takes hold of the line with his fingers and follows the line down underwater. Now he gets his head wet as he swims into this gooey, slimy mud. He's right by the shore now, but it's deep enough that he's completely underwater. But your dad, with his dad yelling at him to untangle the line, traces the fishing line to where it is snagged. Ray can tell it's caught on something big and heavy as he pulls on the line from under the water. Your dad thought it was probably a large log submerged in the mud. He yanks and yanks on that line expecting a piece of the bark to rip off, but it doesn't, for a good reason."

"Like I said, I don't like where this is going," Audie interjects for a second time.

Will smirks at Audie's words; it's the look of someone who knows something that no one else does. "You've got good instincts, Audie," Will tells him.

By now, even John is enthralled by the story and wants to find out what their grandfather's fishing line was snagged on.

Will continues on. "No bark or wood rips off, but the object buried deep into this mud and slime near the shore line starts to move a little at Ray's pulling. Ray's head comes out of the water and yells to his dad that he's getting it. Your granddad asks him if it's unsnagged, and Ray says not yet but the thing it's snagged on is moving and he should have it unsnagged in just a second. With his father urging him on, Ray submerges back under the water, and then with one strong thrust the object comes tearing from the mud and muck right into your dad's view. Then because of the muddy waters he can't get a good look at it until it's staring him right in the face."

"And…" John says as Will takes a frustrating pause for effect.

Will flashes another big grin at the boys, thoroughly enjoying having them in the palm of his hand. Will, always a story-teller, has forgotten how great a feeling it is to have an audience hanging on every word you say, as the boys are right now. "I guess you probably want to know the rest of the story, as the late great Paul Harvey used to say."

John and Audie nod almost in unison so Will begins again. "So right in his face and to your pop's sheer terror, remember he's just a kid right now, about eight, maybe nine, is another face staring right back at him."

"I knew it, man! I just knew it was going to be something like this," Audie shouts out, derailing Will again from his storytelling.

But Will finally finishes his story. "The face is half-skeleton by now and a mess, but the eyes your dad said seemed to look right through him. Ray breaks the water screaming for his father to help him. Your granddad not the most sensitive of men for sure, could still see something was really wrong and that his son was in trouble. So he jumps into the water and swims over to Ray who meets him half way. Ray's crying and hysterical by now and struggling to tell your granddad what's under the water. Your granddad grabs him and directs Ray to swim back to the boat, and then your grandad goes under to get a closer look. A few hours later that shoreline is covered by law enforcement of many stripes, as they pull that body out from the muck and mud and to dry land."

"Wow, man, what a story," Audie responds, wondering if it really happened.

Will assures him it's all true, at least according to their father.

"Did they find out who the person was who died?" John asks Will.

Will nods. "Have either of you ever heard of Juan Corona?"

"Isn't that a famous coffee brand, or is it a beer brand?" Audie actually responds, having no idea.

"Yes, I think I have, wasn't he a serial killer in these parts?" John replies.

Will offers John a gold star for his answer before giving the boys a history lesson. "He was a mass murderer in this area back in the early seventies. He killed a bunch of migrant workers and buried them around this area. That body your old man found snagged onto his father's fishing line was one of many victims he had buried right here on the shores of the Feather River. For days and days after that your pop and granddad came out here to this area and watched as local cops, state authorities, and even the F.B.I. tore this area apart looking for more bodies, and sadly they found many."

"Unbelievable! How did Dad never tell us that story?" Audie can't help but wonder.

Frankly, John kind of wonders the same thing.

Will has no answer for that. All he can think is that being it was such a traumatic event for Ray, that maybe he didn't believe they were old enough to hear the story. "That day scared the hell out of your dad. Maybe he was waiting till you got older to share it with you."

John and Audie think that's a plausible explanation but really no one will ever know for sure the real reason for Ray not sharing the story with his sons.

"Enough chewing cud, should we get some fishing in or what?" Will declares. "I haven't even caught a fish yet, hell I haven't even had a bite yet."

John and Audie grab their lines and reel them in to check their bait. They then cast them out again to a different spot, hopefully a better spot in the river where the bass are biting. Will is about to do the same thing, but first he proposes a toast. He lifts his can of Coors in the air. John and Audie follow suit and lift theirs. Will tells the boys that it is only fitting that it is Coors beer that they salute their father with since it was Ray's beverage of choice. "To Raymond Barrett, a hell of a fisherman, a hell of a drinker, and by god, a hell of a fisherman when he was drinking!"

All three men say their cheers and then down their beers almost simultaneously. Will then gets something up his butt and decides another part of the river is where the fish are really going to bite, so they start up the boat motor and begin looking for that other part.

John and Audie exchange glances as the boat they are passengers in races away. It's not much, just a quick look between two brothers, but each one can tell the other's having a good time. John still manages to whisper to his brother to watch the alcohol, Audie just smiles.

LATER IN THE EVENING, BACK AT WILL'S APARTMENT, A full-fledged party has taken off. Will invited a few servicemen from Beale and few of his retired friends still in the area to come over and meet his oldest and dearest friends, two boys. John and Audie feel like the guests of honor or something, as every airman coming through the front door wants to meet them and shake their hands. News of the event spreads like a California wildfire, and soon every serviceman living in the apartment complex has jammed into Will's modest-sized domicile.

Will talks the boys into hanging up their boots there for the night before heading for Nevada in the morning and the next name on their list. Soon Will's place is filled to the brim with airmen and some of their girlfriends half-baked from booze and more booze. Cigar smoke fills the place, floating from room to room. Men are sprawled out in every room of the apartment trying to stay conscious enough to continue their poker, darts, and slot car racing.

Will is schooling John at the complexities of seven card stud at the kitchen table while three other airmen are playing as well. Two of the guys' girlfriends are hanging out and watching.

Audie's in the game room in the back taking bets on his slot car. Will doesn't know, but Audie's racing the famous "'shadow car'" that he and John brought to Will as a gift from their father's estate. Audie, drunk as a skunk, is amazingly still on his feet. So far this evening, Audie has not yet lost a single race while behind the wheel or at least the gun trigger of the "'shadow car'".

Will and John can hear Audie yelling and gloating at his latest race car victory from their spot in the kitchen. Before dealing the next round of cards, Will asks John if he needs his next beer yet. John puts his hand up to say he's had enough for the night. "I've got to drive in the morning. I don't need a hangover."

At the same moment John's saying that, Audie yells joyously from the back once again.

"I can see that your brother is the one who takes after Ray when it comes to putting them away, ay?" Will concludes as he antes up.

"Yeah, I guess so," John replies as he matches Will's ante.

"I always warned your old man about his drinking, how it could get the best of him if he wasn't careful."

"Did it make a difference with Dad when you told him that?" John asks.

Will laughs before answering, "What do you think, son, ha ha."

John then confides to Will he wishes that it had. In John's mind if his father had not had such a bad drinking problem, maybe his downward spiral wouldn't have continued to the point where he thought the idea of abandoning his wife and kids was a reasonable one.

After John discusses those same thoughts with Will and everyone else at the kitchen table, the mood of everyone sitting there is brought down, and the joy in the air is sucked right out in an instance. Will tries to lighten the mood of his guests by joking about how Ray Barrett would often respond when asked by his friends if he had a drinking problem by saying, it's not a problem. I'm actually quite good at it. The three airmen playing poker at the table in their drunken stupor don't really get the humor, but the two girls sitting there laugh hysterically. John just looks amused.

Will can see the pain that John carries with him from his father's abandoning the family. A knife sticking out of John's back wouldn't be any clearer. Will leans in toward John and says, "Everyone has their demons to deal with, John. Your father did. I'm sure your brother probably does, and even you and me do. But you and your brother have one big advantage that your pop never had."

John waits to hear what that advantage is.

"You and your brother have each other to fight for, to help make each other better men. Your dad, God rest his soul, he had only himself. Ray didn't have a reflection to look at. He didn't have a mirror to show him he was screwing up. You and your brother can be those reflections for each other. It won't be easy, and you probably won't like each other much when you make the other person look in that mirror, but it's the best thing you can do for each other."

When John offers up his mother as someone his dad could have talked to about his demons, Will shoots the idea straight down. "There are just things a man won't talk about to a woman, even if it's his wife. One of those things, John, is his weaknesses or failures; it just goes against the grain for a man to disclose those to a woman."

John listens, not sure if he agrees or not with Will's statement. Although Darlene's past words to him about not talking or communicating what's bothering him are playing like a radio station in his brain right now, so maybe there is something to what Will's saying.

"Men are not wired to show their weakness." Will continues. "It's just the way it is."

The girls at the table don't seem to agree and just laugh off Will's comments as an old man who is out of touch. But

Will is certainly making John consider some things.

In the game room, a particularly inebriated airman is sick of losing money to Audie's black race car and challenges Audie to tell him how he keeps winning. Audie who is in worse shape than even the airman, after taking shots for hours, bursts out in laughter at the request. He staggers as he answers, "I have no idea. I have no idea at all!"

"How can that be," the airman wants to know, getting hotter under the collar by the second.

"Hell if I know, dude. I guess you just suck at this or something," Audie slurs back at him.

The airman, about a foot taller than Audie, grabs for Audie's black race car to check it out. Audie pulls it away from him making the airman even more suspicious about the car. "This is a special car, man. My dad use to race slots with one just like this, years ago."

The airman is even angrier as he thinks that Audie is basically admitting the car is better than all the other cars on the track and therefore the races are fixed. He again reaches for the car, and again Audie pulls it away. The airman staggers toward Audie who backs himself all the way into a corner in the room. He's still refusing to let him handle his "'shadow racer'".

Audie and the airman's confrontation can now be heard all the way through the house. Will tells John they better see what's happening back there and so they rush to the game room with all the other inhabitants of the apartment who are still conscious enough to do the same. Will and John walk in just as the airman reaches one last time for Audie's slot car. Audie plays keep away, but this time the guy grabs Audie, picks him up, and slams him into the wall that he's cornered in. Audie slides down the wall in a crumpled heap still clutching the "'shadow.'"

John seeing this happen to his little brother wastes no time to rush to his defense. John comes up from behind the huge airman and taps him on the shoulder to get his attention. "Hey, asshole, that's my brother. Why don't you pick on somebody your own size?!"

When the drunken airman turns around, Will comments to John the obvious, "I don't think there is anyone here his size, John."

John never one to back down from a fight, doesn't wait for the guy to get the first punch in, he rears back and lands a hard punch, straight onto the man's chin. With alcohol already doing most of the damage, the airman is ready for night-night and falls like a tree backwards to the ground, after the punch. John rubs his fist, now hurting from the blow.

Will orders a few of the other airmen still sober enough to do so, to carry their fallen comrade out of the apartment and back to his place.

John tends to his brother still crumpled in the corner on the floor.

"Hi, Johnny," Audie says slurring his words. "You missed it, man. I won every race tonight and made a lot of money. And this big old Air Force guy wanted to take my car, the "'shadow'" car, but I wouldn't let him, Johnny."

John looks back at Will and just shakes his head.

"You may have to carry him to your truck in the morning," Will asserts.

John agrees and looks back to his brother who in just the few seconds of John turning to look at Will, has passed out and is dead to the world. "Should I put him in a bed?"

"Nah, I would just leave him there for the night," Will responds. "He's dead weight in that condition. Nothing could stir him. Just let him sleep it off, and make sure he's got his sunglasses for the trip in the morning. He's going to need them."

John and Will share a laugh at Audie's expense. John knows that Will is exactly right. Tomorrow is going to be a long day for Audie and his pulsating head.

AUDIE SOMEHOW MANAGES TO WALK BY HIS OWN POWER and reach John's truck the next morning. He plops himself down in the front passenger seat with little to say and even less that he wants to hear. The volume control on his ears seems to be broken this morning. Audie begs for only words between John and Will that are low frequency because any increased audible sound sends his alcohol-induced migraine into overdrive. Will and John do their best to please him as they say their goodbyes quietly. Will stands by the truck and shares a few more things he wants to say. "Try your best to forgive your father for all the mistakes he made John."

John isn't sure what Will wants to hear from him but tells him that he will at least try.

Will speaks through the driver's side window and reminds John of one more fact. "One thing I've learned in my many years of life is this. It's a damn sight easier to forgive our own mistakes and justify the reasons for why we made them than it is to forgive someone else's mistakes against us and try to understand why they did them. It's food for thought, son, that's all."

John shakes Will's hand and thanks him for all his hospitality and for putting up with his brother lying here next to him. Will chortles and tells him it was nothing. Will then wishes them both a safe trip and tells them they are both good sons to be doing all this for their dad. "Ray would be very proud of you boys."

John says thanks before backing up and driving away. Will watches as they go down the street. He looks up in the sky and speaks to only himself. "God it's hot. This is a perfect day for a little fishing."

LORINDA CAN SEE THAT SOMETHING IS BOTHERING Darlene and has been itching to talk to her about it all morning. The café has been crazy busy all morning long, with the after-church crowd filling up all the chairs and booths. Finally there are a few minutes of slow time before the masses looking for lunch start coming in. Lorinda pulls Darlene into the back. She takes her into a makeshift employee's lounge, which is really nothing more than a storage area next to the employee bathroom that houses a small table and a couple of old ripped-up chairs. Lorinda pushes Darlene to sit down on one of the chairs before starting the interrogation. "I know we haven't known each other very long, but I can still tell something is eating you up inside and it's not Bill's homemade chili," Lorinda jokes trying to lighten the mood.

Darlene stares at her wondering what she wants from her. Lorinda keeps pushing her to open up and let whatever it is that is bothering her, out. But it is hard to talk about something that is bothering you if you're not really sure what it is. Darlene signals at Lorinda's demands. "I don't know what's going on with me. I wish I did."

Lorinda sits down beside her in the other ripped-up chair and looks her straight in the eyes. "Is it because John left yesterday? I mean it's only been a day, honey."

Darlene isn't even sure if that's it or not, but there's something gnawing at her insides. "I've hardly seen John the last couple of months since he moved out. With his job at the saw mill and his side business, me and the kids hardly ever see him. So I don't understand why his leaving for this trip with his brother would bother me."

Lorinda gives thought to what Darlene just said before throwing out her best guess, which proves to be surprisingly accurate and stirs some things up in Darlene. "Maybe this is different because…there's no chance of seeing him, where before there was at least the possibility."

Darlene really considers Lorinda's thought. "Maybe, I don't know, maybe, I think I'm kind of worried that this separation from him will kind of be like the final straw."

Lorinda tries to help Darlene see that this might be better seen as a fresh opportunity at a new perspective on life, and men.

"What do you mean?" Darlene asks her to spell it out.

"I mean, like I told you the other day, maybe it's time to see what else there is on the menu to order."

"Not again with this," Darlene tells her.

But Lorinda asks her to put her biases away for the moment and just rationally give it some thought. "Go out on some dates, enjoy the company of some other men, and see how it makes you feel."

Darlene stands up and brushes aside Lorinda's idea. She proclaims it's time to get back to work.

Lorinda isn't about to give up trying to persuade Darlene, however. "Just think about it, honey. This is the best opportunity you're going to get to try and find out if there is something or someone else out there for you."

"How do ya' figure?" Darlene answers.

"Come on, girl. Grants Pass is a small town. With John traipsing across the country with his brother, there's no way you will happen to run into him if you go out with some other guy, is there?"

Darlene shrugs in response again and heads out to wait on customers. Lorinda follows behind still touting the merits of her idea. Then as fate often does in these situations, Mike Stillman comes walking in and conveniently sits down at one of Darlene's stations. "Shit!" she says at the sight.

"We have a new special tonight on our menu," Lorinda whispers in Darlene's ear as she walks by.

CHAPTER 6

A couple of hours have passed since leaving Will's place in Yuba City, and now on the outskirts of Lake Tahoe, Audie is finally perking up.

"Morning, sunshine," John greets him with as Audie attempts to wipe the sleep out of his eyes.

Audie asks where they are, and John informs him that they are just arriving in Tahoe, their next destination. Audie barely remembers leaving Will Aldrich's place. "I must have had a little too much to drink last night."

"Oh, you think?" John responds sarcastically.

"I didn't do anything stupid last night, did I?" Audie inquires of his brother.

"Nothing anymore stupid than I have seen you do before," John answers.

Audie howls at his brother's response, but his own laughter makes his head hurt even more.

John asks him if he's up to helping him or not. Audie, of course, sits straight up and says he is. He's not about let his older brother think less of him than he already does.

John dictates that Audie put the address they are looking for into his cell phone's GPS and get them directions to follow. Audie does as he is told and soon a soothing female voice directs them right through the city of Lake Tahoe and to the address they are seeking. John parks the truck and gets out and waits as Audie slowly extricates himself from the passenger side door.

"Remind me what the lady's name is again?" John asks his brother.

"Minnie Radford," Audie replies.

John and Audie walk up to the front door and knock, but there is no one coming to the door. The doorbell doesn't help either. "Now, what?" Audie asks.

Before John can answer, a neighbor comes from next door. He asks what the guys want. When they tell him they are looking for Minnie Radford, the man informs them that she's working at a nightclub over in Reno. The man tells them the name of the club and what it is next to in Reno. John and Audie thank him for the information. "Should we head over to Reno where she works or wait around and come back here later?" Audie challenges his big brother with.

John gauging the heat is in no frame of mind to just hang around and wait for her. He doesn't want to come back to see her here either. So he tells Audie to get back in the truck. They'll just drive over to where she works and introduce themselves. John thinks maybe they can mark this person off the list quickly. However, Audie reminds him about the fishing obligation. "Maybe we'll get lucky and she won't want to go fishing," John says hopefully.

Audie thinks it's possible as he gets back into the truck with his brother. The Barrett brother's next stop is Reno.

—————

Mike is finishing up his club sandwich and about ready for his bill. Darlene asks him if there's anything else he would like, dessert or another cup of coffee. A crooked smug look takes control of half of Mike's face. "There is one thing you could do for me if it's not too much trouble?"

Darlene as is her duty as his waitress responds appropriately and waits for him to tell her what he wants.

So Mike does. "Why don't you let me take you out and let someone else serve you meals and wait on you for a change?"

Darlene is taken off-guard by Mike's request. She's already had a few guys at the café proposition her since she started working there, but they were usually half joking. If they weren't joking with her, it didn't matter because Darlene didn't take them seriously anyways. But this is different. Mike is serious. Mike waits for her response; he's waiting for her to say anything at all. She's standing there looking at him silently, like a game show contestant who has been stumped by a really hard question. The fact is, this sort of thing hasn't happened to her since high school and before she fell for John. She stumbles over her words as she thanks him for his offer but at the same time tells him that it probably isn't something she could do at this time.

Mike feels like she just rejected a business offer he made, not an offer to go out to dinner. Mike, who grew up in Grants Pass and went to school with both John and Darlene, has heard about her separation. "I'm sorry, Darlene. I thought you and John were split up and all."

He knows, of course everyone knows everything when you grow up in a small town, Darlene thinks to herself. Now she's on the spot to say something about her "'marriage situation'" and it makes her more than a bit uncomfortable. "John and I are trying to work things out still."

Mike gives her an understanding nod. "I think that's great," he says. "I'm not trying to mess that up or anything. I just thought you could maybe use a fun night where someone waits on you for a change. I mean, just as old friends, you know."

Mike's sweet words make her stop and think. Why not go out and just have a dinner? After all she wouldn't be breaking the law or anything. It doesn't have to be a real date, does it? Then she ponders whether it does. "Mike, it's sweet of you to ask me, but I can't see anyone else when John and I…"

Mike cuts her off and lets her know right up front it wouldn't be a date, date. "Just two old friends who went to the same schools and who knew the same people, and know where all the bodies are buried in the small town they grew up in, that's all."

Darlene has to laugh. She again lets him know if she agrees to dinner it would be as one old friend meeting with another. Mike tells her to relax. "I get it, Darlene. We'll just go and have a nice time and reminisce and laugh about old times. We can compare stories of people we went to school with, like the other day, and then laugh about where they are today."

She has to admit that any time without the kids and with adult conversation, and someone serving her, would be a nice change. "Ok, why not, Mike," she tells him.

"Yes, why not. We'll have a nice time. I know you've been working real hard and so have I, driving up and down I-5. I think we could both use a night out," he replies. "I'll call you later when I know my schedule better for the next few days, and we can talk about what night works best for you."

Darlene says sure and lets him have her cell phone number. It seems so strange to be doing this, giving out her number to another guy to call her, to make arrangements for getting together. She reminds herself that Mike is an old friend, but that doesn't make the strange feelings go away. For a second, she panics that John won't understand her having a friendly dinner with Mike, and then for better or worse she remembers he's off on his trip. So there's no chance of that happening, but still Darlene's feelings persist.

She goes to get Mike's bill, her mind overflowing with thoughts and her senses going places they haven't gone in a long time.

Lorinda grins, having eavesdropped on the whole conversation, as Darlene walks by her. Darlene doesn't even notice her.

JOHN AND AUDIE ARRIVE AT THE CASINO IN RENO WHERE the man told them they could find the next name on their father's list. They go inside, and it looks like any other casino, except smokier than most. John looks for someone who works there to ask if a Minnie Radford is working today. He and Audie wander over to the sports bar next to the buffet-style restaurant. They wait for the bartender to get free of patrons and then move in to ask him if he knows Minnie. He chuckles at the question. "Everybody knows Minnie." he answers. "She's been working here forever."

"Is she here now?" John asks.

The bartender directs them to the other side of the casino. "She's over there getting ready for the next show."

"Is there always so much smoke?" John asks the bartender.

Stoically he answers, "Welcome to Nevada, where everything goes."

John tells Audie to follow him in the direction the bartender pointed. It takes them to a room where shows are playing all day, about every hour. The performers are acting as famous celebs of the past, the poster on the outside of the club shows Marilyn Monroe, Elvis, James Dean, and many more. The boys head inside to check it out.

Once inside, they sit down at one of the numerous round tables that remind the boys of the kind of tables you see in the saloons, in western movies. A small stage is in front of them, and as they wait for the next performance, a gal in skimpy clothes comes over and takes a drink order. Before the drinks arrive, a narrator's voice fills the room and music starts letting everyone know the next show is about to begin. For the next two hours performers pretending to be music and acting icons of the past, sing, dance, and act.

John orders his little brother to watch the alcohol intake and Audie annoyed at his brother's bossing him around, pledges to have just one to get John off his back. The boys end up having a late lunch or maybe it's an early dinner, as the show starts.

The showroom is pretty well filled, and when the performances come to an end, the audience stands up and gives the performers a standing o.

John asks the barmaid whose been serving them where they might find Minnie Radford. She tells them that she was the one who played the part of Mae West in the show. So after the show ends and the performers head back to their respective dressing rooms, John and Audie try to sneak backstage. They're stopped by a muscle-bound Italian-looking guy wearing a black t-shirt that looks like it is two sizes too small for him. He's guarding entry to the back of the stage area and stops the guys in their tracks. "Can I help you fellas?"

Audie can't help but stare at the size of his pecs, forming two small mountains under his shirt. Audie decides to let John do all the talking. John asks him if they could speak to Minnie Radford. But the security guard tells them sorry. They will have to wait for a few minutes when the performers have a scheduled time to come out front and meet patrons and sign autographs. Audie grabs at his brother's arm. "We better just wait, Johnny, until she comes out here."

John isn't so sure that would be a good idea. "This gal won't be able to talk to us when she's busy signing autographs and talking to everybody. We need to speak with her now or we'll end up like stalkers hanging around her house all day and night."

Audie hears what his brother is saying but wonders what else they can do. John turns to him and says bluntly that they can speak to her now. John walks back to the Incredible Hulk. "My man, could you just give Minnie a message for us?"

"I already told you guys, you'll have to wait until the performers come out."

"Just a message, my man. You see, we're old friends. I promise she will be happy to hear from us," John guarantees him.

Finally the mountain of man shows a tiny amount of compassion on John and Audie's plight and gives in. "Alright already! What's the message?"

"Can you relay to Minnie that Ray Barrett's out here and he wants to see her?" John says.

The big man repeats the name back to them and then shaking his head, walks back stage.

"What if she knows Dad's dead?" Audie asks.

"How could she? That's why we're here, right?" John responds as they wait to see if Minnie answers their invitation.

Audie chuckles at his own absent-mindedness. "But what if she doesn't come out because she hates him now?"

John snickers at his brother's comment and admits knowing their father that could be a real possibility.

A few more minutes go by, and then a dark-haired woman wearing a satin robe comes strolling from the back room with the Incredible Hulk at her side. The security guard directs her to John and Audie. She gives the boys a quick look over and then asks where Ray is.

"We're his sons, ma'am," John tells her. "I'm John Barrett, and this is my brother, Audie."

Minnie is welcoming and shakes both their hands before again asking where Ray is.

John then breaks the sad news to her.

Minnie covers her mouth with her fingers and shakes her head in shock. A tear trickles down one of her cheeks. "I don't understand. Why are you telling me this?"

John thinks about if there might be a better place to talk, in private.

Minnie asks the security guard for a piece of paper and a pen. He quickly grabs both from one of the barmaids in the club. Minnie jots down her address and tells them to meet her at her house around six o'clock. "My last show is over about five, and I don't have to do the meet and greet afterwards if I don't wish to. I live in Lake Tahoe, but I should be able to make it home by six. If I'm a few minutes late, just wait for me."

John assures her they will.

Minnie heads back to her dressing room, still upset by the news, to put on her white wig and Mae West outfit, and prepare for meeting fans and signing autographs.

Audie comes up with a great idea. Since they have three and a half hours to kill and slot machines and card tables all around….

John quickly, seeing that look in his kid brother's eyes that means trouble, cautions him about blowing his money for the trip.

Audie scoffs at the notion. "Just some nickel and dime stuff, that's all."

John demands he keep his word about that. He doesn't want Audie losing the little money he brought along with him on just the second day of the trip.

Audie again guarantees he'll be smart. "Bro, you can watch me if you want."

John isn't excited by that prospect. "You can cruise the strip for the next two hours and then we'll meet right here at the front door of this club."

Audie happily agrees to John's plan. "You're not much for gambling Johnny. What are you going to do?"

John agrees he's not. "I'll get us a motel room for the night. I guess right here in Reno even though we have to drive back over to Tahoe."

Audie recommends Reno as well. "I love the lights and sounds, the whole bag, man. Yeah, let's stay in Reno tonight. I wonder if Minnie is going to want to do the fishing thing or not?"

"I guess we'll find out about all that tonight," John replies.

Audie and John then say their see-ya's and go their separate ways. Audie to have some fun, something he's always ready to do. While John will find them a place to stay for the night, being the responsible one, something he's always known he has to do.

⸙

Darlene gets off work by mid-day and drives home to find Rose cleaning everything in sight in Darlene's house. Darlene asks her not to overdo it, but that's the only gear that Rose knows.

Rose asks her if she wants some tea. Darlene is a fan of Rose's British hot tea, but she doesn't enjoy it in the heat of summer the way John and the kids do. Darlene can only stomach ice tea this time of year, something that is a foreign item to Rose. For Rose, real tea is hot tea. So Darlene turns down the tea and instead grabs a diet soda from the fridge. She collapses at her kitchen table as Rose wipes down the kitchen counters in front of her. "Rose, come sit down with me."

Rose pokes her head up from her paper towels long enough to respond to the request. "Is everything okay, dear?"

Darlene answers that it is, but would just like her to stop cleaning for a second and sit down and relax.

Rose sees that it is important to her, so she stops cleaning and sits down, as Darlene asked.

"How did the kids do today?" Darlene starts out with.

Rose tells her they did fine and are playing in their room's right this moment after eating too many cookies she baked earlier.

Darlene giggles at that. "That sounds like my children alright."

Rose can sense that there are more "important" subjects that Darlene wants to talk about than kids and belly aches. "Something is bothering you, dear?"

Darlene has no idea why Rose is asking that and tells her the same. "Do I look like something is bothering me?"

Rose just smiles. "I've been around long enough to know when something is bothering another woman. Johnny is gone and you miss him. I bet you're probably conflicted because you miss him more than you thought you would, even though it's only been a few days and you've been separated for two months."

Wow, Darlene thinks, can this woman get to the point or what. She isn't sure how much of what Rose just said is true mind you, but boy, no beating around the bush here.

"Am I right dear?" Rose continues on.

Darlene takes a big gulp of soda, maybe to buy some time before answering. But unfortunately for her, it finally makes its way down her throat and she has no excuses. So Darlene clears her head and considers what, if anything, she really wants to say. Then it comes to her in a flash of clarity. Here in front of her is not only the mother of her husband, estranged or not, but also a woman, a woman of vast life experience. Why not lower the bucket down into the well and pull some things up. Why not indeed, Darlene decides, with Rose still waiting for her answer. "Did you ever, I mean before he left you and the boys, wonder if you really loved him?"

Rose takes a deep breath and seems surprised by the question. "There really is something bothering you."

Darlene attempts to laugh it off and bring down the decibels of seriousness filling the kitchen right now, but Rose wants to ratchet it up even a wee bit more. "Have you stopped loving my Johnny?"

Even if the answer is yes to Rose's question, and it's not, Darlene could never say that to her, not with Rose's eyes show-

Andrew Scott Bassett

ing fear for what Darlene might confess. "I'm not saying that, Rose. I still love John; I just guess I wonder if I always will."

Rose is so relieved to hear Darlene say what she just did, the part about Darlene still loving her Johnny. Then Rose realizes she hasn't responded to Darlene's question. "I never stopped loving Ray."

Darlene is surprised by her words. She has heard how much Ray's leaving hurt the family from John since they first started dating in high school. "All these years I thought you hated him?"

"I did. But the stronger the betrayal was shows the stronger the love was," Rose speaks honestly. "Passion is a strange thing that way. The more you care, the more it hurts."

Darlene thinks she understands but isn't really sure. "So if Ray, God rest his soul, somehow was able to walk through your front door right now, how would you react?"

Rose pauses; she gives the thoughtful consideration to the question that the question demands. "I can't honestly say for sure, love. But I will tell you this, ducky, I wish with all my heart I would have the chance to find out. I think that was the most bloody difficult thing about the news about Ray, the fact that he would never come back now."

Darlene chokes up as Rose does. Darlene apologizes for bringing up such things when the pain is so new and raw.

Rose tells her it's okay as she reaches out and squeezes Darlene's hand. "It is painful, duck, if it wasn't then that would tell you all you needed to know, I suppose."

Darlene takes her other hand and puts it over the top of Rose's. She wants to make her feel better after making her sorrow come back in such a strong way in the last few minutes. "Tell me something, a fond memory you have of Ray, maybe a memory from when you first met?"

FISHING *for* SOMETHING   87

Rose beams at Darlene. She seems delighted to try to fulfill what Darlene's asking. She searches her memories for something special like a gold miner digging through layers of soil. Then it comes to Rose. "We had only been married for a few months when I left my family and my home in England behind, to come to America with Ray."

"That must have been real scary?" Darlene replies.

"It was, dear. I was a city girl, and Ray was raised on a farm in upstate New York," Rose continues. "We had been living with his father and step mum just a couple of weeks when Ray was stationed overseas. It was hard to be without him, being just married and living in a different country."

Darlene is smiling and nodding along with Rose's story, fulling invested in it.

"Well then, one morning Ray's dad decides it's time for me to start contributing to the family farm and wakes me up early in the morning. Ray's dad has his wife, Ray's step mum, take me out to the barn and show me how to milk the cows. Now, duck, I'm a city girl. Our milk came from the corner store right. I don't bloody well know anything about milking cows!"

Darlene can't help but giggle a little as she visualizes Rose trying to squeeze the teats of a cow.

Rose goes on, "Well, of course, I'm bloody well struggling to get anything to come out of the tits of the beast, while mind you Ray's awful step mum is getting impatient with me and starting to raise her voice."

"She sounds like a sweet lady," Darlene quips.

"Awful, a real beast, love! So she's raising her voice and getting madder all the time at me and I'm freezing my bum off because it's upstate New York and its winter time."

Darlene laughs out loud at that. "So what happens?"

"Well the witch, she gets so mad at me she runs out and gets Ray's dad."

"So? What does he do?" Darlene asks.

"He comes storming into the barn and begins to scream at me about helping out around there and how lazy the English are, all this rubbish."

"Wow! So what did you do?"

"I stood right up to him, that bloody bastard, and I said if you want milk so bad you can milk the tits of the cow yourself, starting with the one you're married to!" Rose says emphatically.

Darlene bursts out laughing even louder. "Oh, my god, then what did he say?!"

"It isn't what he said duck." Rose remembers. "It's what he did."

Darlene demands to know what that was.

Rose tells her. "He was so shocked that I stood up to him like that. He couldn't believe it. It just made him very mad, so he reared up his right hand and began to swing it at me like he was going to hit me in the face."

"Did he?" Darlene responds, on the edge of her kitchen table seat.

"He was going to, I think, but he didn't get the chance. Ray had been granted leave for a few weeks for being newly married and having a foreign wife who had just been brought to a new country. He came back to surprise us, walking up behind his father, just as his dad was about to hit me."

Darlene just shakes her head at the story. It's so amazing a tale to her.

"Ray told him, in no uncertain terms, that if he hit me it would be the last thing he ever did. Ray's dad stopped and stormed off. We moved away from their a few days later, and Ray and his father only saw each other a few times after that. They never really had a relationship after that."

"And this is a good memory, why?" Darlene has to ask.

"It's a good memory, duck, because it showed how much Ray loved me. He was afraid of his father his whole life. But that day, his love for me was greater than his fear, and he stood up for me and protected me. I was the most important thing then. It was the best feeling in the world."

Darlene thinks she understands.

"I know Johnny would do anything for you if came down to it," Rose sums up.

Darlene doesn't disagree with Rose openly. But in her own thoughts Darlene thinks if that is true, then why are they still separated and he is still unable to make her and the kids the most important thing in his life.

Darlene worries, and that's all she can do as she squeezes Rose's hand again and thanks her for sharing her memory with her. She knows there is probably a story like that from her past with John, but right now she is in no mood to search her own memories for it.

———— ❧ ————

AUDIE TAKES HIS PHONE OUT OF HIS POCKET AND CHECKS the time. He has to hook up with John soon. After making his way around the casino and plopping a few coins in the slots for a while, Audie made himself at home in his favorite place in a casino, the blackjack table. With John out of the way he can relax and enjoy himself. Audie is three drinks into relaxing. At this point he's breaking even at the table, which for him is doing pretty good. A voice from behind him calls out his name. "Audie, hey, what are you doing here?!"

Audie turns to see an old gambling buddy of his from the many trips to Vegas he has made in the last few years. "Marty? Man, what are you doing around here?"

"The same thing probably, trying to lose all my money, right," Marty says with a laugh.

Audie isn't amused by the lack of confidence in his gambling skills that Marty is joking around about.

"What brings you here?" he asks of Audie, a second time.

"Just passing through," Audie answers. "How about you? I thought you lived in Vegas?"

"Yeah," Marty says with a sigh before disclosing that he's moved to the Reno area for a better business opportunity. When Audie asks him more about it, Marty just tells him it's a bullshit little business his brother-in-law started and nothing to write home about. That's more than enough detail for Audie as he makes his next bet on blackjack. Marty pulls up a seat and invades Audie's space. He and Audie had some good times in Vegas on the strip over the last few years, much of which Audie can't remember anymore.

"Did you ever make things right with Capriati back in Vegas?" Marty asks out of thin air.

Audie stands on twenty and then watches the dealer pull an ace and face card out of nowhere, to beat him. Now irritated he looks at Marty and contemplates why the interest in his gambling days in Vegas. "What's it to you?"

Marty shrugs off the question and just states that he was curious, nothing more, nothing less. "He's just not a guy to screw with, am I right?"

Audie again doesn't join in with Marty's humorous tone. He tells his old gambling buddy not to worry, that he's working on making things "'right.'"

Marty is happy to hear that. "That's good news buddy. I don't want you in Dutch with that bastard. He's a real killer, pal."

Audie thanks him for his concern. Seeing Marty, however, just brings back some bad memories. The memories he can remember are times Audie would like to completely forget. He has a few minutes still before meeting up with John, so he tells Marty he has to get going now. They say their goodbyes and Marty wishes the best for him in the future. "And, man, if you have the chance, Audie, you should head over and check out Tahoe. It's amazing in the summer."

"Yeah, I think we are going to do that, tonight or tomorrow," Audie replies.

Marty hears the "'we.'" "You hanging with some hot babe?"

Audie smirks at the compliment. "I wish. No, I'm hanging with my brother."

Audie insists that he has to get going and meet up with his brother. Marty wishes him the best and tells him how great it is to see him again. Audie says the same thing to Marty as he walks off. Marty watches him leave and then reaches for his cell phone out of his pants pocket. The dealer at the table asks him if he is in on this hand and needs some chips. Marty without hesitation tells him no.

"No, pal, I've got work to do."

JOHN, HAVING ALREADY BOOKED A MOTEL ROOM FOR the night and still having a couple of minutes before he has to meet Audie, decides that it might be a good time to call Darlene. Her cell phone rings three times before she answers. "Hey, it's me," he says.

Darlene doesn't sound as happy to hear from him as he would like. "Where are you and Audie at?"

John tells her Reno.

"Somebody on the list lives there?" she comments.

"Yeah, how are you and the kids doing?"

"We're good, thanks. How about you and Audie? How many people have you met with so far?" Darlene asks.

He tells her that the lady here in Lake Tahoe will be number two. Darlene asks how the first person they met with took the news.

"He took it alright, I guess," John replies. "I miss you and the kids."

It gets quiet on the line for a moment after John says that. Darlene isn't sure how to respond to that. And then she does, but it doesn't make things better, only worse. "The kids are missing you already, too."

John hears very well, and what he hears is nothing about her missing him. He wants to directly ask her if she does, but he's afraid to hear her answer. So he chickens out, "Well… make sure and tell the kids I miss them, too"

Darlene assures John that she will. She asks him if he wants to tell the kids himself. With the wind taken out of John's balloon, he really doesn't. He makes up an excuse for having to get going.

"You and Audie be safe, okay?" Darlene says.

It's the warmest thing that she's said to him since he moved out of the house. John says okay back and then works his way off of the phone call. Afterwards, he just sits there in his truck with his phone in hand, wondering why he even bothered to make the call in the first place. He starts up his truck engine and drives away to meet Audie.

On the other end of the call back in Oregon, Darlene isn't feeling great either. She knows how cold she just was to him and for the life of her has no idea why. It's as if she wants her pound of flesh from John for any past sins he's committed against her and is going to get it no matter what. At that moment, their oldest boy, Cody, comes into the room and asks her who she was talking to. Darlene almost lies and says it was someone else, before admitting it was Dad.

"I wanted to say hi to Dad," Cody confesses to his mother.

Her boys' proclamation makes her feel even worse. Darlene comes up with a quick and handy excuse why John had to get off the phone quickly and couldn't talk with Cody or his brother or sister. Cody to her pleasant surprise believes it. "Well, next time he calls, Mom, can you make sure I get to talk to Dad?"

Darlene promises him she will, and she means it. She's already feeling guilty for her little ice queen routine toward John and the casualty it left behind, namely their son. Then as Cody goes outside to play and leaves her by herself, Darlene considers just what John must be thinking right now after their short and curt conversation. She vows right then and there to try to treat John better the next time he calls her. "He's not your own personal punching bag," she tells herself out loud risking that her other two kids might hear her. They don't. "Oh, John, how did we get things so screwed up between us?"

JOHN STILL HURTING FROM DARLENE'S INDIFFERENCE

Andrew Scott Bassett

parks his truck and heads to the casino front doors to meet up with Audie.

"Let's get going," John greets Audie with, still annoyed by the phone conversation with Darlene.

Audie does as he's told and follows behind John. They hop into John's truck, back-up, and drive down the street. They don't notice the black sedan with tinted windows tailing them from behind.

Marty, Audie's old gambling buddy from Las Vegas stands in front of the casino watching as the two vehicles head down the road. His cell rings as he watches. He pushes the name on the cell's screen to take the call. "Hello, Mr. Capriati, how are you? Yes sir, they just left with your guys following. Don't worry about it, sir. I'm just happy I could be of help to you and any appreciation you could give me sir, well… that would be appreciated. Thank you, sir, thank you very much!" He ends the call having scored points with one of the heavy hitters of organized crime in Nevada. Marty tries to put his Judas act behind him and walks back into the casino to lose whatever self- respect he still has, to gambling and booze.

John looks often out his rear view mirror but notices nothing. Audie is chilling, listening to his tunes saved on his phone. They have reached Tahoe and the area of homes where Minnie Radford resides. Neither brother has noticed the car that has been following them all the way from Reno. John pulls onto the street where Minnie lives and slows down to find her house. The two men in the black sedan see them turn into the street and follow them, ready to do the same. Before they can make the turn, however, there is a loud grinding sound followed by the car slowing down with a will of its own. The two larger-than-normal-sized-men in tailored dark suits jump out of each side of the sedan to see what happened.

"Son-of-a-bitch!" one of the men screams up into the sky. "God dammit, we've got a flat tire!"

The other man with him says nothing about the flat only about losing sight of John.

"The boss isn't going like this, Harry."

"No shit, Sherlock," the man called Harry answers to his partner.

"Should we go on foot and see if we can spot them?" the other guy asks.

Harry shakes his head about this latest event before telling his partner Bob no. "We could be walking for hours trying to find out which house they went to. No, we'll fix the flat first and then drive around here and see if we can spot them or their truck."

Bob agrees and catches the car keys Harry throws him so he can get the spare and the jack out of the trunk.

"We better find them, or our asses will be on line," Harry says to himself, but purposely loud enough for Bob to hear as well.

"Shit!" he yells again, his frustration boiling over.

Bob just keeps his head low, keeping good and clear from his frustrated mate. He focuses on wrestling the blown tire off its axle as Harry watches, getting more pissed by the second at the two of them being such victims of random circumstances.

JOHN AND AUDIE CAN'T TELL IF MINNIE IS HOME OR NOT.

Andrew Scott Bassett

They don't see a car parked anywhere. John knocks on the door, and she opens it almost immediately. The brother's look at each other and wonder if she was just waiting next to the door for them to knock.

After being invited in, John and Audie sit themselves down on Minnie's loveseat in her living room. The guys can't help but notice what Minnie is wearing, or not wearing, whatever the case may be. Her white denim short shorts reveal a little too much body and not enough shorts. Even for a young woman, it would be questionable, but for a middle-aged woman like Minnie it is really pushing the envelope. But as attention getting as the bottom half of her is, it's nothing compared to the top half. Her cleavage claws its way out of her skimpy pink top that is also too tight for its own good. Audie's mouth is gaping open at the sight. When John sees this he reminds his brother that this lady is old enough to be their mother. That adjusts his little brother's thinking real fast.

Minnie is wiping tears away with tissues as she sits down across from the boys. The Mae West wig is gone revealing her true hair color, the dark brown they saw at the casino. "I cannot for a second believe that Ray is gone," she cries, fighting back more tears. "But how did you boys find me, or even know about me?"

John has Audie hand him their father's list of names for the trip. "You were the second closest to where we started from."

"From Oregon?" Minnie guessed, knowing more than John or Audie thought she did.

"That's right. How did you know?" John inquires.

Minnie smiles at the question. She knows the answer will give details of her relationship with their father that she's not sure they need to hear. "I knew your father for a long time and I knew he left you two and your mother in Oregon many years ago."

John doesn't quite know how to say what he says next, so he just lets it spill. "Did you have a relationship with our father?"

Minnie is more direct. "Are you asking me if we were lovers?"

Audie turns to see his brother's reaction.

John sheepishly indicates that he is.

"It's times like this, boys, when I really wished I hadn't stopped smoking, you know?"

The boys are amused at her remark but still waiting for her answer.

Minnie can see that and she does her best to delicately give the boys some background information. "I don't know what it was with your dad and I," she starts with.

She certainly has the guys' attention as she gets up and begins to pace around the room, her boobs bouncing a little with each step she takes. "I never tried to put a label on what we had, Ray and I. We just really enjoyed each other's company, so much."

John at this point has to interrupt and for clarification, ask if their father was married to their mother when all this was going on. Minnie admits he was. "It's probably not a comfort to you now, but your dad really loved your mom. And I knew from the beginning I was never going to replace her in Ray's eyes."

With that nugget, Audie joins in on the conversation. "So, Minnie, excuse me for asking and all, but why did he fool around with you if he loved our mom so much, like you're saying?"

Minnie chuckles and grins at the question. She challenges them, asking if they ever had feelings for another woman while in a committed relationship with a woman they believed they were in love with. John quickly and self-righteously says no. But Minnie isn't buying it. "Then that's probably because you never had the chance."

John doesn't agree and disputes her notion.

"I mean, young man, you probably never had another woman come up to you and excite you and make you think there was something more than what you already had. In other words, John, you didn't meet somebody like me."

Her smugness starts to annoy John, and he comes back at Minnie about if she is the reason for their father abandoning his family and their mother.

Minnie seems taken off guard by the question. She makes a face as if she's surprised that he doesn't already know the answer to his own question. "Your father didn't leave your mother because of me and head back to the East Coast."

"So you weren't the reason he left?" John asks her point blank.

"No. No I wasn't, John. Your father left me behind, too. I wanted more than he could give me. I wanted the whole shooting match, but he still loved your mother more than me. When he went back East, he left me behind as well."

Minnie has to ask if there is more to the boys arriving at her home than just sharing terrible news with her.

Audie steps in and tells her about the fishing thing and that their father wanted them to give her a gift to remember him by. Minnie is anxious to see what it is, the gift that is.

Audie searches for it and finds it in the large backpack that holds all the items for people on the list. He finds a box wrapped in tissue paper and hands it to Minnie. She takes off the paper and opens up the box. The contents inside bring a look of delight to her face. She shows the boys. It's a wedding cake topper, a bride and a groom.

John and Audie aren't sure how they are supposed to react to the object.

Audie wonders why their father would want her to have such an item if he never was interested in marrying Minnie.

"I didn't say he wasn't interested Audie. We came close once. He considered divorcing your mom and marrying me, but he couldn't do it. He loved your mom too much," Minnie discloses.

"So why this?" John asks pointing to the cake topper.

"Like I said, we got close to doing something. We made plans together, we picked out a cake and a topper that looked just like this."

"So what happened?" Audie interjects.

"Like I said, boys, your dad loved your mom more. I threw a cake topper just like this one at your father's head when he told me he couldn't marry me. It broke into pieces. I guess this was your father's way of telling me he still remembered that time, that time when we were so crazy about each other."

When Minnie starts to sob some more, thinking about those days, Audie tries to console her by telling her that their father must have cared for her very much. John looks at his brother wondering why he would even say such thing after what this woman did with their father, behind their mother's back.

Minnie thanks Audie for his kind words before getting up and walking over to him and demanding he let her hug him. Awkwardly he does. He can feel John's eyes piercing through the back of his head. When they break their embrace, Minnie announces it's time for a celebration. John and Audie aren't sure what she has in mind but politely listen. "We'll throw a big party over here, a fishing party in honor of your father!"

"Do you have a boat, or something, Minnie?" Audie asks.

"We don't need a boat, boys. Follow me," she tells them as she leads them to the back of her house. She then opens up the sliding glass door and takes them out to her back balcony, which just happens to hang out over Lake Tahoe.

"Wow!" John exclaims at the beautiful sight of the lake at her back door. "I never knew the lake was back here from the front of your house."

"I'll start making the calls, boys! And if you have fishing poles, you better get them. The rainbow and brown trout have been biting like crazy this summer."

CHAPTER 7

J ohn and Audie do as told. Audie because he's always up for a party and John because it's what their dad wanted them to do and he is a man of his word, even if fulfilling his word means partying and fishing with his father's mistress for an evening.

———

JOHN IS SITTING OUT ON THE BACK BALCONY WITH HIS fishing pole in hand. The party is going on inside the house where Audie is hanging out with much of the cast of Minnie's Reno show and a few others. Inside the music is blaring with an eclectic mix of old school rock and modern hip hop. Drinks are flowing everywhere, but no weed as Minnie hates the smell.

John is by himself. It's peaceful out here on the balcony. The music just a few feet away is muffled by the large sliding glass doors. The water is calm at the lake. With the full moon shining on it, the lake almost looks silver in color. The stars are out in full force. When combined with the moon, the reflections off the water make one think they are seeing the Reno strip just a short drive away, but without the crowded streets and trashy neon signs.

The music invades John's space when Minnie opens the sliding doors and makes her way out to where John is. When she closes the doors, it's a relief to John.

"Any bites?" she asks, as she sits down next to John.

"Not yet," he tells her as he holds his pole tight.

She laughs as she recalls how good a fisherman his father was.

John tells her he remembers.

"How old were you when Ray left?"

John thinks for a moment, before answering that he was sixteen.

Minnie follows that up with asking when the last time he saw his father was.

"Sixteen years old, as well," he says stoically.

Minnie thinks about how hard it must have been for John to so suddenly become the "'man in the family.'"

"You do what you have to do," John responds with no emotion.

"I guess you do," Minnie agrees, feeling sorry for what this young man has had to go through. "Still it must have been very difficult for you."

John shrugs. "It's just the past now."

Minnie can see the burden from all those years ago is still being carried by John to this day. She wishes she could help, but with her history with John's father, she's probably the last person he wants help from. Instead she decides to confess to him something she's shared with no one else, except John's dad, ever before. "I need to tell you something about your father and me. I know it is important for you and your brother to know."

John stands up and begins to reel in his line as he tells her okay and braces for it.

Minnie struggles on where to start and how to say what she wants to say. Finally after making no sense, Minnie starts over. "I told you your father and I came close to getting married?"

"Yes, the time when our dad considered dumping our mother, the first time," John spouts off with sarcasm.

Minnie ignores his tone and continues with her story. "Anyway, the reason your dad almost did decide to do all that wasn't just because he was crazy about me, which he was, but also because he felt obligated."

That last word gets John's attention. He asks what she means by it.

Minnie swallows hard before continuing. This is something she's never uttered to anyone before, except Ray a long time ago.

John still is staring at her, waiting for the definition of obligated.

"You have a sister, John."

John is shocked and unable to come up with any words at all in the moment.

"The girl that you saw playing Marilyn Monroe in the show is my daughter, Angie. Angie is your half-sister," Minnie says, the emotion of the disclosure after all these years causes her to tear up again.

John is still in shock as Minnie looks at him for any response at all. Finally, John says the only thing that comes to mind. "Does your daughter know who her father really is?"

Minnie replies to John that she doesn't. "When Ray decided he couldn't leave your mom and you boys for me, he became Cousin Ray, my distant cousin who would come and visit us every once in a while."

"Oh, so she thought he was some family member who liked to come and see you guys," John responds to Minnie's words.

Minnie apologizes for dropping such a bombshell on John, but she tells him she thought he should know about having a sister.

John is then curious about how often Minnie and her daughter, his sister, would entertain these visits from his father.

Minnie recollects for a second before speculating that it was probably around twice a year, give or take. She goes on about his father's generosity toward his daughter. "He would give me large sums of money every chance he could. He always told me he wanted Angie to be taken care of, and if she ever needed anything to contact him and he would be there for us."

John is blown away to hear all this. Dad certainly never sent his mother lots of money and visited Audie and him. John can't help feel a bit jealous of this woman who he's never even really met, even though he tells himself in this moment, that he doesn't.

"Would you like to meet Angie?" Minnie suddenly asks him.

John smiles at the invitation and of course says he would, although only half of his being really wants to. The other half of John would like to let childish jealously fester while throwing a toddler-style tantrum. That last half John hides from Minnie.

"She's only in the next room," Minnie tells John, excited at the prospect of the two of them and Audie as well, finally about to meet.

John, first however, would like to have a second alone to

gather his thoughts before meeting her. Minnie is happy to grant him his wish. She goes back into the house to locate her daughter and see what she's up to. But after searching through the bodies filling up her living room, Angie is nowhere in sight, and strangely enough neither is Audie.

⸺⧟⸺

"IT'S CRAZY HOW BEAUTIFUL THIS LAKE IS TONIGHT," Audie exclaims as he walks along the beach with a beautiful young woman who he just chatted up at the party upstairs.

With more than a few rum and Cokes in his system to help build his confidence, Audie turned on the charm on the prettiest face in the room. Somehow it actually worked, and she invited him on this walk on the shores of Lake Tahoe. Audie stops to pick up a piece of driftwood that came ashore. He throws it back into the lake as if trying to impress her with a feat of strength. "Nice throw," she says.

"I've always been pretty good at that, good arm for things for sure."

"I bet there are a lot of things you're good at," she flirts back to him.

Audie can't believe how much this chick seems to be into him. "I'm not much for one bragging about himself, but yeah, I've got some skills. Mind you I'm not Liam Neeson or anything, but I've got some skills."

"I bet you do have some skills, Audie. Maybe you could give me a small demonstration," the girl playfully adds as she slides her fingers up and down his arm and then moves in close for a slow, wet kiss.

Audie is so thrilled by the surprise lip lock that he thanks her for it. "You're a really good kisser."

"I get a lot of practice in our Reno show. Marilyn Monroe kisses lots of men," she confides to Audie.

Audie then in that moment realizes that she knows his name, but he has no idea hers. After apologizing for such rudeness, Audie asks her.

"I'm Angie. Minnie that you're here to see is my mother."

Audie had no idea she was Minnie's daughter. "Dude, that's crazy. We're here to see your mom, and now I meet you."

"Maybe it's just fate. Do you believe in fate, Audie?" she asks him as she snuggles up closer.

Audie, with a big smile from ear to ear on his face, has to admit he's a big supporter of it right now.

She giggles and asks if he would like to take a swim with her. Audie is not about to say no. He can tell when a woman has the "hots" for him. Angie tells Audie that there is a place around the bend of the shore, away from all the houses view, where they can swim "privately," if he would like to go there? "Giddy-up," Audie responds with a childish laugh as she takes him by the arm and leads the way.

They pass some teenagers hanging out on the beach enjoying the night with a cooler full of beers, hoping no law enforcement will catch them in the act.

A happy Audie waves to them and tells them to party on as he and Angie walk on by. The teenagers whoop and holler their agreement, waving bottles of beer in the air and toasting Audie's declaration to party.

JOHN WALKS INSIDE AND MEETS UP WITH MINNIE. HE'S prepared now to make the acquaintance of this half-sister of his. The problem is that Minnie can't find her or Audie for that matter.

She begins to ask around and quickly is told that Angie and Audie went outside together. One of the guests, the Elvis impersonator still wearing his sideburns which turn out to be real, shares with Minnie and John that he heard Angie inviting Audie for a walk on the beach out back. John isn't sure why, but Minnie is suddenly concerned about this walk and grabs John by the hand and drags him down to the beach.

When they get down there, there is no Audie or Angie in sight. "We better find them right away," Minnie declares.

John is confused about what Minnie is worried about and asks her if everything is okay. She reluctantly tells him what her worst fear is. When hearing it John agrees. "You're right. We better find them right away."

Minnie thinks she might know where they went and directs John to follow her, which he urgently does as they both walk as fast as they can without actually starting to run. Minnie shouts to John that she only hopes they get to them before something "bad" happens.

"YOU HAVE TO LOVE THIS COUNTRY," AUDIE WHISPERS under his breath as he watches the spectacle of Angie tossing off her clothes, all her clothes, and frolicking into Lake Tahoe's now- dark waters.

Her skin glistens from the sand sticking on her and the moonlight reflecting off of the water and then her. When she dives face first into the tide, Audie's head bobs up and down mimicking her perfectly proportioned bottom doing the same as it enters the lake and then goes under. Audie always wondered what it would be like to make it with some big-time sexy movie actress, and who could be bigger than Marilyn Monroe, or at least the next best thing, he rationalizes.

When Angie comes up for air, her hair is soaked and hanging down straight, and like the lake waters of Tahoe, her hair is dancing around her more-than-proportioned upstairs. She calls out to Audie to follow her lead. "You mean au naturel," Audie responds to the request.

"Like yeah, that's what I was thinking. What's wrong? Are you a shy guy?"

Audie searches for a witty comeback but has nothing. So he speaks about how amazing the full moon is tonight and how it's almost like God left on the porchlight. Angie giggles at what seems to be his timidity for his own body. "If it makes you feel better, I'll close my eyes," she promises him.

Audie yells out, "It's a deal," and waits for her to cover up her peepers with her hands. Angie does, and Audie as quick as any human being possibly could, sheds all his clothes throwing them with all his might into a heap, away from the water. Then Audie with the speed and agility that only embarrassment can give someone, dives into the lake and swims out to where Angie is wading in the water and waiting for him. Audie could see her take a sneak peek through her fingers right before he dove in.

<hr />

JOHN IS STILL FOLLOWING AFTER MINNIE, NOT SURE where they are going. When they come across a group of teenagers partying on the beach Minnie asks them if they have seen a couple that matches the descriptions of Audie and Angie. The half-inebriated kids think for a second and then remember they did just see a couple go by that sounds like it could be them. They let Minnie and John know they are going the right direction, the same way the couple went. Minnie thanks them, and she and John continue on their way.

WHEN AUDIE BREAKS THE SURFACE OF THE COOL LAKE water, Angie is there to meet him and immediately engulfs him with her legs and arms. When he starts sinking in the water, unable to touch the bottom, Audie pleads for her to get off of him for a second. Angie hearing this instantly lets him free of her embrace. "Like really? You don't like that?"

Audie can see that he just annoyed the crap out of her and tries to justify himself. "Sorry, I'm not the greatest swimmer, you know?"

Angie flashes a look of disappointment. The mood has been broken. She's about to call it a night and swim back to shore. But Audie is not about to let a little thing like drowning ruin such a great opportunity. He swims back over to her and doing the best he can to keep himself above water, grabs her by the legs and pulls her to him. Angie is excited by his change of heart and rewards him by once again wrapping her arms and legs around him and giving him a full-court press on the mouth. Audie struggles to keep both of them above water while fully enjoying the moment at the same time. Finally Angie gets how much he is struggling and let's go of him long enough to guide him to a spot closer to shore where their feet can reach bottom. Audie thanks her as much as he can between the brief moments where she isn't covering his mouth with hers. He feels dominated and a little weak, but not so strangely, the way she's making him feel he can live with gladly.

"I don't know what it is, Audie, but there's just something

about you, like I've known you my whole life," she confesses to him when her lips finally leave his.

Audie doesn't know what to say, and at this time most of his blood is nowhere near his brain, which makes it even harder to come up with something. "Wow, that's really cool!" he replies stupidly.

"I'll show you something more cool," she tells him as she grabs a hold of his nether region.

For a brief second Audie worries that a large fish or even a snake has a hold of him and a chill runs down his back. It's both a pleasure and a relief to discover that it's her that's got a hold of him. She grabs his hand with her other and begins to guide it where she wants.

"Angie! Angie!"

The yell of her name from her mother's familiar voice instantly makes her let go of Audie and push him away in the same instant. "Mom, what are you doing out here?!"

Audie turns to see John walking right beside Minnie. Audie bellows out to him, "What the hell, man?!"

Minnie orders her daughter out of the water right this moment, but Angie first wants to know why. Audie is wondering the same thing. Minnie realizes she's going have to just tell them both the truth, right now and here. She looks over to John who gestures that it's fine with him, in fact better if she is the one to breaks the news.

"What is it, Mom?!" You're like freaking me out right now!" Angie screams from the water

Minnie tries to explain herself but it only makes things more confusing. So she just musters up the courage to spit it out. "Audie is your half-brother!"

If the lake's moving waters make any sounds at all, no one can hear them right now. Everything stands still as

Audie and Angie in bewilderment stare at each other standing in the waters of Lake Tahoe, both naked under a full moon that was a second ago kind of magical, but now only awkward and embarrassing.

"What are you talking about, half-brother?" she demands to know from her mother.

Minnie tries to clarify. "His father was also your father, Ray Barrett."

"You slept with your cousin? That's so gross Mom!" Angie blurts out with disgust.

"No! No! Ray wasn't really my cousin. He was an old boyfriend and he was the father of both Audie and John here," Minnie discloses.

At that moment, Angie, filled with so many questions, and Audie, still in shock over the announcement, realize the impact of what just almost happened. "Oh, my god, I kissed him. Oh, my god I touched his…and we were about to…oh my god!" Angie screams out.

Audie asks his brother if this is all true, and John tells him it is. John suggests to Minnie it would probably be wise for them to turn their backs allowing Audie and Angie to come out of the lake and get dressed. "Yes, of course, you're right," Minnie responds to him.

Angie now more disgusted than anything else, tells Audie to go first. She has no desire to let him get another look at her body. Audie politely agrees, goes first, and rushes to throw his clothes on. And then with no one watching, making sure Audie also has his back turned, Angie makes it to shore and does the same thing.

Then all four of them begin a very awkward and uncomfortable walk back to Minnie's house. Angie purposely walks on the opposite side of Audie with Minnie and John between her. It's quiet as no one really knows what to say next.

⎯⎯⎯⎯ ⌾⌾⌾ ⎯⎯⎯⎯

It's silent night all the way back to Minnie's house. Angie announces she's going home right away. She's just going to grab her car keys and flee. Minnie implores her to stay and talk through all this with her and the guys, but humiliated, she wants no part of that. Minnie and the guys watch as Angie races the down the street trying to get away from them as fast as she can. "She's a little shook up right now about all this," Minnie tells them, asking for them to forgive her behavior.

Audie says nothing. His mind is still on the fact that he almost had 'relations' with his half-sister.

John acts like it's no big deal, doing his best to squash the awkwardness of the situation.

Minnie asks if they want to come inside and talk about all this. She believes they still have many more things they want to know.

Audie still in a daze looks to John for direction. "Sure, Minnie, for a little while I guess," John decides.

This makes Minnie happy. She tells the boys that she will shut down what's left of the party inside and send everybody home so just the three of them can chat. But before she can turn the knob on the door, two nicely dressed men interrupt their plans.

"Audie," the taller and skinnier of the two men says to them.

Audie looks right at him and asks how he knows his name. "Who are you guys?"

"We just need to talk to you for a minute, alone," the man answers.

FISHING *for* SOMETHING 113

"About what?" John interrupts. "And how do you know my brother?"

"And that's what we want to talk with you about, alone," the man replies dogmatically.

"Yeah, it'll only take a minute," the other guy in the suit standing next to him says.

Audie tells John it's okay. He tells the two men he'll talk to them away from John and Minnie. So he walks away with the two of them, just far enough that his brother can't hear their conversation. John has a bad feeling about all this but allows Audie to do it. Minnie, who's lived in Nevada with gambling and prostitution all around her for a long time, has a pretty good idea what these two guys are all about. She asks John to excuse her for a minute while she goes upstairs into her house. John nods, while not taking his eyes off of his brother, now standing outside of earshot of him.

The taller man with a big old smile covering his face, as to not tip off Audie's brother that anything is at all wrong, does all the talking. "I think you know why we are here, Audie."

Audie tries to play dumb but is unconvincing to the men.

"Mr. Capriati wants his money, and he wants it now," the guy threatens to Audie.

Audie attempts one more time to play the clueless card but to no avail.

"Now, since I'm sure you don't have the money on you, you have a couple of ways to go right now. You can come with us nicely and take us to where ever the money's at so we can take the money back to Mr. Capriati. Second option: You can go back to Vegas with us and contemplate how you're going to pay Mr. Capriati off if you no longer have the money available. Third option is we can make you do either of the first two options by messing up your brother real bad, right here, right now."

Audie considers their kind offers, but being the smart-ass that he inherently is questions why the man said there was going to be a couple of offers when in actuality there were three.

The man's pleasant look vanishes for a second as he doesn't see humor in Audie's joke. He quickly puts his smile back on for show, as to not tip off John on the tone of the conversation.

Minnie comes back out this time with the Elvis and John Belushi performers from her show. She leans into John's ear and whispers, "They're wise guys, you know."

"You mean, like as in the Mafia?" John asks her.

Minnie says to him that is exactly what she means. "Your brother either owes somebody he shouldn't a lot of money, or he slept with somebody's woman that he shouldn't have slept with."

"Both are possible," John replies.

"So what's it going to be?" the man asks Audie one last time.

Audie looks back to John. The last thing he wants is his brother to get hurt over the stupid mistakes he's made in his past. "I'll go with you guys to see Mr. Capriati. Just leave my brother out of all this. It has nothing to do with him, man. Just let him go and we're cool, alright, okay?"

The two men agree to that, not looking to make a mess out of the situation with witnesses now watching their every move.

Audie walks back over to John and Minnie. "Hey, bro, I got some business I need to take care of with these fellas. It'll probably take a few days, so you might as well head back to Oregon."

"What the heck are you mixed up in?" John wants to know.

Audie tries to shrug it off as nothing, but his brother isn't buying it. Minnie breaks into the conversation and asks Audie how bad a situation it is. Audie isn't about to tell her with John standing right there. He knows his big brother would jump in and try to stop him from going with the two goons and probably get hurt, or worse. "It's no biggie; I just need a few days that's all."

"Well, the hell if I'm going to let you go with these guys. Minnie says they're Mafia," John tells his brother.

Audie tries to calm his brother's fears. He assures him again that he will be alright and that he will hook back up with John back in Grants Pass when he is done.

Minnie looks at Audie and says, "It must be bad. You are protecting your brother, aren't you?"

John raises his voice and demands the truth from Audie. Minnie winks to her fellow performers, Elvis and John Belushi look-a-likes. The two performers begin to walk toward the thugs in fine tailored clothes. Minnie's friends shout out their thanks for the party and tell her they'll see her on Wednesday. They greet the two men in suits as they walk by them. "How's it hanging tonight?" Belushi says.

The wise guys smile a tiny bit without saying a word back. They're focused on Audie who's still trying to convince his brother that it's okay if he goes with these guys.

"Howdy, boys," Elvis says to them with his classic Memphis drawl.

Again, hardly any response, as the Mafia lackeys keep their eyes on Audie, making sure he doesn't make a break for it. Then with the wise guys backs to them, Elvis and Belushi stop, turn back toward them, and take out small wooden bats from their shorts. In one strong swoop, they slam those bats to the side of the heads of the men in suits, making them crash to the ground without as much as a whimper.

Minnie hollers out with glee at the sight of the fallen wise guys. She orders John to take Audie and get as far away as possible. John is worried about her. "What about when they come to? If they find out you had something to do with this, it could be big trouble for you."

Minnie roars at the suggestion. "I haven't lived most of my life in Vegas and Reno without making some connections of my own, John. I'll make a few calls to my friends, and these guys and whoever their working for will be scared shitless to mess with me. No, you and your brother just need to get out of here and stay clear of these guys, alright?"

"Sure," John answers.

Audie thanks her for saving his ass.

"Thank me by getting out of here now," Minnie tells him.

John asks about Angie and having a chance to sit down and talk with her in the future.

"In time, I'm sure she'll be interested. We'll stay in touch, John," Minnie promises. "Now, both of you get going."

John grabs Audie and they start to run back to the truck, thanking Elvis and Belushi as they run past them. John's truck tires screech as he peels down the road heading back to Reno and their motel room which they now won't dare use. They grab their stuff and head south on their way to Arizona and the next name on the list. The guys hope they won't come into contact with the two goons in the suits again. "I want to know what they wanted you for," John demands of Audie.

"It's a long boring story," Audie responds.

"We've got all the time in the world, brother, all the time in the world," John replies, keeping his eyes on the road forward, but also behind, hoping to see no one following them for the rest of the trip.

Andrew Scott Bassett

CHAPTER 8

The guys have been on the road for a couple of hours, leaving Reno, Tahoe, and all the crazy happenings behind them. John has tried to get Audie to open up about the Mafia goons, but Audie has bullshitted him with a story about how the goons' boss just needs some papers signed by Audie. John can hardly believe his brother can make up such crap and spew it with a straight face. But he lets it go for now. He's exhausted and doesn't have the energy to force the truth out of his brother. Audie can see John is wiped out and makes a suggestion that they pull over, off the desert highway and camp out for the night.

"We'll just make it to the next town and get a motel?" John suggests.

Audie counters that might not be a good idea, "The men we left at Minnie's house could be checking the motels for our vehicle. Might be better, Johnny, if we just camp out in the desert. We could pull the truck far enough from the side of the road that no one would see it."

John shakes his head in frustration at Audie's words. "So these guys are just wanting you to go see their boss and sign some papers, but we have to hide from them?"

Audie knows at this moment he's trapped himself in his own spin and lies. There is no easy way out. Not to mention he's too tired to keep up his storytelling. "Okay, okay, what do you want from me, John?!"

For John that is an easy reply. "The truth, that's all, but it's always been so hard for you to do."

Audie is quiet, trying to come back with something smart to say, but too fuzzy in thought from fatigue to come up with anything.

"Maybe a night under the stars out in the fresh air would do both us some good," John decides as he pulls his big old truck off the highway and down into the desert below.

"That's all I'm saying," Audie lets out as they find a flat area to park and set up camp.

———— ⊙⊙⊙ ————

"You better call him now, Harry," Bob pleads with his partner. "We've been checking every motel in the area, and they're nowhere to be found."

"Yes, I know. I'm sitting in this car right next to you, aren't I?" Harry cracks back.

"Mr. Capriati's going to be pissed, and he's going to be more pissed the longer we wait to tell him," Bob continues.

"I know, I know, quit nagging me! You are like an old woman or something!" Harry complains as he pulls out his cell and makes the dreaded call.

Both men swallow hard as they wait for their boss to pick up.

"What?" comes the voice from the cell.

Harry with trembling in his own voice, begins to break down the events of the evening. Mr. Capriati doesn't want a play-by-play and demands that they cut to the chase. "Do you have Audie Barrett or the money he owes me, or not?"

If sweating could be heard it would be the sound that Harry's voice is making right now. "Not yet, sir, but we're working on it."

Mr. Capriati is less than thrilled. "I don't know what happened, boys, and I don't give a shit. You bring that little ass wipe back to me or the money he owes me or you two better start shopping for funeral lots so your loved ones will have a place to visit. You got that?!"

Harry and Bob, more than get that. They assure their boss that there's nothing to worry about. "We'll have that punk in no time, boss," Harry promises.

Mr. Capriati again lets them know in no uncertain terms that they better, and then hangs up on them. The two men look across at each other from their respective car seats. "What are we going to do, Harry?" Bob asks with fear in his voice.

"The only thing we can, Bob," Harry answers defiantly. "We're going to find this Barrett asshole."

<hr />

JOHN COMES PREPARED AS HE ALWAYS DOES. HIS TENT, sleeping bags, matches, even pieces of rolled-up newspaper to help get a fire going, are all inside his truck camper. The Nevada sky is so stunning, putting on a show with the stars that the boys decide to pass on the tent and sleep outside in their sleeping bags next to a fire John starts. Both of them are kicking back and relaxing on their make-shift beds, lying on the ground. John's eyes are fighting to stay open; it's been a long couple of days of driving and craziness. Audie, however, is wide awake and bored. He starts up some small talk with his brother. "You really are a lot like him."

"What are you talking about?" John growls, half-asleep by now.

Audie elaborates. "Dad, you too man, just so much alike, from what I remember."

"Are you trying to piss me off?" John responds, not appreciating the comparison.

Audie smirks at that and then continues his train of thought. "No, dude, I mean the way you are so comfortable in the outdoors, mister fisherman and hunter guy. You know, if Dad had stayed around, he would still be trying to turn me into an outdoors guy. You two would be so close."

John knows that Audie has always resented him for being the older one and the son who got the most time hanging out with their father. Their mom had told him as much when Audie had confided it to her. But this is the first time that he and Audie have ever talked about it. "You never told me yourself about how much you missed out on with Dad leaving," John says.

"I didn't think you'd want to hear about it," Audie answers.

"And why's that?" John asks.

Audie feels like he's being cross-examined and doesn't like it. "Maybe we should just call it a night, bro."

But John insists. He wants to know why his brother never talked to him about things relating to their father.

"Why the hell would I? You hate the guy. I assumed it would just piss you off or something."

John is a little pissed off now with this talk. "I never said I hated our father."

Audie sneers at John's assertion. "Right, dude, you only basically spit when you say his name."

"That's not true!" John challenges. "But why shouldn't I be angry at the man for abandoning us, our mom, leaving us to starve. He didn't give a damn about us!"

"So you admit you hate him," Audie contends.

John attempts to regain his composure. He knows his temper can get the best of him. He struggles to justify himself. "I hate the things he's done to us, that's all. And yeah, I'm real angry at him, not that it matters anymore, and you should be to."

Audie notices what he's seen for years when the subject of their father comes up around John. He sees the teenage boy still living inside the grown man, the boy still hurting and angry from his father's betrayal. Audie was hurt and angry too, but being younger not as much as John. When they were boys, John being older and so much more interested in the same things as their father, spent a lot more time with him than Audie did. Audie would often stay at home with Mom while John and Dad went fishing and hunting and generally exploring nature and all its mysteries. John was closer to Dad, and maybe that's why the bitterness seems so much deeper imbedded in him.

"I just thought it was time to heal the wounds and talk with Dad. That's why I tried to reach out," Audie contends, trying to define his reasons for trying to reconnect with their father.

"Good for you," John says as he rolls to his side and acts as if he's serious about getting some shut eye.

"So we're done here?" Audie tosses out into the Nevada night for John to respond to.

"Goodnight," John answers.

"I'll take that as a yes, man," Audie proclaims as he settles in for the night.

Audie is still awake a few minutes later when he can hear John snoring across from him.

Audie's mind is racing with so many things happening. Capriati's guys almost dragged him away to what could have been possibly death, or worse. Well, that really tops the list, and Audie can't stop thinking about it. Having a sister that he and John never knew about is somewhere in there, too. When he gets his share of his inheritance, it will be enough to pay his debt with Capriati. Audie wrestles with that and the fact he wants to keep the money, not pay Capriati back, and try to get ahead for once. Being always in between jobs and places to live is no easy thing, and that fifty thousand dollars could help him change things in a big way.

"Man I need a drink," he says under his breath.

The alcohol from Minnie's party earlier is starting to wear off, and Audie can feel reality creeping in now, and he doesn't have the chemicals in his body to stop it. Stressed out and sober has never been a feeling he likes.

Then Audie ever so quietly, being careful not to even step on a twig that might break and wake John, slowly and slyly finds his small duffle bag that he brought on their journey for just such occasions. Inside it is some of the booze he picked up at the truck stop on Saturday. He takes a big swig from the bottle in case John wakes up and he doesn't get a chance for anymore. He knows how John already thinks he's got a problem with the stuff and will badger him for drinking too much. Then just as quietly, with bottle hidden in his pocket, he works his way back to his sleeping bag and lies down. He glances over, and John is still snoring away. Intent that he's not in danger of being seen, he takes another big gulp from the bottle and then another, and then finishes it off. In a few minutes, he feels the edge of everything coming off, at least a bit. Audie can now close his eyes and do his best to slow his thoughts. Now, if only his brother would close his mouth maybe he could get some z's himself.

———— ✻✻✻ ————

DARLENE SLIPS INTO HER HOME LIKE A CAT BURGLAR. She ended up switching shifts with another girl and working the late shift at the café. A few minutes before leaving she calls home and gets a status report from Rose. The kids, who went to the city's public pool and swam all afternoon, have crashed for the night. Rose asked her to be very quiet when she makes it home. So that is exactly what she is doing as she tiptoes to the family room and greets Rose who's working on her crossword puzzle book. The house is strangely peaceful with no children or televisions making any noise. Rose asks her how her day went before describing all the fun the kids had swimming the day away. Then the subject turns to her John.

"I was wondering, dear, if you have heard from Johnny."

Darlene lies and says she hasn't yet. "It's par for the course," she tells Rose. "John has never been one to be big on communicating. You know that."

Rose knows that, but it's her son and she will always judge him through her own special rose-tinted glasses. Rose would argue that is something Darlene should already know.

"I just thought since it's been a few days, maybe he texted you or something," Rose adds.

"Not yet, nothing so far," Darlene replies with a look of disdain covering her face.

Rose can't help but notice her look and her body language. It speaks volumes. Darlene has never been one to shield her emotions from view, and she doesn't now.

"Well, I'm sure dear that Johnny and Audie are just really

busy with all they have to do," Rose offers up, trying her best to defend her son's inaction.

Darlene isn't even in the mood to really discuss his personal flaws. All she does mention is the importance of John keeping in touch for their children's sake. She tells Rose, once again, that it is just the norm for John to not think of his family before himself. "If our situation is very different when he gets back, that's his own fault," she informs Rose.

Those are ominous words, and Rose certainly doesn't like the sound of them. She interrogates Darlene on what she means by what she just said. Darlene for a micro-second almost explains, but then remembers just who it is that she is talking to, namely her husband's mother. "It doesn't mean anything, Rose. I'm just frustrated with John like always and really tired from a busy day at work. If you don't mind, I'm going to follow my kids lead and go to bed."

Rose wishes her a goodnight and then packs up her crossword book and all her other stuff and leaves. Darlene is sitting on the edge of her bed still thinking about the conversation that just ended. She shakes her head and sighs as she thinks about John and how she and the children have always taken a backseat to his plans, dreams, and interests. "Maybe it's time to think about myself for a change," she says out loud, only to herself. "Maybe Lorinda's right, maybe it is time to make some big changes."

Her bitterness gets into bed with her as she takes off her work clothes and crawls under the covers. She lets out a few more sighs and gasps a bit more, but then passes out, letting exhaustion do its job.

⸺⸺⸺

AUDIE TWISTS AND TURNS IN HIS SLEEPING BAG. HE'S

been in and out of sleep for hours after finally ignoring his brother's snoring. John finally stops and is dead to the world in his bed for the night.

Audie suddenly awakes. The sounds of animals in the distance cause him concern but the burgeoning needs of his bladder demand relief. He knows John placed his rifle and a handgun close to his sleeping bag just in case some critters or wise guys make an appearance in the middle of the night. Audie contemplates grabbing the handgun as he looks for a decent place to relieve himself. But since he is not weapons savvy like his brother, Audie is afraid he might end shooting himself and not some wild animal who wanders by.

Since the campfire burned out hours ago, it's much darker than it was when Audie finally fell asleep. Now he wishes the fire was still going. He sneaks over to John and looks for his brother's flashlight, but it's nowhere in sight. "Whatever," he whispers under his breath as he does the best he can with the little bit of visibility the stars in the sky leave him with.

Slowly he walks away from John and their camp. Audie measures each step carefully because of the darkness that has engulfed the desert floor. He certainly doesn't want to step or trip on something he can't see. Suddenly, after several minutes of exploration away from John and camp, Audie is satisfied to find some bushes to take a whizz on, and relieve the pressure in his loins. It's a strange fact with men that it's always more enjoyable to pee on something than just the ground when one has to relieve himself in the great outdoors.

It takes a moment to get going after holding it in for so long, but when it comes it's like a monsoon hits the desert. A look of relief comes to Audie as he zips up and begins the trek back to camp. On his way, he sees what looks like another bush in his path, but there's a problem. This bush is moving, and then he hears it. The rattling starts, and Audie with fear running through his body like blood runs through one's veins, makes a dash past and around the object.

Audie, scared to death, fails to see a large rock in his way and trips over it like a drunken sailor on leave. He fights to get back onto his feet as quickly as he can as the rattle seems to follow him

Then it happens, a pulsating sensation in his backside, doom in his derriere, a pain in his ass. He reaches back, half expecting to find something attached to his bottom. It's a relief there isn't anything there, but he still runs for all his worth back to camp and to his brother. When he reaches camp, he dives towards and makes a successful landing on his sleeping bag. Audie grunts and moans, but still doesn't disturb John's restful slumber. When he reaches back again to touch the spot of his discomfort, a whole new level of pain rears its ugly head and Audie yelps out.

The noise wakes John like someone poked him with a stick. He rolls over to see his brother writhing and squirming. "What's wrong?" John asks.

Audie answers between clinched teeth the best he can. "I've think I've been bit!"

John jumps up and out of his bag and races to his brother's side, "By what?!"

Audie still for some reason keeps feeling his wound, which only makes it worse. "I think by a rattlesnake!"

"Here in camp?!" John responds as he immediately grabs his handgun from under his pillow.

"No! No!" Audie yells back. "I went for a pee, and it happened! It hurts like hell man!"

John puts down his gun and instead grabs his hunting knife and kneels down next to his brother. John slaps away Audie's hands and makes Audie drop his pants. "Let me take a look," John says as he places the beam of his flashlight directly on the sight of Audie's pain. "Yeah, you've been bit alright. And whoever got you has some damn big old fangs."

"Shit, it hurts!" Audie blurts out as John further examines the wound.

John can already see with the help of his flashlight, the area around the bite marks is getting redder. This is not his first rodeo when it comes to such matters. He's seen this once before on a hunting trip with some buddies, and unfortunately he knows what his choices are. "The venom's spreading fast. We got to get it out."

"Shit! There's venom spreading man?! I got to get to a hospital!"

Out in the desert, it might take too long to get to the next city or hospital, John makes plain to his terrified little brother. "It's too risky to drive anywhere," John tells him.

"Well, then what the hell am I supposed to do, die?!" Audie demands of his brother.

"I did consider that option," John answers with a chuckle. "Considering what the alternative is, Audie."

"What alternative, man?!"

"This one," John says as he reaches for his hunting knife and then asks Audie if he just "'happens'" to have any alcohol lying around. John assumes he might. Audie directs him to where another bottle of "Jack" resides. John grabs it and opens it up. He pours it over the wound and his hunting knife. Audie is now figuring out what is about to happen next and pleads with his brother for another way. "Let's just try to find a hospital, dude; there is probably one just down the road."

John makes it clear to him there isn't time for that. "We've got to get the venom out right now."

John gives Audie his leather knife sheath and orders him to bite down on it with all his might. John then carves into the two bite marks on Audie's buttocks with his knife. Audie screams like a little kid chased by a bee. The leather sheath and clenched teeth barely dim the squeals. When John is done, he's cut big enough into the holes to do the unpleasant next. He gives Audie a chance to rest for a second and regain a trace of composure. After that John demands for the next and most important step, that his brother stays still. Audie feeling like a Thanksgiving turkey, promises to do his best.

John then grabs him by the hip with one hand while using his other hand to steady the area around the wound. "Now hold still, this is hard enough as it is!"

Audie isn't sure what's next but braces himself for whatever it is.

"Shit, what are you doing man?!" Audie yells as he spits out the leather sheath from his mouth.

"I'm getting the venom out," John declares as he covers the two bite marks with his mouth and begins to suck.

Audie wiggles with both disgust and embarrassment. John grabs him by the hips and squeezes hard to make him stay still. The squeezing hurts and Audie hollers from it, but he gets the message now with the full understanding how repulsive a scene this is. Audie lies still and lets John finish his mission.

John stops only to spit venom from his mouth and then continues to suck out more. Finally he's done, confident he got most or all of it. John gargles with what's left of Jack Daniels in the bottle. He hates whiskey, but it beats the alternative that's been in his mouth.

When he realizes his brother is finished, Audie collapses on the ground. He's still in pain and wiped out from all he's been through.

John grabs a first aid kit he keeps under the front seat of his pick-up and begins to clean and seal the wound. He tells his brother that they have to head to the nearest hospital and have him checked out. Audie protests for a moment worried that they may be spotted by Capriati's men.

But John shuns such a possibility. "Those guys have no idea where we are. Hell, I don't have any idea where we are. They certainly won't be searching every hospital in the state for us."

Audie nervously agrees, and with John's help limps over to the truck and climbs into the backseat. John packs up the camp and starts up his truck. "We've got to make sure that all the venom is out of you."

Audie grimacing from pain every time he moves his position in his seat, for the first time thanks his brother for what he did. "I never thought all that rugged outdoors crap would come in handy, but it actually did. Thanks, John, for doing what you did. I know it couldn't have been fun, bro."

"Let's just never speak of it again, how's that?" John answers with a smirk.

Audie agrees. "Well, anyways, it is ironic."

John wonders what he means as they get back onto the highway.

Audie expounds. "All my life I've been a pain in the ass to others. Now I literally have a pain in the ass. I guess that's Karma."

Audie's comments put a smile on John's face. "I couldn't have said it any better."

Audie and John both enjoy a laugh as they speed through the darkness of the night looking for the next town of any significance, that the highway leads them to.

⚮

"Why are we here again, Harry?" Bob asks as they have been sitting in the same club where Audie Barrett was spotted for over two hours.

"I told you. We need to find out where Barrett went or where he's living, or whatever. If we don't bring him or his money back, Mr. Capriati is going to be using our balls for dog toys."

"But why here? He's not stupid enough to be coming back here, is he?" Bob states.

Harry annoyed by the question from his partner tells Bob to leave the thinking to him. At that moment one of the guys from Minnie's party walks by. He's here to get ready for the show that starts in about an hour. Harry recognizes him as one of the guys who plunked Bob and him on the beach last night. Harry gets up and walks over quickly to catch up with the guy. Bob follows closely behind. "Hey, pal, remember me, John Belushi?"

The guy, of course, does and pulls his arm from Harry's tight grip. "Yeah, maybe, what are you guys doing here?"

Bob wants to threaten the guy but Harry is quick to point out their surroundings, namely a crowded public place. Harry takes a more subtle approach. "Look, pal, we owe you from last night, but I am more than willing to let that little transgression go if you answer some questions for me."

"What if I say no?" the performer challenges.

"That would not be a very smart thing to do, Mr. Blues Brother. Our boss is not the kind of guy to piss off, if you know what I mean."

The show performer knows exactly what he means. He tries to push all this off onto Minnie since it was her party and her guests that they're after, but Harry sets him straight. "Your friend Minnie is connected all over this state. She's untouchable, but, pal, I'm guessing you aren't. So tell me where can I find Audie Barrett."

The guy has to first ask who that is. After realizing who these guys are questioning him about, he admits ignorance, at least at first. But with a little more threatening his memory becomes clearer. "Look, I do recall overhearing the guy say they started out from Oregon. I think he said Grants Pass Oregon, wherever the hell that is."

"What else? Jog your memory, or I'll do it for you," Harry threatens.

With that threat guiding him, the guy tries hard to remember anything else he might have overheard from the party last night. Then something does come to mind. "One of the guys, I think the one you're talking about, said something about being here because of his father's will or something like that."

"His father's will, you say?" Harry mutters back, finding the point an interesting clue. "Anything else?"

The performer swears that's all he can remember, so Harry and Bob let him go on his way.

"Go take a piss if you need to, Bob."

"Why?"

"Because we're heading to Oregon, Grants Pass, Oregon, that's why," Harry answers.

"Right now?" Bob responds.

"Right now, so use the head if you need to?" Harry orders.

Bob, as usual, does as he's told and heads for the nearest men's room.

Harry standing in the club's lobby alone waits for his partner. He talks to himself. "We've got to get this guy. I can see Mr. Capriati playing fetch right now with his Rottweiler and using my testicles to do it."

CHAPTER 9

Darlene is carefully pouring water into one of the café's coffee makers when she receives a solid jab in her side from Lorinda. She spills some of the water on the counter and whines at Lorinda for causing it.

"Look, who's here, darling," Lorinda says in her defense.

"Who?" Darlene responds before turning to see Mike Stillman heading her direction.

"You're waiting on what tables, may I ask?"

Darlene looks pleased at his inquiry. It's nice to have someone preferring her for a change, she thinks to herself. Then she points to one of her tables, and Mike gladly sits down there.

When she hands him his menu, he can't help but ask the question he came in specifically to ask today. "Darlene, I was wondering. I mean, I know its short notice and all, but my schedule is light tomorrow so I was wondering if tomorrow night you would be up for a little dinner?"

Darlene considers his request for a second. Frustrated with the "John situation," she decides it sounds fine to her as long as she can get a babysitter on such short notice. She informs Mike the same before Lorinda butts in and offers to babysit for them. Mike thinks it's a great idea, but Darlene isn't so sure about Lorinda watching her kids. "You've never even met my kids."

Lorinda quickly comes up with a solution for that. "I get off at the same time as you do tomorrow. I'll just go straight to your house and you can make the introductions."

Darlene still isn't convinced although Mike tells her that he thinks Lorinda would probably be great with her children. But since Lorinda has never had any children of her own, and never ever even talks about kids, Darlene has her doubts.

"I'm a fun person. Kids love me," Lorinda says for all the customers in the restaurant to hear.

Mike again supports the idea of Lorinda watching Darlene's children.

Lorinda grabs Darlene by the arm and takes her into the back to discuss the babysitting situation without Mike and anyone else, listening. "Come on now. You can't have your mother-in-law watching the kids when you go out with Mike."

Lorinda has a point. The last thing she wants is for Rose to know about this dinner with Mike. So she reluctantly gives in to the pressure to let Lorinda watch the kids. Lorinda is excited that Darlene agrees to let her babysit while she goes out. In fact, Lorinda is so excited, Darlene isn't sure if she's more excited about her going out with Mike or because she trusts Lorinda enough to put her kids under her charge. Either way, Mike is thrilled as well that the date for tomorrow night is on. "How about I pick you up about seven?"

"Sure," Darlene says. "Should I dress casual or more formal?"

Mike thinks about the question for a second but then he declares, "Let's go barbeque and let it all hang out. What'd ya' say?"

Darlene is okay with barbeque as long as there are plenty of napkins around when they eat.

"Wet naps, now that is the ticket, sweetheart," Mike believes. "Dry napkins don't do the job when you are talking about barbeque joints; it's got to be wet naps."

Darlene looks amused as she offers her approval. She's never really seen anyone so passionate about the use of wet naps. She's not sure if that's a good thing or a bad thing.

"So casual it is. Now, Mike, what would you like for lunch?"

Mike is so happy about nailing down the dinner night that he completely forgets he hasn't even ordered yet. "Just get me anything on the order that you like. I trust your judgement and I know that you have very good taste," he says with a laugh.

Darlene giggles a bit, but inside her mind she's trying to decide if what he just said is sweet or creepy. She decides to hold off on her judgement until after they go out. As she walks back to the kitchen area she passes Lorinda who is grinning ear to ear and acting like a small child who is hiding something they did wrong. "Tomorrow night!" Lorinda bursts out loudly.

Darlene just smiles.

⸻

JOHN AND AUDIE ARE PASSING THRU LAS VEGAS ON THEIR way to Flagstaff, Arizona. It's been almost half a day since they left the hospital in Hawthorne, Nevada. All the venom that remained in Audie's buttocks was drained, and he was given shots and then patched up for his wounds. He's sore and resting in the backseat, and after a nap for a few hours is now wide awake. He sits up to see the Vegas sights which are nothing to look at in the daytime compared to at night.

"Well, we've only got, what, four hours to Flagstaff," Audie broadcasts from the backseat.

John isn't sure about that, but since Audie often made the trek between the two states, he assumes his brother knows what he is talking about. "How you feeling?"

"Foolish," Audie responds.

"Why, what happened to you could happen to anyone," John points out, hoping to make him feel better about it.

It doesn't. Audie is still reliving and thinking about everything they have gone through in the last few days. He realizes as usual, that his screw-ups have caused his brother problems. "It's good we're getting paid for all this, bro. Otherwise it wouldn't be worth it to you."

John sort of agrees, keeping his focus on the traffic around the city.

"I mean, I know what you're thinking, and you're probably right."

John really has no idea what Audie's rambling on about and tells him so. "I'm not thinking about anything. I'm just glad you're alright."

This makes Audie feel even guiltier for the happenings of last night. "I can tell you, man, I got my wake up call. The alarm has really went off for me."

"Audie, what are you talking about?"

"I mean I'm figuring things out. I know I can't keep living the way I have in the past," Audie tries to rationalize. "And I just want you to know that and understand, dude, after what you did."

John laughs at his brother's incoherent thoughts that seem to be just leaking from his head. John could start preaching at him about the evils of over drinking and owing the wrong people money, but is tired after the night they just had and doesn't have the energy to do so. Instead, he offers his brother his encouragement and tells him he's glad he's seeing things more clearly.

Audie, feeling a bit better, turns his thoughts to his brother. "So we haven't really talked much since we left Oregon."

John doesn't say anything. He isn't in the mood.

"What's the deal with you and Darlene?"

This is the conversation that John has been dreading since they started the trip and is surprised it took this long to get around to it.

"I'm no expert, bro, but I was picking up some negative vibes from her when we left Mom's house."

Oh god, John thinks, as he has no interest or desire to discuss any of this with his kid brother, now or ever.

Audie keeps it up though. "Talk to me, man. I'm your brother and a man. I know how crazy women can be."

"We're just working on things, but thanks," John whispers back.

"Any progress because I didn't like the vibes coming from her when we left?"

John implores Audie to stop saying vibes in regards to Darlene. "I think there is, but it's going to take time, that's all," John assures.

"Mom tells me it's about you working too much and Darlene being pissed about it," Audie continues to probe.

John shakes his head and wonders if he should reach for his gun and end his misery. He tells Audie he would rather not talk anymore about his marriage with him. Audie listening so well, asks him why not. "Because, I don't, alright!"

"It's not good to keep it bottled up, man. I don't want to piss you off anymore, but don't keep it all inside. It's good to talk about this stuff. It helps to talk about this stuff."

John lets him know he appreciates his concern, but now is not the time.

"I'm there for ya' when you do think it's the right time, bro, okay?" Audie lets him know.

John thanks him again for his interest and then makes am obvious effort to change the topic once again. "Who are we seeing next in Phoenix?"

Audie buying the switcheroo, reaches for the backpack with their paperwork. He finds the list of names and scours it. "It's a Colonel, Chuck Whiffen."

"Wait a second," John responds, "I remember meeting him when I was a kid a few times."

"Oh yeah, what was he like?" Audie asks.

John skims through his memory banks trying to recall. "From what I remember, he was a war hero, a big tall guy. He was pretty funny if I remember right."

Audie hopes he still is. He and John could both use a little light-heartened humor added to this journey of theirs.

"It's been hot this whole time so far," John quips as they are now on the outskirts of Vegas, and ready to leave it behind.

"It is summer, man, and we have spent most of our time so far driving through the desert, so…"

"Smartass!" John fires at his brother for saying that.

Audie just grins, not offended at all. Then John begins to chuckle along with him. Audie is right; a little humor on this trip could be nothing but good.

"By the way, man, have you called Darlene since we left?" Audie asks him, bringing the lightheartedness to a screeching halt.

John says he has but should probably make another call soon.

"I'm no expert, but I think you better do that, man," Audie nags.

John already feeling guilty about it reluctantly admits his brother might be right. He vows to when they get to Flagstaff.

"Good, man, that communication thing is important, at least that's what women always tell me right before they dump me," Audie says with a sarcastic roar.

John looks at his brother as if he's wondering if he really just said that. John starts to laugh again at Audie's relationship commentary. This gets Audie to laugh even harder and then both are laughing loudly, together. Audie for the moment forgets how sore his bottom is. Humor really is the best medicine he thinks to himself.

AFTER STOPPING MANY TIMES TO TAKE A BREAK AND give Audie an opportunity to stretch his legs, and more importantly let his sore butt get a chance to move around, the boys arrive in Flagstaff, Arizona. Audie as co-pilot uses his phone's GPS to direct his brother where to go to find the next person on their father's list. When they arrive at the correct address they are surprised to find it is a senior retirement community. It's nearly seven o'clock in the evening, and the sign on the front door of the place states that visiting hours only last until eight. The boys have to decide if they want to squeeze in a visit in just an hour. "We should probably come back in the morning," John decides.

Audie can't disagree with that. An hour just isn't enough time if the first few visits from the list are any indication. So they instead will find shelter for the night in Flagstaff.

After getting checked in, showering, and finding a decent place for some grub, the guys return to the motel room for the night. Audie notices that his brother has still made no effort to call his wife or kids. He brings up the subject randomly, watching for John's response. Strangely there isn't much of one. "What gives?"

John looks at him with an expression as if he has no idea what his kid brother is going on about. This doesn't deter Audie from continuing to press him. "This is a good time to call Darlene. No craziness going on right now. I'll step outside for a moment and grab a smoke."

"You don't smoke," John answers.

"Then I'll start. Whatever it takes to help my big brother," Audie responds with a laugh.

"Ha ha," John says.

Audie stops his laughing long enough to ask his brother straight on why he seems afraid to call Darlene again. Audie is taken back a bit when his question seems to stop John in his tracks. John runs his hands through his hair doing his best James Dean, like the old song says. He seems to be searching for words. Audie now for a reason, even he's not real sure of, is a little concerned for his brother. "What's up, man, spill it. I am your brother."

John acting vulnerable and almost weepy lifts his head and looks straight through Audie as if measuring his soul. "I'm afraid."

Those are words Audie's never heard his brother utter before, and it's strange to even hear them come out of his mouth. John has always been the rugged, tough, macho kind of guy who patriotic songs about America are written for. Audie tells John it's okay to talk about this stuff.

"I'm afraid that the next time I talk to my wife, she's is

going to tell me it's over."

Audie isn't sure how he's supposed to respond to all this. His normal smartass kid brother joking around response, a default response he has with John, isn't going to work right now, and he knows it.

"We can't live in our fears, man," Audie finally speaks. "I heard that from somebody who is a lot smarter than me. It might have been Oprah you know, and she's never wrong."

John grins at Audie's attempt to make him feel better. "I don't want to lose her."

"You haven't yet. And the fact you still care this much is a good thing, man. I wish I cared or had someone who cared about me that much," Audie reveals.

John thanks his brother for that. He knows Audie is right, but it still doesn't deal with his very real fear of losing his wife, the only woman he's ever loved.

"First up, dude, you've got to call her and let her know how much she means to you. From what Mom has told me, I think she's wondering, man," Audie bluntly says.

John gets it, but it's hard doing that. "I'm not good with expressing myself. That's something you've always been good at, but not me?"

"I guess so," Audie answers. "But you've got to let her know. You've just got to let her know, man."

John wants to know how. Those kinds of words don't come easy for him. They will come out sounding corny or silly or something, he fears.

"Just call her up right now, man, and let her know how much you miss her and the kids. Let her know how you can't wait to get home and see them again, even though it's only been three days."

Audie's right. John musters up his strength and politely

asks if Audie can leave the motel room for a moment so he can make the call in private. Audie as he just said a few minutes ago, is more than happy to give John his space to make the call, so he gets up and leaves.

Darlene's cell phone rings as John waits for her to answer from the edge of his motel room bed. "Hello, John?"

"Hi, it's me. I just wanted to call and see how things are going," John tells her.

"Things are fine here. How about for you and Audie?" Darlene asks politely.

"Okay so far. We're on the third person on the list. Right now we're in Flagstaff."

"I bet it's really hot," Darlene replies, making her best attempt at awkward small talk.

"Yeah, it is most definitely. Anyhow, I just wanted to call and see how you and the kids are doing."

"We're fine. The kids keep asking me if you've called again. I just made up some excuse about how busy you and your brother are right now." Darlene declares, taking an indirect jab at how long it has taken John to call and speak with the children.

John is not oblivious to her shot, but he lets it go. The last thing he wants right now is to start another fight with her on the phone. "Yeah, I'm sorry for that. Are the kids around to talk to?'

"No, they're all asleep right now. They had a busy day having fun outside," she reveals.

John asks her to tell them how much he misses them and can't wait to see them again just as Audie said to do. Darlene, speaking like they are co-workers, agrees to do that.

Now, the hard part for John, telling Darlene how much he misses her and can't wait to see her. He faces his fears head on. "I really miss you, too," he tosses out like a hand grenade that he hopes won't blow up in his face.

After a few uncomfortable moments of silence from Darlene's end of the line, she speaks. "I hope you and Audie are having a good time on the trip."

"Bam!" The grenade goes off, John thinks, as she gives him nothing to hang his hat on. He repeats that the trip is going okay, so far. She tells him without emotion, that's good, now it is John, who has nothing to say.

Darlene cuts into what should have been his time to speak. "I better get going. I have work early in the morning, and it's getting late."

John tells her he understands and apologizes for calling so late.

"You take care of yourself, John. And, John, please call us and keep us informed where you are and how everything is going. It means a lot to the kids."

"A lot to the kids" is all John hears. I guess it means nothing to you, his thoughts surge through his mind. John wants to tell her that but doesn't want to start World War Three with Darlene. They say their goodbyes, and John is left sitting on the edge of his bed, his fears no less real. He wanted to say so much more to her. The woman in his life who he has shared everything with now talks to him like he is a stranger. This second phone call that was supposed to make him feel better about things has only made him feel worse.

Thirty minutes later, Audie opens up the front door and finds his brother still sitting on the edge of his bed with his cell phone lying next to him. He doesn't have to ask how the call went. He can tell just by looking at him. He wants to question John about details, but thinks better of it. "Bro, it's time for bed. Another big day ahead of us, Johnny, you know."

John grunts something. Audie's not sure what. John slips under his covers and turns in for the night. Audie turns off the lights and does the same. No more words are spoken. Right now is not the time for more words. Now is the time to try and get some sleep and hopefully dream about different things.

⎯⎯⎯∞⎯⎯⎯

ROSE HAS HER HANDS FULL OF DIRTY LAUNDRY WHEN she hears the doorbell at John and Darlene's house ring. Cody offers to get the door, but Rose stops him. Even in relatively peaceful Grants Pass, Oregon, Rose still has a thing about the children opening the front door to a stranger. She gets the door herself. She opens it to find two men, dressed to the hills in nice suits and ties, waiting for her. They introduce themselves as insurance agents seeking to speak with Audie Barrett. Rose tells them immediately that Audie isn't here right now and won't be back for a couple of weeks. When she asks them what their visit pertains to, the taller man who is doing most of the talking tells her that it is in regards to Audie's father's will and estate. Rose has no reason not to believe them, so she does. The taller man who says his name is Harry and introduces his colleague as Bob, explains that it is of the upmost importance that they meet with Audie as soon as possible. Rose asks them about the estate and if she can help in any way. She offers to give them Audie's cell phone number, which they gladly accept. Harry asks her if she knows where Audie might be right now. She doesn't, she tells them. "I would give him a call. Is this something he can do for you over the phone?"

"No, not really." Harry answers. "We really need to meet with him in person. We have some very important papers for him to read and sign. It could be worth a lot of money from the estate for him."

"What about for his brother, Johnny?" Rose asks, since the men haven't mentioned John at all.

"Who ma'am?" Bob, the other guy responds.

"My other son, Johnny, he is also left money from my former husband's estate."

Harry looks at Bob and pretends to confide in him for a moment about the make-believe details of their cover story. "Oh yes, madam," Harry says. "We forgot there is another person who is a beneficiary to the estate, a John Barrett, right?"

Rose gets a strange feeling down her spine that something isn't quite kosher here, but she has no real reason to question the "nice" men's motives for showing up at her home. But she does ask them how they got this address for Audie when he lives in Arizona. "This home belongs to my son John Barrett and his wife Darlene. Did you think this was Audie's address?"

"Yes, I'm afraid that's what we thought, ma'am. There must have been a mistake made in our paperwork," Harry replies, covering their tracks. "Any idea where your sons might be at this moment?"

Rose thinks about it and then realizes she does have one thing in her possession that might shed some light for the men. She still has in her purse a copy of the list of names from Ray's will. The list of people the boys are going to see across the country. She asked for a copy from Audie to see if there were any names she recognized. There are a few familiar names on the list that she heard

Ray talk about years ago. She shows the copy to the two men. Harry takes it from her hand and studies it for a second. "Could we get a copy of this, ma'am? It would be a big help to us."

Rose says sure but questions what they can do with it when her sons are already so far away from Oregon.

"We have branch offices, ma'am, all over the country in fact," Bob interjects.

Harry following his lead adds, "Right, we can fax the paperwork that needs to be signed to an office near where your sons are and have them go in and sign."

That sounds plausible to Rose.

"Could we trouble you for that copy of this letter, ma'am," Harry asks.

Rose knowing Darlene and John have a printer on the desk inside their extra bedroom tells them she is happy to make them the copy but is curious why they don't already have one.

Harry makes up some story about how the letter has nothing to with the life insurance policy and any conditions involving it. Rose accepts their answer as fact and heads back to the bedroom to make them the copy. Cody, who has been standing there the whole time listening to everything that has been said, is still there quietly watching and studying the two men in his living room. His presence is a bit unnerving for Harry and Bob. "Kid, do you mind?" Bob asks him.

Cody says nothing, just stands there like a statue. Harry smirks at him and nods. The uneasiness lifts when Rose walks back in with the copy and hands it to him. "Thank you so much, ma'am. This is going to help both your boys very much," Harry tells her.

Rose is happy to hear it. As a parting shot she asks the men if they can do her a small favor if they do happen to talk to either Audie or Johnny.

"What's that, ma'am?" Harry asks her.

"Tell them to please call their mother and let her know how they are doing. Would you do that for me, dear?"

Both Harry and Bob promise they will. Rose thanks them and sees them off.

Walking back to the car Bob has to question how this long trip to Oregon to get a list of names and addresses has really helped them. "We still don't know when they're going to see these people, Harry."

Sometimes Harry feels like his partner has nothing going on inside that large round head of his. "We don't have to get to one of these people at the same time as they do. We just get there before they do and then stake out somebody on this list. Do you get it now, Bob?"

Bob considers it and chews on Harry's words until it starts to make it into his grey matter sufficiently enough. "I get it, Harry, I get it. So where are we going first?"

Harry pulls out the list of names and places, and studies it for a moment. "They probably already made it to Flagstaff, Arizona. How does South Texas sound to you?"

Bob says it sounds fine. "I love the Tex-Mex down there Harry."

"Shut up, Bob," Harry replies. "Just please for all that is good and merciful, shut up and drive. I'm tired of you thinking with your stomach again."

Bob does as he's told. They take off for the Lone Star State.

—————

FISHING *for* SOMETHING   149

JOHN AND AUDIE ARE UP BRIGHT AND UGLY THE NEXT morning. Neither of them got much sleep to be truthful. Now parked out in front of the retirement home, they wait for the clock to reach the time for visiting hours to begin. When it finally does, they toss into the backseat the empty remains of their coffee cups. When they reach the ladies at the front desk, they ask to visit a Colonel Charles Whiffen. When asked if they are friends or family the boys look towards each other for the right answer to the inquiry. "Our father was a very good friend of his," John tells them.

"Yep, we are here to pay our respects to the colonel, and we have come a long ways," Audie affirms.

The receptionist asks their names and then sends off an employee to inform the colonel they are here to see him. John hollers to the man to drop their father's name when he tells the colonel that he has visitors. "What's the name?" the employee asks.

"Tell him we are the sons of Raymond Barrett," John says.

The orderly says okay, and John and Audie find a seat and wait.

In a few minutes a woman in her thirties comes out to meet the guys. She tells them she is the colonel's daughter. "So your father is an old friend of my dad's?"

"Yes, that's right," John answers.

"Is he with you?"

"Is who with us?" John responds.

"Your father?" the colonel's daughter asks.

"No," John answers. "I'm afraid our father passed away a few weeks ago. That's kind of why we're here."

The woman doesn't understand, of course, what John is talking about but warns them both not to upset her father who is in grave health himself. "I will let you see my dad, with me present. But he has an aggressive kind of cancer he is fighting and is very weak. The last thing I want is for anything to upset him, I hope you can understand that."

The boys, of course, can and agree not to upset him. The woman introduces herself as Wendy Martin. She has them follow her to her father's room. She goes in first to make sure her father still is in the mood for visitors. A few minutes later she comes out and invites them in. They find the colonel sitting in a recliner in a large room with a television blaring in front of him. He tries to force himself up out of his chair, but it is obvious that it is a struggle for him. John sprints over to him to shake his hand and tell him that there is no need for him to get up.

The guys introduce themselves to the colonel and again announce who their father is.

"Hells bells, you're really the sons of Ray?!" the colonel announces loudly not sounding sick in the least. "I haven't seen you boys since you were yay high to my kneecaps."

John and Audie look amused at his declaration. Only John remembers meeting the man before.

The colonel asks them where there father is. It seems that, Wendy has not yet told him about their father's death, so it is up to them to do so. "Colonel, sir, I'm afraid our father passed away a few weeks ago," John informs him.

"Hell no," the colonel calls out as pushes back into his easy chair and his eyes look to the ground. He says nothing else as he adjusts to the knowledge of his good friend's demise.

Wendy is already giving both John and Audie the evil eye for upsetting her dad.

Audie sees that and tries to lighten the mood in the room. "Sir, even though our dad is no longer with us and that is a sad thing and all, we're here for a good reason today."

Audie's hopeful statement gets the colonel to lift up his head and make eye contact with the boys.

"Yes, sir, our father, your friend, asked us to come see you in his will," John chimes in.

"He did?" the colonel responds. "Why did Ray want you to do that?"

Audie tries to reason why. "We figure Colonel, sir, because you meant so much to him. You were one of just a handful of people that he wanted to make sure we personally informed of his passing."

The colonel is touched that his old friend would think of him in his last days.

"So you've told me, and I do appreciate your driving here to see me, boys, your father was one of my favorite people."

"There is more, sir," John lets him know.

The colonel turns his attention to John and listens. John begins to expound about their father's wish for them to go fishing with each person on the list. Audie tells the colonel about an item they are to give to each person, named on the list. The colonel laughs when he hears about the fishing. Wendy quickly intervenes to tell the boys that her father is in no shape to go on some fishing trip. When the colonel tries to tell her that he would be fine to go fishing, she talks over him and insists that he can't go. He asks her to leave the room for a few minutes so that he can speak with John and Audie alone. At first she refuses, again arguing with her father that he is not strong enough for any fishing trip. When he agrees with her and tells her he won't go fishing with the boys, she finally honors his request for a few minutes alone with them. She tells everyone that she will go and get herself an expresso from a nearby Starbucks and be back in a little while.

When finally left alone, the colonel apologizes for his daughter's bossy nature, "She's a worry wart, boys, but she can't help herself, I don't think she can come to grips with the idea that I'm dying and there is nothing anybody can do about that."

The guys don't know what to say, so they just say they are sorry to hear it's that serious.

"It is, what it is, boys," the colonel says matter-of-factly. "In this life you control what you can, but you better damn well respect those things that you can't. Now where did Ray want me to take you fishing?"

Audie looks at the list. "Lake Powell, your colonel, sir, but what about your daughter and everything?"

The colonel chuckles as he thinks about the question. "If it was up to her, I would never be allowed to get out of bed. But as long as the good Lord leaves me some lead in my pencil, I am going to do what I want to do."

John and Audie think it's great to see the colonel's resolve, but they wonder how all this is going to go over with Wendy.

The colonel senses their concern and responds to it. "She'll be upset for a few days and then she'll get over it like she always does. You know, boys, it's one of the few things good about dying."

The boys wait for the punchline.

"You can get away with a lot more than you can when you're healthy. No one can stay mad at someone who is about to die," he enlightens the brothers with.

"That does make sense, sir," Audie has to admit.

John cuts into the banter between his brother and the colonel long enough to ask him when it might be a good time to go, later today would be great with Audie and him, or tomorrow?

The colonel catches them by surprise with his answer. "Right now, I'll get my stuff together, and we'll need to let the front desk know, and then boom we're gone."

"But your daughter, sir, shouldn't you talk to her first?" John asks with concern.

"Why the hell should I? She would just try to stop me from going, and it would be a big old argument. Now, get your car and meet me out front in five minutes," the colonel orders.

"Are you sure about this, sir? Are you sure you're up for all this?" John asks him nicely, worried about the colonel's health and their responsibility for it.

"As sure as a dog flicks it's fleas onto the carpet," he replies.

The colonel again asks them to go get the car and meet him out front in five minutes. He calls for a nurse to come to his room and help push his wheelchair.

The colonel is right on time as he is pushed out to meet John and Audie at their truck with only seconds to spare. The nurse asks him if all this is okay with Wendy, and he is quick to lie and say it is. Then he climbs into the front passenger seat next to John, with Audie in the backseat. The nurse puts the colonel's gear into the back of the truck under the camper shell.

"I am already having more fun than I have had in a helluva long time, boys," the colonel offers up with a grin from ear to ear.

As John drives them out of the senior retirement center's parking lot he sees Wendy pulling in. John has a bad feeling about this even as the colonel is acting like a kid going to Disneyland for the first time. For John it's the third or fourth time on this trip he's had a bad feeling about something. Maybe he should just get use to the feeling, he considers to himself.

CHAPTER 10

Wendy Martin discovers her father is gone quickly after arriving back at the facility. She demands information from the front desk, and they quickly fill in the details of how he left with the two young men who had been visiting him. She is so furious that they left with her father that she demands that all local law enforcement be called at once. When one of the receptionists asks why, Wendy screams that her father has been kidnapped by the two men. This doesn't make sense to the nurse who pushed her father's wheelchair out to meet the men's truck. "The colonel seemed pleased to being going with them, Miss."

"That's because they tricked him. Now do as I say and call all the local authorities and law enforcement immediately!"

The facility manager just told of the situation, orders the front desk to make the calls.

"And tell them to especially keep a look out for my father and his kidnappers at any lakes in the area. Tell the police to contact state authorities who man the lakes in this area to keep a lookout for my father. And remember to tell them all, that he is a war hero. Don't forget to share that with all concerned," Wendy dictates to those making the calls. "My father is in no shape for this sort of thing, no shape at all."

It takes a couple of hours, but the boys and the colonel finally make it to one of Lake Powell's marinas. This one is on the Arizona side of the lake. The colonel slowly and methodically walks to the main office at the marina with both brothers at his side. Then he whips out his wallet and rents a small houseboat. "What do you think, one or two days?" he asks John and Audie.

They answer back that one day is all the time they really have before they get back on the road. So the colonel pays for the one day with his credit card. John wants to chip in on the price while Audie wonders if they need something so big for just a "'little fishing.'"

"I'm already a fugitive," the colonel mocks as the man renting them the houseboat in the marina office watches and assumes they're just fooling around. "Don't worry, boy. It's on me. I can't take my money with me now, can I? So let's stock up here on some grub and drinks and make this into a helluva good time. And since this could well be the last fishing trip I ever get to make on this side of heaven, I am going to make it count. Fishing out here is a perfect tribute to your father. This lake is legendary for two things. First they filmed the original 'Planet of the Apes' here, and two, there is some monster-sized catfish living in these waters."

John and Audie aren't sure about either bit of trivia, but they can still see the delight in the colonel's eyes as he gets the ship's keys. Another younger guy working at the marina guides them to the correct houseboat. After throwing their gear onboard, they're off, ready to embark on their fishing adventure.

John and Audie are immediately blown away by the red rock formations that surround the lake. They can see why Charlton Heston filmed his ape movies here many years ago. This lake feels like you've entered another world.

John looks back to see the colonel smiling. He is studying the terrain as he is driving the boat. He's in his glory. The old man might barely be able to walk anymore, but he can still captain a ship with the best of them, John comments to his brother.

"If this is his last time out on the water, I hope we can make it awesome for him," Audie replies, as they both are now enjoying watching the colonel steer the boat to who knows where.

<hr />

John and Audie wonder if the colonel is ever going to stop the boat and drop anchor. They can see that he is reviling being out on the water, but it's been over an hour. Finally John asks him about finding a place to fish. If his days are indeed numbered they aren't going to pressure him too much. After another thirty minutes of touring Lake Powell and all its otherworldly rock formations, the colonel finally finds a place he is satisfied with and brings the houseboat to a stop. The Arizona heat is blazing as usual even in this northern-most part of the state. The colonel purchased a cornucopia of beverages and food from the marina's store before they left the docks and now is excited to partake in some cold brew. Audie grabs him his can of beer and takes it to him. The colonel using anything he can grab onto to steady his walk finds his seat at the back of the boat. The boat is now anchored in a nice cove with the deep water suitable for the fishing he wants to do. He invites the boys to join him and grab a seat. John and Audie are happy to oblige after grabbing some cold ones of their own. John, trying to lead a good example for his brother, grabs a soda instead of a beer. Audie says something derogatory, but to please John he does the same thing and settles for a can of Coke. John applauds Audie's self-control and ignores the wise crack. Both of the guy's head over to where the colonel is sitting and grab a seat next to him.

"Boys, this is wonderful. Thank you so much for this. You have no idea how much this means to an old sailor like me."

"I thought you were in the Air Force like our father?" Audie responds to the colonel's declaration.

"I was," the colonel says with a laugh, "But I always wished I could have been some big-wig ship commander of a giant battleship. I always saw myself leading men into battle on the seas like Burt Lancaster or the like."

"It sure is peaceful out here," John chimes in.

"That's what makes fishing so special. The peace and tranquility of being out on the water with nature, brushing up your shoulders with the almighty himself," the colonel opines.

"That's a cool way of looking at it," Audie tells the colonel.

After barely breaking a sweat in downing his first can of beer the colonel asks if he can trouble the boys for a second one, and a sandwich. He has them bring over his fishing pole and tackle box. John is especially enjoying watching the colonel prep his pole for the catfish John's been told populate this lake.

What happens next surprises even a seasoned fisherman like John. The colonel had the guys buy some chicken thighs with the rest of the groceries from the little market near the marina. They assumed this was for human consumption, but they assumed wrong. The colonel starts cutting up the thighs for bait. John says okay, he can see that, but the next thing the colonel does really throws him for a loop.

"Hand me that can of WD-40 over there, would ya," the colonel asks John.

John hands it to him wondering exactly what he is going to do with it.

"And hand me that little container of garlic powder," he asks John as a second request.

"Usually you want to let this stand overnight, but what the hell. You play the cards life deals you, am I right boys?"

John and Audie are mesmerized as they watch the colonel first spray the WD-40 on the chicken and then rub the garlic powder all over it.

"The stinkier the better with catfish," he teaches the guys. "And always use big chunks of meat if you want to catch the big fishes."

"I get the garlic powder, colonel, but what's up with the WD-40?" Audie just has to ask.

"Just an old trick I learned from some catfish fishermen, a long, long, time ago," the colonel shares.

The colonel orders the guys to do the same thing if they want to catch a big one. He tells them to cast their lines out in different spots around the boat, almost in a triangle formation. This is again a technique he's learned from his many years of fishing for catfish in lakes. "It's nice and muddy down below in this cove, just the way we need it to be, boys."

John and Audie can't argue that and wouldn't even if they could. Now all three men settle down and wait for the fish to bite. It's hot but the cold drinks are helping. Audie is working on an egg salad sandwich when John asks the colonel how he and their father first met. The colonel is more than happy to take a trip down memory lane.

"It actually had a lot to do with this lake right here," the colonel remembers.

"How so, sir?" Audie eggs him on with wanting to know more.

The colonel sits back, and with fingers rubbing his chin the way people do when trying to concentrate on something, he summons the flood of memories back to his consciousness. He starts out recalling a poker game a long time ago at a house on Luke Air Force Base near Phoenix. This was the first time he laid eyes on a young airman named Raymond Barrett. They were both stationed at Luke at the time, and as the colonel recalls, his first impression of Ray was he's a cocky S.O.B. "He thought he was smarter than everyone else back then, and that annoyed the hell out of everyone around him. He wasn't the biggest guy in the room and I remember thinking this guy has the classic 'Napoleonic Syndrome' going for him."

With no action yet from any of their fishing poles, John and Audie listen intently to every word of the colonel's history lesson.

"But even with all that pain in the ass that was your dad, there was something about him that made you love him. He had that, what do you call it... charisma, that's the word."

"Yeah, we've heard colonel about his popularity with women already," John interrupts.

The colonel just grins at John's statement admitting that all the stories are true. "The ladies did love him, and he loved to have a good time with them. Sometimes too much I think. Often I think he acted like he was trying to prove somebody was wrong about him. He had a chip on his shoulder that was more like a boulder."

Audie asks how they became friends after such a negative first impression the colonel had of their father.

"Let me continue, son. So you see, your dad ended up cleaning everyone's clocks that night at the poker table. He was real good at cards. All the other guys including myself were angry about losing all our money to him and we demanded a chance to recoup our losses. So I set up another game the next week and suggested we drive all the way up here and rent a houseboat, and party."

"So that was the how you and my father first got together on a houseboat here at Lake Powell?" John considers.

"Exactly, my boy, howdy doody, what a time that was," the colonel exclaims as he chuckles over the mere thought of the event. "We all chipped in and rented a huge boat. And we needed all the room we could get, I'll tell you that."

"Lots of women?" Audie excitedly asks.

"Oh my, yes indeedy, and being it was a hot Arizona summer day like today, lots of bikinis and boobs to behold. We had the boat for the weekend, and it was one helluva two days to remember. The cards were flying, the booze was flowing, and the ladies were willing."

"Did you get your money back from dear old Dad?" Audie inquires.

The colonel just shakes his head. "No, Ray kicked our asses again. I'll tell you he had his pick of the ladies that weekend."

John then interrupts again. He's still wondering how they became friends.

"Oh that. Well as I recall, as good as your dad was at cards that weekend, he wasn't so good at holding his liquor. Don't get me wrong. He could put down beers like there was no tomorrow, but he couldn't handle the hard liquor, just wasn't use to it," the colonel continues. "That first night he got plastered, drunk off his butt. Ray passed out on the top of the houseboat, the roof where he had been fooling around with a gorgeous blonde. I was sleeping down below and there was bodies sleeping all over that boat, where ever they could find a place. Anyways, in the middle of the night, one of the girls who was sleeping in the cabin inside the boat, right below where your dad was, she woke up and saw rain falling down her little window next to her bed. Rain in Arizona in the summer is about as rare as vegetarians eating at McDonalds. So she jumps up and starts running around yelling that it's raining, it's raining, waking everybody up! I hop up to inspect this miracle of moisture for Arizona and of course see that it's not raining at all."

"So what was it on the window?" John speaks up.

The colonel before he reveals it, starts laughing hard just thinking about it. "So I yell at the girl. I tell her it's not raining and ask her what she's ranting about. So she takes me over to the window and shows me the evidence. It's streaked with something, but it ain't rain. I get a closer look and I realize exactly what it is."

John and Audie don't say a word. They wait for the explanation, he has their full attention.

"There is bits and pieces on the window, not just liquid. What the girl thought was rainfall was actually your dad's vomit from above."

"You mean he…" Audie interrupts.

"Yep, Ray upchucked down the side of that window from the roof and was so sloshed he went right back to sleep. I checked on him and he was sleeping like a baby. He had the worst hangover the next day on the boat. I spent that second day sitting next to him, talking with him, getting to know him and his past. He let down his ego then and we talked all that day. Beneath all the bravado, he was a good guy and we became fast friends from that day forward."

For the next several hours the colonel weaves numerous stories about John and Audie's father and their exploits in the Air Force. Most of the tales the boys have never heard before, and it shows another side of their dad they didn't really see as kids. He was often strict and serious about most things. Rarely did John and Audie see the fun-loving, have-a-good-time-guy that the colonel is describing. After another hour goes by, the colonel and the guys begin to take notice of something they hadn't up until that point. Their respective fishing lines were seeing no action. Nobody has got a single bite in over two hours. And so far, the day of fishing is turning out to be a real dud with not a single fish caught. Audie can't help but wonder if this lake is all it's cracked up to be. "So, sir, you and Dad use to do pretty good here?"

The colonel tells then they did, but when he begins to think back he does remember a day just like this one. His recollection brings about another story from the past. "Your dad and I were out here, just the two of us that day. Just like today, the fishing was shitty. Well, we both kind of noticed how quiet the lake was that day. We had hardly seen another boat out and about on the lake. So your dad suggests playing some music. He thinks it might bring the fish up from wherever they are hiding to start biting or something like that. Ray had a boom box with him and starts to play his collection of cassettes and cd's. He loved rock and roll and starts to play all his favorites, but the fish still didn't show any life. Tape after tape he tries, and no bites. Finally I said to him, why don't we try something different? Ray looks at me like he has no idea what I am talking about. I say what about some good old-country tunes, some old-time country. I thought maybe that would wake up the fishes and get them to start to bite. So I look through the small collection of cassettes that I have, and then I see the one. I see the one so different and unique from all the rest of the stuff we've been playing that I think, maybe it has a shot."

John and Audie wait patiently to hear what this unique music is. The colonel purposely holds off from giving them the title. "So I turn on my cassette, and it's like a freakin' miracle from heaven above or something. In no time at all the fish are attacking our lines. It's mostly catfish, but some other kinds as well begin to bite and grab our hooks. As God as my witness, it was like the fish were jumping out of the lake and into our boat."

Then the colonel looks at them squarely in the eyes and asks, "How do you feel about yodeling music?"

"What?" Audie responds.

"Eddy Arnold, we played his greatest hits. He was a big star in country music back in the sixties and seventies," The colonel educates them with.

"I've heard of him, sir," John responds, "but my brother probably hasn't."

"Well anyways, Eddy Arnold was a very big star, and he yodeled in some of his songs, and I think the fish really liked that," the colonel continues.

"This really happened, the fish biting like that to Eddy Arnold or whoever's music?" Audie asks.

The colonel laughs as he remembers. "I swear to God it did. It was Eddy Arnold's Greatest Hits Record. I even remember we kept testing it by putting other music on to see if the fish would keep biting, and you know what, as soon as Eddy stopped yodeling the fish stopped biting. Then we would put old Eddy Arnold on again and they would start right back. I think the fish loved the yodeling and his mellow relaxing music."

"That's a pretty hard story to believe there, no offense. You are an awesome story teller, though, I have to say," Audie voices.

The colonel isn't offended at all and has to admit it was pretty hard that day for him or Ray to believe it either.

"Have you tried it since?" John is curious.

"Nah, I haven't, son. If it didn't work, I always thought it would kind of tarnish my old memories of that day."

Audie pleads that they should, and right now for that matter, if the colonel happens to have some Eddy Arnold music lying around in his fishing gear.

The colonel at first resists the idea but then begins to warm up to it. "What the hell. I don't have much time left, so why not. Let's see if we can catch lightening in a bottle again."

John asks if the colonel still has any Eddy Arnold music with him. The colonel then remembers the tape ripped years ago. "I guess we're screwed boys," he says.

"Who needs an old tape, fellas. We've got my phone," Audie tells them as he pulls out his cell phone.

As the colonel and John watch, Audie searches for Eddy Arnold and his greatest hits collection. He finds it and downloads it and tells them when the download is complete. "Ready for some Eddy Arnold, colonel?"

"Load it up, son," the colonel replies.

Then it happens, and the air is filled with the silky soothing sounds of Eddy Arnold. At first there is no change, and the fishing lines remain dormant. But then slowly and in a calculated order every pole gets hit. The colonel and the boys grab for their fishing poles and begin to try to first hook their prey and then reel it in. When the first catches are safely in the boat they cast out again and in no time are reeling in more. Just as in the story the colonel told, the fish, mostly catfish, seem to be under the spell of Eddy Arnold. After filling their buckets up, Audie tries other styles of music, and even other performers of country music. It's not easy for Audie to stomach, and still nothing. When Eddy stops, the fish stop biting just as the colonel said they did all those years ago. When Eddy's music comes back on, so does the fishes' appetites for baited hooks and committing suicide.

John and Audie look at each other like they are living through a "Twilight Zone'" episode, and maybe they are.

AFTER CATCHING ALL THE FISH THEY COULD EVER WANT or need, and with the afternoon winding down and the sun setting, the guys decide to start thinking about dinner and what to eat. The colonel with an assist from John gets on his feet and makes his way to the little kitchen area on the houseboat. He starts rummaging through the groceries they bought before boarding the boat. "You guys don't know how much this means to me, today. When you're staring your own mortality in the face, you wonder if you're ever going to have a day to remember again. I was beginning to think I wasn't going to have another day like this. But I'm out on the water, the blue sky all around. I'm getting to go fishing again and knocking down some beers with good company. This is a special day guys. The only thing missing is some pretty girls to flirt with."

Andrew Scott Bassett

John and Audie's attention is pulled away from the colonel as they hear voices in the distance, yelling something. At first they can't make out what is being yelled, but slowly they decipher it. They hear distinctive calls for help, mixed in with other shouted words. The colonel is oblivious to all of this as he is still talking in the kitchen, working on making something to eat. John and Audie have to get his attention so he can hear the voices as well. When the colonel finally does hear the chants for help, he gets behind the captain's chair and starts up the boat and drives them in the direction of the voices. It doesn't take long for them to find those in distress. It's another houseboat, a much larger one just around the corner from the cove that the guys were fishing in. This boat is floating in the middle of the lake, and as they approach, the colonel and the boys quickly see the smiling faces and waving hands guiding them toward their boat. Something else also stands out, to, The waving hands and smiling faces are overwhelmingly attached to bikini-baring gorgeous women. Audie speaks out what his brother and the colonel are already thinking; this must be their lucky day. The houseboat is full of women having a party before their boat's motor died. The colonel pulls their boat alongside the other boat. John and Audie board the houseboat and are welcomed by the beautiful ladies, a couple of geeky-looking guys, and a couple of built-like-rock-statues men. "What's going on?" Audie greets them with.

One of the geeky-looking guys, talks about the engine just dying a few minutes ago, leaving everyone stranded.

"Why didn't you call the lake patrol?" John asks.

He returns the question with a nervous leer and buck teeth. "Well…we just didn't think that would be the prudent thing to do with our little party and all, if you know what I mean."

John isn't sure if he does, but he guesses that the strange little guy is worried about what law enforcement might find if they do come onto the boat.

"What kind of party is this, man? Are you swimsuit models or something?" Audie asks the bevy of bikini-clad gals.

"No!" one says with a laugh. "We are playmates from the Playboy Mansion."

Audie thanks God in a whisper that only he can hear.

One of the geeky guys asks John if he or Audie know anything about boat motors. Of course John the outdoorsman tells them that he is does. The colonel lends him a few tools that he has with his fishing gear. The colonel slowly makes his way aboard with the help of a redhead on one arm and a blonde on the other. While John checks the boat motor, Audie checks out the girls and begins to mill around. It doesn't take John long to dissect the problem and get the motor going. Both Audie and the colonel would have liked to have seen him take a little longer fixing the problem. But no matter, the geeky guy who seems to be in charge of the girls and the party boat is so thankful with their help that he invites them to join in for food and partying. John doesn't think it's a good idea but is quickly out voted by his brother and Colonel Whiffen.

Now as the sun is starting to go down, the music and fun on the houseboat is just starting up. Audie is apparently able to dance with as many as eight women at a time and is enjoying every moment of it. The colonel who can barely stand is doing his best to dance with two. The redhead and blonde who helped him onboard are now his crutches. He's never enjoyed being an invalid more in his life than at this very moment. John is sitting down with ladies on both sides of him smiling and chatting away at him. With the dance music blaring so loud, he can barely hear what they are saying but acts like he can. The scene reminds him of all the times he pretends to be listening to Darlene when he really isn't. This pretend listening skill of his does come in handy he thinks to himself. Then in the midst of all this body tan and silicon, John's thoughts flee back to his wife. Right this second, John would gladly leave all these Botox babes behind if he could just be with his Darlene. He wonders want she's up to at this moment.

⊶⊷

DARLENE IS TRYING TO RELAX AND JUST BREATHE IN. Mike Stillman will be arriving to pick her up at her home at any minute. Lorinda hasn't shown up yet either. She's late for her babysitting duties. A rhythmic knock at the front door interrupts Darlene's next deep breath. She knows it must be Lorinda because Mike is going to text her on her phone when he pulls up to her street. Lorinda pleads for forgiveness when Darlene opens the front door to her. She asks if Mike is here yet and of course Darlene reminds her that he wouldn't be in the house with her. Darlene is not going to let her children meet any guy, especially when things with their dad are so muddled and hazy right now. Not to mention the fact that Darlene has no idea how this first dinner with Mike is even going to go. Darlene at this point isn't really excited about the notion of getting serious with anyone, including John.

After being given a tour of the place and introduced to the children, Lorinda does her best to try and reassure and relax Darlene. She tells her to just fly by the seat of her pants and have a good time. When the oldest child, Cody, asks his mom what she's doing tonight, Darlene just makes up some story about having a meeting with her boss. She gets across to Cody how she's going to receive some more waitress training and that she might be home kinda' late. An instant feeling of guilt invades her senses as she realizes she is lying to her son. It feels like someone just pricked her with a needle.

Then her cell alerts her to the fact that Mike is out front. Lorinda again assures her that everything at the house is under control and that kiddies will be just fine. Darlene thanks her again for watching them as she takes one last look at herself in her hanging mirror by the front door, making sure she still looks alright, and then heads out to meet Mike.

Mike has parked in front of the neighbor's house as Darlene requested, to make it impossible for the kids to see him. When she tried to justify her reasoning for this, Mike cut her off and told her he understands more than too well. He jumps out of his driver's side and runs around to open the passenger door for her. Darlene appreciates his being a gentleman. She can almost remember the last time John did the same thing for her. After a few minutes of driving, Mike surprises her with a small corsage to pin on the front of her dress. Darlene whoops when she sees it. "We're not teenagers going to the prom are we?"

"No, of course not, but I thought it probably has been a long time since someone has treated you special like that," he gets across to her.

Though it is a little kooky to Darlene she appreciates his thought and gladly pins it on. He then tells her his plans for dining have changed to a small elegant Italian restaurant and then some dancing, country style at a club on the outskirts of Grants Pass. It's been a long time since Darlene's has been dancing, probably four years ago at a friend's wedding. If you don't count wedding receptions then a whole lot longer than that.

In that moment, Mike can see Darlene pressing because she's nervous, even her laughter is sprinkled with anxiousness. "It's okay," he tells her. "We are just going to have a nice time. Don't forget I'm the same guy you've talked with in the diner many times, and you're the same women I've talked to just as many times. This is no big deal tonight, no big deal at all."

Darlene appreciates him saying that to her. Maybe there is more to this man than she thinks. Whatever, she is going to take his advice and try to relax and enjoy herself tonight. God knows it's been a long time since she's gone dancing or been to a restaurant that didn't have crayons on the table.

JOHN FEELS LIKE HE'S ON THE OUTSIDE OF ONE OF THOSE snow globes that you shake. As the party rages on everywhere on the houseboat, everyone seems to be getting sloppy drunk and happy, even the colonel and certainly Audie. John watches it. He's there, but not really. He stopped drinking after one glass and has been in no mood to honor the many times he's been asked to dance. The girls have stopped asking and are enjoying his brother's company much more than his. Hell, the colonel is having a great time, and he deserves it, John has to admit. John also has to admit to himself at this moment that he is for one of the first times in his life, just a bit jealous of his brother. Mostly just how free and unconcerned Audie is. Audie doesn't care what others think is the right thing to do or say or the right way to act. This has been to his detriment for most of his adult life so far but not always and not at times like this. John can't just let everything go like that, push his problems from his thoughts and adjust the way he feels. The pangs of longing for his wife and his kids are starting to get more real, and all the bikinis in the world are no substitute for that, not for John anyways.

John watches as Audie dances like a whirling dervish near the edge of the back of the boat. He's got two girls he's dancing with as the music plays faster and faster. Audie spins one girl in a circle and then grabs the other and pulls her close. When he spins the other girl the combination of booze and gravity are too much and she hits the rail and falls over the side into the dark black lake. Audie blitzed himself, stares overboard not saying anything as if someone has captured his tongue for the moment and isn't about to give it back. The best he can do to the others around him is point at the water. But John, having seen the event unfold, leaps into action and dives off the side of the houseboat to near where the girl fell. She surfaces grasping for air and screaming for help. John is there to grab hold of her in a second. He asks her if she can swim and gets no real answer, so he pulls her arms around his neck and guides her back to the ladder at the back of the boat. Now everyone knows what has happened and dazed or not, are watching as John pushes her onto the boat. A couple of the security guys there for Playboy help her up and take her inside the cabin of the boat to lie down. Audie and others clap for John as he pulls himself up onto the boat. The colonel with assistance from his two bikini babes comes over and congratulates him for being a hero. "Now that is something your dad would have done, with one difference."

"What's the difference?" John responds.

"Your dad would be in the cabin right now personally taking care of the young lass," the colonel wisecracks.

John has no comment. He is just amused as he grabs a towel to dry himself off with.

"Chivalry is not dead!" the colonel yells for all to hear. He commands that the music be turned up even louder and that the dancing resumes.

John sits back down at the other side of the boat and studies the Arizona sky. This is as tranquil as tonight is going to get, he says to himself.

Everyone else follows the colonel's orders and gets back to partying.

CHAPTER 11

D arlene complains that she has a cramp in her side and asks Mike if they can sit the next few songs out. All this dancing after a big meal that she thoroughly enjoyed at the Italian restaurant, is having its toll on her stomach. Mike agrees, and they sit themselves down at a little table in the back of the western bar. Darlene is more than a bit surprised that she is having such a fun time with Mike. He's been funny, interesting to listen to, and much more than she ever expected.

"I got to tell you, Darlene, I have to wonder why we didn't hook up back in the day."

"What do you mean, like back in school?" she quizzes him.

"Yeah", he says, "How did I let you slip by me and let you hook up with John Barrett?"

Darlene doesn't have a sure and fast answer but thinks it might have something to do with Mike being a playboy in high school who chased every girl who was "willing," around. When she brings these facts to the conversation, Mike starts laughing out loud. "Was I really that bad?"

She giggles and tells him that he was indeed.

"I was a real horn dog, you're saying?"

"Yes, you certainly were," Darlene answers.

Mike lifts his beer to make a toast, and Darlene recip-rocates. "To silly old memories and youthful indiscretions. May we learn from our stupid youth, never to repeat the same mistakes."

"I'll say yes to that," Darlene replies.

"Any regrets for you?" Mike slips into the conversation.

"Everybody has regrets," Darlene responds. "And I defi-nitely have mine, as well."

"I guess now with everything that's happened, John might be one?" Mike concludes.

"No, he's not a regret. Things just change over time and people change with them. I probably don't want to talk about these things with you…it's personal you know," Darlene attempts to get across.

Mike says he understands and asks her something else. "So give me your verdict."

Darlene looks straight at him. She doesn't understand the question.

"About tonight, did you have a good time tonight or not?"

Darlene has to answer that she has had a good time tonight because she has.

When Mike offers up more dancing, she again points to her side. "Too much pasta I think. I'm sorry, Mike," she tells him.

Mike is fine with that as he orders another beer. "We'll just sit here and have another drink and just talk. I'm having a good time, too."

Darlene is happy to hear it. And she has to admit it's a good feeling to have some fun again. It's been a long time since she's had this much fun, and she kind of likes it.

JOHN POPS UP OUT OF THE BOAT CHAIR HE FINALLY FELL asleep in last night. The early-morning sun made sure he would sleep no longer. He seems to be the only person on the entire houseboat awake. He looks amused at the site of bodies scattered everywhere around the boat. It reminds him of a war movie, and their side lost. John shuffles along trying to get his morning sea legs as he searches for Audie among the "'casualties.'" A second shake of the head follows as he finds Audie at the back of the boat lying in the middle of three Playmates. They are all fast asleep and dead to the world. John contemplates what his brother must be dreaming at this moment and although he's tempted to wake him, he decides to show mercy to his kid brother and let him continue to snooze away.

John begins to look around for the colonel. The last thing he can recall is the colonel sitting down with one girl on each arm and another sitting on his lap. But before John finds him, the colonel helps John by letting him know exactly where he is. "Somebody help!" a girl yells from inside the boat's, cabin area.

A second yell from the girl and now everybody on the boat is awakened. John quickly makes his way into the room. He finds the colonel trying to sit up but not being success-ful in his attempt. The girl who yelled for help is crouched down next to him and is motioning for John to quickly come over and check him out. John gets on his knees beside him. He is struggling to catch his breath. "Colonel, what's going on? Is it your heart, sir?"

The colonel between breaths tells John he's not sure but that he's in trouble and John better head the boat back to the marina and notify the authorities to have medical personnel waiting when they get there. John is amazed at how even at this moment, as the Air Force colonel struggles just to bring air into his lungs, he can still make orders and direct people into action. John wastes no time to do just as the colonel told him. Walking out of the room John passes Audie and directs his brother to stay with the colonel and help him anyway he can. Audie doesn't hesitate to listen and runs to the colonel's side. One of the Playmates also heads over to help him out. She lets everyone know that she has nursing experience and asks if the boat has a first aid kit.

John, now in the captain's chair, has some of the security guys pull up anchor as he starts up the motor and gets the houseboat moving as fast as he can to the marina. On the way he calls in and tells the authorities exactly what's going on just as the colonel wanted. Now, John only can hope that the colonel will still be okay when they make it back to the marina.

⚬⚬⚬

WHEN DARLENE GETS TO WORK IN THE MORNING, Lorinda is smiling ear to ear. Darlene told her nothing about last night's date when she got back to the house other than she had a good time with Mike. Since it was late and they both had to work the next morning, Lorinda let it go at that and didn't press for more lurid details. But now with both of them having a good night's sleep under their respective belts, Lorinda wants details, details, and more details. The café is just slow enough for Lorinda to demand them right now. Darlene isn't sure what to tell her, however, other than she had a fun time with Mike and the food at the Italian restaurant was very good. Also the western dancing for as long as she could do it was loads of fun. But of course, Lorinda is more interested in not what they did, but chemistry. She wants to know if Mike lit a match in her or not. Did he start the flame a blazin' or did her embers stay cold. "Well, what do you think? Could Mike be that new choice from the menu?"

Darlene laughs, more menu metaphors. She thought they were all done with that by now but apparently not. "It's way too early for that kinda' of talk. It was just one dinner," Darlene makes plain.

"Every great romance starts with just one dinner, sugar, but were there sparks or not?"

Darlene can't say one way or the other. "I had a surprisingly good time, and let's just leave it at that, shall we," Darlene pleads mildly.

Lorinda half-heartedly agrees but can't help cover up her disappointment. "Is there going to be a second date or not for me to annoy you about?"

Honestly, Darlene's not really sure. She will leave that decision up to Mike if he wants to call her again or not to.

Lorinda takes that as a very positive sign. "So if he calls, you would see him again?"

"Yes," Darlene responds. "If he wants to go out again, I'm okay with that, I guess."

"Well, that's just great, I guess," Lorinda responds, sort of mocking Darlene's calm, cool demeanor about a second date with Mike.

"What about John?" Lorinda has to ask.

Darlene wants to know what she means by that.

"What happens when he gets back from his big trip?" Lorinda inquires.

"What do you mean?" Darlene responds.

Lorinda goes further with her line of questioning. "Would you still see Mike if John is back in town, that's my bottom line question..."

Darlene is taken aback by the question and hasn't played things out that far in advance. After all, it has been only one date with Mike so it is way too early to cross those sort of bridges that are on fire, she considers to herself. Her answer to Lorinda says the same thing and isn't very satisfying for her friend to stomach. "We'll just have to see what happens, I guess. You know I still care about John he's the first and only man I have ever loved, so things are far from settled with him."

Lorinda signals her understanding. "But Mike's awful cute," she reminds Darlene as she heads over to a table occupied by two diners who just walked into the café.

"Yes, he is..." Darlene says to herself under her breath, making sure no one hears her, especially Lorinda.

———⨀⨂⨀———

WAITING FOR THEM AT THE MARINA IS A LARGE GROUP of first responders as John pulls the houseboat into the dock. The colonel is still kicking, although his breathing is still strained and he is still unable to move. EMTs and firemen carry him off the boat in a hurry and get him to the waiting ambulance to check him out. John and Audie follow behind them, leaving the houseboat full of Playmates and the men watching over them behind. Audie winks and waves to some of the more special girls, if you know what I mean, as he strides right behind his brother. Then out of nowhere, cutting John and Audie off from their path, comes the colonel's daughter, Wendy. She is accompanied by a well-armed swath of law enforcement officials. "Here they are, officers, the two men that kidnapped my father and have now put his life in jeopardy!"

Speechless at the charges, John and Audie watch in shock as they are quickly detained and questioned by the officers. They are scurried toward a police car that happens to be parked next to the ambulance where the colonel is still being checked out. Audie pleads their innocence to anyone willing to listen, which at this point looks like no one. But as their respective heads are being pushed down so they can get into the car, the colonel with as much breath as he can now muster raises his voice in their defense. It's not quite William Wallace screaming freedom, but it still gets everyone's attention, including his daughter who rushes to his side.

"Dad, please don't exert yourself! You need to rest!"

The colonel motions for his daughter to come closer. She expects a whisper of words from him, but instead he yells in her face. "Let the boys go this minute! They didn't kidnap me. They showed me a great time! Wendy, dear', it was the most fun I have had in a long time."

Wendy is still not convinced. Her anger at the events of last twenty-four hours or so is still fresh in her mind. "They took you from the center and told no one where you were going. Dad, I have been worried sick about you!"

The colonel props himself up. Even in his weakened state he won't be denied defending the boys' honor. "Listen to me, Wendy. I'm sorry I didn't tell you where I was going, but I knew if we did, you would have stopped us and dragged me back to the home. My days are numbered, and God knows I won't have many more opportunities like this to have a good time that reminds me of the old days."

Wendy in that moment with her dad struggling to breathe, with that old familiar spark in his eyes that she has missed seeing for so long, can see how much this fishing trip has meant to him.

One of the police officers comes over and asks her if she still wants to press charges against John and Audie. Even the officer can see that John and Audie have done nothing other than show a dying man a good time.

"No, I guess not. You can let them go," she tells him.

The colonel thanks his daughter for her change of heart. He reaches out his hand and takes hers in his. "That's the girl I raised," he says as he flashes a loving look in his daughter's direction.

Wendy kisses her dad on the forehead and asks how serious his condition is. She is told that it's his heart and that he needs to be checked out at the hospital, and right away. But they think he is stable and out of danger for the moment. Wendy will take any good news about her father's health that she can get.

"I would like to speak to the boys before you usher me off to the hospital," the colonel tells his daughter.

Wendy agrees to it and has the officers release the brothers. They are told to come to the back of the ambulance.

John leans over toward the colonel. "How are you feeling, sir?"

"Physically like crap, but thanks to you and Audie, pretty damn lucky," the colonel answers.

John apologizes for anything he and Audie have done since yesterday that caused problems for the colonel or his daughter, but the colonel won't hear any of that kind of talk.

"All I know, John, is you treated me not like a terminally ill man, or an old relic of a man, but like a guy who likes to fish. Swapping stories and baiting hooks with you boys is the most fun I have had in a long, long time. I thank you for that, and my daughter will in time, too."

John tells the colonel he hopes so. Then Audie comes over and puts out his hand. Audie and John both forgot to give the colonel the item their father had wanted him to have. Now remembering, Audie hands it to the colonel. The colonel unwraps the small item and lets out a howl of a laugh as he see what it is. "An Eddy Arnold cassette, just like all those years ago, ha-ha!"

"Dad remembered, too." Audie mentions as he sees the cassette in the colonel's hand.

"He did, good old Ray." The colonel adds.

The colonel asks the boys to promise him one thing.

"When I finally do croak, I want you to promise to take my ashes right out here and spread them out at sea, or in this case at the lake."

John winks as he shakes the colonel's hand. "Just don't make it too soon, sir," John tells him.

The colonel laughs at John's request, as the EMTs tell them both that it is time to get him to the hospital for a full evaluation.

John and Audie watch from the parking lot as the ambulance drives away followed by the police and the fireman still remaining.

"Do you think we'll see the old colonel again?" Audie asks his brother.

John can only say he hopes so. Audie asks John what he thought about his request to them, in the back of the ambulance. "I think it's an honor that he trusts us with something like that," John answers.

"It might be hard, bro. Who's to say the next time we are going to be in these parts."

John looks at Audie and grins. "A promise is a promise Audie. I'll find a way. Now let's get on the road. We've got places to see and people to meet."

John and Audie go back to the houseboat and collect their things. In a short time they are back on the road and heading for the next name on the list, still with the colonel in their thoughts, hopeful they will see him again.

⎯⎯⎯ ⚬⟩⟨⚬ ⎯⎯⎯

DARLENE IS ABOUT TO CALL IT A DAY AT THE CAFÉ WHEN Mike makes a surprise drop in. He wants her to know how great a time he had last night, and since he had a short haul today with his trucking business, he wanted to see if she could catch a movie with him later. At first Darlene hesitates. She's not about to leave the kids with Rose while she goes out on a date with a man who isn't Rose's son. Not to mention she tells him that leaving her kids at home for two nights in a row isn't something she's real comfortable with. But before she can make up her mind and render a decision for Mike, Lorinda overhearing the whole thing steps in and pulls Darlene to the side. "I can watch the kiddies again."

Darlene is thankful for the offer but still not sure she wants to be away from the kids two nights in a row. Lorinda presses her case. "It's only a couple of hours, girlfriend," Lorinda says sarcastically with an ethnic twang. "I'll feed them some pizza, you know Abby's deep dish. They'll love it. I'll even play video games with them, which you know I hate."

Darlene only has one question for her friend, why all this trouble.

Lorinda analyzes. "The way I figure it, honey, you've got about a week or so before John gets back, and you need to find out if Mike or any other guy does it for you, if you know what I mean."

Darlene thinks she does but isn't really sure.

"So go out with Mike tonight and have a good time while you can. I know you already well enough to tell that you aren't going to want to do anything with anybody when John gets back to town."

Maybe she's right, Darlene considers. Mike might not be the right guy, but maybe more important is the idea of finding out if anyone other than John could be. "I guess it is only a couple of hours," Darlene replies. "If you're really okay with watching the kids two nights in a row I know you must be tired, too."

Lorinda gives her a big-squeezie hug like you give to long-lost family members you see at a reunion. "It's no problem at all honey. You go out with Mike and enjoy yourself. God knows you deserve it after the last few years."

Darlene thanks her and then reports the news back to Mike. He's as happy as someone winning big on a lottery scratcher. "Same deal, Darlene. I'll pick you up by the side-walk a couple of houses down?"

Darlene says that's perfect. A little tingle makes its way down her spine. She thinks to herself that maybe she had an even better time last night than she let herself believe. Before Mike finishes his meal, Darlene feeling guilty for not dancing more with him last night, apologizes for being a "party pooper." Mike sweetly won't hear of it. "Nothing to be sorry for, Darlene, I know you work hard on your feet here all day. I would have loved to dance the night away with you, I have to admit though."

A delighted look takes over Darlene's face. She is touched and a little stirred by Mike's enthusiasm and sentimentality. "That sounds good to me, too," she confesses.

"Great!" Mike exclaims. "I'll pick you up in about ninety

minutes or so, if that works for you?"

It does for Darlene and Lorinda the babysitter. Mike leaves the café with a smug look on his face and a skip in his step.

❧

John and Audie pull off the highway near El Paso, Texas as they have successfully navigated their way into the tip of Texas after ten hours on the road. They find a little tin diner in the sticks off of the highway outside of El Paso and stop for a bite.

John is worn down and can't stop yawning, as the many days of driving are beginning to catch up to him. He falls into the small booth seats with their fifties style red cushions and a white table top. Audie can clearly see his brother's condition and offers to take over the driving for the rest of the day and night. John gives Audie's offer all the consideration it merits in his eyes, before saying no way.

"Why, man? Are you afraid I'm not going to take care of your truck and crash it or something? Or do you think you're the only one who can drive it?" Audie wants to know.

John, rubbing the tiredness out of his eyes as another yawn comes, tells him it's the first one.

Audie calls John a "macho man" wannabee. "You're such a redneck, man. You think you're the only one who can do anything."

John denies the characterization. "I just don't want you driving my truck, simple."

"We're driving across the friggin' country and you would rather do all the driving than let your brother help out by driving some of the way?" Audie states sarcastically.

John acknowledges that's right before questioning if his brother even has a current driver's license at his disposal.

"I have one, man!" Audie fires at John, getting pissed at his brother.

"Is it current?" John follows up.

Audie doesn't answer directly. "I'm a good driver, dude! That's all you need to know, man!"

John knows Audie well enough to know that the answer is he doesn't have a current license. The reason why doesn't matter to John because there's always an excuse with Audie for everything.

Audie's just tells him to drop the whole subject. "If you want to drive and wear yourself out, that's fine with me, Johnny."

"Good," John responds. "Now we have an understanding."

Audie is rebuffed when he tries to order a half-calf caramel latte from the middle-aged waitress working their table. This diner only carries regular coffee, although bowing to the times they do carry those little French vanilla creamers that you can mix into your coffee.

John makes it easy for the lady; he always orders his coffee black.

Audie is tired to and more than a little sick and tired of his brother's sanctimonious ways. "You always did think you were smarter than everyone else."

John can't believe what Audie just said and denies the description. "I do not."

"Yeah, you do, man. You've always been that way. Darlene's probably tired of it, too."

"Shut-up about my marriage, Audie. I'm serious. Don't go there," John demands with a threatening tone.

Audie is tired, waves the white flag, and drops the

subject. After ordering their food, the two brothers sit across from each other silently, waiting for their meals to arrive. Each man is sick to death of the company of the other.

Half way through the meal, Audie breaks the silence with what's on his mind. "Can I just say one thing?"

"Not so far," John spouts off with a chuckle between bites.

Audie continues, not letting John's negativity stand in his way. "I think right now, man, I know why dear old Dad had us make this journey in the first place."

John won't give Audie the satisfaction of knowing he's listening, but he is.

Audie again. "I'm totally serious. I think Dad wanted to throw us together in this little adventure for a reason."

"And what's that?" John just has to ask, he can't help himself.

"I think..." Audie elaborates, "to see if all this will bring us together, make us closer, or tear us apart!"

"Really, that's what you think?" John responds.

With a philosophical voice, Audie tells him he does. He analyzes, "And here we are, and we are getting tired, and are at each other's throats. This isn't what Dad would have wanted. I think he would have wanted us to get closer, man. And you know what, Johnny, so do I."

John has no idea what to say next. He has no idea what Audie wants him to say either. So Audie keeps talking. "This fighting right now, this is not cool, man. You know what, Johnny..."

John actually at this second knows nothing.

"I'm going to make you real uncomfortable, bro."

John says nothing. He knows more is coming. He can just feel it.

"Right now, right here, I am pledging to you, my brother that I am going to do everything in my power to get to know you and understand you better."

John for the record, right about now is wondering if there is a school somewhere where they send men to learn how to talk like Audie. A place where a man checks in his testicles and all semblance of being a man and talks like this. Of course, John can't mention any of this to Audie. John just has to let Audie blather on and on and on. Finally, after ten minutes or so, Audie is done. He's waiting for John to reciprocate. But John has other thoughts to point out.

"I don't know what our dear father wanted from this trip. Since he abandoned us and Mom more than fifteen years ago, it's kind of hard to say," John begins with. "But I can tell you this, brother of mine, I don't care."

Audie is staring right now at John wondering where he's going with all this, why his brother is being so negative. "What are you trying to say, man?"

John leers back. He feels like he's talking to Darlene and having one of their numerous "discussions," the kind he always loses.

Audie presses him to define himself further. "You don't want to get closer to your brother? You don't want to bond with me, your brother?"

"No," John answers abruptly. "I don't want to talk about it. I don't want to talk about any of this stuff."

"That's why you're having so many problems with your wife, dude. You're all pent up inside. Johnny, you can't discuss anything with anyone, man," Audie diagnoses to John's disgust.

John's had enough and let's Audie know it. "Okay, that's it. I'm done. Order your food, eat it, and shut up already. No more psychoanalyzing me or my marriage, alright?!"

Audie puts up his hands and shows he surrenders for now. He can see it's useless to go further about this with John not willing to talk about anything, so he lets it go as John ordered.

After they get their food served to them and are almost finished eating, Audie decides to risk breaking the silence once again and starts a different conversation. "Crazy all the stuff we're learning about Dad though, you've got to admit?" Audie blurts out into the air like a trial balloon.

John looks up from his plate long enough to give Audie a look that says why are you even talking to me right now. Audie doesn't let that deter him. "I mean we're just learning things we didn't know, you know?"

John breaks his silence. "Like what, Audie? That Dad was a major league womanizer and cheated on our mom, even having a daughter out of an adulterous affair. Or that as we already know he was a drunk who was screwed up by his drill-sergeant like-dad, so of course he screwed us up as well. Is that the kind of things you're talking about that we've learned so far?"

Audie knows he needs to step lightly right about now. Talking to John when he is like this is like tiptoeing through a mine field. He has to choose his words carefully. "I only meant, Johnny, well whatever. One thing at least, Dad seems to have made some really good life-long friends."

John between bites doesn't respond to that point.

"I mean, it's more than I can say. I don't have any real good friends like that, you know? How about you?"

John actually gives consideration to his brother's query. "I've got a few buddies in Grants Pass, but that's about it."

"Well, that's one thing Dad had on us for sure. I wonder how he did it." Audie questions out loud.

"Did what?" John asks.

"You know, how he made friends and kept their loyalty for like ever, dude," Audie responds. . Both guys think about that for a second before John takes a stab at the answer. "Well, he certainly was a charmer, our father. You've got some of that in you," John tells Audie.

"I don't know about that, man. I just have enough charm to get myself in a shit full of trouble, Johnny," Audie observes.

John insists he thinks Audie inherited the charm gene from their father.

"Well, my personality might be a little more like Dad, but if he was here right now he would want to spend his time with you, brother," Audie contends.

"And why do you say that when you've gone out of your way to try to reach out to him over the years and I haven't," John points out.

"That's only because you still hate him so much for everything. And it's also because you don't want to piss off Mom. That's why you never made any effort at all."

"Why should I have?" John barks back. "He left me and you, and Mom, and didn't give a damn what happened to us."

Audie tries at that moment to justify what their father did, that maybe if they could have just talked to him. John clearly isn't ready to hear any of this.

"I'm really tired. I'm going to finish my meal and find us a cheap motel to crash in for the night. Let's go back to the blissful silence, shall we," John insists mildly.

Audie agrees. Any hopes that this conversation was going to add anything positive at all just went up in flames. Audie knows when it's time to quit when you're behind. He just wishes that he could get a drink. A beer or two could take the edge off now. But in the mood John's in, the last thing Audie wants to do is get a temperance lecture from his brother when he's already angry about so many other things, so he thinks better of it. No, Audie like John finishes his food quietly, with no talking to get in the way. After that they find that cheap motel and just as quietly fall into their respective beds for the night. There are no that words that can take you to places you don't want to go when you're asleep.

———∞———

MIKE PUSHES THE BAG OF POPCORN TOWARD DARLENE, and she happily snags a couple of kernels. He then nuzzles into her, close enough that she can feel his breath on her neck. "It's a pretty good flick, don't you think?" he whispers to her.

Darlene agrees, contemplating that warm breath that sent a shiver down her back more than any moments in the movie they are watching together, on this their second time out. A few minutes later, he moves in again to tell her how much he is enjoying spending time with her. Darlene thanks him with a gracious look.

"How about you?"

Darlene isn't sure what he's asking. So she politely asks him. "What?'

Mike asks her again. "Are you enjoying spending time with me?" he whispers in her ear.

She can sense him lingering there longer than completely necessary. And he is doing just that, gladly taking in whatever enticing fragrance Darlene has deposited on her neck for the evening. As uncomfortable as it might make her feel for the moment, she doesn't want to embarrass him by bringing up how awkward it is for her to have him hovering over the back of her neck.

"What are you wearing tonight?" Mike, out of the blue brings up.

She looks down at her clothes wondering if in the dark of the movie theater he can't see her outfit. Mike reacts to this by chuckling and translating himself better. "No, I mean what perfume do you have on tonight?"

"Oh," Darlene says as she suddenly gets his meaning. "It's called White Diamonds."

Mike notes how much he likes it as he makes another maneuver toward her neck. Darlene is still trying to not act bothered or behave in any way that makes him feel awkward like he is doing something wrong by admiring her scent. But when he pecks her on the neck with his lips, all bets are off. Without thinking she pulls away from him and slides to the other side of her seat. Mike quickly apologizes for doing what he did and lets her know it was just an impulsive thing. He didn't mean to come on so strong, so fast, and act like one of "'those guys.'" Darlene tells him it's okay. "Let's just watch the movie," she says.

Mike reluctantly agrees as they both slide down into their seats and enjoy what's left of the film, before Mike takes her back home.

The drive back to Darlene's place is a quiet one with Mike feeling foolish for the whole neck peck and Darlene embarrassed that she made him feel that way. Mike parks as he did the night before, a couple of neighbor houses down the street. He gathers his courage enough to tell her how good a time he had tonight and again apologizes for the peck on the neck. "Well, have a goodnight, Darlene, and thanks for tonight," he forces out of his mouth.

Darlene can see the discomfort over him like a cheap suit a size to small. The only emotion he is stirring in her right now is pity. She takes his hand and holds it in hers. Then feeling sorry for Mike, and without thinking, she slides over to him in the front seat of his pick-up and kisses him on the lips. He barely kisses her back he's so surprised by her move. Darlene looks him straight in the eyes and flashes her warmest expression before whispering to him that it's okay and that there is nothing to feel bad about. When Mike tries to respond by kissing her back, she pulls away. "I'm still not sure about all this," she gets across to him. "So can we take it slow, please?"

Mike matches her gracious look with one of his own. He takes her hand as any gentleman in the textbooks is supposed to and kisses the top of it. "Of course," he responds.

Mike escorts Darlene as far as he can without being seen from the windows of her house by her kids. "You have a great night, Darlene and I'll talk to you real soon."

Darlene wishes Mike the same and agrees they will talk soon before making it back to her home where she knows that Lorinda will be waiting, wanting to know every detail.

CHAPTER 12

"Finally, man I need to stretch!" Audie declares loudly. John pays little attention to his brother even though he certainly could use a good stretch of his limbs and a repositioning of his backside himself. The boys are thrilled that they have finally reached their next destination after over ten hours of driving across Texas. The guys headed southeast from the southwest border of the state to near the Mexican border. Audie's been whining about the drive all day, and John is fed up with listening to him. After hours multiplied by many more hours of driving through the huge state while seeing nothing much but a little town, and then more miles of nothing, they finally reach the tiny town of Zapata. The next name on their list resides here, a man by the name of Bobby Johnson who both boys remember their father speaking about many times when they were kids but whom they've never met.

Audie again uses the GPS on his phone to guide them to Mr. Johnson's residence. When they arrive, they only see a large wall with a metal gate and speaker box to greet them. The guys hop out and try to un-stiff their stiffness. Simultaneously Audie grabs at his lower back as John does the same with his extremities.

"I heard Texas was big, but this is ridiculous," Audie complains to his brother.

John orders Audie to stop complaining as he studies the front gate and locates the big button that seems to be calling him to push it. When he does, nothing happens, so he tries it again.

"Maybe nobody's home," Audie reckons.

"Maybe," John responds as he tries the button a second time. This time a voice comes from the other side. "Can I help you?"

"Is this Mr. Bobby Johnson?" John asks.

"Who wants to know?" the voice comes back with. "Are you guys selling something?"

"Kind of," Audie says, which instantly irks his brother.

John tries to spell out their purpose for standing at the man's front gate but makes it sound even more like they are a couple of sales people when he asks if they can have just a few minutes of his time.

The voice thanks them in a nice way and turns them down before wishing them both a blessed day.

Audie pushes his way in front of John and pushes the button again while blurting out their father's name.

"What did you say?" the voice they assume is Bobby Johnson's, comes back with.

"We're here because of Raymond Barrett," Audie tells him.

"Is he with you?"

"No, sir," John chimes in with. "We are his sons, and we would like to speak with you, if you are in fact Bobby Johnson."

The man tells them to give him a minute and so they wait patiently outside the front gate unable to see anything that resides behind it. Then the sounds of the gate opening start and the gate does indeed begin to open. John asks if they should drive their truck down the driveway or leave it parked on the street. They are told to drive it into the property, and so they do.

They discover behind the large gate a huge manufactured home, one of the biggest either one of them has ever seen, accompanied by a large shop area and a massive yard to boot. An older black gentleman comes out of the home to meet them. His hand is outstretched in front of him, and he is wearing a face that shows he is very happy to make their acquaintance.

"Our redneck dad had an African-American buddy?" Audie whispers to John as they watch the man walk towards them.

"I guess so. What's the big deal?" John quietly answers back.

"Nothing," Audie responds. "Just surprising the way I remember Dad was, you know."

The man firmly shakes both of their hands and acts shocked that Ray Barrett's sons are standing before him. "Your father is one of my dearest and best friends."

John and Audie turn to each other. Both are happy to receive such a warm welcome.

"It's a pleasure to meet you, Mr. Johnson," John says.

The man then apologizes for poor manners and asks them to come in. He invites them to follow him into his home. He's tickled pink to meet them, so much so that the brothers wonder why.

It doesn't take long after sitting down on Bobby's couch for John and Audie to be faced with the difficult job of sharing the news of their father's death with his good friend.

Bobby is asking so many questions about their dad that they really have no choice but to quickly "get it over with." Bobby acts stunned by the news, and his mouth which was running a mile a minute only moments ago, is now stopped in its tracks. He is even more concerned about how the boys are taking the news. "This is a shock, isn't it? Such a shock," he stutters, as he digests what the guys just told him.

John and Audie give him their condolences. This man, who probably hasn't seen their father in many years, seems much more troubled by the loss than they are. "You two were real close, I guess?" John directs to Bobby.

"Like two peas in a pod," Bobby replies.

"How did you two meet?" Audie interjects.

Bobby laughs as he remembers back. "We were both in the Air Force, stationed in the same place in Arizona."

"Luke Air Force Base?" John guesses.

Bobby confirms that's correct and continues with his story. "I was having lunch in the cafeteria one day, minding my own business as I usually did. You have to understand that even though this was a base in Arizona, not Mississippi or the like, there was still a lot of redneck, big ol' white boys running around, who didn't much care for black men like myself."

"Wait a second," Audie interrupts. "This is the eighties?"

Bobby confirms it is.

"It sounds like the nineteen sixties or something, man," Audie states.

Bobby puts across that sometimes with the right crop of white boys together in the same place at the same time, even in the eighties it could be an uncomfortable existence for a dark- skinned man. He continues. "So I got up to get seconds, and as I am passing by one of the other tables this tree trunk of a big ol' white boy sticks his leg out and trips me up."

"Oh, shit," John exclaims.

"Oh, heck yes," Bobby agrees. "I go tumbling down face first onto the floor with my tray of food breaking my fall. As you could probably assume, I was a sconce perturbed at this event and even more when I heard the bastard laughing with his buddies at my expense."

Both John and Audie in unison want to know what Bobby did next. Bobby is happy to oblige. "Well, I was young and not the calm sophisticated man you see before you today. So I jumped up with fists a ready. Big ol' redneck starts in my direction with two buddies, their fists a ready to go."

"Well, you're still with us so I guess they didn't kill you or anything," Audie says with a laugh.

"Well, I might not be if it wasn't for your dad," Bobby continues. "Ray jumps in between me and tree trunk and his friends and tells those guys what's what. I mean, Ray starts talking like a crazy man or something and threatens all three of them with the wrath of God if they even lay a hand on me."

"No way!" Audie interjects again, surprised by the twist in the tale.

"I swear it!" Bobby says, promising the boys that he speaks the truth.

John asks him what happened next.

"Well, your dad wasn't the biggest of men, but he was a tough son-of-a-bitch and everybody knew it. And with his acting crazy and all, those redneckers just backed off and left me alone. Me and Ray were fast buddies from that day on."

"You guys think that's kind of funny that your father stood up for a black man, don't ya'?"

John doesn't answer that, but Audie does have to admit to Bobby he is surprised since his dad could often tell off-color jokes and say some things that were in poor racial taste.

Bobby for one isn't surprised by Audie's revelation about his dad. "Your dad and I would razz each other all the time. He would make his jokes and comments about black people, and I would make mine about white folks. It was in fun, we were friends, and we loved to do it."

"And nobody's feelings would get hurt?" Audie is interested to know.

Bobby laughs off the assertion. "No! We weren't all uptight like people today are. We could laugh at each other and all the prejudices we grew up with and have a good time. He was raised, your dad to not like blacks and I was raised the same toward whites. We both knew it was stupid, and we laughed about it all the time."

John is still surprised to hear all this, but happy at the same time to know there was another side to his father, a better side.

"Your father was a good man, no matter what you two boys might think. Ray got along with anyone and everyone. He could fit in at a Southern Baptist convention or a Hells Angel's rally. Everybody liked Ray Barrett," Bobby says with glee in his eyes.

Bobby asks if there is more to their visit that just breaking the sad news to him. Audie is reminded right now of the gift he has in the backpack for Bobby, and he pulls it out. It's one of the biggest things in the backpack. It's wrapped in plastic. Audie hands it to Bobby.

FISHING *for* SOMETHING   199

"My, I wonder what it might be," Bobby says as he takes it from Audie and begins to unwrap the plastic.

"It's a tray, that makes sense," Audie spouts from his mouth as Bobby makes the same discovery.

Bobby laughs as he gives it a good look, up and down. It's just like the tray that Bobby fell onto all those years ago at Luke Air Force Base when Raymond Barrett came to his aid.

"Good old Ray. I guess he remembered how we first met, too," Bobby muses as he studies the gift some more.

Bobby thanks the boys for the trip down memory lane even if it began with them having to tell him about their father's passing.

"There is one more thing," John gets across to him.

Bobby asks what that is as he still is studying the cafeteria tray.

"Dad wanted us to take you fishing before we left," John tells him. Bobby laughs and isn't surprised. After all, he and Ray fished as often as they possibly could whenever they got together. "Did he give any details in his letter about this fishing trip?"

"He said in his letter that he wanted us to go to a Falcon Lake down here," Audie responds.

"Well, of course. That's just down the road. We are right next to it here," Bobby declares to the guys. "We can take my big old boat; it's got a motor on it like a rocket ship. You boys are going to love it. We could leave right away."

John and Audie are surprised Bobby is ready at such short notice and they tell him as much.

"What's there to wait for? If there is anything your dad has just taught us it's this. Life is short and you shouldn't take a single day for granted," Bobby preaches to the brothers.

John informs him that all their fish and tackle is in their truck. So Bobby tells them to gather it all up and meet him at his bigger truck parked in the back of the place. In only about ten minutes, the electric gate in the front opens and Bobby leads the guys to their next fishing stop on Falcon Lake.

DARLENE HANGS UP HER KEYS AS SHE ENTERS HER FRONT door. When she turns from the key hook she is startled to find Rose standing directly in front of her. Rose who is known for her warm greetings doesn't seem herself. There is a reason for this, and Rose wastes no time to put it in plain English for Darlene. "I hear, duck, that you went to the cinema last night."

Uh oh, Darlene thinks as she can see where this talk is going, and she certainly doesn't like it. Darlene at first plays dumb, but she can tell that Rose is having none of that. "A lady friend of mine saw you and some man at the movies last night," Rose vents with obvious disdain coming from her words.

Darlene knew that in a small town like Grants Pass that something like this could happen. She even considered her different scenarios for trying to justify her way out of just this type of conversation with Rose, but she still isn't ready for all this. "Alright, Rose, it's true. I went to a movie last night with an old friend. Is it really the end of the world?"

The answer to that for Rose is yes, and she makes that very clear to Darlene. "How could you do this? John is out of town for a short, bloody time, and so you think now is the time to cheat on him!"

Rose's anger rising is not helping either of them at this moment.

Darlene isn't sure what to even say, so she shoots for the truth since it doesn't appear lying is going to work. "John and I have been apart for some time now, Rose, and I have been lonely."

"Oh, my God, you're already sleeping with other men!" Rose yells in her face before looking to see if the children are in earshot of any of this. Fortunately for both Rose and Darlene they don't seem to be. "I can't believe you would do something like this," Rose says as she chokes up on her words.

Darlene feeling about a foot tall right now, even though in her mind she really hasn't done much, puts down the second charge thrown her way about sleeping with other men. Rose stares at Darlene like she is trying to see through her.

"It's the truth, Rose. This date last night was only the second one I've been on, and both with the same man."

Rose hears the part about it being a second date more than the part about her not sleeping with anyone.

"It's nothing serious, a dinner and a movie that's all," Darlene tries to put across.

But Rose is concerned that it could be and lets her know that. "How would you feel if Johnny was seeing other women without you knowing?"

Darlene tries but has no great comeback for that. She just indicates that right now there is nothing for Rose to be concerned with.

Rose pushes for a promise there won't be in the future and hopes that Darlene and John will be able to make things better and get back together. Darlene who thinks the world of Rose would love nothing more than to guarantee to Rose that she and her son will live happily ever after and all that muck, but she can't. Darlene feels like she at least owes Rose the honest truth, no matter how painful. "I am so thankful to you, Rose, for taking care of the kids all the time, and frankly being so kind to me all these years. Even when John moved out, you didn't turn on me when so many mothers-in-law would have, in defense of their sons. I really respected you for that and still do."

Rose is no psychic, but she knows a but is coming in a second.

"But, John and I have to work out all this on our own," Darlene says, as Rose expected.

"I know you want us to make it all work out and get back together, and I understand that," Darlene expounds. "And part of me wants that, too, but I don't know if that's how it's going to work or not. John has to make changes in his life. He's got to realize that I am not going be just something that he enjoys when it's convenient for him and when he can spare the time. The kids and I are not something sitting on a dusty shelf somewhere that he can show interest in, only when he feels like it."

Rose cuts Darlene off and asks her if she is being a bit melodramatic. Rose tells her squarely that it's never only one side that needs to change in a relationship, that it's both. Darlene surprises her by not disagreeing. Darlene agrees it takes two, but sometimes one person is trying a whole lot more than the other and she feels in their marriage that person has been her. Rose is ready to defend her son's honor, to challenge Darlene's words, but then she stops herself. Fighting with Darlene isn't going to help anything, especially when she has to see her at least five days a week while watching the children for her. Instead Rose reminds her how much Johnny loves her and wants nothing more in the entire universe than to be back with her and the children.

Darlene is touched by Rose's sincerity, but reality is reality, "I know John loves us. I have never doubted that, Rose, but sometimes good intentions aren't enough. I need actions from John. Do you understand, Rose, what I'm saying?"

Rose does, but not completely. She asks Darlene flat out if she's going to keep seeing this new man. Darlene in all honesty isn't really sure and she tries to explain that but Rose wants to hear none of that. "It's your life dear. I only know that Johnny is a wonderful man who would do anything for you and the children; he's not like his father at all. I only wish I'd, had a husband like John," Rose voices in speech-like form.

Darlene gives her an uncomfortable hug and thanks her again for her help with the kids. She tells Rose that she promises to give John every chance to work things out with her if he is willing. Rose thanks her for that and asks if she has had another phone call from John. Darlene has, but it didn't change anything. "He's probably out having the time of his life with Audie right now."

BOBBY AND THE BOYS HAVE BEEN CRUISING FALCON LAKE for about an hour. Bobby's searching for the perfect spot to anchor and fish for bass. When he finds it he pulls his boat in and has John climb to the front and tie some rope onto a dead tree sticking out of the calm waters.

"That should hold us, fellas, should keep us from drifting too much away from the shore," Bobby tells the guys.

Audie is impressed with Bobby's boat and tells him.

"Thanks, this is my pride and joy. I only wish I could take it out more than I do."

John wonders why he can't, being Bobby is retired and all.

"Oh, I don't like to go out alone anymore. I have a problem you see," Bobby discloses.

John and Audie exchange glances. They can't help but be curious if Bobby is willing to discuss.

"Is it serious?" John asks as subtly as he can.

Bobby's permanent smile he seems to wear disappears from his face as he confides his affliction. "I suffer from narcolepsy, I'm afraid."

"You can't help yourself from stealing drugs, man?" Audie responds.

"No, you idiot! It means he falls asleep sometimes and can't control when or where." John says, trying to educate his brother.

Audie nods. Now he understands.

"Yeah, I've been dealing with it for about ten years. It just came out of the blue and started to kick my butt," Bobby teaches.

"That's gotta' be pretty rough," John says.

"It's no picnic that's for sure. Anyways because of the narcolepsy I'm afraid to go out and do anything alone, even fishing."

John and Audie can certainly understand that.

"But it sure is beautiful out here, and I sure do miss getting out on the water. Your dad and I fished this lake many times back in the day," Bobby tells the guys. "The last time I recall my whole family was out here with us, even my wife at the time."

"Not married anymore." John inquires. It's a popular topic with him these days.

"That's why I said at the time, John. I tried it once, but it didn't take. Now I'm probably too old to meet another, or at least too old to charm another."

Audie snickers at Bobby's words. He tells him he's likely better off for it.

Bobby smirks and howls back, "You're probably right, you're probably right."

John steers Bobby back to the story about their father and Bobby's family.

"Oh, it was like a Johnson family reunion that day as I recall. About thirty black people and your dad."

"How did dear old Dad do with that?" Audie is interested to know.

"He had a great time! My family loved him. My great aunt called him the Johnson family's token white family member. Like I said, your dad could get along in any group. He was like a chameleon with a great personality."

The reference brings grins to the boys' faces.

Bobby scans the beauty of the lake. "You'd never think that this could be a dangerous place by looking at it, would you?"

"What do you mean?" Audie questions after hearing the word dangerous.

"You know," Bobby says, "about some of the craziness that's gone on down here."

John feels he can speak for both himself and Audie when he says, no, they don't know.

Bobby is surprised the boys haven't heard about some of the "incidents" at the lake. "Part of Falcon Lake, obviously the southern part, crosses into Mexican waters. There are some pretty bad people running around that part of the lake."

"How bad of dudes?" Audie wants to know.

"Well, real bad son. We're talkin' drug smugglers, gang members, Mexican Cartel members, real bad people," Bobby tells him.

"But we're okay right here, right man?" Audie asks nervously.

Bobby assures both John and Audie that there as safe as a baby in a cradle as long as they stay out of the Mexican waters.

John and Audie take another look around. They hope Bobby knows what he's doing.

"Enough talk, boys. Your dad, Ray, wanted us to come out here and fish and that's just what we are going to do!" Bobby promises loudly.

John hands Audie his pole and tackle box and then grabs his own. The brothers prepare their lines for the large-mouth bass that reside in these waters. Bobby on his way out of his house grabbed snacks and drinks for the day. He begins to dole them out to John and Audie. Audie reaches for a beer. He's been craving one all day, but John tells him to not even think about it twice. Instead Audie takes a can of soda that brings a satisfying grin from his brother who appreciates his effort.

"Let fishing commence!" Bobby shouts to no one in particular. "To you, Ray, wherever you are, my friend, God's speed," he toasts lifting his beer can in the air.

John and Audie toast once again to his memory, clanging their soda cans together.

DARLENE KEEPS CLOSE EYES ON HER THREE CHILDREN as they run and jump into the city's public pool. Between sips of ice tea, she yells at them to be careful and watch out for other kids. She doesn't want to see them land on others and get themselves or somebody else hurt. Lorinda is stretched out in a lawn chair next to her. Darlene with the day off is only a few hours removed from her challenging talk with Rose. Lorinda just got off work at the café about an hour ago and agreed to come over and hang out with Darlene by the pool. Darlene needs someone to talk to about the Rose conversation, and who better than Lorinda who knows all the details of what's going on.

"It sounds like to me, sweetie, that you handled everything perfectly with your mother-in-law," Lorinda calculates, puffing up Darlene's confidence a tad.

"You really think so?" Darlene answers, still feeling insecure about the whole episode.

"I really do, girl. That's a tough one, with Rose being John's mom and all, and you trying to figure things out and what you want. No, I think you were straight up with her the best you could be. You told her the truth, and that's what she needed to hear."

Lorinda's statements are certainly encouraging and definitely making Darlene feel better about herself. There is just no easy way to try and deal with a separation from your husband with his mother watching your every move, and Darlene knows this all too well. Lorinda in a flash, changes the course of the talk by bringing up the other elephant in the room, Mike Stillman. "How does Mike fare in all this, sweetie?"

Darlene looks at her wondering what exactly she means.

"You know what I'm asking? How are you feeling about Mike?"

Darlene reminds her friend that they have only been on two dates to this point but that doesn't really answer the question hanging out there in the air.

"You know what I am saying," Lorinda insists.

But Darlene insists just as forcefully that she doesn't.

So Lorinda spells it out for her. "Do you think Mike could turn into something serious or not?"

Darlene with one eye on the kids in and out of the pool, and one eye on Lorinda, tries her best to give an honest answer. She isn't sure yet. It's way too early to even know what might happen between her and Mike. But Lorinda is quick to point out that she didn't say it couldn't turn serious. Lorinda chortles back at Darlene's defensiveness as she tries to dampen any talk of things turning serious with Mike Stillman.

Lorinda teases her about liking Mike a lot more than she is telling. Without notice by either woman, another voice enters the fray. "Hello, ladies, are we having a good time or what?"

Both Darlene and Lorinda look up to see Mike Stillman standing there, smiling away. Lorinda immediately wants to know how long he was standing there and how much he overheard. Mike acts like he heard nothing. "I just got here, why? Is there something important that I missed?"

It's been a long time since anything in life has made Darlene blush, but Mike showing up like this was definitely doing it for her. "What are you doing here?" she asks him directly.

The question catches Mike off guard. He hadn't thought about having a good story on why a single man without kids would be at public pool like this. Darlene and Lorinda can see Mike's grey matter mashing together as he struggles for a reasonable response to the inquiry. Finally, with nothing really coming to him, he gives in. "I saw your car in the parking lot and just wanted to see you."

Darlene's son Cody happens to walk up at that moment to ask Darlene something. He soon forgets what that something is as he examines the strange man standing in front of him, talking to his mother. Darlene talks him back into the pool. Then with Cody unable to hear, she says, "Mike, I'm flattered and all, but my kids are here. This isn't the time or place for you to just drop by."

Lorinda interrupts Darlene to say how sweet she thinks it was for Mike to come here, but Darlene has other ideas. "I'm sorry, Mike. I'm not trying to be mean or rude to you. I'm really not."

Mike cuts her off. "No, I get it. It's too soon to meet your children. I get it, Darlene, and sorry for pushing things a little too fast for you."

Darlene is touched by him being so understanding about everything. "I'll call you later, Mike, okay?"

It's more than okay for Mike, and he tells her so. He'll be looking forward to the call. Mike gracefully exits the pool area and the ladies.

"He's a sweetheart," Lorinda declares, making sure that Darlene hears her.

Darlene isn't disagreeing, but she also isn't ready to say anything else about Mike that might put her in deeper water with Lorinda. "He's a nice guy and his coming by to see me is flattering. Let's just leave it at that, Lorinda, okay?"

Lorinda shakes her head. She thinks Darlene has no idea how great a catch Mike could be for her.

"Who say's I'm even fishing. John is the one on the fishing trip right now, not me," Darlene offers as a humorous take.

"Maybe you're both on fishing trips right now except John knows he's on one and you don't," Lorinda hoots right back at her.

"Whatever," Darlene sarcastically replies. "Whatever."

⸺⸻⸺

THE PEACEFUL QUIET OF FALCON LAKE IS ALMOST THERapeutic to John and Audie as neither says a word. They just sit back and watch their lines as they probe the lake water for bass. Finally after more than hour, Audie has to comment on how he gets this "'fishing thing'" and why John and their father both loved it so much. "It's like you leave the real world for a while, and you forget all the stuff that pisses you off."

John likes how he put that. "It's kind of like a great exhale from everything that stresses you out or pisses you off."

"Yeah, it is," Audie agrees.

"Now, if we could actually catch some of these fish we have been hearing all about from Bobby, that would complete the day," John says loudly so Bobby will hear him.

When there is no comment back from Bobby, John and Audie turn back around to see what he's up to. He has his back to them as he faces his pole and the water. Audie yells over to Bobby but he doesn't respond. "You don't think…"

Before John can answer his brother, he makes his way over to Bobby and finds him unresponsive.

"Is it the narcolepsy thing, or man is he dead?" Audie asks John.

John wants to know why Audie would even say something like that. "Well he is a little old," Audie voices in his defense.

John checks Bobby for a pulse and finds one. "Why does somebody have to get sick every time we go out on a boat now?"

Audie says the same thing. "We've got to quit fishing with these older dudes, Johnny."

John finds his pulse, and it's working like it should, he thinks.

"What should we do, bro? I mean, how do we know he's going to be okay? He might need to be at the hospital right now, Johnny," Audie spits out as panic begins to take hold.

John tells Audie to calm down and get a grip, but he has to admit that Audie does have a point. John agrees that they should probably take the boat back to the marina and have Bobby checked out by medical personnel. "First the colonel and now this," John says in disbelief at the situations they find themselves in.

"Did you happen to catch the way we came from?' Audie asks John.

John believes that it's no big deal and that he can easily find his way in, but really he wasn't paying much attention either as Bobby drove the boat. John was too busy listening to Bobby's stories. "It can't be too difficult. I'm pretty sure we came from that direction," John indicates as he points with his index finger to the way he thinks they must go.

Audie has no idea, so he's ready to go along with whatever John thinks. John mans the driver's seat and starts up the motor. He soon has them going in the direction he pointed to so confidently. Unfortunately for John and Audie, and even fast-asleep Bobby, John is wrong and they are headed the opposite way. They're ripping through the water but going farther and farther away from the marina and U.S. waters. By the time they realize something is wrong and make the decision to turn around, Audie spots a large power boat heading their way. The boat is coming their direction at breathtaking speed. "Johnny, I don't like this, man," Audie whispers to his brother as if trying to not let the inhabitants of the power boat, still a fair distance from them, hear him.

John doesn't say anything, but he's not wanting to see why the boat is heading their way either. He quickly whips the boat around and starts in the opposite direction, picking up speed as fast as he can. The boat chasing them is gaining ground as Audie tries in vain to wake Bobby.

Audie is starting to freak out, but John won't let that distract him, as he pushes Bobby's boat as hard as it will go.

"It's closing on us, man! I bet we wandered into Mexican waters and those guys are drug smugglers or coyotes!" Audie screams over the boat motor's noise.

John steadfastly, without hesitation, keeps his head down and his eyes forward as if trying to will the boat back to friendly waters. Then a sound echoes across the lake. A couple more times a popping sound is heard and the glass at the side of John, on the starboard side cracks. "They're shooting at us, man!" Audie yells at his brother as he lies down on the bottom of the boat.

John not knowing Audie already has, yells for him to get down. The other boat is getting closer and closer as Bobby's boat is no match for the speed of the boat pursuing them. John knows he's outclassed, and his mind races with many thoughts. Is this how this is all going to end, he thinks, on some lake between Texas and Mexico, a half a country away from his wife and kids.

"Hey, man, it's another boat!" Audie yells, pointing in front of them.

John sees it too, but since it's not a sheriff or border patrol boat, he wonders what difference it makes. Then another sequence of gunfire pops in John's ears, this time followed by a strange sensation in his shoulder. He reaches back to feel the spot, and when he pulls his fingers back they are bloodstained. Then with cold shock, John realizes he's been shot. It's funny there was no pain until he realized it. Now he's feeling the pain and can sense his is blood seeping out of his body. Wooziness slowly starts to set in, and John hollers for Audie to take the wheel. Audie is hunkered down protecting himself from the shots, so John screams at him a second time. Audie slithers like a snake across the bottom of the boat to John. When he gets up close he can see the blood on John's right shoulder. "Oh, my God, you're shot!"

"Nothing gets past you," John responds. "Now take the wheel. I feel like I might pass out."

Audie can barely breathe at this moment but does as John directs as his brother slouches down next to him, and next to the driver's seat. More popping sounds and more glass breaks around them. "We're not going to make it man," Audie yells as he steers straight ahead.

"What are they doing?" John asks Audie as he's getting weaker by the second. "Why hasn't the boat in front of us turned around?"

Audie is wondering the same thing. The guys are about to become a marine sandwich between the boat heading at them and the boating firing away at them from behind. Audie can barely make out the two guys in the boat in front of them, but he sees one of them is standing up with a large handgun steadied by his hands. He is firing the pistol but not at them, but at the boat chasing them. Even after his glass is shattered by return fire, the marksman in the front boat continues to unload his clip at the boat behind John and Audie's. Then, even farther in front of them, Audie spots a border patrol boat coming full steam ahead in their direction. When Audie looks quickly back behind he sees the boat pursuing them is turning, and heading back the other direction. "Yeah! Alright!" Audie yells at the top of his lungs at the sight.

The other boat, the one in front of them that had come to their aid, is also turning and heading back the other way away, distancing itself from the border patrol boat. The border patrol doesn't pursue them but instead continues on their path toward John and Audie. By the time they wave Audie to a stop and board their boat, John has blacked out and misses the entire rescue. So, too, does Bobby who has slept through all the excitement. The two guys in the other boat who had come to the boys' aid have slipped away, out of sight. Apparently the authorities didn't see them firing their guns at the Mexican boat. By the time Audie discloses what happened to the border patrol agents, there is no sign of the two men who saved the boys' hide. They have vanished into thin air.

CHAPTER 13

"Hold still, it's just a scratch!" Harry raises his voice to his partner as he bandages his wound.

"It still hurts a lot, Harry," Bob moans as Harry seals the bandage to his skin. "Maybe I should go into the hospital and have it checked out or something. I could get an infection."

Harry shuts down that idea immediately as he explains the report of a gunshot nick like the one Bob has on the side of his arm would bring all kinds of unwanted attention to the two men. "You're fine. Quit being a big baby!"

Bob's wining doesn't help him if he wants Harry to quit teasing him. "So if we can't go in, then how long are we going to stay out here just sitting in the hospital parking lot?"

The question irritates Harry even more. He's already told Bob several times what the plan is. They'll sit and wait until the two brothers come outside, and then they'll grab them. Harry can't fathom why that is so hard to understand.

"Damn Mexican smugglers! I hope I hit a couple of those filthy bastards when I returned fire!" Bob exclaims, as he goes over the earlier moments at the lake when he and Harry opened fired on the boat full of Mexican coyotes who were firing at the Barrett brothers. One thing still bothers Bob about what unfolded at the lake, however, and with the painkillers Harry gave him finally kicking in, he has his wits about him enough to finally ask. "Harry, why did we even bother to save those guys? It seems to me we would have been better off if we just let the Mexicans do our job for us."

"No, no, no!" Harry responds emphatically. "That's why I do the thinking around here!"

Bob asks politely what he means.

"If we had let the Mexicans get them, Mr. Capriati would wonder if we just let them get away or something. He wouldn't go for that, Bob. No, we need to bring them back to Vegas to Mr. Capriati, in person, one way or another."

"Dead or alive?" Bob asks.

"Preferably alive. Mr. Capriati wants that douche Audie Barrett to pay what he owes him," Harry renders.

"Well, how long do you think we'll be just sitting here?"

"I don't know, Bob. This is a stake-out scenario now, and we'll be here till the assholes come out of the hospital!" Harry promises.

"Great," Bob frets. "We could be here for days or longer."

Harry says otherwise. "That Audie guy wasn't hurt. It was the other one that was shot and we don't need him. The Audie prick will come outside for food or something and then we'll grab him. You got it, Bob?"

Bob does, but he doesn't have to be happy about it. Both men settle in their seats. It might be a long wait.

A BRIGHT LIGHT THAT SEEMS TO COME FROM THE SIDE of John, stirs his eyes to open to a squint. Then beeps, hums, and other sounds push him to awaken even further. A familiar voice is talking to him, but John isn't sure exactly who it is until his eyes open wide and he takes his first peep in over eight hours. Audie's goofy face greets him. "Hey, man, you're back with us in the land of the living, bro. You had me worried for a while there, dude."

John struggles to clear his throat and find his voice, but eventually does. "What's going on? How long have I been here?"

Audie lets him know it's been since late afternoon when the ambulance brought him to the hospital from Falcon Lake. "You passed out at the lake from shock and some blood loss and then kind of fell into a 'small' coma."

John fights to sit up in his hospital bed and look at his brother face to face. He trips one of the sensors that sets off a loud alarm, which he is told will bring a nurse shortly to check on him and turn it off. Like clockwork, the nurse comes into the room and does just that.

"What time is it now?" John asks his brother.

"It's late, man. I think it's about three in the morning," Audie answers.

John spots Bobby Johnson sitting in another corner of the room. Bobby says hello and tells him how glad he is that he is doing alright. Bobby apologizes for dozing off at the lake and missing all the excitement.

"It's okay. Bobby. You certainly didn't need to stay here all night like this," John tells him.

Bobby won't hear of it though. "Your dad is one my best friends. I know if one my kids were in trouble, he would have done the same thing."

John, just the same, thanks him again for staying at the hospital and watching over him. John asks Audie how they got out of the situation at the lake. "The last thing I remember was seeing blood on my fingertips and realizing I had been shot. I know we were getting chased by that boat. What happened?"

Audie explains about the other boat that came to the rescue and fired on their pursuers. "Then the border patrol agents came, and the drug smugglers turned and ran."

"Who were the other guys who were shooting at the Mexican boat?" John asks.

Audie isn't sure but would love to be able to thank them in person for what they did.

"That's crazy!" John acknowledges. "I am lucky to be alive."

"We all are," Audie agrees.

Bobby agrees from his corner of the room, too.

"You know when I was laying there in the boat, bleeding, and wondering if I was going to die, things became clear. For the first time in a long time, things became really clear to me," John discloses, gaining the full attention of his brother and Bobby.

"What are you saying, Johnny?" Audie asks, interested in where this is going.

John considers his thoughts to himself for a moment before tossing some more out there for Audie and Bobby to consider as well. "It's just that I really thought this might be the end. And you know, Audie, when I thought that, only a few things mattered to me."

Audie of course, wants to know what those things are, those few things.

John confesses to his brother as his voice becomes more quiet and serious. "All that mattered right at that moment was Darlene and the kids. I thought I might not ever see them again, and they're all that mattered. I didn't think about my business, or my future, or anything else."

"Well, that's a good thing, man," Audie says. "That might be something to tell Darlene, when you see her next, Johnny."

"No!" John shouts. "I need to let her know right away. I've taken things for granted long enough. Everything else in my life I've obsessed over but not them. Darlene's been trying to get that through my thick skull for years, but I wouldn't listen. I thought she was trying to control me. But when I thought I would never see them again, none of that other stuff mattered."

Audie can't remember the last time he's seen John like this. Oh wait, never really. When John wants to call Darlene up right now, Audie talks him out of it because of the late hour. He gets John to wait until the morning as not to worry Darlene about why he's calling so late at night in the first place. John agrees to the morning call but is still worked up about spilling his guts to Darlene after his near-death experience. Audie tries to calm him down. He doesn't want John's phone call to his wife to come off like his brother has become unhinged.

"Look, I've just got so much I want to get off my chest. I want her to know that I get it, you know!" John professes to anybody in earshot of his room.

"I know, bro. Just think through what you want to say to her before you make the call," Audie replies. "And, Johnny, realize that her reaction may not be what you hope for."

"What do you mean?" John questions not understanding what his brother is trying to say.

"I'm just saying, man, it's still phone a call, and it's still just words. It might take some convincing, you know?" Audie continues to try and clarify and slow down John's giddy expectations.

John is like a kid on a sugar high right now and thinks he's found a miracle cure for all that ails his marriage. Maybe he has, Audie has to consider. Maybe the fear of

Andrew Scott Bassett

death staring him straight in the face at Falcon Lake was what it took to get everything in the right perspective. These thoughts are too deep for Audie to wrap his mind around right now. Audie just needs to get his brother out of this hospital room and back onto the road, to finish this trip and get the money waiting for them in upstate New York. John's nurse comes back in and brings some sedatives with her to help him get more sleep. She assures Audie that if the doctor on call in the morning gives his brother the okay, he could be released later in the morning. Audie offers a pleased look in Bobby's direction at the news, as John falls back to sleep.

"That's good news, son," Bobby says to Audie. "Your brother is going to be okay it looks like."

Audie is relieved but hopes that John snaps out of his deliriously happy state of marital revelation and morphs back into his regular old brother by the morning. Audie is worried about the morning phone call. "Darlene might think he's went off the deep end if he comes on to strong with all this turning over a new life crap," Audie whispers to Bobby, who agrees with him.

⸗⸗⸗

THE NEXT MORNING, JOHN HAS ALREADY DRESSED HIM-self and is anxious to leave the hospital. John and Audie have already said their goodbyes to Bobby and are ready to get back on the road. They have a long drive in front of them, all the way to Miami. Audie steps out of the room to give his brother some privacy as he makes his phone call to Darlene. John first calls her on her cell phone but gets only the voice mail. He then tries the landline at the house that they still have, just because. The phone rings several times, and John waits for the message recorder that used to be the whole family speaking but now is just one of those annoying generic ones. To his surprise, his mother picks up. "Johnny, dear, how are you, honey?"

John isn't about to tell his mother that he is sitting in a hospital room in South Texas after being shot the day before, so he lies. "Everything is great, Mom. You're watching the kids today, I see?"

Of course Rose is, as Darlene is at work. Rose chides her son for taking so long to call her to let her know how they are doing. She asks him about Audie and how the trip is going, but John is barely listening. All he can think about is what he wants to say to Darlene, but she isn't available to listen. His emotional gun is locked and loaded, and he can't even fire. After a few more minutes of the normal pleasantries between a son and mother, John is ready to hang up, but before he can, Rose butts in and lets him know in no uncertain terms that there is something she is dying to tell him. Usually when she gets like this it means Darlene has done something that Rose isn't happy about, and she can't wait to share the "dirt" with John and try to get Darlene in trouble. John normally brushes his mom's gossipy ways off and doesn't hear it. But this time she gets his attention quickly. "You need to get back soon, Johnny. Your future depends on it."

Dramatic words, for sure, John thinks. When he presses Rose on what she means she takes her time to spit it out, as she makes a spirited trip around Farmer John's Barn. Finally getting perturbed with all of it, John demands for his mother to just say it, and so she does.

"Darlene has been on dates. I'm so sorry, Johnny," she tells him as dramatically as a person can.

There is no response or even sound from John's side of the phone. He struggles to digest the information. It's going down his craw like a chicken bone right about now. "With who?" he manages to ask.

Rose isn't sure of the name but confirms the validity of her juicy facts by all the eye witness sightings by her chatty girlfriends. The news hits John like a two-by-four from his blindside. All the good feelings, all his future hopes and declarations to make everything right with his wife, in a flash are gone. The only thing John can thing of after he says his goodbye to his mother and hangs up is how his wife has betrayed him. He wonders how long all this has been going on and if Darlene just couldn't wait for him to leave with Audie to flaunt this "new" man for all of Grants Pass to see. By the time Audie gets back to the room, John is in a "wonderful" mood. It takes only a few seconds for Audie to tell John's delirium has left and been replaced by foulness. "What's wrong, Johnny?"

John only mumbles and groans, nothing is coherent enough to decipher his dramatic change in attitude. When Audie pushes him to talk,, he shuts down even more and snaps at his brother about not wanting to talk about anything. When Audie asks him about the phone call to Darlene, John's mood gets even more grim. This tells Audie all he needs to know. The phone call must have turned into the disaster that Audie thought it would. After the doctor makes his appearance and checks out John, he gets the okay to get dressed and leave. Audie is hoping that getting back on the road and back to business will put his brother in a better mood. At the very least, hopefully, getting on the road again will take his mind off his problems, whatever they might be, Audie hopes.

Thirty minutes later, the guys are discharged and heading for the front doors of the hospital. Audie is whistling an up tune that has the opposite effect on his brother. John gives him a look that says shut the hell up, so he does. "Whatever you're going through, man, I hope you can talk to me about it. You know, we've both been through a lot already, man. Geez, we've both made visits to the hospital since we left Oregon. You know you can talk to me about anything."

Standing at the doorway John stares at his little brother, shaking his head. "Thanks," John speaks, "but no thanks. Let's just find my truck and get the hell out of here."

Audie agrees. Whatever helps to get Johnny out of his dismal mood is okay with him.

※

IT'S LATE MORNING WHEN BOB IS AWAKEN BY TAPPING on his passenger-side window. Harry is standing there, hands full with two cups of coffee using his elbows to tap. The look on Harry's face let's Bob know that he did indeed catch him dozing in the front seat of the car when he was supposed to be watching the front of the hospital for any signs of Audie Barrett. Bob starts the engine with the keys still hanging from the ignition. He quickly makes his window go down and grabs his coffee from Harry. "You fell asleep!"

Damn! Bob thinks. I'm screwed. He's justifying as fast as his brain will let him, tells Harry that he just dozed off a second before Harry tapped on his window, and that's all. Harry isn't buying. "Now you are going to have to go inside the hospital and make sure he hasn't already left."

Bob considers arguing the point but thinks better of it. Bob likes his front teeth and would rather just keep them where they are. He delicately places his plastic coffee cup on the dashboard and hops out of the car to do as Harry told him. Only a few steps to the front entrance and he spots their prey coming out the front doors. He runs back to tell Harry, but he already sees the same thing and is climbing out of the driver's side, the two men speed-walk straight toward Audie Barrett now. Harry and Bob grip their pistols from the holsters inside their blazers. Harry orders Bob to let him do all the talking. The closer and closer they get, the more the heat and humidity of this Southwest Texas summer day hits them in the face like a frying pan.

Amazingly, neither Audie Barrett nor his brother walking slowly beside him has taken notice of them yet, as they are now just thirty feet away. "I'll put a gun in Audie's ribs and you put one in his brother's," Harry demands of his partner in crime.

But out of nowhere, two city cops walk up to Audie and John. Harry slams on the imaginary brakes in his shoes and stops Bob with his left arm. They both quickly release the handles on their guns and remove their arms from their jackets. Harry orders them back to their car as fast as possible. "But don't look like you're going fast," he barks at Bob. "Just walk normal, alright."

When they get back to the car, Harry can't help but let his partner know his disappointment at this set back. "Shit! Damn cops! They would have to show up now. Just like the police to screw everything up, first at Falcon Lake, and now!"

Bob tries to calm him down, but it doesn't help. In these situations Bob has always found it's better to let Harry works these things out in his own head and then he usually calms down. As normal, Harry does just that. "Why am I getting so upset? The cops will leave, and we'll nab them, right?"

Bob agrees lightning fast, all part of the process of helping Harry cope.

"Shit! Now what?!" Harry's blood pressure begins to rise again. He gestures to the brothers who are now being escorted to their vehicle by the local law enforcement.

The taller of the two officers holds the passenger door to the truck for John. John hurting, moans as he slides into the passenger seat. Audie is more than happy to occupy the driver's side even if John is terrified at the prospect. With John still hurting and banged up from the shooting, he has no other choice but to let Audie drive, but he doesn't have to be happy about it. The police officers have some questions for the brothers about what happened at Falcon Lake. John in his condition does his best to answer them. The officers have more things to ask but seeing John's struggles, agree to make it quick. They have already interviewed Bobby Johnson, who of course had little to say since he slept through the whole incident. The border patrol had already spoken with Audie at the hospital, so he thought they were done discussing the events of Falcon Lake, but local police now want more detail. John and Audie tell them everything they know and answer all their questions to the best of their ability. The officers are satisfied.

Before the officers can leave Audie has a question for them. "Did you find out who the guys in the other boat were, the guys that saved us?"

The officers tell Audie they didn't but are still investigating that part as well. "Maybe good Samaritans, you know," one of the two officers considers.

"Carrying guns on the lake and firing away like that," Audie considers. "We don't see a lot of that where we're from."

"This is Texas, buddy," the other officer makes plain, putting his two cents in. "Everybody has a gun here."

John interrupts and thanks the officers for everything and assures them if he or Audie recall anything else they'll be in touch right away. The officers wish them a better rest of their trip than the last twenty-four hours. Audie and the policemen share a laugh at that one. The officers watch as John and Audie drive away leaving the hospital parking lot to get back onto the main roads. What the officers don't notice is the four-door black sedan with dark tinted windows in hot pursuit.

CHAPTER 14

John and Audie fail to notice the car that has been tailing them for almost three hours. Audie informs his brother that the gas tank is bone dry, so they pull into a gas station off of the interstate. The two men following close behind do the same thing. "It's a good thing they're stopping, Bob, because we're almost out of gas ourselves," Harry admits, as he follows the Barrett brothers into the gas islands.

Harry makes sure to park at a gas pump far away from them on the other side of the islands. He watches as Audie gets out and pumps the gas while his brother slowly strolls into the large convenience store. He can't take the chance to be spotted by them in such a large, public place, and with so many people around. When Bob gets out of the car he asks Harry if they are going to grab Audie Barrett right here, but Harry analyzes why they can't in a place like this. "We've got to grab them in a place without all these witnesses," Harry says.

"But what if we can't, Harry? What if they keep stopping at places that are crowded, just like this one?"

Harry assures his partner that they just have to be patient and wait for the right opportunity to present itself. "They'll slip up sooner or later, and then we'll grab them, or at least that Audie asshole."

With Audie now joining his brother in the convenience store Harry thinks the coast is clear and begins to pump gas into his car. Bob asks him where they're heading to next, the brothers that is. Harry lets him know that the next big stop on their trip is Miami.

"How far is that?" Bob responds.

"About another twenty hours or so," Harry tells him matter-of-factly.

"Twenty hours!" Bob blurts out in shock. "And we have to keep tailing them the whole way?"

Harry tries to soothe his partner's concerns. "It won't be that long. They'll have to make a lot more stops along the way, even find a motel to stay in tonight. We'll nab them soon enough Bob," Harry promises with confidence.

Harry's words bring some comfort to Bob; he certainly hopes he's right about that. The last thing Bob wants to do is to have to drive all the way to Miami. His girlfriend has already yelled at him on his cell several times for being gone from home this long. "What about Mr. Capriati?"

"What about him?" Harry asks his partner.

"What are we going to tell him, in regards to why it is taking so long with this guy?" Bob challenges Harry, as he looks in the direction of the convenience store.

Harry shrugs off Bob's worries. "I know what I'm doing. When we come back with Barrett, all will be fine. If we don't, Mr. Capriati might plant us like a cactus in the Nevada desert."

For some reason, Bob is still concerned. Then, at that moment, they both spot Audie and his brother leaving the convenience store and heading back to their truck. Harry and Bob get inside their car with its tinted windows, which make it impossible for anyone to see them inside. They start their car and slowly follow behind the Barrett brothers' truck as it leaves the gas station's parking lot and heads back to the interstate. Inside the car, Harry tells Bob to get comfortable because it might be a long haul before another stop. Bob says that he understands, but all he really can think about is being planted in the Nevada desert next to some cactuses.

⸺⸺∞⸺⸺

JUST AS HARRY PREDICTED, TWO-AND-A-HALF HOURS later, and the Barrett brothers have to make a stop for food. This time it's at some out- of-the-way, dimly lit, dump of a burger joint. Harry and Bob wait on a dirt road that lies between the burger joint and the road that leads back to the highway. Harry has already instructed Bob how this is all going to go down. "You're sure no one will spot us when we grab them?" Bob asks.

"Positive. It's desolate out here, just like we wanted. There's hardly any cars coming or going. We'll bide our time, and when they leave the burger joint and head this way, we'll do as I said. We'll force them off the road and then throw them in the backseat with you. The next thing you know, Bob, we're in Vegas."

"Good! My girl back there is getting more pissed off by the second," Bob confides to Harry.

"Don't worry, my old friend. In no time, we'll be getting toasted by Mr. Capriati for all our hard work in bringing this parasite in," Harry exclaims happily.

Bob sure hopes he's right. Their celebration is abruptly ended when another car pulls up behind them and stops. "What now?" Harry says as he and Bob watch a gorgeous young woman escape the driver's side of the car.

"She's a looker, Harry," Bob says as the beauty with clothing not suitably covering her body slinks their way.

Harry can't argue the fact that she's fine, but tells his partner they don't have time for this right now, not with the Barrett boys probably heading this direction at any moment.

The young woman knocks on Harry's tinted window as if to see whose inside. He rolls his window down to see what she wants.

"I'm so sorry, guys, but my car started making strange sounds a little while back, and I just don't know anything about such things. Would it be possible for you wonderful fellas to take a look see"

Harry remains composed, purposely trying his hardest not to peek at her proportions staring him in the face. Bob, on the other hand, is swallowing hard and straightening his tie. He is locked in on the target that is presenting itself through Harry's window. "Well, maybe a quick look," Harry offers her as he begins to open his car door.

The woman stops him for a moment. "Oh sorry, these darn high heels of mine are so hard to walk in on dirt roads. Let me take them off real quick."

Harry waits to open his door while the woman crouches down to remove her shoes.

"That's much better," she says as she stands back up and gets out of the way of Harry's door.

Bob gets out from his side, and the two men escort her back to her car all the while watching for any signs of the Barrett brothers heading their direction. Then the young woman, with her denim cut-off shorts playing peekaboo with her butt cheeks, shows the guys where the latch is to pop the hood of her car. "Do you want me to start the engine?" she asks Harry in a voice that could melt a snow cone.

Harry clears his throat before telling her yes. He instructs Bob to take his eyes off the gal for a moment and keep them on the road that leads to the burger joint. Bob does his best to follow orders but still steals a glance in her direction as often as he can. Harry tinkers with the few things he actually knows about while Bob stands watch. She starts the car, and it starts right up.

"I don't hear anything unusual, miss, I think your cars fine now." Harry yells to her over the sound of the revving engine.

"Are you really sure about that because I'm really worried about getting broken down out here?" she hollers back.

Harry listens closely but still hears nothing, and the vehicle seems to be firing on all cylinders. Bob grabs at Harry's arm. He sees Audie and his brother getting in their truck at the burger joint. Harry notices the same thing. He closes the hood and tells the woman she has nothing to worry about as she thanks them whole-heartedly, for taking a look. Harry excuses himself and Bob as she drives away, leaving them running for their car.

"Here they come, Harry!"

Harry starts up their car, planning to follow close behind them and then run them off the road. They watch in their rear-view mirrors as the Barretts pass by them. Harry puts the car in drive, and they begin their pursuit. It doesn't take long to see, however, that their car is sluggish and something is wrong. A loud grinding sound is coming from Harry's side of the car and forces him to pull back off the road as John and Audie get farther and farther out of sight. Harry jumps out of the car to see the cause of the vehicle's problems. "We've got another flat!"

"What?!" How could this happen again?!" Bob hollers out.

Bob comes around the side to see what Harry is talking about and is surprised by what he finds. Harry is crouching down, studying what's left of the tire.

"It's practically shredded," Bob observes. "You don't think the gal..."

Harry cuts Bob off not willing to entertain his theory. "Why would she do this? No, this is just one of those things that happens, that you can't predict," Harry contends, regaining his composure. "Help me with the spare in the back. It looks like we're heading for Miami after all."

Bob drops his head in disappointment. "She's never going to forgive me for this Harry," he says, talking about his already exasperated girlfriend waiting for him back home in Nevada.

Harry tells him to shut-up and help him with the spare. Their trip just got even longer.

CODY BREAKS AWAY FROM THE VIDEO GAME HE'S PLAY-ing with his younger brother and sister and walks into the living room to talk to his mother. Darlene is folding clothes that just came out of the dryer when Cody interrupts her. He asks her for his dad's cell phone number. Darlene is happy to give it to him. "You're really missing your dad, aren't ya'?"

"Yeah, and I know he's not going to call you, so I figure I better call Dad myself," Cody suggests.

Darlene has no idea what he's talking about, so she asks him why he thinks his dad is not going to be calling.

Cody is reluctant at first to spill the beans, but after more coaxing from mom he finally does. "After hearing what Nanna said to Dad, I don't think he is going to want to talk to you."

Darlene has to know now exactly what it is that Nanna said and Cody overheard. She prods him to tell her, and he finally breaks down to her pressuring and divulges everything. Darlene is beside herself that Rose would gossip about her, especially to John. She's even more upset that Rose would allow her grandson to hear the conversation. As awkward as it is to try to translate to her eleven year old, she does her best. "I just had dinner with a man who is a friend of Mom's from work. We also did go to a movie, and that's all."

Cody wants to know why she would do that when she knows it would make Dad so mad. This is now a talk that might be too difficult for Darlene to really help her eleven year old understand. She tries her best to make plain but to no avail. At this point Darlene apologizes to Cody, though she's not exactly sure why. "If I upset you, I'm so sorry," she tells him. "I would never want to do anything that would hurt you or your brother or sister."

"Are you going to say you're sorry to Dad, too?" Cody would like to know.

Darlene changes her tone when answering that one. "That's adult talk. That's between me and your father. But I don't want you worrying about it, okay? I will work things out with your dad. Don't you worry about it."

Cody only has one more thing to add, but it's a doozy. "Are you going to go out to dinner and a movie with this other man anymore?"

Darlene pauses to come up with the right response. She isn't one to ever lie to her kids. On the other hand, she doesn't want to make a promise that she isn't sure she can keep. She pulls Cody close and squeezes him up against herself. She can't believe how big he is suddenly getting. Darlene tousles his hair as she deliberately looks him straight in the eyes. "I don't know. But, Cody, honey, I won't do anything else until your dad and I work things out, okay?"

Cody looks pleased. He seems happy to hear what he thinks she just said to him. He wants nothing more in the world than Dad back at home. To Cody, Mom and Dad figuring things out, has to be a good thing.

Darlene sends him off to go play something with his brother and sister. Now what about Rose? Should she confront her about this phone call to John or not? Darlene isn't sure. She needs Rose to watch the kids while she is at work. Darlene knows how wonderful Rose is with her grandkids. She decides to let it go for now and not let Rose know that she knows about the call to John. But then what to do about Mike Stillman? Darlene will spend much of the rest of the night tossing and turning unable to sleep, contemplating that one.

———⊲⊳⊲⊳———

"I THINK I'M DONE, DUDE," AUDIE SAYS TO HIMSELF AND to his brother. "I can't drive anymore."

The Barrett brothers have been going all night and are now just a few hours from New Orleans on their journey to Miami. With John's injuries, Audie has done all the driving and now it's morning. He's ready to let his head hit a soft pillow as soon as possible.

John has at least gotten a few winks, maybe actually a little more than that through the night as his kid brother drove. "You did good Audie. I think we both need to catch some z's."

"There's a little town coming up soon called New Ibera. I say we stop there and get a motel room and sleep for a while," Audie suggests.

John agrees, and they book a small motel room with a couple of beds. Not the heat of summer or the bright sunlight that comes with it, stop the guys from falling off into a deep sleep as soon as their tired bodies hit the slightly too firm mattresses.

Audie is the first to wake up. He's startled to see when he checks his cell that's it's nearly four-thirty in the afternoon. Audie considers stirring his brother from his rest but then thinks better of it. After all John's been through the last few days, he'll just let him sleep. Audie Googles on his phone and finds a café nearby within walking distance of their motel. All the driving in the last twenty-four hours has built up a pretty good appetite in him, and he's doesn't feel like waiting around to see when John is going to wake up before getting something to satisfy his cravings. So he leaves his brother a note on the bedside table, runs a comb through his hair, and takes a swig of a small bottle of mouthwash he brought with him on the trip. Then he's out the door, hoofing it for his next meal.

⸎

ONCE INSIDE THE SMALL, QUAINT, WOODSY COFFEE SHOP, Audie finds himself a booth in the corner and seats himself. The coffee shop is mostly empty with just one young couple occupying a booth on the opposite end of the place from Audie and a small group of old timers spewing their thoughts on politics and the news of the day at the café's bar. A waitress quickly comes over and takes his order for a cheeseburger and fries. Audie waits quietly for his food to arrive. He spots an old-fashioned juke box by the hallway that leads to the bathrooms and goes to check it out. Predictably, it's filled with lots of country music, which disgusts Audie, but some classic rock tunes as well. He digs for some quarters inside his pockets and makes his request. "'Lay Down Sally'" sounds good right about now. When the song comes on, it's like sweet relief to his mind and spirit.

When the front door opens next, the cowbell attached to it lets everyone in the place know someone has entered. Audie looks up to see a stunning blonde in denim short-shorts coming his way. She's heading for the bathroom but has to comment on his great taste in music as she passes by. For a second, Audie is frozen in time. The woman messes up his thoughts. Now what was I doing, he thinks to himself. Oh yeah, he remembers as he goes back to his booth and sits down.

By now Audie's food is served, but before he can take his first bite, his attention is diverted as the woman exits the bathroom hallway and sits at the restaurant's bar, not far from the old men. She turns to look over in Audie's direction and offers him a big smile. Man, she has white teeth and lots of them, Audie wisecracks to himself. He fumbles to return her warmth with his own but only gives back a goofy grin. In a moment she looks again, smiles again, but this time she does even more, she gets up and walks over to him. A lump forms in his throat. Audie only hopes that she isn't a hooker. "Please don't let her be a hooker," he says under his breath.

"Would you like some company?" she asks.

Oh, god she is a hooker, damn it, he thinks.

"I know, I for one really don't like to eat alone, how about you?"

Audie can't resist. He directs her right into the booth, and she sits across from him.

"You're staying at the same motel as I am, the one right around the corner, right?"

"Oh, yes," he answers, feeling sweat beading up on his forehead from his nervousness.

"You must be like me, traveling somewhere?" she follows up with.

She can't be a hooker if she's staying in the same motel as me and John, Audie considers. Could she actually be this hot and be interested in me, a complete stranger? "My brother and I are driving to Miami."

"Really," she responds with excitement. "I'm trying to get to Nashville where my uncle is going to record my music for me and help me get my foot in the door."

"You're a singer then?" Audie guesses.

"I am hoping to make a career of it too. That's why I'm heading to Nashville," she goes on to detail.

The waitress spots the woman's change of seat and brings her food over to her. Both Audie and the girl laugh together when they realize they ordered the exact same thing. The woman realizes she hasn't even formally introduced herself, so she does. "I'm sorry. I'm so impolite. My name is Kitty, Kitty Colbert."

Audie shakes her outstretched hand and then comments on her name. "Like in 'Gunsmoke'?"

Kitty laughs at the connection that is already familiar to her. "Exactly, my grandfather was a big fan of the old show, and my mom gave me the name to make him happy."

Audie has to remark on how coincidental that is since that was also his dad's favorite all-time show and supposedly their grandfather's as well. "My brother John and I were named after John Wayne and Audie Murphy, so I get where you are coming from with your story."

"Wow! That is so weird! And they don't even hardly make western movies or television shows anymore, you know?" Kitty states.

"No, not much anymore," Audie agrees. "So you're into country music then, I'm assuming, since you're going to Nashville?"

"That's right," she answers. "You listen to country, Audie is it?"

Moral compass time, Audie debates inside his brain. He can tell her the truth and possibly throw water on this electricity they have between them, or he can lie and tell her he actually doesn't hate "'hick'" music as he calls it. Since lying has always come too easy for Audie, he chooses the latter. "Yeah, Johnny and I like it a lot, country music that is."

"That's awesome! I knew you had good taste when I heard you playing 'Lay Down Sally.' That's such a great song," she praises him.

Kitty then reveals the real reason for her sit down. "Are you and your brother in a real hurry to get to Miami?"

The question comes out of left field and makes Audie have to think for a moment before answering. "Pretty much I guess, why?"

"Well, it's just that I'm actually hitchhiking, all the way from Utah. I was wondering if you and your brother could be kind enough to take a small detour and drop me off in Nashville, on your way to Miami. I would pay you for it of course, your gas and food."

Audie again has to think hard before opening his mouth. First of all he has no idea where Nashville is in relation to here or how out of the way it is as far as driving to Miami is concerned. Kitty fills in those details for him. Her details aren't good news. It's about eight hours in the wrong direction from where they are right now. And then Nashville to Miami is about another fourteen hours or so, the other direction.

Kitty looks at him, waiting for his answer like a kid waiting for their first present on Christmas morning. Audie is stuck between really wanting to make her happy and say yes, and then having to defend to John why in God's name he said yes. John would probably never go for it in a million years anyways. Audie says the only thing he can that doesn't crush her hopes right now. He wants to allow them to enjoy the meal, while not promising something he can't deliver. "I'm all for it. But it's up to my brother, we'll have to see what he says."

"Well, I'm not worrying then!" Kitty proclaims with enthusiasm. "If your brother is anything like you, Audie, I'm sure he'll say yes!"

Audie just grins at her confidence and takes another bite. He only wishes he shared it.

AFTER MORE THAN AN HOUR OF TALKING, AND WITH their meal over, Audie walks Kitty back to her motel room. He tells her to give him a few minutes to talk to his brother. He'll ask John about a trip diversion to Nashville. Kitty excitedly thanks him for all he's doing and says she'll be anxiously waiting to hear what his brother has to say. Audie for one isn't so anxious.

When he gets back to his room, he knocks quietly twice on the door before entering. He finds John fresh out of doing a half-ass job of cleaning himself around his bandages in the bathroom sink. "I read your note. You've already eaten, I guess?"

Audie confesses he has, but he also reveals to John that he met someone at the coffee shop who's staying in the same motel. John barely listening, talks about what he wants to eat since Audie already has. Audie again begins the story about the woman he just met at the restaurant. After his second telling, John asks what he's talking about.

"She's a singer, and she's going to record music with her uncle. Hell, she might turn out to be a big star or something."

John looks at his brother with a stare that says he's less than interested. In fact, John assumes he knows why Audie is sharing all this with him. "She must be pretty good-looking?"

Audie gets self-righteously indignant at the accusation that his motives aren't pure and honest. "Her looks or whatever, man, have nothing to do with anything, dude," Audie says back.

"Right," John replies with a chuckle.

"Whatever, she's hitchhiking all the way from Utah, and she just needs a lift to Nashville and I thought…"

John cuts him off right there. "Wait, you didn't promise her that we would take her…"

Now it's Audie's turn to do the cutting off. "No! Who do you think I am, man? I told her I would run it past you, and you're a good-hearted guy and all."

John wants to know how far Nashville is from here in Southern Louisiana, and just how far out of their way it would be. Audie quotes the numbers right away off the top of his head. They don't help his case with John.

"Eight hours! That's not a little out of our way, Audie. That's like half a day!"

Audie tries to pander to his brother's softer side. "What's eight hours more, and it would be really cool to see Nashville."

"Why?" John wants to know. "You hate country music."

John's got him on that one, even Audie has to admit, searching for a comeback. "It's more than just music, it's the history of the place."

John just shakes his head, irritated. He again comments that she must be a real beauty. But Audie argues that's it's the right thing to do and that's his motive, nothing more, nothing less. John actually takes a minute to consider. Audie is almost waiting for smoke to come from his ears at any time. Then to Audie's surprise, John says okay. "What the hell, we've come this far. But she sits in the backseat, not in my seat."

"Absolutely," Audie responds with delight. "You order some food for yourself at one of the nearby restaurants, and I'll pick it up for you."

John still shaking his head reaches for his phone to find out what's available to eat in a small town like this.

"I'll be right back, man," Audie tells him as he leaves their room and scoots down to Kitty's.

She hears him coming to her door and lets him in. She is more than thrilled by Audie's news and leaps into his arms almost by instinct. She apologizes as she breaks his embrace. "Sorry about that. I'm just kind of emotional and don't always think before I act, you know."

Audie tells her it's no problem at all as they enjoy an awkward moment.

"When are we leaving?" Kitty is eager to know.

Audie and John didn't actually discuss that, but knowing his brother, if it's not tonight, which it doesn't look like it will be, it will be early tomorrow morning for sure. "How about six in the morning. Is that too early?"

"Not at all," Kitty answers. "I always get up early."

"Then it's a date, so to speak," Audie concludes, nervous with his choice of words, not trying to be forward with her.

"It's a date," Kitty agrees as she grabs both of his hands and shakes them.

That lump reappears in Audie's throat, and he can physically feel his heart beating faster as they are both standing there, hand in hand. As the second awkward moment passes, Kitty releases her grip and calls out for both of them to remember that they need to get some sleep, since they have to get up so early the next morning. This is her way of saying goodnight, see you in the morning, but Audie, hoping and wishing to stay a little longer, needs stronger directions.

"Goodnight then, Audie," she whispers like vapor in the air.

It hangs in the atmosphere for a second and then falls like rain. When it hits Audie, he finally breaks out of his little trance and excuses himself. "In the morning then," he declares as he leaves her room and heads back to his own.

"He's cute," Kitty says to herself as she closes the door behind him.

Audie isn't skipping back to his room, but he's darn close.

DARLENE CAUGHT A CLOSING SHIFT AT THE CAFÉ AND IS wiping down tables and putting things away for the night. The café closes in about twenty minutes and has been basically dead for the last two hours. Lorinda, who is filling in for one of the other waitresses, who called in sick, is helping her get ready for closing. Darlene has been debating in her own mind since yesterday about Mike Stillman. Her talk with Cody has been heavy on her heart, and she's been waiting for the right time to discuss it with Lorinda, about the only person in her life she can talk to about this sort of thing. Now seems the perfect time as they are working side by side and there is no one in the restaurant to have nosy ears. "I haven't told you yet, but I've been really thinking about myself and John and other things."

Lorinda who is replacing ketchup bottles, looks up to give better attention to her friend. Lorinda asks Darlene if Mike Stillman is one of those other things.

Darlene looks amused by Lorinda's remark. "Maybe so," she replies.

"What's there to think about? You and Mike are having a good time so far, and no one is worse for the wear," Lorinda brings out.

"It isn't that simple," Darlene attempts to discuss. There is more than just her and Mike now involved. Lorinda knows about Darlene's mother-in-law finding out about Mike, but Darlene now discloses to her about Cody knowing and Rose speaking to John about it.

"Wow," Lorinda says when hearing all this. "Have you talked to John?"

"No, I tried, but he's not picking up his phone or returning my texts," Darlene reveals.

"Well, can you blame him," Lorinda says with little laugh that does not help the situation in the least.

Darlene gives her friend a dirty look. "Since I had my talk with Cody, this is all I've been able to think about."

"Well, darling, that is totally understandable," Lorinda responds, trying for a more helpful stance. "But you have to make yourself happy, too. You also deserve to be happy, Darlene."

Darlene understands what she is saying but thinks it's a lot more complicated than that. Darlene knows that Lorinda has never been married or had children, so living for just her own happiness probably comes a hell of a lot easier for her than it does for Darlene.

"I'm going to tell Mike I can't see him anymore, at least until I figure out things with John," Darlene declares to her new close friend.

Lorinda immediately tries to talk her out of her decision. "Honey, that's not fair to you or Mike for that matter. You two are just getting to know each other and having a good time."

"You don't understand…" Darlene interrupts only to be interrupted herself.

"Yes, actually I think I do! You're being a martyr for John and Rose and everybody else! John has had his chance all these years. Now it's your turn!" Lorinda says her voice rising with emotion and frustration.

Darlene goes for the you-don't-understand card once more but Lorinda won't listen to it. She's ticked at Darlene's decision and doesn't want to talk anymore about it, or for that matter talk much more at all tonight with Darlene. Lorinda quietly focuses on getting the café ready to close in a few minutes. When Darlene makes overtures to her, Lorinda rebuffs her. "Darling, it's your life not mine. I only know that when you get a chance to be really happy you should take it, the hell with everyone else!"

Darlene leaves her be. She can see there's no more discussing it with Lorinda tonight. All Darlene knows is that it's easy for someone like Lorinda to say the hell with everyone else, but a whole lot harder when you're a mother responsible for three young children and have been with the same man for basically your whole life. And when those kids love their father, deserving or not, decisions like this are anything but easy and your own desires are not all that are at stake. Darlene only wishes she could get Lorinda to see that. But Darlene determines in her own mind as she watches Lorinda ignore her, still upset with her, to make her own decisions, no matter what her friend thinks.

———⁂———

"SHE BETTER BE READY," JOHN LECTURES AUDIE AS HE climbs into the passenger side of his pick-up and waits for his brother to go fetch this woman he's been hearing about since last night.

Audie knocks on her motel room only once as Kitty opens the door immediately. "Oh, good. You're up," he greets her with.

She hoots at his surprise and reminds him that she told him last night that she is a morning person.

"That's right," Audie remembers. He grabs her couple of travel bags and directs her out to their truck, and to his brother, who is waiting for them. Audie is quick to introduce Kitty to him.

"Nice to meet you," John responds, forcing a manufactured smile to his lips.

Kitty says the same and tells John how thankful she is for the ride to Nashville despite the inconvenience it brings.

"Sure," is John's only comeback, and it's not the warmest comeback at that.

Kitty informs the guys that she just has to turn in her door key card with the manager and she's ready to get going. John and Audie watch as she walks to the motel office.

"Her name is Kitty?" John remarks to his brother.

"Yeah, man," Audie replies. "Just like in 'Gunsmoke', Weird isn't it man?"

"Named after Miss Kitty?"

"Yeah, by her mother to please her father, she told me," Audie details.

That is a little funny John has to admit. John also is fast to tease his brother about Kitty's looks. "You are such a sucker for a pretty girl."

"What are you talking about, dude? I am not at all that way," Audie challenges.

Audie's lame defense causes John to laugh. Then they both hush up and change the conversation as Kitty makes her way back to the truck.

"All set," she says out loud for both guys to hear, as she hops into the backseat while again thanking John for doing this for her.

AFTER ABOUT FORTY MINUTES DOWN THE ROAD, JOHN looks behind him and spots Kitty with her earbuds on listening to her phone. She sees him spying on her and pops her earbuds out. Audie is driving and has his eyes focused on the main road but hears everything being said.

"Did you say something to me, Johnny?" she asks him.

"No," he answers as he asks her to call him John.

Kitty is quick to apologize. "I'm sorry I heard Audie call you that."

John tells her it's no big deal. It's only that his mother and Audie call him that, for everyone else it's John. "Even with my wife, it's John."

Kitty says sorry again and promises to make the adjustment.

Audie just looks annoyed by his brother making such a big deal over such a trivial thing.

"Listening to some tunes, I'm guessing?" Audie interjects

to change the subject.

"I am, I hope that's okay?" Kitty demurs.

Audie, of course, tells her how great that is for killing time when you're traveling or anything else for that matter. His small talk with Kitty makes John chuckle. He's thinks Audie is being so phony.

"Any songs that I would know?" Audie continues.

"Oh, just the standard stuff, you know. I like the giants, like Toby Keith, Tim McGraw, Keith Urban, they're all such great artists."

John can't help but notice that she's talking about country music performers and the irony that this girl that his brother has the hots for loves the kind of music that Audie despises. "You're into country then," John concludes as he gives his brother a look that shows him grinning ear to ear.

"I like lots of styles, but country is probably where I am most moved and inspired. The storytelling is just so wonderful," Kitty tells John.

John then gets a wild hair up his butt and has an idea. "You know, I love country music myself. Hey, I have an idea, why don't we turn on the radio and we can all listen together to some good old country. What do you say, Audie?"

Audie sends a dirty look John's way before disguising it with an agreeable look toward Kitty. "Maybe Kitty likes her own music on her phone using her earbuds."

"No! No!" Kitty chimes in. "I think it would be great to listen to the radio with you guys. I am sure there are some great country stations in this part of the country."

"Then it's decided!" John says with glee in his voice as he searches for a station that comes in well.

"Great, just great," Audie says with sarcasm hiding like snakes in tall grass.

When John finds the perfect station he cranks it up to bother Audie even more. Willie Nelson is crooning his best, so John turns it up louder.

Kitty jumps in and softly shows off her voice to the boys. "On the road again, I just can't wait to get on the road again, the life I love is making music with my friends and I can't wait to get on the road again!"

John is quick to compliment her on her singing. Audie is equally fast to follow suit.

Kitty humbly thanks them for their kind words.

John asks her to sing some of her own songs if she has any.

"Are you sure you want to hear that?" she asks John.

John, to irritate his country-music-hating brother, insists that he does and eggs her on to sing.

Audie goes along with it. What else can he say?

"Alright then," she says as she starts to sing some of her own country songs.

For Audie, it's like nails on the proverbial chalkboard, but for John it's a whole lot of fun just watching his little brother squirm. John looks back to Kitty and tells her how glad he is that they could help her by giving her a ride to Nashville. He is enjoying annoying his brother, and this has annoyed the snot out of Audie.

She stops her singing just long enough to thank him again. Then she starts up where she left off.

"She sings like angel, doesn't she, Audie," John teases.

"She sure does," Audie agrees, giving John another dirty look.

"Only about seven-and-a-half hours to Nashville, guys," Kitty reports happily before starting her next song.

Audie only hopes she doesn't have seven-and-a-half hours of country songs in her repertoire.

CHAPTER 15

D arlene feeling a slight headache coming on, takes off from working early with her boss' blessings. All the stress from earlier is finally catching up to her as she walks through her front door. Rose is there reading a story to Darlene's daughter, Courtney. Darlene is sorry to interrupt but she does when Rose stops to ask her why she's home so early. For the last few days Darlene has had an overwhelming desire to talk to Rose about the Mike Stillman situation and Rose's phone call with John. The time has never been quite right, nor has Darlene's attitude, which she is well aware of. But maybe now after making the decision to cool things with Mike, maybe now is the time, Darlene considers. She asks Courtney to go to her bedroom to play while she talks to Nanna.

"Are you sick, dear? Is that why you got off early?"

Darlene tells her about her headache, which is still pulsating like a mother. But that's not what Darlene wants to discuss, and she lets Rose know that. "Have you spoken to John in the last few days?"

"No, dear," Rose answers unaware of what Darlene's getting at. "Have you?"

Darlene informs her that she has tried in vain to but that John won't pick up his phone or return any of her calls.

Rose has more than a strong hunch why that might be the case, but she keeps it to herself for the moment.

That is until Darlene starts pressing the question. "Why do you think he's obviously avoiding me, Rose?"

Rose shrugs; she pretends to wonder why Darlene would ask her such a thing.

"It doesn't have anything to do with something you might have said to John, does it?" Darlene presses her further.

Rose now suspects that Darlene must know about her conversation with Johnny. How she knows, Rose has no clue. Darlene asks her the same question again this time with a little more pepper sprinkled on her words.

Finally Rose breaks her silence and defends what she did. "I'm sorry, dear, but I felt my son's marriage was in peril, and I thought he needed to know that."

"Peril," Darlene squawks. "Your son's marriage Rose has been in peril for a lot longer than that. His marriage has been in peril since the moment I asked him to move out, to be exact."

Darlene's sarcasm isn't amusing to Rose, and she lets her know as much. Rose once again defends her phone call to John.

"My relationship with your son is my business, not yours, Rose." Darlene insists.

Rose, getting heated up, raises her British voice and fights against the claim.

They go around and around for a couple of minutes, both getting lathered up and on the brink of saying things they will surely be sorry for later. Darlene lets Rose in on her decision not to date or see anyone else until things are settled with John. This changes Rose's attitude instantly.

She jumps to her feet to give Darlene a big, loving, hug. Darlene has to push her away for a second and try to make her understand that this decision doesn't mean that she and John are going to be getting back together. But Rose bubbling over with joy, hears it no other way as she continues to hug Darlene. Darlene, with the stuffing being pushed out of her by Rose, just gives in and denies no more. She returns Rose's hug as tears fall down her mother-in-law's cheeks. Courtney comes back in the room and asks if Nanna can finish reading the story to her. Darlene is happy to let Rose do just that as she heads to the bathroom for some more headache meds. Darlene's headache just got a few octaves higher.

<hr />

Now only three hours out of Nashville and needing to gas up, pee, and get some food, Audie with John's urging, gets off the highway and pulls into a Denny's restaurant sitting lonely by the side of the highway. John is sore from his injuries, and all the driving the last few days has only added to his pain. Kitty can see this and rushes to help John get out of the truck in the parking lot. At first he's not sure what to think of the help, but her gentleness in offering wins him over. She gently pulls him up from under his right arm and helps him to his feet.

"Appreciate it," John whispers to her as if not wanting Audie to hear him. Kitty's face beams. She's happy to help in such situations.

"Do you need me to carry you, Johnny, ha ha?" Audie says, poking a little fun at his brother's condition.

John is not amused and grumbles under his breath, "Let's just get something to eat, alright."

After being led to their table by the hostess, all three of them waste no time rushing to the bathrooms. After five hours on the road they all feel like they are ready to burst. After the menacing calls of nature are adequately silenced, they place their respective orders and then wait for their food to arrive. Kitty is facing both of the guys in the booth and searching for topics to start a conversation with. It doesn't take her long to realize that although she has rambled on with all her reasons for going to Nashville to meet up with her uncle and record music, she hasn't asked why they are going across the states. "What's in Miami?" she asks, getting the ball rolling.

Audie first looks in John's direction to see if he's going to answer the question. When Audie sees John's in no hurry to do so, he does. "We are...well, kind of hard to explain, but we're fulfilling our father's wishes from his will by meeting all these old friends of his from across the country."

"Really?" Kitty responds with interest and curiosity. "So you're traveling across the country because of your father's will?"

Audie confirms that's right as their food shows up at their table.

"So one of your dad's friends is who you are going to see in Miami?" Kitty continues.

"That's right," Audie answers. "We have to break the news to these people we are traveling to see about our father, and then we take them fishing with us."

"Fishing with you? Is that right? Why all the fishing?" Kitty can't help but wonder.

"Well, we're not really sure, but our father loved fishing, and he fished with all the people on this list that he left us with when he died," Audie spells out some more. "That's all we know."

Kitty finds it touching that their father would want them to take one last fishing trip with his old friends. "Is Miami your last stop, or are you going on from there?"

Audie tells her about ending the journey in upstate New York where their father's remains are waiting as well as his estate's attorney.

"That's a long trip from Oregon to New York," Kitty recognizes.

John who hasn't said a word the whole time since they sat down, finally opens his mouth to agree with Kitty's observation.

Kitty asks them both about their families, how much both of them must be missing them. Audie is quick to let her know that he's single, with only his brother here and a mom back in Grants Pass, Oregon. John doesn't really open up about the subject, so Kitty asks him more directly about his "attachments."

"I'm married, but we're separated right now," he informs her.

Kitty is sorry to hear that and lets him know she hopes things work out for the best. "Marriage is really hard in this day and age," she offers as comfort to John, but he's not at all comforted.

"It must be really hard being away from then," she guesses.

John, without hesitation, confesses it is. "It's getting harder by the day to be away from my kids and my wife, although I doubt she's feeling the same way."

The disgust plastered all over John's face is enough to make Kitty leave any more discussion on the topic alone. She quickly does a one-eighty and changes the subject. She goes on about her recording session coming up in Nashville with her uncle. Audie, his mouth semi-full, garbles about how he hopes Kitty remembers him and John, when she is rich and famous.

"Amen to that," she responds with a hearty laugh that gets other diners in the place to take notice.

Kitty and the guys finish up their meals and get back in John's truck and start heading north. Tennessee is a pretty state, and all three of them are enjoying its sights as they drive to the capital of country music, Nashville.

⸙

THE VOICE ON KITTY'S GPS INSTRUCTS THEM THAT THEY have made it to their destination. Their end point is a small house with a garage door on the front of it that seems to be barely hanging on. The dark green paint on the house is peeling away in many places, and the front yard has as many weeds as it does blades of grass. Audie asks if she is sure this is the right address. She checks her letter from her uncle that she has in her pocket and confirms that it is. Audie parks the truck in the street in front of the house. The neighborhood in Nashville is certainly not as glamorous as they all thought it would be. When Kitty gets out of the truck, the guys don't, so she informs them that they are welcome to come in with her. Audie is happy to, but John decides to stay in the truck claiming his injuries feel better sitting down. Kitty buys that and lets him be while she and Audie make their way to the front door. Kitty rings the doorbell and waits. Audie asks her if she has met her uncle before.

"When I was young I met him," she says.

No one comes to open the door, so she pushes the doorbell a second time. This time they can hear someone stirring about inside. The door opens, and a middle-aged man wearing an old stained white t-shirt and a three-day beard greets them. He seems to have no idea who Kitty is.

"Uncle Ralph?" Kitty responds.

"Yes?"

"I'm Kitty, your niece. You invited me to come here and stay with you. You said you would help me with my music."

The blank stare the man is wearing on his face suddenly turns into a half smile as Kitty's words begin to register in his thought processes. "Oh yes, Kitty! You actually came," he says as if he was expecting otherwise.

Kitty happily says she did and is excited to get started. Audie, however, gets a feeling that tells him something is amiss here. He likens it to the robot in "'Lost in Space'" bellowing danger, or maybe Peter Parker's spidey sense acting up, whatever this whole situation doesn't "feel" right.

Kitty's uncle isn't inviting them in or anything. He's just blocking them at the front door. Kitty introduces Audie and asks if they can come inside. Her uncle finally breaks his silence. "Right, of course, darling. Where's my Southern manners."

When they get inside the home, they are met by clutter and downright dirtiness everywhere their eyes gaze. Audie looks at Kitty who is obviously dealing with the dual emotions of disappointment and embarrassment. She asks her uncle where his recording studio in the house is, the one he talks about in his letters. He thinks for a moment, and then says he has one of those recording do-hickeys here, in the backroom. He directs Kitty and Audie to follow him. He guides them to a small bedroom in the back of the house. "Here we go!" he says, pointing in the room.

The small room has an ancient keyboard on its stand, a

beaten-up acoustic guitar in the corner, an electric guitar that looks okay. The recording equipment looks like it was new in the early seventies. All of this is hard to focus on because of the giant brown stain that spreads across the carpet in several directions.

Kitty is speechless as she checks it all out. Her uncle seems proud of this "'music'" room of his, which is even more surprising to Audie than the equipment itself.

"I traveled all the way from Utah for this?" Kitty says with disdain.

"What do you mean, girl?" her uncle comes back with as clueless as possible, and with an accent that seems to be bouncing between a northeasterner and a southern gentleman with ease.

"Do you even really know anyone in the music industry here in Nashville?" Kitty demands.

Her uncle now is figuring out how disappointed Kitty is in what he has shown her and is getting a bit defensive. "I know lots of people, missy!"

"From where?!" Kitty blasts back.

"From my gentlemen's' club, that's where!"

Audie for the first time enters the fray. "Is that code for stripper's club?"

"No!" the uncle discloses. "I only wish we had strippers at the club, right pal," he says with a laugh and an elbow in Audie's side.

"You lied to me?" Kitty accuses.

The mere accusation angers him immensely. "Hey, nobody told you, you had to come here. So if you don't want my help, then get the heck out of here already!"

"What help?!" Kitty yells back at him. "Singing for your drunken' friends at the bar you get sloshed in."

The uncle hearing that screams for Kitty and Audie to leave his home immediately. Kitty in tears is ready to say more or yell more, but Audie grabs her by the arm and tells her it's time to leave. She falls into Audie's arms and cries on his shoulder as he walks her out of the uncle's house with the uncle following behind them, screaming at them all the way. Audie yells back and threatens the uncle if he dares to keep following them. The uncle seems to take the threat seriously as he doesn't take one step past his front door. Instead he tosses a couple more insults their way before slamming the front door behind them.

Audie helps Kitty back to the truck. Still sobbing, he opens the backseat door and guides her in. John still sitting in the front is bewildered by what's going on. John pulls himself out of the truck and grabs Audie. He escorts his brother to a hedge on the side of the uncle's home. "What happened in there?" John demands.

Audie starts to go into detail about what a disappointment everything in the house was for Kitty. This of course brings up the obvious question, now what? And that is exactly what John wants to know, and right now. Audie only wishes he had an answer. "We can't just leave her here, man," Audie pleads to his brother.

"What do you want to do, take her to Miami with us?!" John says as his frustration over the whole situation begins to boil over.

Audie thinks for a moment. He can't come up with anything else, but he won't leave her in this condition, all alone, far from home.

"What happens after Miami, we take her to New York and then back to Oregon with us?"

Audie admits to John that he isn't sure right now, but

he's not leaving Kitty stuck in Tennessee, all alone with her heart ripped out and her dreams crashing down around her.

Audie plays to John's good side; he knows it's in there somewhere. He just has to find it, like digging for gold, elusive but real.

Audie waits for his brother's decision. John hems and haws. He glances back to view Kitty battling to gain control over her emotions in the backseat of the truck.

"John, we've always complained about how Dad was such a cold-hearted bastard for leaving us like he did. We always said we would never be like that. Now we have our chance to prove it. Let's do the right thing and help her out, dude. It's the hella' right thing to do."

If this was chess, Audie just made a masterful move. He's guilted his brother into agreeing with him. As they walk back to the truck with their peace agreement in place, Kitty jumps out and meets them halfway. "You don't have to worry about me, fellas," she promises with the lines from tears still imbedded on her pretty face. "I'll be fine. I can just hitch hike back to Utah with my tail between my legs. I don't want to burden you guys anymore," she fights out, as she chokes up again with emotion.

Audie looks to his brother, waiting for him to say something. John looks back to him and sees he's waiting. "No, it's okay. We want you to go with us to Miami," John informs her.

Kitty, wiping tears from her eyes, smiles broadly at John's words. "Are you sure? You don't have to worry about me," Kitty insists.

"You are not hitch hiking all the way back to Utah," John says. "When we drive back home, will make a detour and get you back to your place."

Kitty, overwhelmed with thankfulness at John and Audie's kindness, does as she is prone to do and lets the rivers start flowing from her eyes once again. And then she hugs John with all her might, something else she is prone to do. She is definitely a toucher. John isn't and is feeling very uncomfortable with the show of affection directed at him, but lets it stand anyhow. John doesn't have the heart to do anything else but let her find comfort in his embrace.

"She's a good crier," Audie notes with a laugh.

John agrees as he pats Kitty on the back and tells this strange young woman that he has only known since this morning that everything is going to be okay.

JOHN IS SNORING AWAY IN THE FRONT PASSENGER SEAT while Kitty is staring out her backseat window. The threesome has been flying down the highways and byways at all speeds. Audie still is doing all the driving as John continues to recuperate from his Falcon Lake injuries. Audie is frankly more concerned with the wounds his brother received from one phone conversation with their mother about John's wife's shenanigans than the drug cartel bullets that found their mark.

Kitty has been talking John's ear off since they left Nashville, and like it or not, she seems to have talked him out of his pit of depression. John, sleeping for the moment, is at least conversing with them, and Audie thinks he even heard his brother laugh once or twice. Audie grins as he looks at his brother fast asleep, soaking up his brother's peacefulness. He turns toward the backseat and Kitty to announce in a quiet voice, as to not disturb John, that he is ready to call it a day.

Kitty is fine with that. She's worn out too from sitting in the car for so long.

Audie finds a small town in Georgia called Adel and decides to stop there for the night. He finds a quaint little single-level cottage motel to stay at. It's about nine o'clock when Audie checks in with the front desk and unpacks the truck. Just as Audie is ready to lock up the truck for the night, John awakes to ask where they are and what time it is. Audie helps his brother out of the truck and into their room. Audie paid for Kitty to have a room right next to theirs. It's only a matter of about fifteen minutes before there is a soft knock at John and Audie's door. John, exhausted from everything, has already turned in for the night and went right back to sawing logs and grinding teeth. Audie opens the door and finds Kitty on the other side.

"Sorry it's so late," she says.

Audie is quick to tell her it's no problem at all. Then he waits to hear what she wants.

"I noticed when we were driving into town that there is a country music nightclub a few blocks from the motel. I Googled it and found that it has live music, dancing, and serves some killer food," she informs.

Audie is still listening.

"Maybe we could go get some late dinner and check it out?"

Audie looks back at John before giving her his answer. His brother's wounds have made him extra protective of him. But for the moment, John is happily snoozing away so a little time alone with Kitty sounds like a winner to Audie. "Sure, I guess I could leave John for a little while since he's sleeping."

"Great!" Kitty responds enthusiastically. "Throw on a nicer shirt, grab your shoes, and let's get going."

Audie quickly obeys his marching orders and they head out the door.

⸙

THE HOSTESS IN THE NIGHTCLUB IS QUICK TO SUPPLY Audie and Kitty with cheap cowboy hats when they enter without them. Kitty comments that she thinks that is a great idea while Audie dreams about whose head has worn this hat before.

The band taking up most of the smallish soundstage is really rockin' for a country group, and that makes this whole experience a little easier for Audie to endure. In fact with the electric guitar solos and pounding percussions, if it wasn't for the ugly shirts, tight jeans, and cowboy lids, you might be able to close your eyes and think you were at the real thing, a rock concert.

Audie can't keep himself from tapping his feet and swaying his head to the songs between glasses of beer. He justifies his first drinks in the last few days for all he's been through. He makes a promise when the first glass is served that he'll only have two, max. He reminds himself of the promise when the third glass is served. "This is my last one!" he says loudly to Kitty over the music that makes it hard to hear anything being said.

"Don't make me stop you!" she hollers back. "You're a big boy!"

"Yeah, but I'm not the smartest boy in the world," Audie replies.

"What do you mean by that?!" Kitty asks him.

Audie has to decide in the next seconds if he wants

to disclose his issues with booze with this woman he has instantly begun to have a liking for, but has in reality only known for about a day. What the heck, he decides. He has so few people to talk to in his life. "I have to watch it."

Kitty immediately gets what he is saying and feels a pang of guilt for leading him on to drink more. "I'm really sorry. I didn't know you had a problem with it."

"It's not really a problem," Audie says with a laugh. "As my father said, I'm quite good at it!"

His making fun of himself and his own problems brings a delighted look to Kitty's face.

"Maybe you shouldn't have this third beer?"

Audie winks at her concerns. "Last one," he promises again as he takes a big gulp.

The music stops and a skinny, odd-looking western chap, supposedly manager or owner of the place, takes the stage and the mic. He gets everyone's attention by telling a few truly stupid and corny jokes. The packed club's crowd groans more than it laughs at his attempts at humor. Then the real reason for his stopping the show is revealed. He announces a live Karaoke competition taking place right now on stage. The band that they have been listening to will provide the musical back-up.

"This is perfect for you," Audie tells Kitty.

Kitty isn't so sure and doesn't seem real interested in trying. Audie eggs her on and tells her that this is good practice. "I'd love to hear you sing, I mean really sing."

The skinny mc is taking volunteers and announces he needs one more for the show. Kitty can't face the puppy dog eyes that Audie is throwing her way right now and reluctantly raises her hand. The man onstage directs her up up on stage. Kitty takes her place sitting in a chair at the back of the stage with the other contestants waiting for their chance to sing. As luck would have it, she would be the last one to perform. Each contestant gets a list of songs okayed by the band before singing. The lyrics are on a large monitor facing them at the front of the stage. Kitty studies the list searching for the right song for this moment. Then with the crowd getting more restless by the second and more buzzed as well, she finds the perfect tune. She points to it on the list and the lead guitarist in the band grins. He likes her choice.

Audie still sitting at their table is getting a little buzzed himself, now on his fourth or fifth beer, but is ready to stop at any moment. Like a teenager looking at his first center-fold, he's excited about the possibilities that are about to be seen. He can't wait to hear Kitty belt out a song. He rubs his sweaty palms together in anticipation.

She slowly strolls over to the mic in the middle of the stage. Audie notices some nervousness in her as she grabs the old-fashioned mic and rips it from its stand. Kitty stares at her feet with one hand on the mic and another hand patting her side as if giving herself a last minute pep talk. Now the band is itching to get going, with its instruments armed and ready to launch their musical attack on the audience. They wait for Kitty's cue to begin. The packed audience in the club starts to get restless wondering when this woman is going to do something, or if she is. Audie is starting to wonder the same thing and begins to gets nervous for her.

Kitty lifts her non mic arm up and then slams it down. This body signal is enough to tell the band to start. The powerful chorus begins, with Kitty leading the way backed by rhythmic drums that everyone in the crowd recognizes, it takes hold immediately. "'SOMEBODY'S GONNA'

HURT SOMEONE, BEFORE THE NIGHT IS THROUGH! SOMEBODY'S GONNA COME UNDONE, THERE'S NOTHING WE CAN DO!"

Before "'Heartache tonight, Heartache tonight I know'" rouses the crowd to join in, Audie is in a trance of Kitty's making. Sure the alcohol he's consumed makes it easier to enter into such a thing to be sure, but still Audie is captured and trapped by Kitty's amazing performance. Even in a country western nightclub like this, the Eagles are gold-standard stuff. For Audie the Eagles classic rock is as close to edge of where he is willing to jump into country music as he can get. No matter, who doesn't love this song that Kitty and the band behind her are belting out to an audience that's eating it up like a fat kid on Easter.

When she's done a few minutes later, she takes a moment to ravish in the crowd's reaction. Kitty begins to make her way off stage before being grabbed by the skinny mc and brought back on. Audie can see that she's spent. All her energy and every inch of musical passion went into that rollicking choice of a song. She's the exhausted runner who just showed how fast she can run. The mc doesn't waste time to bring the other contestants back on stage. He just as quickly announces what everybody in the place tonight already knows, Kitty is the winner.

She gets a check and a small trophy for her work. It looks like the kind of trophy places purchase en masse for things just like this contest. She gladly receives it and the crowd's love, at least most of them, as they stand to their feet to give her even more applause. Finally she makes it back to the table and Audie's warm congratulatory embrace that meets her. After that, they sit down, and Kitty in a flash of movement takes a huge gulp from her beer. She asserts how alive she feels at this moment. Audie isn't sure what to say to that, so he just tells her how awesome she did.

"I feel like celebrating!" she says loudly to Audie even though he's sitting right across from her.

Audie tells her she should feel that way after what she just did. He lets her know how talented she is. "You should go back to Nashville and really pursue your dream. You're incredible. You'll make it for sure."

The kind words meant to inspire seem to pass right through her without notice. "Let's go somewhere and celebrate!

Even in his state, Audie can see that Kitty is quickly joining him in stuporness. He can also see that she has made up her mind. She stands up and grabs him by the hand to escort him out of the place. As they leave, more and more folks praise her and congratulate her on her singing. Audie focusing on walking straight, barely has his wits about him, as they walk on through. When they get outside, the humid hot summer night sobers them up a tad, but only a small tad.

Thankfully they walked to the club and now can walk back to the motel or at least try. And try, Audie and Kitty are going to do. Audie realizes after all the excitement that there is one big fact that will hit him in the face like a sledgehammer, if he's not careful. Kitty asks him what he is talking about. "I'm talking about a large hibernating bear sleeping in the bed across from me in my motel room."

Kitty chuckles in response before realizing that Audie is serious. She grabs him by the arm and assures him that she will take care of everything.

KITTY AND AUDIE QUIETLY TIPTOE PAST THE ROOM JOHN is sleeping in. They hear no sound of life or movement, so they guess it's safe to pass. The full moon in Kitty's room is more than enough light for the avarice adventures she and Audie are ready to partake in. It's kind of weird for Kitty since she is the one pawing at and unbuttoning his clothes instead of the other way around. She can hear his breathing, possibly even his heartbeat racing at her every touch, but he seems reluctant to make the same effort for her. She covers his mouth forcefully with hers, her fingers rolling through his hair, grasping and demanding. Then determined to get things going forward, she grabs one of his hands and guides it to one of her bottom cheeks. This seems to be the start button he is waiting for. Audie pulls her body to his and presses her close to him. Now she can hear his heart beating like a race horse next to hers. Audie kisses her in response, passionately like she kissed him. The two of them entwined together, only half clothed, tumble into her bed. When he reaches for her pants to completely pull then off in furious fashion, Kitty's reason gains a foothold in the world of her senses. She pours as much emotional water on the fire as she can and pleads for Audie to stop everything, and that means everything.

Audie is taken aback, not sure what's wrong, if he did something wrong. He pushes himself off of her and retreats to the edge of the bed. His intoxicated brain makes him fear that somehow he forced himself onto her, and that's something he would never do to any woman. He starts throwing apologies in the air around them like Hail Mary's in a confession booth. Kitty is fast to pick up on what Audie is worrying about and lets him know in no way does she blame him for anything that's happened tonight. "I just don't think now is the time. It's too quick and all," she tries to put across.

Audie is relieved to hear it's not him that's the problem. As he works to take back control of his emotions and thoughts, he tells her it's okay. "I guess the excitement of the night and how much fun you've been to be around the last day or so, well you know, where I'm going with this, I think."

Kitty does. "All the drinking didn't help either, did it, Audie?"

"No I guess not," he has to agree with a laugh.

Kitty buttoning up her top and pulling up her pants acknowledges that she already feels close to him, and not in just a physical way, but something much deeper than that, she says as she leans toward him and thanks him for the night by giving him a kiss on the forehead. "A deposit for some time later," she murmurs.

"Better than any bank," he replies, getting red in the face.

Kitty makes the judgement that Audie probably should try to sneak back to his own motel room for the rest of the night.

Audie can see that she is resolute on this one, so he zips what needs to be zipped and buttons what needs to be buttoned.

After parting ways, Audie tiptoes back over to his room and as silently as possible, opens the front door and tiptoes in. John, who must be completely exhausted Audie thinks, stirs, but does not waken. Audie takes his top level of clothes off and climbs into his queen-size bed. Visions and hopes dance in his head as he falls asleep thinking about the last few hours and this new woman who has entered his life like a missile, destroying everything Audie thought he knew or wanted in its path.

CHAPTER 16

Lorinda and Darlene are both working the early morning shift at the café. As per usual lately, there is no banter or social words between them. Darlene has made overtures to Lorinda for several days, trying to stop the chill that has developed between them since she revealed to her friend that she was ending things, at least for now, with Mike Stillman. Darlene isn't exactly sure why this is such an affront to Lorinda. This is her life and her decision to make, not her friend's. With all she is going through, the last thing Darlene needs is Lorinda being icy to her at work.

Lorinda finds herself standing next to Darlene in the kitchen, side by side. Darlene glances her way and flashes a warm smile that she hopes Lorinda receives in the proper way. Lorinda sort of grins back. It's more of an apologetic smirk than anything else. Then she attempts to thaw the ice. "Look, I'm sorry."

"Me too," Darlene is quick to respond.

"My high and mightiness sometimes gets in the way of things, you know," Lorinda claims in an effort to account for her coldness of the last few days. "I pushed you toward Mike, and I guess I got a little bit butt-hurt when you decided to cool things with him."

Darlene reaches out and squeezes Lorinda's hand as Lorinda continues to reveal her feelings. "It's your life, not my ego that matters. I get that you have to do what's best for you and the kids, I really do."

Darlene moved by Lorinda's honest and humble words, thanks her. She knows that it is not easy for anyone to admit when they are wrong, and it's especially hard for Lorinda.

"When are you going to tell Mike?"

"Soon, you know. But I can't talk to him in the café with everyone around. And I can't talk to him over the phone, not about something like this," Darlene tries to reason out loud.

"Well, you better decide fast," Lorinda tells her.

"Why?" Darlene replies.

"Because Mike just walked in, and I'm pretty sure he's not just here for our multi-grain pancakes," Lorinda says as she pinches Darlene on the arm.

Darlene tells her friend that she might as well get this over with as she grabs a menu and heads Mike's direction.

"Hello, Mike," Darlene greets him.

"Hello, my sweet lady," he greets her back.

She asks him if he wants to sit at the bar, booth, or table. When Mike answers that the bar is fine, Darlene instead leads him to a booth in the corner of the restaurant far from the kitchen and other diners.

"What's up?" Mike says as he's redirected.

"I just need to talk to you about something, and the café really isn't the place to do it," Darlene confides in him.

Mike says he understands, but really he has no clue what she's on about.

"Maybe I could stop by your place after work today if you're not too tired from driving?" she tells him.

Mike isn't busy, he tells her, but wants to know why she can't just tell him right now what's on her mind.

Darlene looks back to the kitchen and sees both Bill the owner and Lorinda watching their conversation closely. This just reaffirms to her that they need a private place to talk.

"You're not going to tell me you don't want to see me anymore, right?" Mike begins to think. Darlene doesn't answer directly and that only throws more logs on the fire that is blazing in Mike's imagination right about now. "You can't be serious, Darlene. I thought things were going so well after our first couple of dates."

"They were, but we need to discuss some things and we need to be alone to do it, okay?" Darlene states before adding "After my shift, I'll stop by, okay?"

"Sure," Mike answers solemnly, sensing that whatever she wants to talk about with him is not a good thing.

Darlene attempts to take his breakfast order.

Mike just hands her back the menu. "I am not really hungry anymore, Darlene," he tells her like a pouting child. "I will see you after your shift." He gets up and leaves.

Darlene knows she's already hurt him, and she hasn't even gotten to the official cooling down discussion with him yet. She can see that this talk with him isn't going to be easy.

Lorinda comes over to ask her how it went. Darlene tells her it could have gone a lot better and that Mike has already figured things out. She tells Lorinda that he is already hurt and mad at her. Lorinda puts her arm around Darlene and tries her best to comfort her. "Why don't you take a short break, go in the back and take a few minutes to gather yourself."

Darlene feeling more upset by the second at Mike's reaction, does as her friend advises. Lorinda goes back to serving some of the café's patrons. One in particular was closely watching the less-than-happy exchange between Darlene and Mike and makes a comment to Lorinda. "Did she just break up with Mike Stillman?"

Lorinda says that she can't say, that it's their business not anybody else's. But the diner continues. "Just tell Darlene to be careful."

"What does that mean?" Lorinda wants to know.

The man confides to Lorinda how he's heard that Mike is not a guy who takes rejection well, if she knows what he means.

Lorinda is afraid she does, but still manages to keep it to herself. With Darlene already upset, she doesn't want to add to her friend's guilty feelings. Mike's always been a nice guy to Lorinda and she doesn't want to start anymore gossip in the café. There's already been plenty of that lately. Darlene comes out of the back, and she and Lorinda go about their usual tasks as if nothing just happened.

"How much farther before Miami?" John asks his brother.

"Just a couple of hours and we are there, man," Audie answers.

Audie turns to sneak a peek at Kitty in the backseat. She's been all that's on his mind since they left Adel, Georgia. She smiles back at him and gives him a wink like a cherry on the top of his sundae. "This next guy on Dad's list, I guess we can plan on seeing him in the morning," Audie thinks out loud.

John reluctantly agrees with his little brother's assessment. "Another city, another night in a motel. This is getting old," John discloses for Audie and Kitty to hear. "I'll be glad when this is over and I can get back to Oregon."

Audie asks John if he has spoken at all with Darlene in the last few days. John curtly says no. Audie suggests maybe he should, since it's been so long since he last talked to Darlene or the kids. John is in no mood to discuss this subject and lets Audie know as much.

Kitty, listening from the backseat, feels sorry for John, even without knowing the full story of his marital problems. She wants to talk to him about it. Maybe she could help, she thinks, but she realizes now is not the time and lets it go.

Audie slowly gets the same feeling as Kitty and stops pushing his brother to open up and confide. "Only a couple of hours and we'll be there, guys. Maybe we will get to do some ocean fishing. That would be pretty cool, Johnny."

"Yeah," John grunts mildly in response to Audie's enthusiasm.

"It would be pretty awesome, that's for sure," Audie replies before again exchanging looks with Kitty. "I'm not big into fishing, but being out on the ocean and trying to catch one of those monsters would be pretty cool."

Kitty agrees, but like Audie she can see that John is hurting and his most painful wounds are on his inside, not the ones on the outside.

Audie fixes his eyes back on the open road. Two more hours, he whispers to himself, two more hours. He and Kitty know it's going to be a long two hours with John wallowing in his misery.

Just as she promised, Darlene stops by Mike's house on the edge of Grants Pass after work. She knocks on his door and hears no response, so she tries a second time. Mike yells for her to come in. When she walks in, she finds him sitting in the middle of his living room at the edge of his brown leather couch, with four empty beer bottles resting on the end table next to him and a fairly full one in his right hand. Darlene says hi to him as she closes the front door behind her. Mike motions for her to sit anywhere she would like. She chooses a recliner on the other side of the end table from Mike.

"Go ahead then," he instructs her.

Darlene hopes he means take a seat. An uncomfortable moment takes hold as she has a hard time coming up with a starting point for what she wants to say.

"Well, go on, you came here to tell me something," he says.

He's tipsy from the booze and not acting like the man she has gotten to know recently. She asks him if everything is okay.

"Of course not!" he answers, raising his voice. "I'm about to be dumped! Why in the world would you think everything is okay?!"

Darlene tries to defuse the situation and just talk to him, but Mike is in no mood for talking. "You women are all alike. First you make a guy think he has a shot and then you just rip out his heart without giving it a second thought."

Darlene tries in vain to show that this isn't the case at all here, but Mike isn't listening. "And you know what the worst thing about all this is?"

She has no idea, but is afraid she's about to find out.

"After all my hard work charming you in the café, and then charming you on our dates, I didn't get anything in return. I didn't even get to second base, or more importantly have you get to second base with me, ha ha!" he cracks himself up with.

Darlene's heard enough and gets up to leave. She can see there will be no reasoning with him or having an adult talk at this time, maybe a few beers ago, but not now.

"Where are you going? We haven't talked about this shit yet!" he says as he jumps up and grabs Darlene by the arm and pushes her back onto his couch.

Darlene, no weak-willed female to begin with, slaps him straight across the face without giving it a thought. Mike smiling after the slap climbs on top of her and pins her down with his knees and elbows. "Finally some action!" he yells as he paws at her waitress uniform and begins to pull it down from her shoulders.

She pleads for him to stop, to let her up, but Mike seems to have no desire to do either one. He exposes her brassiere and is teasing her with tearing it right off of her chest. Then in the midst of Darlene screaming for him to stop and Mike laughing at her complaints, he sees her eyes leave his and stare behind him. Mike stops laughing long enough to look behind himself. Standing there is Lorinda. In all the commotion, Mike didn't hear her come into the house. She's wearing a look of disgust on her face. "You prick!" she yells.

Mike gets off of Darlene who scrambles for the floor. Mike turns around still smiling in his cocky manner when Lorinda hits him full face with a spray can of mace. Mike screams from the burning in his eyes and tosses out profanities in Lorinda's direction. Lorinda helps Darlene up from the floor and pushes her behind her for protection. "One more thing, Mike," Lorinda calmly says, then with all the force she has, Lorinda delivers a hard punch to Mike's chin.

Darlene puts her hands over her face and gasps with both surprise and delight. They watch as Mike falls down onto the floor. He's still crying out from the burning in his eyes when Lorinda clutches Darlene's hand and escorts her from the home. They both drive to a nearby park as

Darlene tries to regain her composure after what just happened. She holds Lorinda for all she's worth and then thanks her with tears rolling down her puffed-up red cheeks.

But Lorinda just apologizes to Darlene. "I should have never talked you into going out with him. It's my fault what just happened."

"No!" Darlene responds. "You just saved me!"

Lorinda dismisses the saving and is still dwelling on her putting Darlene with Mike in the first place.

"You couldn't have known he was like that. I didn't know he was like, and I went out with him," Darlene confesses to her friend.

Lorinda tears up herself a bit as she thanks Darlene for not holding her responsible for what happened with Mike. "You have to call the police on that son-of-a-bitch!"

"Oh, I will, don't worry about that. And soon as I get home, I'll file a report against his ass," Darlene promises.

Lorinda is relieved to hear it but considers where this leaves her friend. "Are you going to tell John what just happened?"

"I don't know," Darlene answers. "John would kill him if he knew."

"Then do me a favor and please tell John all about this," Lorinda says with a laugh.

That brings an amused look to Darlene as she starts to laugh herself.

"Now what?" Lorinda then asks.

Darlene wonders what she means.

"About John, about men, now what?" Lorinda is interested to hear.

Darlene shakes her head wearing a silly look that doesn't reflect what she just endured. "I have no idea really, but when Mike was holding me down on his couch all I could think of was how I wanted John to come walking in that room, right at that moment."

"Really," Lorinda replies.

"Yeah, I know it's not a politically correct thing to say, but that's what I was thinking. I guess after all these years and even after all we've been through, I still need him," Darlene confesses.

"And I'm sure he still he needs you, too," Lorinda says, as she reaches out and squeezes Darlene's hand.

"That I don't know," Darlene whispers with sadness in her voice. "I guess I will find out soon enough. Right now I'm pretty sure he hates me."

Children running for the monkey bars sprint past them both, as Lorinda gives Darlene another hug and lets her cry some more on her shoulder.

───✦───

ANY THOUGHTS FROM AUDIE THAT HE MIGHT GET A repeat performance with Kitty like the night before, end early, as he, John, and Kitty, are all worn down from traveling when they discover a motel in Miami to stay at. All of them go straight to bed after checking in and are soon out for the count.

The next morning, John is reading Kitty the address for the next person on the list, as she speaks it into her phones GPS. The GPS lady, as Audie likes to call her, guides them street by street through Miami and to their next address. When they arrive, they find a bar and grill near the ocean front, a place called the Pineapple Cove.

"So this is it?" John asks Kitty.

Kitty confirms it is, as the three of them get out and make their way into the place. Like the parking lot they just walked through, the bar and grill is mostly empty. A few people wearing flowered shirts seem to work there because they are cleaning and organizing things both behind the large bar area and in the restaurant. One of the employees takes his eyes off his work long enough to spot the three visitors. "Sorry, we're not open for another hour-and-a-half folks."

Audie and Kitty are at first tempted to wait, but not John. He's ready for this big adventure to end. "We've come a long ways to speak with Mr. Ricci," he tells the man behind the bar.

The man doesn't respond to the request, he doesn't even blink. "He's not here, sorry."

Before John can say another word, Kitty jumps in on a hunch. She can see that there is an upstairs up above the bar and reasons that there are probably offices up there. Maybe she thinks, for this Mr. Ricci guy. A twisting old wooden staircase leads to them. "If Mr. Ricci does happen to be here and found out that you didn't even tell him about these two men being here to see him, and you didn't let Mr. Ricci know, he might be pretty upset."

The employee considers Kitty's words and then asks their names.

"It's not our names that will mean something to Mr. Ricci but our father's," John offers. "Our father was a friend of Mr. Ricci's. His name was Raymond Barrett."

The man repeats the name trying to make sure he can remember it. Then he starts up the stairs.

"He's here," Kitty concludes as they watch the man quickly walk up the stairs.

"How do you know?" Audie asks her.

"Because he didn't write Dad's name down. He didn't have to. He knew he would be repeating it to Mr. Ricci as soon as he got to the top of those stairs," John answers, interrupting and taking the worlds right out of Kitty's mouth.

Kitty grins and signals her agreement with everything John just said.

It's only a moment or two later that the man reappears from the top of the stairs and with a much more friendly manner, asks the three of them to follow him up. When they get upstairs the man leads them to a closed door in the corner and after one short knock, opens the door.

John, Audie, and Kitty are led into the room where they find a rotund man sitting at a cherry oak desk with two younger and well-dressed men standing on each side of him. The older fella behind the desk greets them with a "how ya' doin'?" "Raymond Barrett, I haven't heard that name in a long time. And my employee here says you are his kids?"

"They are, sir," Kitty is quick to respond. "I'm just with them."

"You are Ray's sons then?"

John speaking for both himself and Audie says they are.

"Well how is Ray, anyhow?" Mr. Ricci continues.

For both John and Audie this has been the thing they have dreaded at each stop along the way, the moment they share the news of their father's passing.

"He's been better, sir," Audie blurts out without even a smattering of sarcasm.

Mr. Ricci then wants to know what's wrong with him.

"I'm afraid we are here to let you know that our father, Raymond Barrett, is dead," John says directly to Mr. Ricci as if he had rehearsed saying the line all night.

A smile leaves Mr. Ricci's face as he takes in John's words. He can't believe the news about his old friend. "How did it happen?"

The guys tell him that they aren't even completely sure themselves, that they'll find out when they meet with the attorney to the estate, in a few days.

Mr. Ricci gulps down some orange juice from a glass on his desk as he consumes the news. "So you came here to tell me that your dad has passed. I got to say since I haven't seen or heard from Ray in many years, this is shocking news."

Audie begins to disclose about their father's estate and his letter's instructions.

"And I am supposed to take you out fishing? Sounds like Ray," Mr. Ricci says sounding just a bit irritated all of a sudden. "Did your father have anything else for me, maybe?"

"No, I don't think so," John responds.

But Audie remembers the gifts in the backpack and mentions it to Mr. Ricci.

Mr. Ricci is quick to notice no backpack on any of their persons. "So where is this backpack?"

"I must have left it in the truck," Audie confesses.

"Well go get it!" Mr. Ricci shouts before realizing how unkind he is sounding. "Your pop may have left me something very important in that bag, boy."

Audie says okay and heads downstairs and to the parking lot to go get the backpack. Kitty accompanies him, while

John waits in the office with Mr. Ricci.

Audie fumbles for the truck keys while Kitty watches him. Suddenly Audie feels something digging into his side and a person next to him. Kitty is fast to feel the same thing as someone grabs her from behind and muffles her mouth with one of his large hands.

"Hello, kid, how's it hanging for you?"

Audie looks behind in disbelief. "You guys again? Come on dude, all the way to Miami!"

"I never give up kid," Capriati's thug from Vegas, Harry informs Audie. "Now I have a proposition for you."

"What's that?" Audie asks him, in no position to say no.

Harry then makes it plain. "If you don't put up a fight and come peacefully with us right, now, we'll let your little girlfriend go, no harm no foul. What do you say?"

Audie looks at Kitty and sees fear in her eyes. He agrees to the bargain.

"Let's go then, kid," Harry says as he escorts him to their sedan. "Let her go, Bob."

"It's your lucky day, lady, after what you did to our tire before," Bob says as he releases her arms and takes his hand from her mouth.

Kitty watches for a few seconds as they escort Audie away. Then she begins to scream "help" with all her might. John and Mr. Ricci hear her all the way from his office and hurry outside to the parking lot to see what's happening. With John's injuries and Mr. Ricci's weight, it's actually more of a slow jog out to the parking lot.

"What's going on?!" Mr. Ricci demands to know. "Where's the other boy?!" he asks, referring to Audie.

Kitty tells him and John what just happened, and John knows immediately who it is.

"What about the backpack, the gift for me?" Mr. Ricci wants to know.

Kitty lies to him and tells him that Audie has it with him right now, that he grabbed it right before the men took him away.

Mr. Ricci is furious, and even more so when he finds out from John that the guys who nabbed Audie are a couple of wise guys from Vegas. "On my turf? Nobody dares to disrespect me on my turf!"

John and Kitty exchange looks of realization as they just begin to understand that Mr. Ricci, John's father's friend or not, has a lot in common with the guys chasing them all the way from Nevada.

"Don't you two worry about this. I'll have your brother and that backpack here in no time. I just have to make some calls, that's all," Mr. Ricci promises confidently.

Kitty, worried about Audie, falls into John's arms as they wait for Mr. Ricci to make his calls from his office. This is the second time for John to hold a woman in his arms again. It's been awhile since he's held Darlene like this.

"Should we call the police?" Kitty asks him, looking up from his chest.

"I don't know," John tells her. "I think we should give this guy, Ricci a chance first, maybe. It sounds like he's a big wig down here, you know."

Kitty like John isn't sure, but she decides to see what Mr. Ricci can do to help first.

John still has Kitty wrapped around him and is getting uncomfortable with it. He pries her away from his chest. "Don't worry, I'll get my brother back," he tells her. "If they make it out of Miami, I know where there heading."

Before he can say another reassuring word to Kitty,

John is cut off by Mr. Ricci coming back out. "Some of my boys have spotted the car heading for the interstate. They're going to stop the car and hold everybody there until we get there. We'll deal with this mess your brother got himself into when we get there. Now shall we?" Mr. Ricci says as his own black SUV pulls up and he invites John and Kitty into the backseat with him.

⸺⸙⸺

"TRAFFIC IS THICK OUT HERE," BOB STATES AS HE DRIVES toward the onramp to the nearest interstate.

Harry is sitting behind him in the backseat with his pistol digging into the ribs of Audie Barrett.

"I can't believe you guys came all the way to Florida for me," Audie says. "Capriati must really want his dough bad."

"Listen, I would have pursued you asshole to the gates of hell if that is what it took," Harry barks.

"All I can say is he must pay you a lot of money for such loyalty," Audie wisecracks.

Bob from the front seat mentions it could be more, the pay that is. Harry is quick to shut his partner up. "You never mind," he says. "With you, punk, I would have done this for free, especially after all we have been through just to get a hold of you."

Audie isn't sure what they mean but apologizes anyways for any inconvenience he might have caused them. Harry tells him to shut up, and his partner Bob, when he starts to talk about a bonus for all their hard work. "Just drive, Bob, okay? Leave the thinking to me. It's not your strong suit."

"Bam!"

The car swerves from the impact of another car smacking it from the side.

FISHING *for* SOMETHING   283

"What the hell was that?!" Harry yells from the backseat.

"This car came out of nowhere and hit us, Harry," Bob hollers as he regains control of the steering of the vehicle once again.

"Just keep your eyes on the road and get us on the freeway coming up here in a second," Harry orders.

Another car bumps them from behind, causing all three men to lunge forward in their seats.

"What the hell is going on here?!" Harry bellows. "Are these guys friends of yours?"

Audie shakes his head in response. "Search me, man. I don't know anybody around here, I swear."

Now a harder bump from behind is followed by another side swipe on the driver's side, which causes Bob to lose control of the vehicle again. He is able to stabilize it only long enough to see the car hit again from both sides and then forced off to the side of the road only a mile from the interstate's onramp. Their car is surrounded almost immediately, as they struggle to understand what's going on. A third and fourth vehicle show up on the scene to make sure that Harry and Bob aren't going anywhere.

"I don't like this, Harry!" Bob says, stating the obvious.

"This isn't a dream come true for me either, idiot!" Harry hollers back.

Then a voice comes from the outside demanding that Harry and Bob release Audie and step out of the car.

"Do they have any idea who they are screwing with here?!" Harry yells, hoping they can hear him from inside the sedan.

Harry grabs Audie by the arm, and with his gun still pressing against Audie's side, he directs him out of the car. They are met by about twelve guns pointing directly at them.

Bob still sitting in the front seat wets his pants a little from the sight.

One of the men, the one whose voice they heard, does the talking and demands that Harry drops his weapon immediately.

"Look, I don't know who you guys are, but you're making a huge mistake here," Harry says. "If you knew who I was working for, you wouldn't be doing this shit to me right now."

"And if you knew who we work for, you would be dropping your gun and begging for mercy," one of the other men responds.

"Oh God! oh God!" Bob whispers to himself, still nestled in the front seat. "This is just like the end of '"Butch Cassidy and the Sundance Kid.'"

"Drop your firearm, and we may show you some professional courtesy and let you walk away," the man doing most of the talking on the other side tells Harry.

"Screw you! You make any move on me and this kid here gets it! You got it?!" Harry guarantees, acting tough, even as the Florinda sun begins to make him feel a bit woozy.

The stand-off goes on. Finally another vehicle shows up on the scene, and three more heavily-armed men show up accompanied by Mr. Ricci, John, and Kitty.

"Who are you guys?" Mr. Ricci demands to know from Harry.

"It's none of your damn business!" Harry shouts back at him.

John asks his brother if he is alright. Audie tells him he's okay, at least for the moment.

Mr. Ricci approaches the discussion from another angle. "Do you know who I am, dumb-shit?"

"Should I?" Harry responds sarcastically, but still scared to hear the answer.

"Only if you want live for more than a few hours, schmuck," Mr. Ricci retorts. "I am Sonny Ricci, and this is my domain, so to speak. Nothing goes on around this area without me knowing about it and okaying it, got it?"

"You're Sonny Ricci?" Harry responds. "The Sonny Ricci that controls most of the southeast seaboard?"

"In the flesh, partner," Mr. Ricci answers. "Which, you won't be for long if you don't let the kid go and drop your guns."

Harry looks to his partner Bob, still paralyzed in the front seat, before he pleads ignorance to realizing who he is up against. "Me and Bob are just following orders, Mr. Ricci, that's all."

"Who you working for?" Mr. Ricci wants to know.

Harry in quivering voice tells them about Capriati, their boss. He still has his gun in Audie's side without even realizing it.

Mr. Ricci howls with laughter at the mere mention of the name. "That small-time clown! You work for that mental midget! Ha!"

The heat now is really beating down on him, Harry chuckles along with Mr. Ricci, hoping to live more than a few more minutes.

"And you followed this kid here all the way from Nevada on orders from Capriati, the schmuck?"

Harry nods to Mr. Ricci, while shaking in his shoes.

"That's pretty impressive. You fellas want to graduate to the big leagues and come work for a real boss?" Mr. Ricci surprises Harry with.

Since the choices seem to be death or a job change,

Harry thinks it's great idea. He yells to his partner Bob who agrees that it's a fine plan indeed. Bob finally gets out of the car, knees shaking and all, and walks over and stands next to Harry.

"Then it's settled. You boys will come and work for me! That is if you can do one more thing?" Mr. Ricci asks.

Harry and Bob glad to not be fed to the gators, say "anything."

Then Mr. Ricci mentions the gun Harry is still sticking in Audie's ribs.

"Oh, sorry about that," Harry says as he drops his gun to the ground and lets Audie go.

Mr. Ricci immediately tells him to pick it up and put it back in its holster.

Kitty, and then John, both rush to Audie's side. "You alright?" John asks him.

"Still in one piece, man," Audie responds with thankfulness.

"I'm so glad," Kitty says as she holds his hand in hers.

"Now, the matter about this gift from your pop to me," Mr. Ricci asks Audie.

Audie informs him that it's still in the backpack in John's truck back at the Pineapple Cove.

"What?" Mr. Ricci says as he turns to Kitty.

She looks back at him knowing exactly what he is thinking. She then sort of apologizes. "I assumed that you wouldn't go after Audie if he didn't have what you were looking for. I'm sorry, Mr. Ricci."

Mr. Ricci thinks about it for a moment without uttering a word. Then he says, "You played it well, young lady. Now let's go back and grab this magical backpack and get some fishing in. You boys ever ocean fish?"

"A few times back in Oregon, sir," John muses.

"Oregon," Mr. Ricci says derisively. "This is Florida fishing, the best in the world, and today we do it in the memory of Raymond Barrett my old friend, even if he does still owe me twenty thousand dollars."

John and Audie look at each other after hearing that. They wonder why this man is even on the list if their father owes him all that money. But they are not about to bicker with the offer, that's for sure.

"How about you two?" Mr. Ricci asks of Harry and Bob. "You wise guys have the sea in your blood?"

"Whatever you say Mr. Ricci," Harry replies.

Bob repeats what his partner just said.

"Then it's settled, a fishing we will go everybody, a fishing we will go!" Mr. Ricci declares to all his men, and his guests.

CHAPTER 17

The ocean spray feels great as it washes away some of Miami's sticky humidity. Blue sky and bluer ocean welcome John, Audie, and Kitty as they enjoy the pampering from Mr. Ricci's insanely large fishing boat crew. Mr. Ricci has his staff waiting on them for their every need, even some that they don't need. The neck messages that Audie and Kitty got were especially, unexpectedly pleasant. Even Harry and Bob, who have officially decided to quit their jobs with Mr. Capriati in Las Vegas and stay here instead, seem to be enjoying themselves, cruising away from the Florida Coast.

"What am I supposed to tell my gal back in Vegas?" Bob asks Harry.

"Tell her she can come out here and be with you, or not. There's plenty of gorgeous babes out here, Bobby, my man," Harry tells him.

"What about Capriati? He's going to want our heads on a platter for not bringing back idiot boy over there," Bob contends, still worried.

"Don't worry about that. Capriati can't touch us along as we're working for Mr. Ricci here. Ricci's a way bigger fish in the pond than Capriati, and Capriati will understand that and not dare to mess with us, pal," Harry confidently says trying to calm his partners concerns.

"You sure, Harry?"

"No doubt, pal. Now enjoy this beautiful day and shut-up already," Harry orders him.

Mr. Ricci who has been inside the boat's captain's quarters since they left the marina, finally makes an appearance. He pulls up a seat next to Kitty and the guys. "Another mile and we'll set everything up and get some fishing in."

"That sounds awesome, Mr. Ricci," Audie says enthusiastically, although still unsure of his fishing savvy.

"Good to hear, kid, but you guys can call me Sonny, just like your dad did. I grew up with your dad, so you guys are almost like family to me."

Then Mr. Ricci, or Sonny as he wants to now be called, asks Audie if maybe now is the time for the backpack reveal.

Audie isn't really clear want he means, but John steps in to clarify. "He wants to see what Dad left him, that's all."

"Oh," Audie replies as he opens up the backpack sitting between his feet and searches for the item meant for Sonny Ricci. When he finds it, he hands it to Sonny without hesitation.

Sonny opens it up like it's his birthday. Inside is a lump of rubber-banded money, twenty thousand to be exact. Also included with the money is a letter for Sonny. He smiles at the sight of Ray Barrett's debt paid and begins to read the letter silently to himself.

Audie whispers to his brother John. "We had twenty thousand dollars in that backpack the whole time," he moans in disbelief.

"Seems to be the case," John whispers back.

"It's only money, guys," Kitty interjects, which makes both John and Audie look at her like she's from another planet or something.

Then Sonny grabs everyone's attention by announcing loudly how great a man Ray Barrett really was. "It's not enough that your old man pays off his debt to me, and from his grave at that. No, that's not enough, then he leaves me this beautiful letter. I wish to read this to you boys, if you let me do so."

John and Audie, of course, agree to his request immediately.

Sonny takes out his reading glasses, making sure to not get a single word wrong. "Hey, Sonny boy, how you doing? Your pop used to call me that all the way back to when we were kids; he's the only one who ever did. I'm so sorry it took so long but here is all the money I owe you. I hope we can let bygones be bygones. What a guy," Sonny trumpets as he pauses to get a sip of something from a tall glass before continuing. "At my death, I willed my sons who you are with right now to pay you back in full all the money I took from you, to my shame, many years ago. I'm sorry for screwing up our friendship over money and greed, but I hope this makes amends. Sonny boy, you are like family to me and you always have been. An as family I ask you to take care of my boys and let nothing happen to them. At my deathbed it was time to make things right with everyone in my past. So sorry, old friend, my best to you, and tell my boys I love them, Raymond Barrett."

Sonny tears up as he puts the letter down onto a table. "Wasn't that beautiful?"

"Nice, our dad actually wrote that?" Audie responds.

"What he said Sonny, what he said," John echo's sarcastically.

"It's time to celebrate, me getting my money back from your pop, and your father's memory," Sonny shouts for all aboard. "Now we celebrate Ray Barrett style!"

"What exactly would that be, Sonny?" Audie would like to know.

"Why fishing and drinking, my boys, and lady friend," Sonny answers with gusto.

Sonny has one of his girls working for him come over and take orders for drinks. John just asks for water, maybe some lemon in it. Kitty gets a Diet Coke. And then it's Audie's turn. John is closely watching what his brother will do, once again. "What my brother's having, that sounds good to me to," Audie says.

John praises him for his will power.

"What in high heaven are you three doing?! Two waters and a Diet Coke, what do you call that?!" Sonny jokes. "That is definitely not celebrating like your old man would!"

Audie is about to spell out his battle with the bottle when John steps in. "Sonny I'm afraid there is a Barrett family tradition you are probably not as familiar with as we are."

Sonny asks John what it is he's talking about.

"It's called alcoholism," John answers glibly.

"Fair enough," Sonny answers. "We still got fishing, am I right? How about you new fella's, You up for some fishing?"

Harry and Bob answer the affirmative because as of now, their lives are based on their job security. What Mr. Ricci wants, Mr. Ricci gets in their book.

Kitty inquires of Sonny what kinds of fish they would be going after.

"Oh, there's a lot in these waters, tuna, swordfish, mahi-mahi, and many more. And all these fish are fighters, my boys," he says, looking in John and Audie's direction. "So get ready to be strapped down and bullied. This fishing is Florida style, and the fun is about to begin!"

⤝⤞

D**ARLENE FINDS HERSELF STANDING NEXT TO** R**OSE IN** the kitchen. Rose is finishing up some dishes by hand while Darlene makes her lunch for tomorrow. Rose knows nothing about what Darlene went through the day before with Mike Stillman, and Darlene wants to keep it that way. She called the police on him and already went down to the station to tell her side of the case, but Mike is saying that she attacked him and he just pushed her away. Unfortunately for Darlene, there is no evidence that backs up her story of the assault. It is a she and Lorinda said kind of situation. As for Rose, the last thing Darlene wants to hear is how it's all her fault for having the gall to go out on a date while still married to her son. And about that still married thing, since the craziness of yesterday all Darlene has wanted to do is hear John's voice and get the chance to talk to him. She knows John's not willing to talk to her because he won't pick up her calls on his cell or return any of her messages. She has tried texting for good measure and even that brings no response from John.

"Have you talked to John since the last time?" Darlene asks Rose.

Rose tells her no and then asks if she has spoken to him.

Darlene shakes her head and then an idea comes to her mind. "Rose, what do you think about letting me call John with your phone?"

Rose asks if there's something wrong with Darlene's phone.

"No, I just think John would answer his phone if he thinks you're calling him, and I would actually get a chance to talk to him," Darlene explains.

Rose isn't comfortable with deceiving her son and will have to be talked into it. Darlene starts to do just that. "If I'm going to be able to repair this marriage, as I think you hope for, Rose, I have to be able to talk to John."

She gets Rose with that, but Rose still wants to know what she is going to say to John.

"I just want him to know that he's the only one in my life right now. I don't want him to feel threatened by other men. I want him to know my most important commitment is working on our marriage," Darlene claims to Rose, trying to convince her.

Rose couldn't ask for much more than what Darlene just said, so she gladly hands Darlene her cell phone.

Darlene has no idea where John is in the country and dials his number. She never thought she would ever feel nervous about talking to John, but she does. Darlene wonders if he'll just hang up on her or read her the riot act on the phone and then hang up. She wonders if she'll even get the chance to explain honestly how she feels right now about him, and their marriage. It's ringing, so she's about to find out. Rose is listening closely. She may want this phone call to go well even more than Darlene does.

No answer for the longest time, until there is. "Hello, Mom," John finally answers.

"Hi, John it's me, Darlene."

There is silence for a few seconds that feel like minutes. Darlene asks if he heard her, and he says he did. John asks her why she's using his mom's phone to call him. Darlene, never good at lying, tells him the truth. "I didn't think you would answer a call from me."

John doesn't really respond to that. He just lets her know that he can't really talk right now. He's on a boat off the coast of Florida, and he's losing his cell signal.

"Would you please call me, John? Please call when you get a chance?" Darlene straight out asks him.

Again silence, then John stammers he will when he gets a chance. He hangs up.

The call could have gone better, or it could have gone worse. But it certainly didn't solve anything as far as Darlene is concerned. Now that uneasy feeling in her gut she will have to carry with her a bit longer, as she hopes that John does call back.

Rose rubs her back in a show of support. "I'm sure he'll call, ducky," she says with her British accent making it sound more hopeful than it probably is.

"We'll see," Darlene replies. "We'll see."

⎯⎯ ⌾⌾⌾ ⎯⎯

"Darlene?" Audie asks John as he casts his line into the ocean depths with one of Sonny Ricci's staff helping him.

John nods, but says no more.

Kitty once again has the urge to engage him about his marriage but sees that the time is probably still not right and lets it go.

Audie with his pole now secured at the side of boat, doesn't. "You could have talked to her longer than that, man."

John doesn't respond. He just gives his brother a menacing glare, which says it all.

Audie, however, won't so easily back down. "You are going to have to talk to her, and for your sake, Johnny, and mine too, the sooner the better."

That statement makes John speak up. "What's that sup-posed to mean?"

"It means you keep acting like a real asshole," Audie sternly tells his brother.

Kitty does her best to intervene and calm the situation between the guys. But neither one is listening to her.

John gets up from his chair and marches over to his brother and gets eye to eye with Audie's face.

Audie tells him to get it out of his face and chill out. The chill out order makes John angrier. "Stay out of my business!"

"I would love to," Audie answers back. "But unfortu-nately for me I'm stuck with you for the next few days until we finish this little mission we've undertaken, and your business, and your attitude becomes my problem!"

Kitty walks over and tries to get between the guys and separate them like boxers to their own corners, but neither is following her directions.

John shouts at Audie to not say another word about anything to do with Darlene or his marriage. Audie shouts back that he is glad to do just that and why don't they make it any other subject while they are at it, since John is acting like such a miserable excuse for a human being.

"Good! We are in agreement about something!" John yells at his brother before storming off and sitting back down in a chair on the other side of the huge ocean fishing vessel.

John and Audie have both made up their minds to stubbornly say as little as possible to each other for the rest of the trip.

Kitty tries to get them to make up and see how childish they are being, but neither one of them wants any part of making up with the other at this moment.

Sonny suddenly reappears from his cabin, having not heard any of the tiff between the brothers. He comes over to check out the fishing prospects with Audie. He asks John why he's not fishing yet. John has no good answer.

"Let's get you set up with your pole and get you going then," Sonny says.

John still pissed off, reluctantly agrees but asks if he can fish off of the other side of the boat, as far away from his brother as possible.

"No problem," Sonny tells him, oblivious to John's reason for the request.

Kitty implores John to stay on this side of the boat and fish with her and Audie, but he wants no part of his brother right now and tells her as much.

After a few minutes pass, all three of them are set up by Sonny and his "'employees'" and are casting lines into the deep blue depths of the sea. John is on one side of the boat, and Audie and Kitty are on the other.

Sonny takes the opportunity with Audie and Kitty standing next to him, all three of them staring out over the overwhelming mass of waves that the ocean is, to offer some stories about growing up with Ray Barrett. He thinks that Audie might be interested in his father's early days, and he is right.

"Did you know that your pop and I almost became priests together?" he starts with.

Audie has to admit to him that he's never heard that one before. "How did that come about Sonny?" Audie is curious.

Sonny is happy to tell him. "I first met your pop in a boy's home run by the Catholics in upstate New York. We were only about eight years old at the time and full of vinegar. Your dad's mother had died of some mysterious thing about a year earlier, and your grandfather a real hard-nosed military type, wasted no time remarrying a younger broad. Stop me, boy, if you have heard all this."

Audie hasn't, so he doesn't.

Sonny continues. "I, like your pop, had a step-mother, but mine unfortunately, since as long as I can remember, has been ticking me off. That's the first thing me and your pop had in common, a deep hatred for our step-mothers, and boy were they mothers," Sonny expresses with an insidious laugh.

Audie had heard stories about Dad's step-mother, from his mother. His dad had never said a word about her. Now he understands why. Audie wonders why Sonny and his father were in the boy's home in the first place. Sonny is happy to elaborate. "Your pop hating his life on the family farm with his drill-sergeant father and his wicked witch step-mother, kept running away from home. Finally your grandfather sent him to the boy's home hoping to set him straight. My story was similar, except I tried to kill my wicked stepmother. We ended up there together and became fast friends.

"I didn't know anything about that," Audie has to admit. "Where does the priest thing come into it?"

Sonny chuckles as he thinks back. "Well, having seen what women did to our pops, you can see how an occupation without them could appeal to someone like us."

Kitty joins the conversation. She asks when all that animosity toward women changed.

"Like most boys, around puberty," Sonny answers wearing a big grin on his face.

Audie and Kitty laugh.

"In fact, that boy's home is where we first learned how to fish," Sonny remembers.

"I thought it was my grandfather who taught my dad to fish," Audie responds.

Sonny thinks about that for a minute but then recalls that it was the priest who looked out for them in the boy's home who definitely did. "I know as your dad got older, he and your grandfather would go out fishing together. I think that his love for fishing came from his fishing trips with his father. I remember your pop telling me that fishing was one of the only times that he and his dad ever could get along, and that's one of things why fishing meant so much to Ray."

"That's a real nice story," Kitty remarks. "I never heard that about Ray. I mean, I never would have thought that Audie wouldn't have already heard that," Kitty attempts to correct.

Audie confirms he never has heard that before.

"What about you boys?" Sonny asks, changing the subject. "Ever married or just bachelors for life? And how about you, young lady?"

Kitty is quick to say never. Audie says the same as he makes sure not to look Kitty's way.

"Your brother over there I'm guessing has been or is," Sonny observes.

Audie asks Sonny why he thinks that.

"Frustrated, irritable, all the earmarks of a marriage, my friend," Sonny jokes.

"Are you married, Sonny?" Kitty asks.

"Many times miss. I'm on the third Mrs. Ricci right now, and I think I finally got it right, at least I hope so," he says with a humorous groan. "I don't think I have the energy or can afford a fourth Mrs. Ricci.

FISHING *for* SOMETHING   299

Everyone whoops and hollers at his funny diatribe before Sonny asks Audie and Kitty about the two of them and their relationship.

"We've only known each other for a few days," Kitty answers with an embarrassing giggle accompanying her words.

"Yeah, we just met," Audie agrees.

Sonny smiles at both of them and wags a wise finger in their direction. "I don't know I just can see there's a spark here."

"A spark?" Audie repeats.

"Yessiree, something special going on here, never doubt me on such things," Sonny says confidently.

Audie and Kitty can barely look in the other's direction. They are too embarrassed to do so.

Sonny has a good chuckle at how uncomfortable he's made both of them. He's relishing every second of it.

One of Sonny's right hand men points and yells. Sonny turns to him to see what all the fuss is. Audie's pole is bending almost in half.

"Holy shitburgers, you've got a bite, and it's a big one!" Sonny yells out as he directs Audie on what to do.

John hears the yelling and comes over to see what the commotion is all about. He finds Audie being strapped in what Sonny calls his tuna fighting chair. Sonny's men strap him in real good and tight. The fight then begins between Audie and whatever is on the other side of his line.

Kitty cheers him on as John watches, not sure what to make of his kid brother being so over his head. Audie no seasoned fisherman, is holding on for dear life as he is jerked back and forth in the wooden fishing chair. "What am I trying to catch here, man, a whale?!" He yells out.

"Let's hope you haven't hooked one of those, kid, otherwise the whole boats in trouble," Sonny says tongue-in-cheek.

Everyone on the boat is watching now, even Harry and Bob are riveted by the scene, and they know nothing about fishing.

Audie at the advice of Sonny lets the fish have some line to play with before reeling him in again. Audie does the same thing again and again as he tries to drain the fight out of the large animal on the other side of his line.

John isn't saying anything, and he's still not talking to Audie, but he can't help but be proud of the fight his scrawny kid brother is putting up.

Kitty notices one of the brackets bolting down the chair to the deck of the boat is loose. She says it out loud, but no one is really paying attention. They're all too busy cheering Audie on. When she sees a second bracket getting loose, she begins to panic and grabs John by the arm.

"What?!" he snaps at her, acting annoyed that she is interrupting him watching his brother do battle.

"John, look, look at where Audie's chair is fastened," she points out, finally getting his attention.

It takes a second for John to understand, but as soon as he realizes it too, he pushes his way through the crowd around Audie and demands that his brother is pulled out of the chair ASAP.

Audie isn't listening to John. He's too busy being thrust back and forth and hanging on for dear life.

Sonny isn't listening any better, as he's coaching Audie on reeling in his catch. Then in a flash of amazing nature at its best, and in slow motion to everyone with a view, a gorgeous, larger-than-life tuna comes flying out of the water and silhouettes against the blue sky that is a perfect background. The sight takes Audie's breath away as he now realizes what he is up against.

"Hold on, kid! You almost got him. He's wearing down!" Sonny implores him.

"Me, or the fish?!" Audie shouts nervously.

John finally gets Sonny's attention. "Get Audie out of there right now! That chair isn't going to hold!"

Then before Sonny can react to John's warning a snapping sound is followed by the chair being ripped right out from the boat's deck. The chair and Audie still tied down in it, go sliding toward the boat's railing and then fly right over it. John and Kitty both scream out to Audie, but it all happens to fast. They rush to the side of the boat and look over into the ocean.

"He'll drown if we don't find him!" John yells at Sonny.

"We'll find him," Sonny answers defiantly.

Kitty yells out Audie's name over the crashing waves.

Then the tuna breaks the surface of the water with Audie still being dragged behind by his fishing line and pole, still strapped into the chair. He screams out in a blood-curdling way for help, any help. John yells out to him to let go of his pole before demanding a large knife from Sonny. Sonny orders one of his men to grab one and give it to John. They do with breakneck speed.

"What are you going to do, John?" Kitty asks.

"Something probably really stupid," John says back to her, right as he prepares to jump over the side of the boat and swim out to his brother.

Kitty stops him and takes the knife. "You're too hurt, John," she says, as she dives into the crashing waters and swims toward Audie, while Sonny directs the boat to follow right behind her. Audie's wooden chair is bobbing up and down in the water and acting like a floatation device.

When Kitty sees this, she frantically swims his direction. He's still in the chair and beginning to sink. He let go of his pole and the tuna is gone. Between spitting out water, Audie screams for someone to help him. Then he sees Kitty swimming to him.

"Hang on!" John yells to Audie from the boat.

"Yeah, kid!" Sonny yells. "She's almost there!"

Kitty is closing fast, but just as she arrives, Audie, chair and all, goes under like a battleship being sunk. She takes a deep breath before diving under the surface of the water for him.

Every person on the boat is frozen, barely breathing as they watch the situation unfold. Then after what seems like an eternity, it happens. Kitty surfaces, pulling Audie still trapped in the chair up with her. Kitty then pulls out the knife that is strapped on her side and slashes at the straps that have Audie tied to the chair. She furiously cuts him out of the chair and maneuvers him onto her back, while still keeping both their heads above water. Kitty then smacks him on the cheek to make sure he's awake for all this and not just dead weight in the water.

Audie comes to and holds on tight to Kitty. He lets her know that he's with her. "Yeah…I'm still here," he tells her while spitting water from his lungs.

Sonny's boat is right beside them now, and his crew puts out a ladder to pull them in.

"Look out there! Is that a shark fin?! John yells out, pointing to the object he spots.

"It's a big shark, judging by the size of the fin," Sonny trumpets matter-of-factly. "You guys need to get in the boat quick!"

Kitty turns to look behind them and she sees it to. She begs Audie to hold on with the soundtrack to "'Jaws'" playing in her head. She swims to the boat's ladder as fast as she can.

"Hurry up! It's almost on top of you guys!" John hollers to them.

Kitty gets Audie to the ladder, and Sonny's men begin to pull him in. He's pretty much dead weight out of the water, as he is exhausted from all he's been through.

The fin is closing fast toward the boat as Kitty begins to reach for the ladder.

"Too close for comfort, boys!" Sonny yells out as he orders his men to open fire on the shark.

They do as ordered and begin firing round after round at the shark. Harry and Bob scream obscenities at the huge fish as it dares to get close to the boat.

Audie is now lying on the deck of the boat and John wastes no time on checking his condition. The shark in pursuit of Kitty dives under the water as she climbs the ladder to safety. Its fin disappears under the boat. Kitty races to Audie's side. He's okay, just so weak that he can barely lift his arms. She embraces him and squeezes him so hard that it hurts. John is next in line for a hug from the hero. He's both amazed and thankful to her for what she just did in rescuing his kid brother. He asks her how she managed to do something like that. Kitty is quick to give up her secret. "I was a lifeguard from my teenage years to early twenties. I guess all that training paid off."

John thanks her again for her bravery. Audie hears his brother's words and thanks her, too. Sonny orders him to lie down and rest after all that he's been through.

Kitty corners John. "It sure is never a dull moment with you guys, I have to say."

John, starting to feel his injuries acting up once again, can't dispute her point. "You know if it wasn't for bad stuff happening to me and Audie on this trip, it would be pretty boring and routine. God, how I wish for boring and routine."

"Well there is certainly nothing routine about your jaunt across the country with Audie, that's for sure," Kitty interjects with a laugh.

John, sitting back down in a deck chair next to his brother, who is still lying down, agrees.

Sonny suddenly says to everyone that the fishing trip is over after what just happened and they will turn the boat around and head back.

"Wait just a second!" Audie hollers as he rises to his feet. "I came out here to catch some ocean fish, Sonny, and I'll be damned if a little thing like a tuna dragging me under the sea and trying to drown me is going to stop me."

Sonny asks him if he's crazy.

"One hundred percent, Sonny," Audie responds.

"Alright, you heard the man! The fishing trip is back on!" Sonny tells his crew. "Now let's get the lines baited and get a new pole for the crazy son-of-a-bitch here."

John and Kitty wonder if he's up for more of this.

He won't let them talk him out of more fishing. "I've got the sea in my blood, brother," he jokes to John.

"Well at least you have it in your lungs, that's for sure," John replies, patting his brother on the head.

Sonny brings over a new pole for Audie, and the rest of the day's fishing proceeds normally. No huge fish are caught, but many small ones are. For John and Audie on this trip, things going normally aren't normal at all.

THE NEXT MORNING, AFTER A GOOD NIGHT'S SLEEP AT Sonny's digs, Kitty and the guys are saying their goodbyes to him and thanking him for his hospitality.

"I've got something I want to give you guys," Sonny says as he reaches into his pocket.

John reaches out his hand and watches as Sonny places a necklace in it.

"What is it?" Audie is interested to know.

"A Saint Christopher's necklace that Ray gave me many years ago when things weren't going so well for me, I'd like you guys to place it with his remains, or whatever, for me."

John tells him he would be proud to do that for him, while Audie says how much this gesture would have meant to their father if he was still around.

Sonny begins to choke up a little as thinks about his old friend, no longer being alive. It's still hard to believe that I won't see that smartass smile of his again. Life is short, boys. Take care of yourselves in New York, and by the way, who you going to see up there?"

Audie pulls the now-battered paper from his backpack and checks the list. He tells Sonny that the next name is a Father Paul Carson, who lives in New York City.

Sonny grins at the disclosure of the name. "That guy's still kicking, excellent news, just excellent."

John asks how he knows the man, but Audie and Kitty already know the answer. "This is the same priest from the story you told us?"

Sonny nods "The one and the same. He's got to be getting up there in age after all these years. When you guys see him, tell him Sonny Ricci says hi and thanks. Thank him for all he did for me as a kid."

John and Audie promise they will as they say goodbye and begin to walk out to John's truck parked in front of Sonny's mansion of a home. Along their path, with Kitty by their side, they come up upon Harry and Bob. Audie apologizes for being a pain in the ass to the two of them. Bob is quick to tell him no problem, but Harry has more to say. "You're lucky, kid."

"How's that, exactly?" Audie wants to know.

Harry raises one eyebrow and shrugs his shoulders before answering. "Nobody ever got away from me before, and you wouldn't have either if your old man wasn't buddies with Sonny Ricci."

Audie wonders if there is a point to this.

"But you had good luck from your old man, and us getting hired by Ricci, well that's our good luck coming from chasing you. It's a weird situation, but we both benefitted from your old man's connections. So when you see your pop kid, in whatever place he may be in, thank him for me and Bob too, okay then," Harry concludes as he reaches out to shake Audie's hand.

Audie says okay as he shakes Harry's outstretched hand.

"Better get going," John tells his brother as he unlocks the backseat door and helps Kitty in.

"Right," Audie agrees.

John says he feels up to doing the driving again. His brother's near death in the ocean has inspired him. His wounds feel better after spending time with the ocean air.

"You're sure you're up to this?" Kitty asks him as they pull down the driveway.

"Yeah," John answers confidently. "Anyone for the Big Apple?"

"Can't wait, dude," Audie answers.

Kitty says the same.

New York State is their final stop, and both John and Audie are ready for their journey to end and for their lives to get back to normal. That is normal with fifty thousand more dollars in their pockets, of course, a better normal they would both say right about now.

CHAPTER 18

Darlene scoops up the plethora of dirty dishes on the table that her customers in the café were so nice to leave for her. Well, at least they left her a hefty five percent tip on the table for all her hard work. These are the moments when she so enjoys her new profession. Darlene piles the dishes up one upon the other and then balances the glasses on top of them. On her slow walk back to the kitchen and to the café's dishwasher, Marcus, she crosses paths with Lorinda.

"Any news, darlin'?" Lorinda asks walking by.

Darlene shakes her head and drops off her load near the sink. Marcus takes it from there.

"Nothing at all?"

"No, nothing, and it's been since yesterday since we talked and he promised to call me when he got a chance," Darlene reveals with a disappointed tone. "Unfortunately for me, when it comes to John, I'm not that surprised."

"Well, it's still shitty, honey. I don't care what you say," Lorinda complains. "To leave you hanging like this is not cool, not cool at all."

"It sounds like they're on the East Coast now so at least the trip over there is almost done. Then they can drive straight back to Oregon, and then we'll have to figure things out," Darlene confides to her friend.

"You've been through a lot, honey, with John and without him. What's he going to have to say to you for you to take him back and give him another chance?"

The front door opens, and it's time to get back to work. Several couples come in to get something to eat. Darlene is up, so she has no time to give a thoughtful response to Lorinda. So she says the first thing that comes to mind. "I guess I need to be as important to him as he is to me."

With that, she walks out to the front of the café and seats the new diners.

Lorinda considers Darlene's statement and then her own relationships with men. "Fat chance," she says under her breath.

⸻ ⧉ ⸻

THEY'VE BEEN ON THE ROAD FOR SIX AND A HALF HOURS since leaving Sonny Ricci's home. John has driven the whole way and has loved every minute of it. Getting back behind the wheel after a few days of being a passenger while recovering from his injuries has put John in a much better mood. He's been almost melancholy since they left Miami. John even apologizes for his bad attitude toward Audie and apologizes to Kitty as well.

Audie lets him know it's no big deal, nothing to worry about really, but then he brings up the elephant in the room for his big brother. "When are you going to make that phone call to Darlene? Johnny, this might be your chance to get things going in the right direction with her, bro."

Surprisingly John doesn't get angry at the mere suggestion. With a deadpan expression and zero emotion, he responds to his brother. "I don't know what to say to her."

Audie doesn't understand. "Just tell her you miss her, dude."

"Yes, John, sometimes you don't have to say very much," Kitty adds.

John interrupts their "'happy talk'" to get across that they have no idea what he's going through. Audie wants him to bring it out, to open up and help them to understand.

"I don't know. It's hard to even talk about it," John answers.

"Come on, Johnny, whatever it is, it's eating you up inside. Talk to me, man, talk to me, please," Audie insists.

Kitty from the backseat of the truck campaigns for the same thing. "You need to get it off of your chest, John, whatever it is."

John swallows hard as he struggles to find the words. He spits out the truth like he's only has a few seconds to live. "Darlene's been seeing another guy since we left Grants Pass! Mom told me when I called the house several days ago, before the last phone conversation I had with Darlene."

Audie is stunned by the news. "Are you sure, man?"

John affirms that he is, his chin bouncing off his chest with defiance written all over him.

"Is Mom sure?" Audie asks.

John divulges that Mom got the info from very reliable sources. "Some of Mom's friends saw Darlene out with him in Grants Pass."

"Is it serious?" Kitty interjects.

John doesn't get her question.

"What I mean is, maybe he's just a friend and they're just going out for a few laughs, or to have a good meal," Kitty says, trying to justify John's wife's actions.

John has to admit that he doesn't have any real answers for those questions. He doesn't know who the guy is or how much he means to Darlene.

"Then maybe he doesn't mean anything, Johnny. Maybe you're just getting all worked up over nothing," Audie suggests.

For the first time since leaving Miami, John can feel his temperature starting to rise and with it his temper. "Why did she wait until I left town to make her move then? Explain that to me."

Neither Audie nor Kitty, of course, can. Audie still thinks John should make the call and talk things out with Darlene. Kitty repeat's the sentiment.

"I'm afraid to talk to her," John confesses.

"You afraid, well that's a first," Audie has to say.

John continues, "Well, I am. I'm afraid of the truth, I guess."

Audie looks back behind him to where Kitty is sitting. They exchange perplexed expressions. Audie asks his brother on what this "'truth'" he is talking about might be.

John with his hands tightening up on the steering wheel, shrugs his shoulders as he searches for the right words to express it. "I guess… I'm afraid that she's already moved on and just hasn't told me yet."

Kitty caresses his shoulders in a tender way to show her support for how he is feeling. Audie watches her, impressed by her sensitivity.

"Am I crazy, Audie?" John openly asks his brother.

"No," Audie responds. "You're only scared. And you're only scared because you love her so much, and you're afraid to lose her."

With his eyes glued to the road John says nothing. He

just nods in a barely noticeable way. But John can't argue with a word Audie just said, and they both know it.

The seriousness in the truck's air could be cut with a chainsaw, a knife wouldn't do the job.

"Hey, you know what," Audie breaks the ice with.

John looks at him to see what he's talking about.

"On this whole trip we have had one crazy, bizarre experience after another, especially when we've tried to do a little bit of actual fishing," Audie details for the record.

John is still listening as Audie continues. "We've still got a long ways to go to get to New York. Why don't we stop at a cabin or something on our way there, man, and spend the night. We could do some fishing, just you and me. We could roast some s'mores over a fire."

John brings up the obvious flaw in the idea, Kitty.

Kitty to her credit is quick to agree to make herself scarce and get out of the guys' way. "I could stay in the truck, whatever you two needed me to do."

Audie laughs at the notion. "No, Kitty, I mean you too, all of us relaxing, doing some fishing, no goons chasing us, no coyotes shooting at us, and no old rich guys passing out next to us. What do you say, Johnny?"

John admits it sounds simple and appealing after all they have been through. Kitty loves the idea and thinks that the brothers really need this. She encourages John to go along with Audie on this.

He thinks about it for a few moments and then asks, "Where are the cabins at?"

Audie isn't sure, but he'll find some, somewhere on their way to the "Big" Apple. With cell phone in hand, he'll find some.

"You're burning them!" John barks at Audie as they sit by the campfire that they made outside the backdoor of the cabin they rented for the night.

Kitty grabs the skewer away from Audie and takes control of the situation. She's much more adept at cooking over an open fire than he is. Kitty and the guys are all relaxing in lawn chairs, feasting on s'mores. The beautiful summer night is about perfect, they watch the sun go down taking the temperature with it. John admits that this idea of Audie's was a good one.

"There's a small lake down the path here," Audie says as he motions to the direction they would follow to get there. "It's stocked with trout from what the brochure said."

John thinks that sounds great as he sits back and releases a huge sigh. "I wish the whole trip could have been as nice as this."

Audie matches John's sigh with one of his own. "We had some crazy fishing trips with Dad back in the day, too."

John snickers as he recalls some of those adventures with their father.

"You know I heard some stories about your father from Sonny Ricci, but you two must have some great stories yourselves," Kitty observes.

Audie is quick to admit that even though he was a young boy back then, there certainly were a few misadventures with dear old Dad that he does remember. John agrees and thinks back on a few memorable ones for Kitty's satisfaction. "Let's see, there's of course all the times the boat's engine died and we just drifted around. I remember paddling across half a lake in the dark with Dad. I don't think you were with us that day, Audie."

Audie says probably not since he can't recall that happening at all. Audie mentions the deer episode, when coming back from a fishing trip, Dad had a deer plow into the car. "Mom was so angry and upset about me and John that she didn't talk to Dad for two weeks after that," Audie recalls with a laugh.

"I remember that," John says chuckling. "Dad said it was two of the best weeks of his life."

The brothers both laugh at that, but Kitty doesn't get the humor.

"Remember the bear?" Audie asks John.

"Oh… how could I forget," John answers.

Kitty, intrigued by the mention of a bear story, pleads for the guys to tell her all about it.

Audie gives in to her request. "Me and Johnny were with our dad bass fishing in the middle of the night. I really remember it because it was one of the first times I was allowed to tag along with them. I was pretty darn young at the time."

"About seven if I remember," John calculates.

"So it's really dark out on the lake, and I mean really, really dark, it was so dark I was scared. Dad had a small lantern for light on the boat, but it wasn't a gas one. It was battery operated. So, we're out there fishing, all three of us. Dad fixed up my line for me and showed me how to cast. It was all pretty cool, until…"

"Until what?" Kitty wants to know.

Audie can see he's got her eating out of his hand now, and he loves it. He starts up again. "Well, we're out there fishing off Dad's boat at the time. He had many of them over the years. This was a little bass boat, and we were fishing in a cove on the far side of the lake. Suddenly, we hear a big splash not far from the boat. Now this isn't the splash of some fish, not unless dolphins or sharks have found out how to live in freshwater, and this isn't the splash of a deer or any other animal that lives near the lake, except one. Now me and Johnny immediately look at Dad. He's got this weird look on his face, one I'd never seen before."

"Yeah, it's called scared shitless," John asserts, remembering the story of that night well.

"What he said, man," Audie offers up, pointing to his brother.

"So it was a bear and that's why your father was so scared?" Kitty exclaims, really getting into the story.

Audie doesn't directly answer. "Then we hear more splashing, and more, and it's getting closer all the time. My dad grabs his lantern and he aims it in the direction of the sounds coming from the water."

"And then he sees the bear?" Kitty interrupts.

"Not exactly," Audie answers.

"Well, what then," Kitty asks, getting impatient with the story and how Audie's telling it.

John begins to chuckle at her frustration and how well Audie is exploiting it.

"The lantern suddenly stops working. It's pitch black on our boat. The splashing is getting louder and closer by the second. Dad yells to Johnny to get into the storage box he keeps under his driver's seat. Inside it he has a flare gun, a real gun, and some extra batteries, he orders Johnny to grab all of it, and then hand them to him as quickly as possible."

"What about you? You must have been scared to death being you're only seven," Kitty guesses.

"He's was whimpering in the corner as I remember," John says sarcastically.

Audie laughs off his brother's abuse and continues. "So funny man here, Johnny, somehow in the dark fumbles around and finds all three things and hands them to Dad. Dad is frozen on the end of the boat, listening as the splashing gets closer and closer."

"And then it happened!" John broadcasts with glee.

"What?! What happened?!" Kitty begs.

Audie keeps her in suspense for only a moment longer than what is nice, then he movies on.

"We're tossed into the dark black lake, and man was that water cold, huh, Johnny," Audie recalls.

Kitty wants to know the whys and how's.

"Our boat was flipped upside down by something, the something that made all that noise swimming in the lake."

"So the bear flipped your boat over?" Kitty says stating the obvious.

"Yeah," Audie answers. "But we didn't know it was a bear until we swam the short distance to the shore. Since I was so young, Dad came and grabbed me up and let me ride on his back, all the way to shore."

"So I missed it somewhere. How did you know it was a bear that flipped over your boat?" Kitty questions.

John looks at Audie. He already knows the story but is still enjoying listening to Audie tell it with such vigor.

"We get to shore. Dad still has the guns and the batteries in a plastic bag in his hand. He makes sure that me and Johnny are okay, and we are for the most part, other than being really cold because the water was so cold. Then we hear it."

Kitty asks what, not even noticing that she's burned up her marshmallow, right off of her skewer that was cooking in the fire.

Audie elaborates. "We hear a growl in the dark. The growl isn't more than about twenty feet away. Dad somehow puts new batteries in the lantern with all this happening and flips on the switch. He moves the lantern near the growling, and there it is."

"The bear?" Kitty assumes.

"The biggest, meanest brown bear you'll ever see, and it was only one quick dash from reaching us," Audie says with relish.

"Oh, my God, what did you guys do?" Kitty asks, from the edge of her seat.

Audie is thrilled by her interest. "Dad screams for us to swim for the boat. He grabs me and pushes Johnny in front of him, and we go right back into the water and start swimming for the boat. Then in one of the top ten scariest moments of my life, I hear a loud splash from behind. At that instant, I know the bear has jumped back into the water as well and is in pursuit. But somehow we make it to the boat, flip it over, and climb in as fast as we can. The splashing sounds are still heading our way as my dad fumbles for his gun. Then Dad yells, dropping the loudest f-bomb in history. I believe scientists confirmed it was heard all the way into outer space."

Kitty interrupts him. She wants to know about the bear.

"Let me tell you then about mister bear. He reaches the boat and starts to try to climb onto it from the water. Dad yells because he finds out he had no bullets for his gun. Then he did the next best thing."

"What?" Kitty interrupts again.

Audie is getting a kick out of her enthusiasm for his storytelling, but finally finishes the story. "Dad grabs the flare gun. He aims it at the big old brown bear who is still struggling to climb into the boat and fires it right at him. Well let me tell you, man, it was a direct hit. That bear screamed and jumped back into the water and hightailed it away as fast as he could. And that was the last we ever saw of him."

"So your dad saved the day?" Kitty offers up.

Audie and John both ponder that thought for a second. It had never occurred to them like that before. "I guess he did," Audie says after considering the episode.

Kitty mentions that their dad did have his good moments even if they don't think about them as much as the bad times.

John jumps in to say that of course he did, and usually the good times with their dad were related to the outdoors and special occasions like holidays. Audie agrees. He remembers that Dad loved Christmas and birthdays and could be a fun, wonderful guy at those times.

"Too bad he threw it all away with his drinking and gambling," John vents with words tinged with bitterness.

"Like me," Audie says, agreeing wholeheartedly. "Hey Johnny, how about that fishing now? The lake here is just down this path. It's supposed to be real close. How about you. Kitty?"

Kitty reluctantly excuses herself. She's pooped and ready to turn in for the evening. But she does think it would be a great idea for Audie and John to spend some time together, just the two of them, without her hanging around.

John, in a good mood, says why not and grabs his pole. Audie does the same as they say goodnight to Kitty who goes into the cabin. The guys start their way down the dark path.

The sun has fully set now, and there are no lights to guide their way.

"You did bring a lantern?" Audie asks John.

"Of course, and this one's a gas one so no batteries to worry about," John laughs.

Audie joins in and then makes just one wish. He asks that there are no bears nearby tonight.

"No kidding," John says as he lifts the lantern high in front of them and leads the way.

"I GOT A BITE, DUDE! I GOT A BITE!" AUDIE SCREAMS OUT like a scared schoolgirl.

John is amused at how excited his little brother gets at such routine acts. Of course John considers that on this trip, and with all the fishing they have done, he and Audie haven't exactly been filling their respective buckets with fish. Now that isn't important for two guys traveling across the country, stopping only for a day or so with no home nearby but still, for a diehard like John it is a bit strange. John congratulates Audie on his catch. When Audie gets what looks like a trout to shore, he admires it for just a second before pulling the hook out and releasing it back into the pitch-black waters of the lake. He turns to his brother with the cat-that-swallowed-the-goldfish look on his face. "Times like this, bro, I can see why you and the old man enjoyed this crap so much."

John only smirks in response.

"At least you and him had this," Audie vents as he casts his line.

John asks what he means.

"Nothing, it's just I remember as a kid how you two went fishing all the time," Audie clarifies.

John reminds Audie that he was very young back then,

and that Mom would often stop Dad from taking him anyways.

Audie acknowledges all that, but it doesn't change how much he still wanted to go. "At least you still have all those memories with him. I only got to go a few times, like the time with the bear," Audie spews out from somewhere in his guts.

John has never heard Audie mention this before. John has never even given it much thought, how the loss of their father had affected Audie in those terms. John's anger aimed at his dad has steered him away from the good times they had together. Being older he has a lot more of both types of memories, good and bad. "I guess I kind of take that all for granted," John speaks into the night air for Audie's consideration.

"You mean all the good times, fishing and hunting with Dad?" Audie concludes.

"That, and more. You know I built up such a hate and resentment toward the man for so long that I don't even give myself the luxury of remembering anything good," John continues.

There's a silence after that as both men consider the other's words. Audie's always looked forward to reconnecting with his father to create new good times, the kind he missed out on as a kid. While John always contemplated if he ever saw his father again he would list from memory all the lousy things that his father did to him and the family by abandoning them like he did. It is the difference in perspective that six years of age can have between two brothers growing up in the same home and the same circumstances.

Audie poses a question that this conversation brings to mind. What would either of them do if they could see their father one last time? John seems unable or maybe unwilling to even consider the question. Audie for his part at least tries to grapple with it. "Johnny. I think I would just want to know why."

"Why? What do you mean?"

"Why he did what he did, man, that's all," Audie replies.

"Maybe because he was a selfish bastard who cared only about himself," John throws in, with underlying anger coming from his words.

Audie inappropriately chortles at his brother's bitterness. Then he brings up the strange contradiction that this trip has brought to his and John's attention. That is just how many people, at least the people they have come across on their dad's list, seem to champion how good he was.

John is quick to toss out the old standby that they didn't have to live with him. But Audie immediately makes the point that some did.

"He wasn't their father. They didn't have to be sons of his and be left behind with a mom whose heart was stomped on by the man who for good or for worse, she loved," John declares with disdain, his words revealing old wounds.

Audie won't deny anything John is saying. He can't. For John it's all too real. Audie does muse some more about how a man can mean such different things to different people.

John asks that they drop the subject, so Audie does. "What do you think about Kitty?"

"You mean the Kitty that you have known for about two days?" John wiseasses back.

"Yeah, that's the one," an ever-optimistic Audie admits.

"Why?" John asks.

Audie acts like a pre-teen boy talking about a girl he saw at school walk by. John threatens his life if anything resembling a giggle comes out of his mouth.

"No, dude, it's just that we got…"

While Audie fumbles around for the right word, John picks up the scent of something he never thought he would pick up from his brother, infatuation.

"You really like her," John says, getting to the heart of the matter as he likes to do.

Audie nods his head yes. Even after John again reminds him it's only been two days, Audie isn't in the least deterred by the timely fact. "Chemistry!"

John asks him what he means by that.

"I don't know, Johnny. There's just a spark that fires up when I get near her. It's the weirdest thing."

John agrees with him that it is weird and then takes a laugh at his expense.

"I know, man, it makes no sense, and I can't really define it, but there's a spark like I've never felt before," Audie analyzes the best that he can.

John is taken back by his brother's emotions coming to the surface like this. This showing of feelings and other such matters is very un-Barrett like. "So this is new territory for you, when it comes to women?"

"Absolutely," Audie answers without hesitation.

John ponders his next thought as he reels in his fishing line and checks his bait.

Audie follows his brother's lead and does the same.

After a few minutes of returned focus on their night fishing, John comes up with the next important question to ask. "What are you going to do about it?"

Audie swallows hard before responding, "I think I am

going for it, Johnny."

John doesn't know what that means, "'going for it'" so he asks Audie to define exactly what he is talking about here.

While shouting out to John he's got another bite on his line, Audie has the same excitement when he goes into detail about his plans for Kitty. "When we get to New York City, I'm thinking about asking if she would like to head back to Nashville with me."

"Why Nashville?" John responds.

Audie takes his eyes off of his fishing pole and the lake in front of him long enough to make eye contact with John. "Because I've seen her sing, and she's great. I hope with my share of Dad's money we could go back down there, maybe get a place together and I could set up a small recording studio and…"

John cuts him off right there. "Are you sure about this, Audie? This is pretty serious stuff for you."

Audie lets his big brother know that in no uncertain terms, he realizes how serious these ideas of his are.

"How do you think she is going to react? I mean, have you picked up any signals from her or anything?" John asks.

Audie isn't sure, but he thinks the chemistry, the sparks as he says, fire both ways.

John places his fishing pole down securely in the ground. He strolls over to his brother as Audie watches him wondering what he's doing. John puts his arm around his brother and pulls him close. Audie's arms are still down at his side, in a sort of shock. "What's this for, Johnny?"

John still holding him says, "I'm just happy for you. You need this, little brother, and I hope it works with her."

John finally lets him go. Audie doesn't know what to say. John picks up his pole and starts right back up where he left off. Audie once again follows his brother's lead. Finally after a long while Audie thanks him for the kind words. John smiles as he denies the whole thing. "It goes against my image or reputation of being an asshole, so let's just say my encouragement never happened and leave it at that, shall we."

"That's true. No one would believe me if I tried to tell them what just happened," Audie agrees as they then both take part in the humor of the moment.

The rest of the night belongs to stories of their glory days, arguments about fishing lures, and debates about whether country music is about great story telling and if rap is modern-day poetry from the streets of inner city America. You can guess who trumpeted each side.

CHAPTER 19

"Still no call from John?" Lorinda asks Darlene as they are wiping down tables, straightening condiments, and organizing the café's dessert menus.

Darlene shakes her head. The silent disappointment speaks more loudly than words.

Lorinda tries in vain to cheer her up, improve her mood, but Darlene isn't willing.

"Oh, shit! You've have got to be kidding me right now!" Lorinda moans as she notices who just walked through the front door of the café.

Darlene takes a look for herself and has the same reaction. She can't believe he has the nerve too ever show his face in here again. Bill, their boss and the owner of the café, comes out from the back where he was cleaning up the kitchen. He offers to Darlene to toss him out. But before he can take a step in Mike Stillman's direction, Darlene stops him. "I got this, Bill."

"Are you sure?" Bill asks her with concern.

Darlene assures him she does and heads to Mike's table.

"You're not still mad at me, are you?" he greets her with.

Mike shoots for humor, but it's no laughing matter to Darlene or anyone else in the café.

"What are you doing here, Mike?" she wants to know.

He mocks her serious tone. "I'm here to have a meal. I believe this place still serves them, right."

"Not to you!" Lorinda yells from the back.

"Are you going to let your help talk to your good customers like that?!" Mike barks at Bill, the owner, who is standing right next to Lorinda.

Bill only cracks how big an asshole Mike must be to pull a stunt like this and come back into the café.

Mike genuinely acts like this is no big deal for him to be here, as he brushes past Darlene and takes a seat at a table.

"You're a real bastard!" Lorinda tosses in his direction.

Darlene asks him to count himself lucky that law enforcement didn't have enough evidence to do anything to him before she demands that he leaves.

Mike ignoring her on purpose, requests a menu.

Bill has seen enough and pulls a sign off his wall before marching over to where Mike is sitting.

"You see this!" He shows Mike, his voice teased with anger.

Mike looks at the sign in his hand and expresses nothing back.

Bill, unperturbed, continues. "This sign says I have the right to refuse service to anyone, anyone at all."

Mike defiantly offers no response, not giving an inch.

"Consider yourself anyone, Mike, and then get the hell out of here!" Bill threatens as he points to the words on the sign.

Mike then changes course and tries to downplay the incident with Darlene at his house. He resolves that it was just a big misunderstanding, nothing more. Unfortunately for him, no one in the café is buying what he is selling, and Bill again orders him out.

Lorinda has heard enough and threatens to call the police on him.

"Just leave. No one is going to wait on you here anymore, Mike," Darlene promises him.

"Fine!" Mike says with a disgusted voice. "Your food sucks almost as much as your service!"

"Ten seconds, Mike!" Bill tells him. "You've got ten seconds before I throw you out!"

Mike raises his arms like he is surrendering. He flips them all the bird and slams the front door behind him as he leaves. Lorinda tells him to never come back or she'll beat him up again.

"Thanks, Bill," Darlene says. "Thanks for standing up for me like that."

Bill for his part goes all "awe shucks" on her. "I don't need a piece of crap like that in my establishment. Besides, Darlene, he's put a bad name on the rest of us men. You know, gentleman like myself," Bill says with a hearty guffaw.

Lorinda gives Bill a kiss on his cheek. "You're a good man and definitely a true gentleman," she tells him as they share a laugh.

Bill getting a bit embarrassed orders the girls to stop fooling around and get back to work as a couple of diners walk in at right that moment. Darlene is happy to guide them to their table.

THERE IS NO MISTAKING WHEN THEY GET INTO THE CITY. They aren't in Grants Pass, that's for sure. John weaves them through the traffic and to a hotel in mid-town. He has already contacted the next person on their father's list. His name is Paul Carson. He was the young priest who reached out too their father in the boy's home when he was young. Sonny back in Miami had glowingly spoken about Father Carson and all he had done for him and their dad. They would meet with him at his home, an apartment not far from their hotel, tomorrow mid-morning. That left them with the rest of the night and New York City surrounding them after checking into their room, yes, one room for all three of them. The cost of a room in the city was crazy so Kitty insisted that they should just share one hotel room. Audie will sleep in a small pull-out mattress from the couch while John and Kitty take the pair of queen sizes beds in the room. The three of them take turns freshening up in the bathroom. Audie invites John to join in on some Big Apple sight-seeing with him and Kitty. Kitty has no idea that while standing on the shores of the lake last night that John and Audie had plotted out this plan where Audie will ask him to join them only to have John decline his invitation. This way Audie and Kitty get some time alone, and Audie can spring his plans for moving to Nashville to her. The script works perfectly as John tells his brother he's just too tired from all the driving today and wants to take it easy in the hotel room. Kitty asks him if he's sure about that because how often will he get a chance to see New York City. John showcasing some excellent acting chops, still resists, and then insists on staying behind and just watching some hotel TV.

"You two go out and have a good time. You can bring back some cheesy New York City souvenirs for me," John tells then as they are leaving.

"Anything in particular?" Kitty asks him.

John thinks for a second. "How about one of those miniature Statues of Liberty?"

Audie and Kitty chuckle at his pick, but promise to do their best.

After they leave, John considers doing as he said and turning on the boob tube. He props his pillows just right up against the headboard of the bed and flips on the television. But after only about a half hour, he can hear the grumblings in his stomach ordering him to get something to eat. He looks out his room window. Across the street there is a bar and grill advertising the best sliders in town. That or room service he mulls over, before deciding that with Audie not around he could relax and have a few beers across the street without feeling guilty for tempting his brother's weakness. John could also go for one of those sliders they're bragging about with their signs. He throws on some clean clothes and darts across the road dodging traffic carefully.

It doesn't take John long to find a quiet small table in the corner of the place. The lighting in the bar and grill isn't the best, and John is sitting in half light and half shadows. He orders the sliders and a beer and begins nursing the latter when an attractive redhead a few tables from him catches his eye. She lip syncs something in his direction but he has no idea what it is. He points at himself, asking if she's talking to him. She smiles and comes over to his table making it obvious that she is indeed looking his way. She asks him if he is alone while standing over him. John indicates he is, hoping she doesn't see him gulp air from the fit of nerves that has now overcome him because of the attention he's getting from this very sexy woman.

"Would you like some company?" she asks.

"Uh…sure," John musters from his trembling lips.

After sitting down with John, she notices the bandages near his shoulder and asks him what happened.

John tells her that it's a long story, sort of a hunting accident kind of thing. For quite a while they engage in pleasant, particularly generic banter that is until she finds out that he is only in the city for the night. She confesses the same holds for her. "Maybe this is a fortuitous crossing of our paths tonight," she declares to John as she gushes over him with laughter and a smile that could melt cement.

John hasn't been around a lot of women in his life having spent most of his post-puberty existence with Darlene, but he still gets the drift of where this woman is going with all this. He finds himself in the strange place of being both terrified and exhilarated at the same time.

"My name is Bella. What's your name?" she asks with eyes fluttering like they are matching the beats of some familiar song.

She is even more attractive up close than afar as John attempts to organize and manage all his thoughts and all these new sensations flickering in his person.

John introduces himself and nothing else. Name, rank, and serial number he thinks to himself, anything more and he could be in a lot of trouble right now.

"I take it you're single?"

It shouldn't take him this long to answer that, but it does. "I'm not sure, really," he stutters.

"You're not sure? I can't say I've heard that one before," she responds with a laugh. "I was for seven years, and it was like a prison sentence. Now I live for me and what I want. And, John, I never let something good pass me by."

John stammers some more in response even he's not sure what he said.

"It's a little loud in here, don't you think? I've got a hotel room across the street. Would you like to keep me company and have a few more drinks?" she says with a sexy curl in the corner of her mouth.

John bites his lower lip as he considers the offer. Two problems pop into his mind. One, he's only half way through his sliders and still hungry. Second, and a real possibility he thinks, is this gal for real or am I going to get a bill at the end of the night if I actually follow through with her wishes. Oh, and a third important thing comes to mind, Darlene. John knows if he does this he crosses a line that maybe he can't cross back over. But then he thinks she's doesn't want me anymore obviously, so why should I care. Darlene back in Oregon doing God knows what, with God knows who, so the hell with it. He takes a couple quick bites of what's left of his sliders and wolfs them down. "A drink sounds nice," John answers.

Bella whips her head back with laughter. She understands what John is wondering and puts the notion to rest. "You think I'm a hooker! Well, I hate to disappoint you, John but I'm just a woman who likes men and likes spending time with them, and that's all," she says laughing some more. "I really do have a hotel room that is just across the street from here if you are interested," she reveals to John.

John apologizes for thinking anything else, but she doesn't seem offended more bemused by it actually. "It's alright; do you still feel like having that drink with me?" she asks.

A sexy redhead who's funny and has a great smile, why in the world would I not, he tells himself. So John follows her as they exit the bar and grill. He leaves one and a half sliders sitting on the table behind. He may end up leaving more behind by the end of this night.

THE WIND IS WHIPPING THROUGH THEIR HAIR AS THEY look out through the viewers from the one hundred and second floor of the Empire State Building. Kitty gestures to some of the sights to be seen, including Central Park in the distance. After cruising by cab to many of the sights the city has to offer, they ended up here, just as Audie planned. The long summer sun has finally set, and with it now dark, the city is coming to life in all its glory.

"At night the city reminds me of the old Light Brite toy I had as a kid," Audie says as they look out over the glittering skyline.

"That's a funny observation, Audie, I had one of those too." Kitty remembers. "You know a lot of famous movies have been filmed right here."

"You mean in New York?" Audie replies.

"No, silly, I mean here at the Empire State Building," Kitty clarifies.

"Cool, I guess that's true," Audie responds.

Kitty tells Audie that she hopes that John is doing okay. "I wish he would have come with us and had a good time. You don't get to see New York every day."

Audie assures her that John is okay. "He's had a tough six months, you know with his wife and the separation and all that stuff," Audie shares with her. "He's got a lot to work out when he gets back to Oregon."

"What about you? Are you going to stay in Arizona now that you are going to have some money from your father's estate, or go somewhere else?" Kitty would like to know.

Audie couldn't have asked for a better slow pitch over the plate to hit than what Kitty just offered up to him. Now,

FISHING *for* SOMETHING   333

if he can only put his plan into action, or better words. "Funny you should ask," he starts out with. "I was kind of thinking about how much I liked Nashville after visiting it."

"You were?" Kitty responds with surprise.

Audie leans in a little closer to her. "Yeah…I thought maybe you and I could head down there, and I could help you while you try the singing thing."

Audie waits to get the response from Kitty he was hoping for. She seems to be considering in great detail his idea without letting him know what she's thinking. Finally, Audie has to know what's going on in her pretty little head. "Bad idea, maybe?"

Kitty waits, making sure to speak her thoughts carefully. The last thing she wants to do is hurt Audie's feelings. "It's just kind of quick, that's all."

"I know," Audie answers. "We've only known each other for a few days, but…"

Kitty cuts off his next sentence. She puts one finger over his lips in a way that makes her even more desirable to him. "Let's just see how things go, okay. Let's take it slow and get to know each other first."

Audie's head tells him that Kitty is right in her logic, but other parts of him are willing to fight to the death to argue against it. Still he suppresses all that and the disappointment he feels right now and happily holds her hand when she reaches out for his.

"Why don't we get through your father's estate first, and then we can talk about things before you go back," she articulates with reason and wisdom that makes all the sense in the world, but that Audie still hates with a passion.

He agrees, though not happily. "We should take it slow and see how things go."

Kitty is glad that he understands. She then slips into his arms, which only makes Audie feel worse.

"We should probably get back and see how John's doing," Kitty says as she wiggles out of Audie's embrace.

Audie reluctantly agrees. He would love to stay out here and talk her into Nashville and all that it entails, but he can see now is not the time and she's just not ready, so they walk out together toward the elevators.

Kitty stops for a moment before pushing the button to retrieve the elevator. Her stopping makes Audie stop in his tracks as well. She looks at him with an expression that he has in only a short time really began to love. Then she peppers his lips with butterfly kisses. "I had a great time with you today," she whispers in his ear.

Audie in his condition, forces his best pleased look right back at her. "Me too, me too," he says, hoping she doesn't notice how forced his smile really is.

The elevator opens, and Kitty leads him by the hand onto it and back to the hotel.

JOHN TRIES TO NOT STARE AT THE WOMAN'S BODY SO perfectly designed in every way.

He follows her into her hotel room as she requested. He knows he shouldn't be there, but he can't seem to stop himself. Bella invites him to sit down anywhere he pleases, so he sits down in a small chair by a bureau in the room. She asks him if he has any preferences in his spirits to drink, but nervously he tells her anything is fine. His instincts tell him to leave and forget he ever got this far, but his imagination is tantalized by the possibilities tonight might hold. Thoughts dart in his head about Darlene and the kids, how much they mean to him, but then he remembers how much she hurt him by seeing someone behind his back. Bella, this sexy woman he is with, has no idea what is going on inside John as she hands him his drink. "Scotch and water. It always helps relax me and make me loose as a goose," she confesses to John.

Bella takes John by complete surprise when she plops herself onto his lap. "Don't you like scotch?" she murmurs, noticing he has hardly touched his drink.

"It's fine," is all John can think to come back with.

"Your nervousness is very sexy to me," she whispers to him, "very, very, sexy."

"Look, Bella," John fights to say as he struggles against what's about to happen here. But before he can finish his thought, she takes his hand and guides him to his feet. She then destroys the space between them as she presses her body into his. She grabs John's hand and pulls it back behind her and to the zipper keeping her top on. She guides his hand as he unzips her, and then she pulls her blouse off from over her head. Her perfectly posed chest cheers him on from its black lacey brazier.

If this battle inside John were being fought on a hillside, Darlene and the kids would be sliding downhill right about now.

Bella cups both of his hands in hers and leads him to where her impressive assets are barely covered by the black lace.

John can hear his heart racing in his head. When she unzips her skirt, his heart beats a few skips faster. The skirt almost makes an audible sound as it gracefully falls to the floor. John cheats a glance at her bottom half; it doesn't help his cause if he hopes to get away somehow from this temptation he has too easily embraced.

John gets a chill down his back as this gorgeous woman begins to feed on his neck with her lips and her tongue. She seems to be tracing a line from his shoulders to his jaw and back, and he's enjoying every step of her path. Her fingers find the buttons of his plaid shirt and start to undo them. Then with that mission accomplished her nails sink into his chest hairs and tease them for all their worth. Next is the belt holding up his jeans. She wrestles it loose and pulls his pants down with her feet, her lips still locked onto his neck. Urgency begins to drive the engine as she is moving faster now. Bella finishes with his pants and then takes off John's shoes and socks and finally pulls off his shirt.

John is standing before her wearing only his boxers. The last thing protecting his marital faithfulness, not yet torn away from him.

She backs up a few steps, enough for John to get a perfect view of her as she slowly and meticulously takes off her bra and slides her panties down her legs until they are piled up on the floor beneath her.

"Why don't you do away with that and come here," she breathlessly tells John like he's a schoolboy who just got caught doing something wrong.

John reaches down to the elastic band holding his last defense on, but he freezes. Darlene and the kids' faces enter his thoughts at that moment. Why his brain had to pick now, John has no idea. But it's invading his thoughts like an enemy army marching into his territory. No matter what he does, he can't get those faces out of there. By now Bella is staring at him like he's crazy. She's trying to fathom why this man in front of her hasn't taken advantage of the opportunity that most men only dream might happen. "John?"

He struggles for the words to answer her.

She says his name again, wondering if anyone is home inside him.

"I can't do this," he forces out of his mouth.

Bella, this sexy woman, naked before him, is startled by the turn of events and begins to feel a little self-conscious herself. She covers herself with her own hands, the best she can.

"You're incredible, and I am going to always wonder what I missed, but I know what I'm about to lose," John tells her, in a gruff whisper.

"This is the woman that you're kind of single to, I take it," Bella asks him.

John nods as he puts his clothes back on.

"I hope she understands how great a guy she has in you," she professes as she fumbles for her own clothes from the floor, adjusting to the changing situation.

"It's actually the opposite of what you just said," John answers.

"What do you mean?" the woman asks, not understanding.

"It's not how great a guy I am because I'm not. I shouldn't be here with you, but I guess if I can be tempted like this, Darlene can, too," John says with disappointment in himself.

"Darlene's your wife?" Bella assumes.

"Yes, and she's the only woman I've ever really loved, and that's why I can't do this," John states clearly as he puts his clothes back on.

Bella touched by John's loyalty tells him she hopes she finds a good guy like him some day.

Before walking out her door, he tells her she will. "You're a nice person, and with a body like that, I'm sure you will," he says with a grin on his face as he escapes her hotel room alive.

AUDIE AND KITTY MAKE THEIR WAY BACK TO THE HOTEL. John isn't there. They both wonder where he went but assume he got hungry and went out to get something to eat. Before entering the bathroom to get ready for bed, she reminds Audie how big a day tomorrow sounds like it is going to be for him and his brother. She's cheerful and optimistic, but Audie's not feeling it after being rejected when he suggested his "Nashville Plan." While Kitty's still indisposed in the bathroom, John enters the hotel room.

"Where have you been?" Audie greets him.

"Just doing some thinking, brother," John replies back without hesitation.

John is wearing a relaxed, comfortable attitude, which Audie is happy to see. Audie isn't sure if it's of natural origin or chemically created by alcohol, but he's still likes to see it. On that subject, Audie could really use a drink right about now after having his plans squashed by Kitty.

John then recalls Audie's big plans for the night and asks him how it went. Audie is reluctant to spill the beans with Kitty just behind the bathroom door. "You feel like talking, dude," Audie says instead of answering John.

"I guess," John replies. "I've had a real interesting night myself."

Audie declares to Kitty through the door that he and John are going downstairs for a second. Kitty tells them that she may be asleep when they get back, if that's okay.

John butts in to tell her it's no problem, that they will be very quiet when they come back to the room.

They park their seats in some chairs in the hotel lobby. It's getting late now, and only a few hotel employees are mill-ing around. John can see by his brother's countenance that things didn't go tonight as he hoped. "Well, she's still sharing our room so it can't be all bad," John surmises with a laugh.

He doesn't get a like response from Audie. "She wants to take it slow, see how things play out," Audie confides.

John reminds him for the umpteenth time that he has only known this woman for a few days.

"I know, I know, I just thought we had something, you know going," Audie answers with frustration coming from his words.

John does his best to give Audie hope. "You've really connected with her in just a few days, and we still have tomorrow and the next day, who knows, right?"

"I guess, man," Audie conjures up, but with no confidence behind his statement.

"What about you, Johnny? You said you had an interesting night, too. Care to talk? I could use some good news," Audie tells his brother.

John downplays the experiences from earlier tonight and offers no juicy details, which of course there are some, real juicy in fact. "Let's just say I stood on the edge of the abyss, my marriage on one side and a whole different life on the other."

Audie waits for more description, something, but John doesn't offer any.

"And so…?" Audie quietly asks.

John looks pleased with himself as he considers the question. It's a good question, and John's been thinking it through himself since he escaped the redhead's hotel room with his fidelity still intact. He wishes he had a great, wonderful, eloquent speech he could deliver in answer to Audie's probing, but he doesn't. "Audie, I just found out tonight, how much I am still in love with my wife and how much I'm willing to give up to fight for her."

"Well that's a good thing, right?" Audie responds.

John smiles again at his brother before answering. "I hope so because it's all I've got to go on. When I get back to Oregon I'm going to do everything I can to make Darlene understand that she and the kids mean everything to me."

Audie is happy for John's mea culpa and hopes it lasts when faced up against reality back in Grants Pass. "If I have to fight for her against someone else, then that's the way it's going to be, and there's nothing I can do about it," John says for the record.

"She loves you, dude, she always has," Audie reminds. "Why, is a mystery to me, but what can you do."

"Ha ha, you're a real funny man, aren't you?" John responds with a laugh.

"I don't know what I am right now, man, except tired and worn out," Audie answers. "We need to get some sleep. Tomorrow's the big day."

John is quick to agree with Audie. "Last name on the list."

"Yes sir, and then Dad's attorney and finally we get our money," Audie sums up.

"Well, it's been a hell of a trip," John throws out there for consideration or consternation by his kid brother.

"That it is, that it is bro," Audie responds with a yawn messing up his speech.

They both then get up and head back to the room. It's been a long journey since Grants Pass, but now at least they can see the finish line.

KITTY AND THE GUYS MAKE A RUN FROM JOHN'S TRUCK

to the apartment building where the final name on the list resides. An out-of-nowhere summer rainstorm has started, and no one in the city including the three of them, was expecting it. Once inside, they work their way up to the third floor of the old building that has certainly seen better days. Paint and molding are both missing in many spots as they find the right apartment number. John knocks on the door. He has already spoken on the phone to Father Carson, so the priest knows they're coming. Father Carson unlocks numerous locks before opening the door. An old man in his eighties long retired from full-time ministry, the silver-haired man meets them with a warm smile and a hearty handshake as he invites them into his modest living quarters. He knows the boys are sons of Raymond Barrett, and he also lets them know immediately that he knows why they are meeting with him.

"Your father wanted you to see me," Father Carson says.

"How did you know that?" John is quick to ask.

The priest is happy to tell them but first insists they find a place to sit and enjoy a pot of coffee with him. John speaking for the others thinks that sounds nice and they are thankful.

With coffee in hand and cookies as well, Father Carson begins to discuss all he knows about their dad, Raymond Barrett, and his list. "I've been friends with your father for a very long time, boys. And I have gotten especially close with him in the last few years."

John wonders if the Father knows of their dad's death.

"I know the whole story, and I think your father wanted you to know as well, before you go upstate and finish up this journey of yours."

John and Audie aren't quite sure what the Father means by the whole story, so they ask him to help them understand.

"Your dad's childhood as you probably already know was a very difficult one. He was sent to live in the boy's home for quite a while. That's where I met him. Then when he went home, it was still very difficult."

"We know about the evil stepmother, Father," Audie interrupts.

"Yes…she put a great strain on your father's childhood and his relationship with his own father, your grandfather. Your grandfather was very strict and uncompromising. Nothing Ray did as a child was quite good enough for him," the priest continues.

"We've already kind of heard all this, no disrespect intended," as John puts in his own two cents. "Is there something more that our dad wanted you to tell us?"

The Father pauses for a moment to dunk a cookie into his coffee; he explains how good the cookies are soaked in coffee. He then goes into detail. "You see, boys, your dad went through a serious health crisis a few years ago. This made him take a new look over his life and all he had done. He confessed to me how much he regretted leaving you boys and your mother behind. He said he had lived as a coward for that act since the day he did the deed."

"Is that all, Father?" John says coldly in response to the priest's words.

Audie is quick to apologize for his brother's tone. John is just as quick to tell Audie that he has nothing to apologize for. "Listen, Father, this isn't about you, but it is a bit late now for our dad to be trying to make amends, if you know what I mean."

Father Carson lets John know he understands the way he feels but that life often turns out different than the way you think it will.

"Well, it's still too late for dear old Dad to make up for ditching his family all those years ago, I'm pretty sure," John offers with sarcasm.

"That might be true, son," the Father challenges, "but it's not too late for you and your brother to put away the hate that can devour you from inside out. You need to forgive him."

"Forgive him!" John says loudly as he stands up and begins to pace like an uncaged animal. "There's nothing to forgive. He never made the effort!"

"Raymond told me that he sent letters and made phone calls many times over the years to you boys and your mother. I believe that he did try to reach out," the priest boldly tells John.

"Letters, what letters, what phone calls, I never heard of any of this," John argues.

John looks to his brother and Audie backs him up. "That's the first I've heard of that, too, Father," Audie contends, agreeing with John.

Kitty then speaks for the first time since coming into the priest's apartment. She says out loud if it's possible that the boy's mother might have kept these attempts at correspondence by their father from them. John and Audie waste no time defending their mother's integrity on a matter like this. "Mom would never do something like that," Audie responds, to everyone in the room. "Not in a million years, man."

Kitty can see that going any further on this subject is not going to be worthwhile, so she says no more. But Father Carson does. "You know if your mother did keep this information from you, it does in no way make her less of a person."

"Our mother is a saint!" John is fast to point out.

The Father doesn't disagree. He does point out, however, that every human being who has been hurt like their mother was by their father, could be tempted do such a thing and that it again wouldn't make them a terrible person, just one that has been hurt and is in pain. "There aren't many saints left in the world today, John. It's people making decisions in their lives that are sometimes good and often bad. You and your brother were hurt tremendously by your father's leaving. And likewise your father, Raymond, was hurt by the death of his mother at a young age, and the difficult life that proceeded with his stepmother and his father. Your dad wanted you to meet with me so you would know that he understood that he hurt you and that he did want to reconcile with you both."

"If this is how he felt, Father," Audie examines, "why didn't he just come and see us, show up on our doorstep?"

Not wanting to anger John anymore, Father Carson makes sure not to bring their mother back into the conversation. But John does it on his own when he considers what Rose's reaction would have been to see their father again. "She never stopped loving him. Oh, she may have hated what he did, and she certainly did, but she never stopped loving him."

Father Carson tosses out a query to the boys. "What do you surmise then your mother would do if your father was still alive and showed up on her doorstep today?"

Kitty thinks that's a great question and is interested to see what the guys think.

The brothers look at each other and give the question serious thought. Finally, John answers. "Well, I have to say if he was genuinely remorseful, sorry for everything that he put her through, she might talk to him. I guess we'll never know."

"But that would only be after she slapped him across the face a couple dozen times," Audie adds, half serious and half joking.

John motions to his brother and has a chuckle himself. He has to agree with Audie's assessment completely.

"It's too bad we'll never get to find out," John says, taking on a more somber mood.

Audie asks the Father one last thing. "So why all this? The list of names, the gifts for people, the fishing trips with everyone, why all of that?"

The priest clarifies the best he can. "Your father hoped, I believe, that if you knew where he came from, you might understand him better. I think he hoped if you saw that to many people, he wasn't this terrible person you believed him to be, you might find it easier in your heart to forgive him. And God knows everyone needs forgiveness for something. Your father returned to the faith of his childhood in the last few years after surviving his serious illness. He felt God's forgiveness in his life, and now he wanted yours."

A quiet moment overtakes the small living room as John and Audie consider the Father's words. They thank him for his hospitality and his time. Audie then realizes that unlike the other people on the list, there is no gift for the Father or a request for them by their dad, to go fishing with him. Audie asks the Father why this is.

"My placement on Raymond's list was not to get something from you and your brother. I'm on the list instead to give something to you, and I think I just did. Now, may God be with you as you continue on your journey. The next step will be the most important."

The guys don't understand, but that's okay to them. Kitty reminds the boys to give Father Carson Sonny Ricci's regards, as they had promised. The mere mention of his name brings an amused look to the Padre's face. "That scallywag, what is he up to these days?"

"You probably don't want to know, Father," Audie says with a laugh.

Father Carson admits he probably doesn't and shares another laugh with the boys and Kitty before they embark for the final stop on their trip and the big payday they have done all this for, at least Audie that is.

CHAPTER 20

A three-hour drive north and they arrive at the private front gate of what looks like a huge sprawling estate. It lies out in the country. The closest town is Glens Falls, not too far from where New York crosses into Vermont. Neither John nor Audie even have to leave the truck as the electric gate opens and invites them in. The road leading to the main house passes several smaller secondary houses that are nicer than John's home back in Oregon.

"Wow, this place is awesome!" Audie exclaims as they make their way up to the main house, before parking.

A man in a three-piece navy suit meets them as they climb out of the truck.

"Dad was filthy rich," Audie says as he studies the huge home standing before them.

It is one of those large log cabin homes you see on television but rarely in real life. But this is a huge log cabin house, not a little one like you normally see.

"I wonder who gets this place?" Audie says out loud as they walk up to the neatly dressed older gentleman.

John orders Audie to pipe down as he introduces the three of them to the man.

"I'm Mr. Monroe, the attorney who put the letter together that led you here," he informs them.

"This all belonged to our father, Mr. Monroe?" Audie has to ask him straight up.

The attorney tells them it will all be revealed to them in a moment. He tells them to follow him inside. Once inside, he leads them through the house. Audie's tongue is almost touching the ground with the hope that this home is somehow going to either him or John. Hopefully him of course, Audie is thinking.

"Now through these doors and into the backyard area, please," Mr. Monroe says.

Another older gentleman wearing an athletic jumpsuit of sorts crosses their path and stops the attorney long enough to ask if these are Ray's boys. The attorney confesses that they are and then leads the boys and Kitty further on.

"Who is that?" John asks of Mr. Monroe.

"Oh that is Mr. Randolph Templeton. He is the owner of this estate," the attorney discloses to John.

Audie stops the attorney in his tracks. "I thought my father owned the estate."

"No," Mr. Monroe answers abruptly. "But you will understand everything in a moment just as I said. Now please continue to follow me."

They do as they are told and follow the attorney into a smaller house behind the main home.

The boys and Kitty are asked to sit down at a kitchen table that looks like it came from a diner in the fifties. Mr. Monroe informs them that he will tell him they are here.

John and Audie look at each other. They both have no idea who this "him" is.

"I thought it was the attorney we were here to meet, Johnny," Audie says.

"I thought so, too," John answers.

Kitty is amused by both of them. She has nothing to add, yet.

Then they hear the front door open and footsteps moving their way. A moment later a familiar man walks into the kitchen. "Hello, boys."

He's a lot older than when they last saw him. He's heavier and well-worn, but they still recognize him after all these years.

"I bet you're a tiny bit surprised to see me," Ray Barrett tells his two sons.

"What the hell is going on?!" John responds.

"Why?" is the only thing Audie can come up with.

Ray runs his hand through his thinning hair searching for the right words. "I just wanted to see ya," he answers.

The brothers look at each other. They're not sure what to think, much less what to say right now. John does his best. "So all this, the will, the letter, it was all to trick us to come out here and visit you?"

Ray shrugs as he tries to explain. "The people on the list are all real. They are all good friends of mine who helped shape me in one way or another. I wanted you to see that I wasn't some kind of awful person to everybody in my life. I wanted you to know that there are people who actually like me and care about me."

"So you tricked us. After all of this you're not even dead," John reasons in anger.

"I did deceive you to get you to come here, but, boys, I didn't see a better way," Ray confesses.

Audie suggests, "How about just contacting us the old-fashioned way, by phone, email, even mail?"

As Father Carson told them that morning, Ray promises that he did for many years try to reach out, but was stopped by their mother from making any contact with the boys. "Your mother said that if I wasn't coming home to stay that she didn't want me to have any communications with you guys. So I respected her wishes, as hard as it was to do that."

"So you're blaming all these years of you being gone, an absent father and husband, you're blaming all that on Mom?" John challenges.

Ray denies that he's blaming anyone but himself. "I'm the one who screwed up and left my family. I've got no one else to blame but the face in the mirror that I have a hard time looking at some days."

"Dad, we almost got killed a couple of times traveling to come here," Audie discloses. "I mean dammit, Dad, Johnny got shot in Texas and I almost became a shark's dinner."

"I know. Bobby called and told me all about it, crazy thing," Ray responds.

"Wait a minute. Bobby knew you were still alive? Did everybody on the list know that this was just a big joke on us?" John wants to know.

"No, only Bobby and Father Carson knew that I was not dead. They were willing to go along with things, to help me out. When I heard about what happened at Falcon Lake, I had somebody, a good friend of mine, keep a watch on you two."

"Who is that?" Audie asks.

To Audie's shock, his father glances at Kitty sitting next to him.

"What?" Audie asks her. "You were hired by my dad to keep an eye on us?"

Kitty nods her head. She can see the look of betrayal in Audie's eyes.

"So you were lying to me the whole time. You were just playing a part. Wow, you're a hell of actress," Audie says, his hurt feelings coming through stronger now.

Ray doesn't help things when he confides that she has been an actress before and a singer and that's why she was so perfect for the job. "She actually works here with me on Mr. Templeton's estate, as an assistant to him. He was nice enough to let her have time off to do this for me. Mr. Templeton paid all her expenses. He's a great man who's helped me a lot."

Kitty tries to justify herself to Audie, but he's in no mood to hear it. He storms out of the room telling John he'll be waiting in the truck for him. Kitty is saddened by Audie's reaction. She tells John, as she chokes up, that she was only trying to help their father and never meant to hurt Audie. Holding back the tears, Kitty also flees from the home.

It leaves John and his father and a whole lot of silence filling the room. Finally, Ray says he's sorry for everything. "I didn't think the trip would turn out this way for you boys. I didn't know about Audie's gambling debts and who he owed money to, you know."

John shows no reaction to his father's words. He's not sure if it's his time to storm out or not, or even if he wants to, but he does want answers. "And the fifty thousand a piece?"

"I've been working here for five years for Mr. Templeton as his head groundskeeper. I've got about ten thousand each saved up for you boys. It's not a fortune, but it's honest wages," Ray discloses to his oldest boy.

John lifts his hands up in the air. He asks his father who he hasn't seen since he was a teenager but who is standing in front of him right now, "So now what? You got your wish and got us here. Now what do you want from us?"

Ray doesn't hem or haw. He gets straight to the point. "Let's start small. How about dinner tonight? We can discuss all this and what comes next, maybe," Ray responds. "If you can talk Audie into it?"

John thinks they've come a long ways to not at least hear him out. John tells his father they'll stay for dinner, but if things go south, he and Audie will just drive back to Oregon and forget that any of this ever happened.

"Fair enough, Johnny," Ray replies. "Mr. Templeton is going to let us use the big dining room in the main house for dinner tonight. His personal chef is going to cook up something special for us all."

John isn't in the right attitude to be excited by what his father just said, but out of courtesy and manners he tells him they will be there at the appointed time. John excuses himself and goes back to the truck to try and talk a wounded Audie into staying for dinner and at least hearing what their father has to say. Funny how the tables have suddenly turned, John considers, as now he is the one reaching out more to their father.

———⊂∞⊃———

"Everything looks wonderful, don't you agree?" Ray observes, as he tries to break the ice.

Reluctantly, John and Audie pick at the steak and potatoes dinner that has been laid out before them by their father and Mr. Templeton's personal chef. Audie's eyes are mostly looking down at his plate; the revelations from earlier in the day have sapped the usual optimism right out of his person. While he sits next to his brother at the large log-cabin-style dinner table, Kitty sits across from him, next to Ray. She takes peeks at him, hoping to make eye contact. Once in a while it's successful, but Audie is quick to look away when their eyes do meet.

John wants to cut to the chase. He asks his father to get to the point of this dinner.

Ray receives that like a body blow to his ribs. He's ecstatic to be sitting down with his two sons after all these years, even if they don't feel the same way. Ray studies the room. Only he seems to be happy to be present.

"I want to thank you boys for staying for dinner. This means the world to me," he shares with them. "I know how much you hate me for what I did, and you have every right."

John sarcastically thanks him for giving them that right before again pushing his father to get to the "'meat'" of what he has to say to them.

Ray takes a swig of something from the table that's from a bottle. It's a last-ditch effort to find some courage before he speaks his mind.

"Two years ago the final curtain almost came down on my life, and while I lay in what I thought was going to be my deathbed, I took a good long look at my life, and hated what I saw."

Ray's opening salvo has at least gotten the boy's attention as even Audie looks up from his plate to watch his father speak.

"When we were kids and we'd play a game if something happened that didn't seem fair or outside the rules, we'd yell do-over," Ray continues. "After lying there for months on end and looking at my life, I told myself if I got a second chance, I'd want a do-over."

John butts in, "I'm sorry for what you went through, but sometimes it's too late to change what's happened."

Ray with his hand stroking his chin, considers John's declaration. Then he argues against it. "It's never too late if you still have a heart that's beating and air in your lungs son."

"A second chance, Dad, is a two-way street," John contends.

Ray has to laugh at his oldest boy's resolve. "You're just as stubborn as your mother, and I love it. But you are right, Johnny. It is a two way street and that's why you and Audie are here today. That's why I went to all this effort and trouble to get you here. And, Audie, don't be angry with Kitty. She was just doing me a big favor by keeping an eye on you boys and helping to steer you two here to me."

Kitty reaches out and squeezes Ray's hand, her way of thanking him for his kind words. Audie, still grim faced, like John pushes for his dad to get on with whatever else he has to say before they head back to Oregon.

"I want you boys to give me a do-over. I've wanted it for years actually even before I got sick. I respected your mom's wishes and stayed away, but I don't want to stay away anymore. I want whatever time I have left to be spent with my family, my boys and maybe…" Ray answers.

The brothers glance at each other. Audie has for so long wanted to have his dad in his life again. John, however, is a much harder sell.

"Look, I don't want to be a cold-hearted bastard, Dad, but you're asking a helluva' a lot," John says honestly. "I've gotten use to hating you for a long time now."

"I know," Ray replies.

Audie asks his father what exactly he wants from them. "We can't just act like all these years since you left never happened, Pop."

Ray understands and doesn't expect them to. He asks them for an opportunity, not a promise of results. "I'd like to go back to Oregon with you boys. Beyond the ten thousand dollars I've saved for each of you, I have also saved some money up for myself. Mr. Templeton has been nice enough to give me a paid leave of absence from here."

"I don't know," is all John can come up with.

"Just an opportunity, Johnny, like I said, nothing else, like going fishing, boys, I just want to cast my line, be patient and see what happens," Ray tells them.

Audie says he's willing to take his father up on his offer. John, however, thinks about his mother and as he always has, defends her. "There's one problem. Even if we were willing to give you a chance, Mom might be to hurt by all this. And after all that she has endured because of you, I won't let you hurt her again, and I am definitely not going to betray her trust."

Ray assures John he does not want him to. "When I get to Oregon, I want to make things right with your mom, the best that's possible."

For the first time during dinner, laughter of any kind is heard as Audie imagines what their mother's reaction might be to seeing their father again, in the flesh.

"I'm going to apologize and make peace with her. She can spit on me, even shoot me as long as it's only a flesh wound. It's all okay. I can't say I don't have it coming," Ray tells his sons.

"Ha, that's good Dad, because she might do all those things to you and more, man," Audie responds still chuckling at the thought of a reunion between his father and mother.

Ray asks his sons once more if they'll just give him one more chance.

The guys glance at each other again before giving their final answer. Audie again agrees to it. "You went to lot trouble for this, and even though you tricked us in coming here, I guess your motives were good. I'm willing to give you a chance."

Then it's John's turn to decide. He finds it ironic that his old man is sitting before him alive, after all these years, asking him for the same thing that he will be asking Darlene for when he gets back to Oregon. Can he turn down his father's request for a second chance when he wants one so badly from his wife? John decides he can't. "Okay, we'll give this a whirl and see where it leads us. I hope you like sitting in a backseat. It's a long drive back to Oregon."

"Oh, we're not driving, son," Ray answers confidently.

"We're not?" John replies.

"No we're flying. In fact first class thanks to Mr. Templeton," Ray surprises them with.

"What about my truck?" John asks.

"An auto delivery company will bring it out to you in Oregon," Ray spells out.

John and Audie look at each other and at the same time and say, "Mr. Templeton!"

"Wow, Pop, this boss of yours if a helluva guy," Audie has to say, for all he's doing for their father.

Ray admits he is more than a boss, but also a good friend. "He gave me this job and helped me get my act together. I owe him a heck of a lot. So, we leave tomorrow morning for Oregon."

John has just one more thought, though, that he has to add. "These flight tickets, you already had them it sounds like. How did you know we would say yes?"

"I didn't," Ray answers, "but I assumed God spared me for something two years ago, plus I'm not an idiot. The tickets are fully refundable, even the day of."

Everyone laughs at Ray's honesty and stab at humor. Ray tries to remember the last time he enjoyed such a laugh with his boys. He really can't because it's been such a long, long time.

Hours have passed since dinner. Audie is lying in bed, a bedsheet up to his chin. He's in one of the main house's guest bedrooms. There's a television in the room, but he hasn't even thought about turning it on. He's thinking, just thinking, trying to absorb the twists of the day when there is a quiet knock at his door. "Yeah?" he answers, interrupted from his daydreaming.

"It's Kitty, can I come in for a minute?"

Audie isn't sure he wants to say yes, but he's too good-natured to say anything else.

Kitty makes herself comfortable on the edge of his bed. She bounces playfully a few times up and down and declares how cushy the bed is. It's her attempt at thawing things between them. She wastes no time in apologizing for her deception. "I'm sorry I hurt you Audie, but I couldn't tell you the truth without giving away your father's plans and jeopardizing you and John coming here."

Audie listens as he stares to other parts of the room.

Kitty admits that she was more than a little flattered and touched by his offer to move to Nashville for her benefit.

That one sentence gets his attention immediately. "Really?"

"Really," she answers without any hesitation. "You're a sweet guy, and you have a great heart, and I've seen that in just the few days we've known each other."

"But," Audie interrupts.

"But nothing" Kitty continues, "I just wanted you to know those things, and if you still can find it in your... you know you still kinda' like me, maybe we could talk about that."

Her charm reminds him of why he liked her in the first place. She asks Audie if maybe they could just start over. Audie still feeling that chemistry between them says he would like that. A relieved Kitty confesses that Ray has invited her to fly back to Oregon in the morning with them.

She will only go if Audie wants her to. He is thrilled with the news. He figures she must really like him if she wants to fly back to Oregon with him. He tells her that's about the best thing he's heard in a long time.

"So you really want to fly back to Grants Pass with us?"

Kitty flashing her pearly whites and her beautiful baby blues, a combination any man would risk his life for, promises to Audie that she does.

Now with the chemistry back in place, Audie has a few things he's been wondering about since he found out about her working on behalf of his father during their trip here. "How long did you study singing and acting because, boy, you are good at both?" he gushes over her.

"Throughout high school and college, I really did want to make it as singer." she confides.

Audie wonders what stopped her.

"Believe it or not, stage fright. I was terrified the whole time during that karaoke contest."

Audie laughs at the revelation. He never would have known that by watching her.

"Your father and Mr. Templeton thought I would be perfect for keeping an eye on you and making sure you made it all the way here," Kitty discloses.

Audie is interested in the man in Nashville who played her uncle and why the elaborate staging of something like that.

Kitty shares that it was just a local actor they paid to perform the little skit. "We did that so you and John would really believe I was who I said I was. Ray thought it would be a good idea."

Then the tough one, at least for Audie, to ask Kitty about the night in the motel room after the karaoke contest, was that real or just acting, he wants to know.

"No," Kitty doesn't hesitate to answer. "That was very real, and that's why I had to stop."

The room got a lot warmer all of a sudden as Audie has only one more question for Kitty.

"So did they pay you well for all this?"

"Mr. Templeton did. He made all this happen for Ray. He really cares about your dad, and he wanted to do everything he could to help Ray reunite with you and John," Kitty responds.

Audie has to admit that Mr. Templeton seems like a one-in-a-million kind of guy.

"He really is," Kitty says.

"Any more questions, I'm happy to tell you whatever you want to know, Audie."

Audie tells her no. He thinks he understands it all now.

Kitty playfully slides her body toward him at the head of the bed. She leans forward, face to face. "I'm really glad we had this talk. And I'm really glad I'm going to Oregon with you."

"I am too," Audie tells her.

"Do you want me…" she pauses for effect, "to stay here with you tonight?"

"Yes," Audie whispers. "Yes, I do, I really do. If you want to that is."

"Good," Kitty replies back as she leans in closer and closer, culminating with her lips slithering between his.

"I'll take that as a yes," Audie says with a laugh as he kisses her back.

Kitty pulls away for a second, long enough to go and lock the bedroom door.

Audie, his heart pounding, watches as she climbs into bed with him.

"I have never really felt like this about anyone else before," Kitty confides to him as she snuggles up with him under the covers.

"Me neither," Audie whispers back as he takes her in his arms.

Audie and Kitty are interrupted when John knocks on the bedroom door.

"Are you asleep?" John calls out to his brother.

Audie tells him no and asks him what he wants.

"Not much," John tells him. "I just thought I'd check on you, that's all."

Audie's not sure what to make of that but thanks his big brother just the same. "You okay, man?"

John answers that he thinks he is after the crazy events today. John is still in shock that their father is still alive after being duped into thinking he wasn't.

"You worried about what happens when we get back to Oregon?" Audie asks John through the door.

John's admits he is and asks he if can come into the

bedroom. Audie wants to say no for obvious reasons, but Kitty won't let him. "It's okay," she tells Audie.

With that Audie gets up and unlocks the bedroom door. John comes walking in only to be surprised and a little embarrassed to find Kitty with his brother.

"Oh, I'm really sorry," he tells them both. "I should go."

Kitty tells him not to. "I'm the one who can be scarce for a few minutes. You guys talk about what you need to, okay," she says to both of them.

Audie sighs with frustration as he sits up in bed. Kitty leaves for a few minutes. Audie reaches out and squeezes John's arm and tells him, "This better be important dude."

John looks at his brother and playfully smacks his cheek. He tells Audie it can wait for another time, but his brother insists that he talks about it now. "You interrupted nirvana, the least you can do is tell me why."

John grapples for the right words, but Audie already knows what all this is about. "I know you are afraid, Johnny. There is no shame in that. Just pour out your heart and soul to Darlene. That's all you can do."

John asks if Audie thinks that will work to win back his wife.

"If it doesn't, man, then nothing will, but at least you fired all your bullets," Audie says to his big brother.

"You're right," John answers as he thanks Audie for talking to him. John then asks if he wants him to tell Kitty that he and Audie are done with their little talk.

"What do you think, bro," Audie replies, with a laugh at the obvious.

They say their goodnights, and John goes to track Kitty down.

CHAPTER 21

Rose is in the laundry room taking clothes out of the dryer at John and Darlene's house when the doorbell rings. She yells to the kids that she will see who it is. Rose finds a place to put down her folded clothes and makes her way to the front door. She looks through the peephole, and there standing on the doorstop is John with Audie by his side. A happy yelp comes flying out of her mouth as she hurries to unlock and open the door. "My boys!" she yells as she falls first into John's arms and then Audie's.

Audie kisses her on the cheek as he tells her it's good, so good to see her. Rose yells to the children playing in their rooms that their dad is home. John's kids hearing this, come running to greet him. They almost knock him down as they gang hug him for all its worth. "Daddy! Daddy! You're finally home!" Courtney screams loudly with childish delight.

Cody and Kyle are thrilled to see him to, and let him know as well. John couldn't have wished for a better homecoming as he squeezes all three of them with all of his might.

"Where's Mommy?" John urgently wants to know, while still holding them close.

"Mommy's not here," Courtney says in her sweet little voice.

Cody explains that mom has gone shopping with her friend Lorinda.

John asks if anyone knows where they went.

"Gooseberries, dear, Darlene said she was going to Gooseberries," Rose remembers.

John acknowledges the information. He has a determined look of somebody who is on a mission, maybe because he is. He squeezes the kids one more time and tells them that he'll be right back, but first he needs to go see Mommy, right away.

Rose inquires why he can't just wait till she gets back, not wanting him to leave so fast.

"Some things just can't wait, Mom," he tells his mother.

Audie reminds John of the couple of somethings still in the rental car out front.

"Right," John responds, "Mom, we've got something to tell you and you might want to sit down."

"Oh, my God!" Rose says with alarm in her voice as she collapses down onto John and Darlene's couch. "What is it?"

John and Audie look at each other hoping the other one has the right words to say it. Unfortunately both guys are at a loss on how to get started. Audie always the better talker of the two, takes a stab at it. "Mom, you're a person who believes in forgiveness, right?"

Rose has no idea what he's talking about but offers a positive answer.

"You believe people deserve a second chance, maybe a third or fourth if they're sincere?" Audie heralds.

"What are you getting on about?" Rose wants to know.

"Mom, just try to keep an open mind and be as civil as you can, please," John says to her, making her even more confused about what her boys are talking about.

Andrew Scott Bassett

"This is a definite Band-Aid situation," Audie cracks to his brother.

John asks him what he means.

Audie tells him that they could talk until they're blue in the face, but it isn't going to matter so they should just get it over with. "It's like a Band-Aid. Its hurts less if you just rip it off fast and get it done with," Audie thinks.

John agrees with his brother, and besides he wants the rental car right now so he can go and see Darlene, while he still has the courage to do so. He tells Audie that'll he'll go get them as he races out the front door.

"Get who, dear?" Rose asks Audie.

"You'll see in a second, Mom, and remember what Johnny said," Audie pleads.

The sound of a car starting up in the front as John drives away is followed by a knock on the front door. Audie is quick to answer it, but he opens the door only a small crack to see who's up first. He lets Kitty slip inside through the door. Rose asks who this might be.

Audie introduces Kitty to his mother.

"I don't understand, dear. Why would you think I wouldn't be nice to this lovely young lady here?" Rose asks.

Kitty jumps in to help Audie. "I'm sorry but it's not me they're worried about you having a problem with, Mrs. Barrett."

"No? I don't understand," Rose replies.

"Band-Aid time," Audie says to Kitty as he opens the front door a second time.

"Hello, Rose, it's been a long time," Ray says as he takes a measured step inside the house.

Audie and Kitty marvel as Rose's pupils seem to double in size before their eyes. She says nothing for what seems like minutes but is only really about thirty seconds.

"Oh, my gracious goodness," she finally utters in strange voice.

"How have you been?" Ray follows up with.

"How have I been? You are supposed to be dead," Rose shrieks at him.

Kitty suggests that she and Audie and the children should give them a little space to talk. Audie is quick to agree with her. He herds up his two nephews and niece with Kitty's help and leads them back to Cody's bedroom.

"Surprised, I imagine?" Ray nervously asks her.

"Blimey, it's bloody well more than that!" Rose tells him in no uncertain terms.

She demands to know why Ray made everyone believe he was dead, why he made their boys travel across the country to see him.

Ray looks down searching for the right words. Now is not the time for smartassness, that's for sure, and Ray knows that. Sincerity doesn't come second nature to Ray, never has, but he needs that to be his pitch to Rose right now. He starts with putting across his desire to see his boys again and knowing they would probably never agree to see him if he was living. "I can only guess how much you and the boys have hated me over the years for leaving, so this seemed like the only way I could get Johnny and Audie to come meet with me."

Rose shakes her head in disgust. She's always fantasized about seeing him and letting him know in a hurtful way how much damage he had done to their family, to their sons. She agrees with Ray about the hating all these years, but not so much about them not wanting to see him if he was alive. "Boys need their fathers, boys want to be loved by and spend time with their fathers. If you had tried hard enough, they would've seen you."

Ray then reminds Rose, wise or unwise, how much he did try for a few years after leaving to connect with his sons. "You didn't want me to have anything to do with them, remember? You forbid me unless I came back to you and made things right with you. I wasn't ready back then."

"Can you bloody well blame me?!" Rose comes back at him, her voice rising with anger.

Audie and Kitty are eavesdropping from the backroom. Audie whispers to Kitty that things don't sound like they are going well. Kitty isn't too shocked. She can hear the pain in Rose.

Ray's next words are critical, and he knows it. He tells her that in all honesty he used to blame her for not letting him have a relationship with their children, but that doesn't matter anymore.

"You have a lot of nerve blaming me for anything!" Rose hollers at him, her past hurt flowing from her voice and words.

Ray tells her she is right. He tells her he has no one to blame but himself. "Life wasn't good back then, and I screwed everything up. I thought I wanted a different life, Rose, than the one I had with you. Well, I got it, and with you and the kids not in it, it was pretty empty."

Rose isn't sure why he is even telling her this now, after all these years.

"Because," Ray answers, "why do you think I'm standing here before you right now?"

Rose tells him she isn't sure.

"I got to finally see my boys in New York," he says and then pauses. "I came to Oregon to see my wife," Ray says with as much sincerity as he can muster.

Audie and Kitty do their best to try to get the children to be quiet as they wait for Rose's response. She seems not to have one. Finally she offers an I-don't-understand defense.

Ray does his best to explain himself, for what it's worth. "I'm here, Rose, because of you. Leaving you was the biggest regret of my life. And now seeing you again, after all these years, well, I know it was the biggest mistake I ever made."

Rose asks him if he really thinks his pretty words make up for everything. She crosses her arms in a stance of defiance in front of him. Ray remembers that stance from their marriage, oh so well.

"I'm not here to say I can make up for anything," Ray declares. "I know I can't. I'm just here to say I'm sorry. I'm not the same man I was all those years ago. Hell, I'm not the same guy I was two years ago when I almost died. The self-indulgent, selfish bastard who thought he knew everything and had every answer, he's been dead for a long time now, Rose."

"So who's this standing before me then?" Rose asks, her arms still crossed.

Ray has to think about that. He's spent so much of the last few years thinking about the past and what he isn't anymore. He hasn't given a whole heck of a lot of thought about who he really is now. Standing dumbfounded, he has no easy answer.

"I am sorry for what I did to you, Rose, I'll go outside and call for a cab. I can get a flight back to New York," Ray tells her, giving up on any other plans he had for this trip.

But before he can turn the knob on the front door, Rose stops him. "I'm not sure I'm ready for you to go yet. I might be in a few hours, mind you, but not yet. I'd like to get to hear about this new fella you're speaking of," she tells Ray offering him a stay of execution of sorts.

Ray turns to her and releases the doorknob. He smiles as he says how much of a pleasure it would be for him to introduce her to this new gentleman that she has only briefly met in the past.

"Well, then," Rose says, "why don't you have a seat? I'll make you and Audie and the girl something to eat. You must be famished."

Ray sits down and is quickly greeted by Audie, Kitty, and by his three grandchildren who heard the whole conversation, the three grandchildren he has never met before. Audie makes the formal introductions.

"Are you my dad's dad?" Courtney asks him.

"Yes, he's our grandfather," Cody is quick to tell her.

Ray smiles and pats her on her head. "I am your grandfather, young lady, and it's nice to finally meet you."

<hr/>

As soon as John enters the Gooseberries Grocery Store, his eyes dart from one side of the store to the other in search of Darlene. No luck at first, and since she's not driving her car, John has no idea if she's in the store or not. He starts making his way past one aisle after another. Eventually John spots her and another woman on the last aisle he checks. The two ladies are in the corner where the dairy products are sold. John sneaks down the aisle that is before theirs, in hopes of getting the maximum surprise value for being home. He makes his way to the end of his aisle and peeks around the corner. He sees Darlene talking with her friend. John can hear every word they're saying, they're debating flavored coffee creamers and other things as he listens intently.

"Some of these are just too sweet for me," Lorinda tells Darlene.

Darlene says it depends on the flavor for her.

"Well, I don't mind my coffee being tasty, but I don't want it to taste like a milkshake either," Lorinda opines with a snort.

"John's the same way. He always tells me that we should be able to taste the coffee that's in our coffee," Darlene jokes.

Lorinda mentions to her friend that his name has come up about eight times since they left the house. Darlene isn't aware of that and hasn't noticed it.

"You are really missing him, aren't you," Lorinda says.

Darlene would like to pooh-pooh Lorinda's intuition but doesn't have the energy or the will to do it. If she can't tell Lorinda what she's going through, who can she, Darlene decides.

John's ears perk up as he listens as Darlene discloses her feelings to her friend.

"It's the strangest thing," Darlene starts with. "Before he left on this trip with his brother, he irritated me almost every time I saw him."

"And now?" Lorinda asks.

"Now, knowing he's not around, I don't know, I guess I miss him more. When he was here I knew I'd see him. With him gone I find myself thinking about him all the time. Kinda' crazy isn't it?" Darlene reveals as she grabs one bottle of coffee creamer and puts back another.

Lorinda tells her she doesn't think it's crazy at all. "So what do you miss most, and don't say sex?"

Darlene chuckles under her breath, just a tad; she admits she does miss the intimacy a whole bunch. But there are many other things, too. She begins to roll out a list of things from her memories, mostly the little moments in life that you give only small thought to when they're happening, but realize their significance when they're gone. One of them she states in more detail. "Eighties movie night."

"What do you mean?" Lorinda replies. "You mean movies made in the eighties?"

"Every once in a while, John and I would just binge on old movies. I mean not too old, like I said, usually the eighties movies were the ones we would agree on," Darlene expounds.

"Really, are we talking chick-flicks or action films, horror, comedy, what?" Lorinda questions, wanting more info.

Darlene says it was a lot of everything, but that John was good about suffering through her girly flicks.

Lorinda is surprised. "What chick-flick did you both like?"

Darlene thinks for a minute, but quickly comes up with an answer. "An Officer and a Gentleman," she says. "John and I both liked that one."

"Oh, that was a good one," Lorinda has to admit.

"I still get a little goosepimply about the ending," Darlene says remembering.

"Oh, where Richard Gere goes in and gets Debra Winger and…"

"Yeah…" Darlene responds cutting off Lorinda's words. "That was so romantic; they just don't make movies like that anymore."

"They sure don't," Lorinda agrees, before spouting off, "Richard Geres are extinct, too."

John hearing all this, knows what he has to do. He comes out of hiding from the next aisle and surprises the girls.

"John! I didn't know you were back!" Darlene offers up in shock.

"Well, I guess I am," John replies, right before saying hello to Lorinda. "I just got back."

Darlene isn't sure what to say. A moment ago she was missing him and fantasizing about good times with him, but now reality kicks her in the teeth and he's standing right in front of her. "You never called me back."

Lorinda excuses herself from the situation. She escapes over to the bakery to give the two of them a chance to talk.

John apologizes for that. He admits to being angry with her before seeing things clearer. "It took me seeing myself for who I am, the good and the bad, before I could appreciate what I had in you."

Darlene has never really heard John talk to her like this before and doesn't know how to take it, or more importantly react to it. His talking about feelings is a new deal for sure.

"I know you're seeing another man, whatever, but I'm not going to give you up without a fight," he tells her boldly. "I want you back."

Darlene tries in vain to interrupt him long enough to let him know that the other man thing is nothing to worry about right now, but she is talked over by John who is determined to say his peace.

"I'm madly in love with you, always have been and always will be. Even if it took me spending a couple of frustrating and even painful weeks with my kid brother, where I was shot, chased, and almost bled to death, I still finally figured it out," John tells her emphatically.

Darlene goes on to say something, but is again cut off by John who is charged up like a new car battery.

"All I need to know is that you still somewhere in there," he says pointing at her heart, "still have the smallest, tiniest, smattering of love for me, and I'll do what you want. I'll quit my side business; I'll focus everything I have and dedicate my life to you and the kids. I will prove to you, that you and the kids are the most important thing in my life."

Lorinda, unable to not hear this, even from a distance in the grocery store, like most of the other shoppers, is touched. She says quietly to herself, "Wow."

Everyone on that side of the store is waiting for Darlene's response. Darlene is waiting for her response, too. She shakes and paces, trying to conjure up the right words as John waits for it. There's dead silence in the market as Darlene reaches out to cup John's hands in hers. "You were shot and almost bled to death?" It just hits her.

"It takes a lot for me to get my mind right," John confesses with a laugh.

Darlene grins as she guides his face to hers. She kisses him like she hasn't kissed him in years. A reward she tells herself for John being brave enough to do a very un-John kind of thing, and let his feelings spill all over the floor of "Gooseberries," like he just did.

John has tingles from his chipped toenails to his receding hairline, but still wants an official answer to his question. "So?" he says.

Darlene smiles and shakes her head like even she is surprised by what she's about to say. "John, even when I've been mad at you and I have many times in the last few years, I never stopped loving you," she tells him as she leans up to him and kisses him once more.

"Well alright then!" John hollers as he grabs her and picks her up off the ground.

Darlene between giggles asks him what he thinks he's doing.

"You just bring the Richard Gere out in me," he tells her as he steals another kiss.

Lorinda claps as they stroll by her and Darlene waves to her friend. "I'll see you tomorrow at the café," Darlene tells her as they pass.

Lorinda waves back and tells Darlene she's lucky.

As they walk through the front doors Darlene informs John that he can put her down now. But John insists that he won't. "That's not the way an officer and gentleman would do it. He would take you all the way to the car, although my arm that got shot is hurting."

"Well then put me down! Don't hurt yourself, John!" Darlene orders him with concern.

John just laughs. "It's okay, honey, you're worth it."

John refuses to put her down as he carries her to his rental car and to a new start, a fresh start.

"Plop!" The sound the line makes as the fishing lure and sinker hit the surface of the water. Audie waves from the small fishing boat drifting about fifty yards from shore. He's joined on the boat by his father and John.

Kitty waves back to him from shore. She's helping Rose and Darlene make lunch for everyone while Darlene's kids play a game of go-fish on an old picnic table beside them. Lorinda has tagged along and is helping little Courtney beat her older, more experienced brothers, in the card game.

"It fills me with joy to see you and Johnny together again," Rose tells Darlene as they put the fixings together for sandwiches, for everyone.

"I know, Rose," Darlene responds. "I have to be honest; John is trying really hard to make things better. He's only going to be working at the mill for now. He wants to be at all of Cody's games, and we're going out just the two of us, tomorrow night."

"Am I watching the children, dear?" Rose is interested to know, since this is the first she's heard about tomorrow night's festivities.

"Nope, it's covered, Rose," Darlene answers, as she gets a thumbs up from Lorinda, willing and ready to serve.

Lorinda affirms for Rose's benefit, that it is no bother at all for her to watch John and Darlene's kiddies since she's the only one here at the moment without a man in her life, before starting to laugh at her reality.

Rose laughs with her and promises that she will soon, being such a pretty woman and with such a great sense of humor.

"Speaking of that, Rose, how are things with you and Ray, two days and counting now?" Darlene acknowledges.

Rose chuckles once more as she gathers her thoughts. "It's complicated, dear, after all these years. Ray's still a charmer, and he has been sweet. We're not even taking it day by day at this point; it's more like minute by minute. After all the terrible things that are in the past and after how long I got use to the idea of hating him, it's complicated."

"I heard from John that Ray wants you to go back to New York with him," Darlene notes.

"So he tells me," Rose says as she finishes up the last sandwich.

"I think you would really like it there, to visit," Kitty interjects into the conversation, not trying to eavesdrop on Rose and Darlene, but doing so just the same.

"I'm sure I would, dear. We will have to see." Rose replies. "Like I said, it's complicated, this forgiveness muck."

"Well, so far so good, and I'm proud of you and the way you're handling things with Ray," Darlene let's Rose know.

"It's not easy, God knows. One minute I want him to hold me in his arms and never let go, and the next minute I want to jam a bread knife into his neck for the past, complicated," Rose shares as she starts a hearty laugh.

The other ladies can't help but join in and enjoy the humor of the situation.

"I think that's how every woman feels about her man," Darlene says, laughing even more.

Kitty feels comfortable enough to join in. "I have to say that Audie has been so great. We've only know each other for a short time, but it seems like I've known him forever. He wants me to move here to Grants Pass and be with him," Kitty tosses into the conversation pit.

"Audie is planning on staying here?" Darlene asks. It's the first she's heard this.

Kitty says yes. "John told him he can get him on at the mill, so that's what he's thinking."

"So are you going to move here?" Rose asks her, hoping the answer is positive.

Kitty smiles, "It sounds kind of silly since like I said, we haven't known each other for very long, but if it's okay with you ladies, I think I'm going to. I hope that's okay with all of you?"

After that announcement Rose and Darlene rush over and give Kitty a big hug. Rose tells her that she thinks she is wonderful and is thrilled that she is moving to Grants Pass. "I have always dreamed that Audie would meet someone like you, my dear," Rose happily tells Kitty.

Lorinda feeling left out, comes over and gives Kitty one more hug of congratulations. "I don't know all the details girl, but it must be good news for Rose and Darlene to be hugging on you so much. I better do the same."

Kitty thanks her to, for her best wishes.

Audie observing all this from the fishing boat comments on the splurge of hugs going on between the girls. John and his dad admit they notice it too.

"I guess it's a good that they're all getting along so well," John surmises as he casts out another line.

Ray agrees before announcing, "It's a beautiful day for Oregon," as there is hardly a cloud in the sky. "I never thought I would be back here, fishing with my two sons by my side, while your mom is on shore, fixing up something good for us to eat."

"Yeah," John responds to his father's words, "a few days ago and I don't think anyone would have taken that bet."

"Smartass," Rays directs at John, chuckling as he does.

"Speaking of the women in our lives, how are things with you and Darlene? I'm picking up good vibes with you, too," Audie says, hoping to make his older brother feel embarrassed.

"Pretty good," John answers. "Pretty good so far, you and Kitty?"

Audie considers what is the best metaphor to describe the current state of their relationship. His surroundings lead him to it. "It's kind of like bringing in a big old fish. It's so big you're worried it's going to break your fishing line if you're not careful. So you reel it in a little at a time, and then you give it some slack, and then you reel it in a little more and then you give it a little more slack. It's slow and deliberate and takes a long time to reel it in, but you keep doing it trying to wear it down. That's about where we're at, dude," Audie confesses.

"You're a master with words," John jabs as he asks Audie what he means.

"Kitty's about worn out, and if I don't break the line, I'll catch her," Audie declares.

Ray laughs as he can't make sense out of where all these fishing metaphors come from, since Audie is not exactly Mr. Outdoors as far as he can see and after what John has told him.

"How's the battle with bottle? Any desires?" his father inquires.

"Still got the desire, man," Audie discloses.

Audie's brother and dad look at him with concern.

"But fortunately, a much bigger desire not to," Audie tells them, quenching their worries.

"Good for you, son!" Ray says as he toasts him with some ginger ale.

John does the same and shares with Audie how proud he is of him.

"To better days ahead for all us!" Ray toasts a second time as John and Audie join in.

Ray tells his sons, in a sermon-like voice, how much he loves fishing.

That reminds John of something he's been meaning to ask his father since New York, "Dad, I get the traveling across the country and meeting the people who were so important to you, by the way we still need to discuss our new sister. I get you wanting us to have a better understanding of who you are and all that, but why all the fishing trips?"

"Yeah, pop, it's not like you got to go fishing with all these old friends of yours," Audie adds, backing up his brother's sentiments.

Ray listens to his sons before clearing his throat. He has his boys look around at the peacefulness and tranquility that few other things in life offer. Then he answers, "I've always loved fishing since I first discovered it as a messed-up kid at the boy's home, back in New York. Fishing for me is like a spiritual experience. It's uplifting, relaxing, and exhilarating, all at the same time. The glorious skies, the mountains and tree lines, the glassy waters that are like a massage for your soul, it all speaks more for the existence of God than anything else I can think of. When I'm fishing, life makes sense, the world makes sense."

John and Audie look at each other impressed by their father's reflections.

"I always did my best thinking in a boat, out on the water, with a fishing pole in my hand. I imagine I thought things would make more sense for you, too, maybe my life would make more sense to you," Ray professes.

There is an awkward moment of silence after their dad's serious observations. Ray and his boys fish quietly for a while without saying a word. Then Audie finally breaks the silence. "Life is kind of a lot like fishing, Pop."

"How's that?" John responds.

"Well, think about it," Audie continues. "You cast your line out into the great unknown, like you do yourself. You patiently wait to see what happens, and you hope it's something good."

"You hope for what exactly?" John's curious.

"You hope you catch something really big," Audie says, on a roll now. "That one great love, a job with a purpose, freedom, whatever it is you're searching for. Sometimes you don't catch anything and sometimes your line just gets tangled all up, with all kinds of problems. Catching a break in life is like catching a fish, part skill, part perseverance, part dumb luck. Life's a lot like fishing when you really think about it," Audie concludes.

John laughs off his brother's monk-like musings. "Dad, I think Audie just fell in the deep water if you know what I mean."

"Ha! Yep, I think you're right, Johnny. I think maybe we should just concentrate less on philosophy and more on catching some fish right now. We can fix the world later. How's that sound to you Audie?" Ray asks.

Kitty interrupts the guys as she yells out to the boat. She asks them how the fishing is going.

Audie yells back that they haven't caught a keeper yet.

Ray turns to John and tells him again how beautiful a day it is. John looks to the shore where his mom and Darlene are now flagging them to come in for lunch and says, "Yes it is, Dad. It's a great day. Now if we could only catch one stinking fish."

From John's lips to God's ears to Audie's fishing line, his bobber sinks. Audie's got a bite, and it's a big one, finally!

THE END